LOST GODS

SUMMONERS
BOOK TWO

A.M. YATES

For information contact www.amyates.com

Cover photographs: *Mt Hood at Sunset with Portland City Center/Krzysztof Wiktor/123rf.com ; Shirtless muscular man looking away/4x6/istock* by Getty Images

ISBN-10: 1-943746-05-2
ISBN-13: 978-1-943746-05-7

LS Print Edition: May 2016

10 9 8 7 6 5 4 3 2 1

For Madre,
who loved books
and me.

PROLOGUE

MAY 2ND

I WAIT FOR HIM.

The rain turns from a soft mist to a downpour. I sit on the deck with my hands between my knees, shivering. Cold seeps into my skin, chilling me, layer by layer. In a few minutes, he'll be with me, and I'll be warm again.

I touch the smile on my lips. The smile grows.

Dad and Tessa suspect something. Dad keeps asking me, "What's up?"

All I can do is shrug. No one but Simone knows I've been seeing Fire Guy every night for the last week. She's worried.

You don't know who's behind the god's guise, she says. It could be anybody. Don't let him kiss you again until he takes off the mask.

What she doesn't know is that I'm the one who kisses him first. The moment he appears, guise of black smoke, eyes vortices of blue flame, I go to him. All the questions about his identity vanish. Who cares what his name is? What his face looks like? As long as he's with me, I know everything I need to know.

It's stupid. I know. And reckless. It's not like me. And yet . . .

Considering the state of the Core—with Lily out there, darkening the horizon, threatening to unleash the storm of storms, and Tessa struggling to control the Tripartite, unable to assume her duties as leader—there's plenty of reason to be wary. I, of all people, should be on guard. It's not like I want to be kidnapped again. I know Lily will be coming for me. I broke her mask. I'm the only one who can fix it.

The Eye has been running background checks on anyone who even walks by the tribal center. I'm not allowed to leave the house alone. Dad's tracking my cell phone. If they knew I'd been secretly meeting with a mystery summoner, allowing him to cross the protective circles around my house and my room and my body, they'd freak out.

I'm not worried though. Whoever my Fire Guy is, I know he's not working for Lily. He saved me from her. He sent Simone the GPS coordinates that enabled my tribe to locate and rescue me.

I'm almost certain he's a member of our tribe. I have a suspect. I can't prove it, but I know, eventually, he'll reveal himself. I understand why he's leery. He stole the mask of an ancient volcanic god. If he's caught, he'll be punished. Big time.

The wind whips icy needles of rain across my face.

Okay, I can wait inside.

I turn towards the patio doors that lead into my bedroom. Pale light seeps around the edges of the blinds. A shadow crosses the light—someone's inside. Not Dad. He's working late. Not Tessa. She never comes into my room.

My summoner must've decided it was too cold and wet to translocate onto the deck like he normally does.

I pull open the door. Warm air rushes out to meet me. On it, the faintest hint of musky smoke and resinous amber—his smell.

My smile fades as I step inside. The room is empty.

Maybe I imagined . . .

I catch sight of a folded piece of paper on my pillow. Shoving aside the rumpled blanket, I sit down on the futon and pick up the paper.

I read the note. Two lines. Handwritten. Black ink.

I can't anymore. I'm sorry.

This is when I start dying.

CHAPTER 1

JULY 1ST

THE CHARTER BUS PULLED UP behind the tribal center. Brakes squealed and hissed. Acrid exhaust puffed across the parking lot. The gray plume drifted up over the iron gates, thinning as it dispersed into the blue summer sky.

"Do I look okay?" Tessa asked Simone, grabbing her arm like they were friends. "How's my hair?"

"The same as it was five seconds ago," Josie muttered.

Tessa scowled over her shoulder at Josie, who sat in the driver's seat, door open, an ancient, leather-bound tome on her lap.

"Is that from the island?" Tessa asked, tapping the page with a fingernail painted pearly white.

Josie drew the book away from her sister's manicured nails. "Yes. And it's delicate."

"Should you have brought it out here then?" Tessa put her hands on her slim hips. "Why are you spending so much time in the archives anyway? Every time we go to the island, you bring back like—a million books."

Josie huddled over the book again. "We have to prepare you for the trials, don't we?"

Tessa recoiled. A breeze ruffled her beach-waved hair. She caught it, smoothing it down again. "What's taking so long?" she said, turning her back to Josie and standing on her tiptoes, craning her neck.

Any time Josie mentioned the trials Tessa changed the subject or pretended like she had an urgent message on her phone.

Simone leaned a shoulder against the SUV, peeking down at the page. Behind her, the sky was flawless blue. Another beautiful summer day in Portland. Not that Josie cared. Rain or sun, she was always cold.

"How's it going?" Simone asked in a soft voice.

Josie ran her finger down the page. Core language—the language of the Corpora Deorum, the summoners of the gods, the Core for short—wasn't spoken. The complex chains of symbology ran in different directions depending on the subject or the god being spoken of—left to right, up and down, in circles.

Josie rubbed her forehead. "I wish someone had translated these into English. Ancient Latin and Greek are hard enough, but Core is the worst. I swear the gods invented this language as an evil prank."

Simone twisted one of her many bracelets, tugging at the rainbow-colored plastic beads. Each bracelet was a charm of one kind or another. Most of them she made to give away to other people. It seemed like she'd made a dozen for Josie just in the last week.

"Seems like forever since I've seen Judah," Simone said softly.

"Lucky you," she murmured.

"Josie . . ."

Josie looked up at her best friend. Hot pink hair spiked in careless clumps, eyebrow pierced twice, old Zeppelin shirt reduxed, exposing her shoulder, Simone's big manga eyes, as always, were concerned.

"Sorry. I forget . . . you like your brother."

She frowned over at Tessa who was rocking from her heels to her toes in her sparkling flip-flops, her lacy white skirt fluttering around her tan thighs. Tessa had spent hours picking out a dress for this occasion. Just for Judah's return from another three week mission. Josie didn't bother saying it was pointless—Judah was never impressed by anything.

"Oh, there he is," Tessa said, stretching her arm up high to wave. Josie peered past her sister's svelte frame.

"There he is," she muttered, spotting Judah. Not that it was hard to spot him.

Adonis Reborn had stopped to help the bus driver unload the bags. He took charge of the younger kids milling around, directing them to form a line. That was Judah, always taking control, whether anyone asked him to or not.

"Look, there's Kai," Josie said.

Simone's face lit up as she turned. Josie almost smiled too.

Kai, lean and black-haired, bypassed the obedient line of kids, snagged his rucksack, and strode towards Simone. Judah shot a look after him, mouth pressed into a disapproving line. For a second, his gaze met Josie's.

All her smiling thoughts withered.

"Do I look okay?" Tessa asked again.

"Tessa, you've been dating Judah for a year," Josie said. "He knows what you look like."

"Almost eleven months," Tessa corrected. "Our one year anniversary is coming up."

"Our two-year anniversary is at the end of the month too. On the 27th," Simone said.

They grinned at each other.

Josie bowed her head over the book again. For the last two months, she'd been researching nonstop. When she wasn't reading up on manifestation, trying to discover a means to prevent a god from taking over a summoner's body, she'd been pouring over every charm book she could get her hands on. She hoped to find a charm that might help her uncover the identity of a summoner—one summoner in particular.

Simone went to meet Kai. He hugged her, picking her up off the ground and kissing her.

They returned to the car. Kai's arm draped around Simone's shoulders, their fingers interlaced. He bowed towards Tessa. "Hey, Mother of Mothers, Divine Voice of the Three Stooges—"

Tessa craned her neck past Kai. "Hi, hi," she said, flapping a hand at him.

Kai's smirk deepened. His long eye, made longer by black eyeliner, moved over to Josie.

"You look good," he said.

"You mean like I haven't seen the sun in six months?" she asked.

"Yeah." He gestured to her dark jeans and black T-shirt. "I see you're finally coming over to the dark side. Excellent."

Josie couldn't help but smile, a little. "How were the redwoods?"

"Woody," Kai said, plunking his bag down on the ground. "Red."

"You didn't enjoy communing with nature?" Josie asked.

"Sure, I sang kumbaya, played the bongos, all while baring my soul to the little childrens. Isn't that right, Tevis?" he called to a shy-looking preteen, who was shuffling by with his parents. Tevis's eyes widened. He hurried away.

"You traumatized him," she said.

"As much as I could," Kai said.

"Why did you go on this mission anyway?"

"Have to put in my time, don't I?" he said.

True, every tribal member was expected to supervise a mission, once in a while. The trips helped younger members get in touch with the gods.

"I figure these last three weeks should clear me from duty for the next decade," Kai said. "What have you been up to?"

"Oh, you know, the usual, waiting to be abducted by a psychotic earth goddess. Maybe you know her? Used to be our tribe's Past Eye, name of Lily, trying to build an army of ancient gods to destroy humanity. Seen her around lately?"

"I wish. I still haven't thanked her for inviting me over the last time." He waggled the fingers that had been broken by Lily.

Months earlier, when Josie had refused to repair Lily's hoard of ancient masks, the earth bitch had kidnapped Kai and threatened to torture him. It had worked. After breaking three of Kai's fingers, Josie had started fixing the masks.

"When I see her, I'll give her the message," Josie said.

Simone gave her stern look. "You're not going to see her again. You destroyed her mask."

"Yeah, so she probably wants it fixed and, lucky me, I'm the only mask-maker in the world," Josie said.

"That's looking on the bright side, champ." Kai gently bumped her chin with his knuckles in a buck up gesture.

"I am really glad you were never my camp counselor," she said.

"Scary, huh?"

"Those poor children."

"Judah!" Tessa called, standing on her tiptoes, like he couldn't see the stunning blonde in a white eyelet sundress, glowing with a fresh spray-on tan and all the power of the Three-Faced God.

She bounded towards him, threw her arms around his neck, and kissed him.

Josie closed the book and stashed it in her bag on the passenger seat. She knew if Judah saw it and figured out what she was trying to do, he'd give her an earful. He'd already made it clear he thought she was pathetic for obsessing over the Fire Guy. If he found out that she'd met with the summoner secretly and that she was determined to see him again—even if the Fire Guy didn't want to see her—Judah might decide to tell the Eye she'd been holding back information. After all, Fire Guy had stolen the fire god mask.

Judah and Tessa returned to the car. Judah wasn't just a perfectionist, he was perfection. From the gold-blond sculpted waves of hair, to the chiseled face, to the lean athletic physique. No one should look so good. It was obnoxious. Even after three weeks in the woods, his jeans and pullover looked pressed and cleaned. Was that possible? Had he used his air god mask to whip up a breeze and remove the wrinkles from his clothes? She wouldn't have put it past him.

Except for the sharp slant of his brow, which was like a Morse code machine, his face was impassive. Most of the time, she was an expert in deciphering his eyebrows' various tilts and angles—not that she wanted to know what he was thinking. In fact, she would've preferred not to.

He hung back behind Tessa, eyeing Josie. "What are you doing here?"

Josie put her hand to her chest, batting her eyelashes. "I missed you."

His brow said, *Not funny.*

"Josie drove," Tessa said. "Dad got her a car." Tessa gestured to the tank of an SUV behind them.

Their dad seemed to think a bigger car was going to offer her more protection from an earth goddess capable of stopping time. The extra space did allow Simone to draw lots of protective symbols in invisible ink and to fill every cranny with charms. Thanks to her, it was about as safe as any place.

Judah's gaze ran over the vehicle and then returned to Josie. "The last thing you need is a car."

Two seconds and he was already criticizing.

"Well, since you haven't been here to chauffeur me around, we didn't have much choice." She flared like she always did when Judah opened his perfect mouth. "Or maybe you're afraid I'm going to get into a car accident and you'll have to play superhero again? Sew my fractured skull shut with dental floss and a paperclip? Free me from the burning wreckage? Well, you know what? Don't bother. If I'm in mortal peril, just let me die, okay? Put both of us out of our misery."

"Josie," Simone and Tessa said in unison. Tessa, annoyed, Simone, fretful.

Judah's brow had gone into blackout mode. "Don't talk like that."

"Gods, I was joking."

Mostly. She felt half dead already. In her worst moments, she wished someone would just finish the job. Those moments came more often these days. Simone insisted it would get better—it had to. But it hadn't—it was getting worse.

"Don't joke about it," he said.

"Is Kai the only one who gets to have a morbid sense of humor?"

"No one cares if I kill myself," Kai said.

Simone smacked his arm. "That is not true. And not funny. No one is going to talk about dying because no one is going to be dying any time soon."

A stifling cloud settled over the group. They all knew Lily wasn't finished. The question wasn't if she'd return—it was when. She'd already killed Josie and Tessa's mom, the previous Triune. She'd made human sacrifices to increase her powers. She'd taken possession of sacred tools, devices of the gods, and used them—all crimes punishable by death. And after death, Oblivion. By murdering a Triune, she'd violated the

Covenant. Her soul was screwed. She had nothing to lose. And she was crazy as shit.

Josie slid back into the driver's seat. "Are we ready to go?"

The boys loaded their bags into the back. As cars streamed out of the parking lot, a single sleek black one rolled in. Josie's heart began to hammer. She knew that car. She hadn't seen it in the tribal center's parking lot for months.

Russell. Fire Guy suspect number one.

The Eye had sent him to Asia. Or that's what she'd been told. She knew her tribe's Eye, the three women who made up the tribe's leadership, were part of a larger investigation into Lily and her followers. Over the last two months, numerous tribal members had gone on impromptu "vacations" and unexpected "business" trips.

Russell's car pulled in two spaces down from hers. She twisted to get a look at him. Judah appeared, blocking her view. He opened her door.

"Let me drive," he said.

Her fists curled. "Do you know what *backpfeifengesicht* means?"

"I do," a voice said from behind Judah. "And she's right, Goodwin, your face is begging for a fist."

CHAPTER 2

JULY 1ST

JOSIE UNBUCKLED HER SEATBELT. Judah had turned towards Russell, placing his hand on the roof, standing in her way.

She pushed against the tense muscles of his back. "Move."

His arm dropped and he shifted, barely. She slid past him.

Russell stood in the middle of the adjacent parking spot. Darkly dressed in slacks and a silky button-down, his eyes were as black as his hair. Tanner and leaner than she remembered, the weight loss made his cheekbones all the more staggering. A girl could jump off those cheekbones and plunge to her death. Seeing him again almost made her want to . . .

She bit her lip to stop the questions from spilling out. Are you him? Why did you leave? Why haven't you come back? Please come back.

"You?" Kai came around from the back of the car. He sneered at his foster brother. "Has it been a month already?"

Simone hurried in front of Kai and to Josie's side, flashing a too-wide smile. "Russell, hi. How are you? We were just leaving. Weren't we, Josie?" She gave Josie's arm a tug.

Josie didn't move. She couldn't. She couldn't even breathe.

Russell's gaze never left her. "Actually, I was hoping I'd run into you, Josie. Can I talk to you for a second?" Finally, he looked at the others. He inclined his head towards Tessa. "Mother of Mothers."

Tessa shifted, clearly embarrassed by the title.

"May I borrow your sister briefly?"

Tessa lifted a shoulder. "Sure, whatever."

Josie started to step forward, but Simone had a death grip on her arm. Her eyes were frightened-puppy wide. They kept flicking over Josie's head.

Josie followed Simone's anxious looks—to Judah.

Judah's glare was trained on Russell like a laser sight. His brow said, *Shoot to kill.*

Simone had told her Judah and Russell had a long-standing rivalry. She'd mentioned something about a competition for a mask when they were younger. But Josie didn't care if Judah's alpha-male dominance was threatened by Russell. And if Russell didn't like Judah, that was fine with her. She didn't like Judah either.

She pried Simone's fingers off her arm. Ignoring Judah's radiation waves of animosity, she joined Russell.

He smiled a little as she approached. His mouth was wide, his lips pouty. Were they the lips behind the Fire God's mask? Why couldn't she tell? Even if she hadn't seen them, she'd kissed the Fire Guy's lips often enough she felt that she should know them by sight.

He led her away from her friends, and Judah. The parking lot was mostly empty now. The bus driver closed the bus's undercarriage doors. Late afternoon sunlight bounced hot off the tribal center's three floors of brick, reflecting mute in the blocks of tinted-black windows. For the first time in months, she was warm. Sweat rolled between her shoulder blades. Her breath lodged in her throat.

"I feel like I owe you an apology," he said in a soft voice as they walked away from the others.

"You do?" Her voice sounded strangled. She cleared her throat. "Why?"

He smiled. "After the Fire God's mask was stolen, I was a bit of a prick."

"You weren't . . ."

He raised an eyebrow.

"Okay, you were a bit," she conceded. Mostly, when she'd seen him, he'd ignored her, but she'd thought it had something do with the fact that he was losing his soul to a fire god.

She felt like she had pretty good reason to suspect he was her Fire Guy.

Only a handful of people had known about the Fire God's mask. Of those, even fewer had known she'd repaired it at the time it was stolen. Of those, he was the only one she could imagine being her Fire Guy. She certainly hadn't been kissing Tessa or Simone.

"I've been working so hard to establish myself as someone who can be trusted," he said. "I was upset when the mask was stolen. I guess I took it out on you by giving you the cold shoulder, but . . . I know it's not your fault it was taken. You were only doing what Caroline asked. I'm sorry if I came off like a jerk."

"It's okay," she said, coaxing out a smile for him. "You're forgiven."

He smiled back. "Just like that, huh? No hoop jumping to prove my contrition?"

"I don't see how tests of agility are going to prove anything," she said, "unless you're a golden retriever."

He chuckled. Her smile lingered, without being forced. It felt good to smile again.

They stopped on the far side of his car, in the middle of the now empty parking lot. The bus had rumbled away moments before. This late on a Sunday, few people were in their offices on the upper floors. Most of the retail shops on the other side of the building were closed. Beyond the chain link fence were train tracks and a host of industrial buildings. Vacated, the neighborhood had a dozy, eerie quality.

Standing in the open lot, Josie's pulse skittered. She hugged herself and shifted into Russell's shadow, out of the sun's light. Even in the tribal center's parking lot, safeguarded by hundreds of hidden protective charms and circles, she felt exposed. She glanced over at her friends.

Simone was worrying her bracelets, watching Josie with a wrinkled brow. Kai's arm hung lazily over Simone's shoulder as he stared down at his phone. Tessa chattered up at Judah. He didn't seem to be paying attention to her. Arms crossed in classic Judah pose, he was too busy glaring at Russell.

An urge to go back to them overcame her. She pushed against it. She hated the feeling of vulnerability and the need for others to protect her. As heir to the Triune, she'd been taught to protect others. Even though she wasn't the Triune, she had a hard time letting go of her training.

Russell put his hand on her shoulder. Warm pulses shuddered through her.

"Are you okay?" he asked.

She was tempted to ask him, flat out, if he was the Fire Guy. But the question stuck in her chest, aching. Everything was complicated. Why did it have to be so complicated?

"Not really."

His hand slid down her shoulder, along her arm. "I was thinking, Josie, maybe we could start over?"

She gazed up at him, searching the deep wells of his eyes for some hint. Was there fire hidden in the darkness somewhere? She couldn't tell, and she felt selfish for looking.

The Fire Guy had told her, even before they'd kissed, that he couldn't be with her.

When she'd recrafted the Fire God's mask, she'd subconsciously tailored it for the summoner's face. How could she have modeled the mask after him, even accidently, if she'd never seen his face before? Even she didn't understand it.

And because the mask was fitted to the summoner, the Fire God was becoming manifest. The summoner, if he wasn't vigilant, could lose his body. The god would take over. The summoner's soul would be pushed out.

As if that wasn't bad enough, the Fire God wanted to be with Josie.

This was why Fire Guy had left her. The god wanted her, but the summoner wasn't sure if *he* wanted her. The blurred desire made it difficult for the summoner to maintain the boundary between himself and the god. If Fire Guy wanted to keep his soul, he needed to hold onto that boundary.

Every time they'd been together, she'd only vaguely wondered who was really kissing her, the summoner or the god. In truth, she hadn't cared. So long as he was there, so long as he was kissing her. She'd been so selfish. It wasn't fair to the summoner. He was losing his soul. He had to protect himself.

When he'd left, she'd felt like she'd started losing her soul too. The hollow ache inside her just kept growing.

So what did it mean that Russell was approaching her now? If he were the Fire Guy, could it mean he'd established a firmer grip on the god? Firm enough that he felt safe returning to her? The wan flame of hope in her wanted that to be the case. She needed it to be.

"I thought," he went on, "we might try being friends."

"Friends?" The word had a disappointing flavor.

His hand fell away from her arm and slid into his pocket. He glanced towards her car. "I understand if you're not... interested." His eyes narrowed, darkening as he and Judah seemed to lock gazes. "I know I haven't made a very good impression. I'm sure your friends haven't had very nice things to say about me. My brother and I have never really gotten along. And Judah—"

"Judah's not my friend," she said. "He's my sister's boyfriend. And I don't get along with either of them very well myself."

"I know you've probably heard some rumors about me, Josie," he said. "I don't go around defending myself anymore, because I realized a long time ago that it was pointless. People are going to think what they want to think. The more you try to defend yourself, the worse you make it."

She snorted. "I know something about that."

A few months ago, most people in the tribe hadn't believed she was really a mask-maker. Not even Tessa had believed it until she'd actually seen Josie make a mask. Russell was one of the few people who had been willing to stay open to the possibility. Josie hadn't forgotten that.

She had heard more than a couple of rumors about Russell. She knew he'd dated a girl, Allison, and then hadn't called her back after they'd supposedly slept together, but Josie didn't know what had really happened between them. No one did, except Russell and Allison.

She could hear her mother's smoky voice reminding her,

The Triune is the law, Josie. Your judgments must be based on the evidence. You'll need to make judgments, sometimes quickly, but don't be quick to judge. Opinions aren't fact, not even your own.

It would've been wrong for Josie to allow rumors about Russell to inform her opinion of him.

"I've made some mistakes," he said. "I admit it. I've had some hard lessons to learn about self-control. And I haven't been very good at dealing with other people. Honestly, I'm still trying to figure it out. Sometimes it seems like the things that are obvious to everyone else . . . I just don't get."

"That makes two of us." She reached for him, hesitating, afraid of what she might feel, or not feel, if she touched him. When her fingers brushed the soft fabric of his shirt, she felt a faint fluttery sensation in her stomach. She didn't know what that meant, but she wanted to find out. "I'd like for us to be friends."

He smiled a little. She smiled back, flutters increasing.

Two deafening pops, like gunshots, rang across the parking lot.

Josie ducked. Russell threw his arm over her head. She grabbed him, heart thundering in her ears.

"What was—?" he started.

"Looks like you got some car trouble, bro!" Kai called, pointing at Russell's listing car.

Russell left Josie and circled his car. She followed. Both tires on the passenger side had exploded. Josie picked her away over the scattered pieces of rubber.

"What the hell?" Russell turned on Kai and Judah. "What happened?"

Judah and Kai exchanged a look. They weren't generally on friendly terms, but in this instance, they seemed to be on the same side—the side of antagonizing Russell.

Kai leaned back against Josie's car. "How should we know? We didn't do anything."

"They didn't," Simone said. "We were just standing—"

Russell kicked aside a chunk of tread and took a few menacing steps towards Judah. "I know you did this, Goodwin."

"No one did anything," Tessa said, folding her arms. "The tires just blew."

Russell's skin darkened in shades of bronze. "Forgive me, Supreme Voice of the Divine, but that's bullshit. Tires don't just blow like that." He pointed a finger at Judah. "You did something, and you're paying for the tires."

Judah glanced away. "Why would I do that?" he said, cool as ever. But Josie knew better. His brow was hard and sharp. A samurai sword had a duller edge.

"Because if you don't, we're going to have a problem," Russell said.

Judah's eyes flashed, like distant blue stars. "I wouldn't want to have a problem with you, would I, Vale?"

Russell snorted. "You've had a problem with me since the first day we met. You think you're so damned superior—"

Simone scurried between them, holding up her hands. "Why don't we all just take some deep breaths?"

"I'm breathing fine," Russell said.

Josie inspected the tires. Russell was right. It was strange that both tires had blown at the same time while the car was parked.

But as clear as their hostility was towards Russell, she couldn't imagine that either Judah or Kai were responsible. She supposed Judah could've used his air god powers to blow them, but he would've needed his mask. When he was in possession he was invisible. She'd been looking right at him just before the tires had blown. He'd been very visible, in all his glowering glory. Russell was right about another thing though too. Judah did seem to think he was superior. His dislike of Russell was written all over his face. Still, she couldn't see how he could've done it.

As for Kai, he didn't have any masks. She could see him slashing his brother's tires, but never in front of Simone. Besides, the tires hadn't been punctured, they'd burst.

Josie scanned the adjacent street, which was quiet. On the other side of the parking lot fence were train tracks, and beyond them, a wide yard full of construction vehicles that appeared to be deserted. Even if someone was lurking beyond the protective circles, they wouldn't have been able to perpetrate a magical attack from outside the boundaries, not even to do something as mundane as pop a couple of tires.

"Maybe it was an accident," she said.

Russell shot her a dark look. All glimmers of friendliness seemed to have evaporated from his eyes. Instead of being offended, she couldn't help but think how fire god summoners were often mercurial. Just one of the many reasons so few summoners were allowed to possess fire god masks. Summoners most in tune with fire ended up being too temperamental to exercise the control necessary to handle a fire god. And she didn't blame him for being angry. She didn't really think it was an accident, but there didn't seem to be any other explanation.

"It *was* an accident," Tessa said.

Josie could tell her little sister was trying to sound commanding, like a Triune should, but from her glossy-pink lips, it came out more like a whiny sixteen-year-old.

"It's no one's fault," Tessa insisted.

"I would expect that from you," Russell muttered.

Tessa's face went white. "What does that mean?"

Russell pressed his hands together at his chest and bowed. "Nothing personal, Divine Mistress, but you're not exactly impartial."

Tessa's fists clenched. "I was standing right here. No one did anything to your stupid car. Are you saying I'm lying?"

"I would never say that."

"But you're implying it."

"You may be the Triune, but you're not infallible."

"I'm not a liar either," she said. Suddenly, her tone dropped—from high and strained to low and thundering. "I am the Voice of the Three-Faces..."

Wind whipped around them. Bits of shredded tire rolled and skittered across the pavement. The green-gold irises of Tessa's eyes began to bleach out.

"Witness to the Covenant..." Tessa's voice splintered into four separate voices, hers the weakest among them.

Kuso.

Josie jammed her forefingers against her forehead. Months of training and Tessa was still losing control over the Tripartite's powers. Unrestrained, the powers of Life, Death, and the Other could kill all of them, including Tessa.

Russell shook his head. "Gods, you're completely out of control."

"Watch it, Russell," Judah said.

"What are you going to do about it?" Russell asked. "The same thing you always do? Nothing? Or are you going to let your girlfriend fight all your battles for you from now on?"

"Bearer of the Divine Will..." the Triune was saying.

Clouds formed overhead from seemingly nowhere. Even nontribe, terrae—as they were more often called—would notice the abrupt blossoming of black clouds in a clear blue sky.

"I'm ready when you are, Vale," Judah said, stepping away from the car.

Russell unbuttoned his cuffs, rolling back his sleeves. "About time."

"Oh, please kick his ass," Kai said to Judah.

"Kai!" Simone whirled around and whacked him on the chest.

"Stay out of this, you twisted little freak," Russell said to Kai. He turned back to Judah. "I'm glad you've finally grown a backbone, Goodwin. I've been waiting for years to bring your high-and-mighty ass back to earth."

Judah held out his arms. "Come get me."

CHAPTER 3

JULY 1ST

FAT DROPS OF RAIN PELTED THEM. A cold wind gusted. The Triune's voices grew thunderous. "Kneel before us . . ."

"Josie!" Simone cried.

Once, Josie would've launched into action without prompting. These days, she could barely muster the energy to leave her room, let alone stop the world from imploding. If anyone else had called to her, she might've ignored them. Let Judah and Russell fight, if that's what they wanted. It wasn't her job to stop them. Besides, she was more concerned about Tessa. But for Simone . . .

Lightning cracked. Blinding and deafening. Tessa began to glow, emanating the power of the Tripartite, even without her mask.

Very bad.

Rain slashed down on them, plastering their hair to their heads.

Simone grabbed Judah's arm, begging him not to fight. He shook her off. Kai pulled her away.

Russell drew back his arm, ready to swing, as Judah surged towards him.

Simone twisted in Kai's grip. "Stop! Don't!"

Josie stepped in. She caught Russell's arm, spinning him, and shoved him back. He stumbled, taken off guard.

She turned. Her forearm slammed against Judah's chest as he continued after Russell. He drove her back. His hands clamped onto her upper arms like red-hot vice grips. Then he looked down at her, like he'd just realized she was there. He halted.

She glared up at him. "Did you notice your girlfriend's about to self-destruct? Or don't you care anymore?" She ripped her arms away, shoving him for good measure. She turned to Russell, giving him a hard look. She wasn't necessarily opposed to him knocking Judah down a few pegs. She fantasized about doing it herself every time she spoke to Judah, but they had more important things to worry about at the moment.

Another crack of lightning. Tessa began to levitate. Her sandals slipped off her feet.

Josie bumped into Judah with her shoulder as she stormed to the car. "Get her down," she ordered. "Before she hurts herself." She yanked open the door. "Or us."

As cool as she was acting, inside her stomach was twisting. This shouldn't have been happening. Tessa had enough practice and training that she should've been able to stop the Tripartite's powers from slipping through like this.

Grabbing one of the crystals hanging from the rearview, she saw Judah take Tessa's arm and guide her back down like a stray balloon. Josie climbed out of the car.

Under normal circumstances, Tessa shouldn't have been able to access the Tripartite's powers without their mask, but she wasn't really accessing them. They were bleeding over and accessing her—somehow. Like Josie's Fire Guy, Tessa was in danger of the Tripartite overwhelming her. But in Tessa's case, if that happened, her brain would turn to goo and she would be dead. The Tripartite's combined power was simply too much. Not that it was entirely Tessa's fault.

Josie was the one who'd spent most of her life on the Triune's interdimensional island with her mom—preparing, training, studying. Not until their mom had been murdered did they learn that there had been a mistake. By then, the Tripartite's powers were already flowing into Tessa. Josie would never have said it, but sometimes she was surprised that Tessa had survived as long as she had.

Josie approached her sister, squinting against the glow. Simone rushed to her side.

"What can I do?" she asked.

"Got a Sit-Bad-Tripartite charm?"

Simone's lip stuck out, apologetic.

"It's okay." Josie patted her friend's shoulder.

Josie dangled the crystal in front of Tessa's face. Judah continued to hold her, keeping her feet on the ground.

"Tessa, do you see—?"

The crystal flared and shattered. Sparkling dust sprayed over Josie.

She wiped the gritty remains of the quartz from her face, along with the streams of rain. Her heart knocked persistently against her chest, like a parent politely, but firmly, reminding her that if she didn't do something soon, there were going to be repercussions. Serious repercussions.

"Should I call the Eye?" Russell asked from behind her.

"They can't do anything—"

"Wait! I have an idea." Simone pulled off one of her bracelets. She dug into her back pocket and took out her mini-engraver, which she carried with her everywhere.

"What will happen if she doesn't get it under control?" Russell asked, now closer to her.

"She'll get it under control," Josie said. "Get me another crystal."

Russell went to her car.

"Mask-Maker." The Tripartite's voice vibrated every particle of her being, from her hair follicles to her marrow.

Judah cringed, leaning away from Tessa.

"That's me," Josie said, leveling her voice in a cool-but-still-pissed-off range. "What the hell do you think you're doing?"

"Bow to us, Mask-Maker."

"You're violating the Covenant."

Judah's brow said, *Are you effin' crazy?*

He would think that. Like everyone else in the tribe, he bowed and scraped to authority, especially the Tripartite's authority. The three gods, Life, Death, and the Other, had been like second parents to Josie. Imperious, judgmental, douchebag parents. Right after her mom had taught Josie respect for them, she'd taught Josie disrespect for them. In the mortal world, the Triune was the master, not the servant.

Maybe that was part of Tessa's problem. She hadn't grasped that the three gods of the Tripartite were subject to her and not the other way round.

Still, this little display was making Josie nervous. It shouldn't have been happening.

Russell handed her a fist full of crystals. Before Josie could lift them, the stones disintegrated and ran like sand into the wind.

Josie handed the dangling cords back to Russell.

The blank white orbs of Tessa's eyes started to cloud up, turning gray.

"Great," Josie muttered as the Other took control. "Hey! You're way out of line, you know that? You weren't invited. Back off and leave my sister alone."

Thunder rolled. Another rush of wind tore down from the sky, shoving at her, but she held her ground.

"Mask-Maker." The Other's voice was a booming murmur, distant and dull. She'd listened to the Other lecture the Core's tribes for hours, like the worst philosophy professor ever. Most of what the Other said was usually vague and contradictory. "Hear the voice of the Tripartite. Hear the Other, Voice of Mystery, Keeper of the Book—"

Josie dropped her head back. "Skip it. What do you want? And hurry up because if you splatter my sister's brains on the concrete, I am going to be pissed."

Judah stared at her like he was afraid *her* brains were going to be splattered on the concrete, which wasn't out of the realm of possibility.

Huddled near the car, Simone was bent over, engraver whirring in her hand. Kai stood guard over her, blocking the rain and eyeing Tessa warily.

"We have warning," the Other said, unnervingly succinct.

Josie shifted and bumped into Russell, who was staring, open-mouthed, at Tessa.

"The Triune is unable to convey our voice," the Other said, "or receive the visions."

The Other rarely spoke in sentences less than a paragraph long. Something was big-time wrong.

"Yeah? So? She's working on it," Josie said, trying to straighten out the tremble in her voice, with little success.

"A possible future appeared to us in which the Covenant is destroyed. Steps were taken, as dictated by the Covenant if such a possibility arises."

The mist of rain formed a corona around Tessa's shining skin. Josie blinked against the glare of the halo.

"What steps?"

"A mask-maker was chosen."

She raked the wet coils of hair off her face.

"You mean—you did this to me? You interfered with the Triune's line of succession?" Her hands curled into fists, shaking. "You violated the Covenant—"

"No violation occurred. All was done with knowledge and agreement of the Triune, as is dictated by—"

Josie's head throbbed, not understanding. "Tessa?"

"Your mother."

She rocked back on her heels. "Mom knew? She let Tessa become the Triune, instead of me?"

"Only the blood of the Daughter of Death could bear the power of mask-maker."

Daughter of Death, the way the gods liked to refer to the Triune and all Triune heirs. The first Triune had been a demigod—the daughter of Death.

Josie pressed her palm to her mouth, head reeling. She put the brakes on the dizzy swirl of revelation. Time to be shocked was later.

"I was chosen to be a mask-maker because there's a chance the Covenant might be destroyed?" she asked.

"Yes."

Josie's stomach turned. If the Covenant—the deal that bound Life, Death, and the Other to the Triune, and all the gods to their masks—was destroyed, then the gods would be free to rove the mortal realm. Free to rule the planet and humanity.

Not good.

"How does being a mask-maker have anything to do with saving the Covenant?"

"The last mask-maker will decide the fate of the Covenant."

She ground her fingers into her forehead, trying to blot out the swell of rage. She didn't need the Other reverting back to its usual vagaries. Not now.

"How?" she demanded.

"Many paths—"

"*Kuso!*" she swore. "Is that all? You endangered my sister's life to tell me the Covenant might be destroyed and that it's up to me to save it, but you're not going to tell me how? Or what I'm supposed to do—"

"We are obligated to warn the Corpora Deorum when dissolution of the Covenant is imminent. Since your sister cannot receive the visions, and the Eyes are blind, we were forced to intercede, as is dictated by—"

"Wait . . . imminent? How imminent?"

"Time is a god greater than ourselves—"

Josie swore again.

Judah was giving her the hurry-it-up look. Tessa's godly light pulsed erratically. They needed to pull her out of this.

"Okay," Josie said, trying to think. Covenant in danger. Josie's fate tied to the Covenant's—somehow. Not surprisingly, now that the Other had relayed the required warning about the Covenant, it didn't seem much interested in answering any other questions. Typical. Gods could be such jerks.

"Who then? Is it Lily? Does she destroy the—?"

Before Josie had finished the question, Tessa's eyes turned black. Josie sank back.

Death's voice was a whisper, seductive and deep, chilled and chilling.

"Josie . . . dearest daughter."

Her heart's knocking turned into an anxious pounding. "Piss off."

"When I am freed from my bondage, the blood of the Core shall pay for Lu-Ji's betrayal. All will bow and beg."

"Leave my sister, now."

"Why? I like your sister. Such a beauty. And so sweet. Perhaps when her time comes, I shall not let her pass through my domain, perhaps I shall keep her—"

"Shut up, you son of a—"

"Josie." Simone pressed a neon-colored bracelet into her hand.

"Passion, ferocity, that's my girl," Death said. "I know you, Josie. I know you fear the cold, the darkness, the emptiness within you, but don't despair. Embrace your pain. Follow it to the depths of its black heart with all the fervor I have imparted to you, that obsessive want, that intractable urge, that unrelenting need. Then, and only then, will you find what you are seeking—"

Josie grabbed her sister's hand and pushed the bracelet onto her wrist.

Death went silent.

Tessa's eyes rolled. She sagged in Judah's arms. Her light waned and went out.

The lashing rain lessened and then petered out. The clouds thinned, breaking apart and scattering into the wind.

Within minutes, the sky was clear and blue again.

Judah eased Tessa onto the ground. He pressed his fingers to her neck, eyes on his watch.

"Nice work, kitten," Kai said to Simone, wrapping his arms around her from behind.

Simone smiled weakly. Water dripped off the end of her freckled pixie nose. "Sleep charm," she said to Josie.

"What just happened?" Russell breathed behind her.

Good question.

Josie knelt next to Judah. Tessa was pale and limp, but her chest was rising and falling. No gray matter leaking from her nostrils.

"Well?" she asked Judah.

"Her pulse is steady," he said.

Josie bowed her head, pressing her hand to her mouth, inhaling deeply through her nose. And . . . out.

When she looked up, she found Judah's eyes waiting for hers.

Perfect blue.

In a voice almost too soft to hear, he asked, "Are you all right?"

Her words came out in a choked whisper. "Not really."

A furrow appeared in his brow.

She looked away. She didn't want his concern or pity. She didn't want anything from Judah.

"I'm calling the Eye," Russell said.

"Looks like they already got the call," Kai said, pointing towards the tribal center.

The side door swung open and Caroline, the Present Eye, appeared.

Kai drew Simone tighter against him. "Let the uncomfortable questioning begin."

CHAPTER 4

JULY 1ST

NANCY'S STEELY BLUE EYES narrowed, her thin lips pursed. Her nails, painted the same silvery-gray as her bobbed hair, drummed the table.

"I don't believe it," she said after a moment.

Josie sank back in her chair, folding her arms over her damp shirt. Sitting to her right, Russell gave her a sympathetic smile, but she couldn't bring herself to smile back, not with Nancy shooting her that suspicious glare.

Nancy leaned forward across the uninspired meeting room table, with its folding legs and fake wood grain. "You expect us to believe the Tripartite violated the Covenant and endangered the Triune's life simply to tell you ... what? That you're a mask-maker?"

"Excuse me, Honorable Mother," Josie said, "but if I remember correctly, a few months ago you didn't believe I was a mask-maker. But I wasn't lying then and I'm not lying now."

Nancy, the Future Eye, stiffened.

Seated beside her, Caroline, held up her hand. "No one is calling you a liar, Josie. It's just that . . . the Other disregarded the boundaries between the realms to say that you were chosen to be a mask-maker to prevent the destruction of the Covenant?"

"More or less."

"That's absurd," Nancy snipped. "The Covenant is in no danger of being destroyed. To make such a suggestion is irresponsible and, frankly, seditious."

At the other end of the table, Gretchen, the Past Eye, leaned back. She planted her boot on the edge of the table. "Seditious, Nancy? We're not in Imperialist Russia here."

"Since you are new to the Eye, Honorable Sister, I might need to remind you that it is against Corpora law to question the existence of the Covenant or to speak of its rescindment."

"I believe the statute states it's unlawful to speak *in favor* of its rescindment," Caroline corrected, not looking at Nancy. "And of course, you're not suggesting Josie is doing that. Because if you were, that would mean you were suggesting she is speaking in favor of murdering her own sister. Is that what you're suggesting?"

Nancy sneered, but didn't respond.

"I didn't think so," Caroline said with a heavy sigh. She sagged. Normally vivacious and bright eyed, she looked tired and ashen.

To Josie's left, Simone twisted her bracelets anxiously. Kai was slouched far down in his chair, like he wished he could melt into the floor. Judah had annoyance on his face, but Josie couldn't tell why. Probably because he wasn't downstairs with Tessa in the first aid room.

Through the tinted blocks of windows, the sun—a faint point of light—was setting over the low tumbles of the cityscape. The Eye's sanctum, a large conference-style room on the third floor, looked like it had been broken into and graffitied. Tribal symbols of every variety in every color were painted on the walls. In front of the windows myriads of crystals were hung. From the ceiling dangled charms of metal, stone, feathers, plastic. Underfoot, a massive protective circle was painted in white. Most of the protections were new. Since they'd discovered Lily, their own former Past Eye, had betrayed them, everyone was skittish. They were right to be.

"Did the Other tell you anything else? Anything useful? Like where we can find Lily?" Caroline asked.

"No," Josie said. "Death butted in."

Gretchen raised a pierced eyebrow. "You spoke to Death?"

"Yeah, and he's a real dick."

Gretchen chuckled.

Nancy scowled. "You shouldn't encourage such disrespect. Especially from this one." She pointed with her tablet stylus at Josie. She lowered the rubber-tipped pen, tapping it on the table. "Perhaps the Other is right. Perhaps there is a way you can assist the Core in bringing Lilith to justice. That is what you want, isn't it, Miss Day?"

"She murdered my mother. Of course that's what I want."

"Maybe we should wait on this," Gretchen said, sitting up and looking down the table at Nancy. The two women couldn't have been more different—Nancy, silk and pearls and steel; Gretchen, tattoos and piercings and eyes as green as ferns in spring. "Until the Triune can join us?"

"Wait for what? The decision has been made. I don't see why we can't inform Miss Day now. Since she's here," Nancy said.

"Inform me of what? What decision?" Josie asked.

Caroline wasn't paying attention, too busy frowning at Judah.

"Caroline?" Nancy tapped her stylus in front of Caroline.

"What?" She glanced at Nancy. "Oh. Right." Her gaze turned to Josie. Judah had her eyes. Caroline's were more fluid and less blue. Her cropped hair was lighter blond than her son's. Her features were just as sharp and dramatic, but her face was more open and expressive. "We want you to repair the tribe's ancient masks, Josie."

A long silence filled the room. The air conditioning kicked in, huffing chilled air over them. Josie couldn't tell if she was shivering with cold or shaking from anger.

Finally, she said, "You can't be serious."

Nancy folded her arms over her chest. Caroline bit her lip. Gretchen scooted her chair closer to the table.

"Josie, try to understand—" Gretchen started.

"Hell no," Josie cut in. "Do you hear what you're asking me? Do you even know what you're saying?"

"We're not asking you anything," Nancy said. "You will do as you are told."

Josie gripped the edge of the molded plastic chair to keep from jumping out of it. "Or what? You're going to throw me in a windowless room like Lily did? Crack a couple of my ribs? Or maybe you want to break some more of Kai's fingers?"

"Hold up," Kai said. "Let's leave me out of it this time, huh?"

Caroline knitted her fingers together, pleading. "Josie, this is not the same—"

"It's exactly the same," Josie said. "You want the same thing she wanted. You want me to build you an army." She shook her head. "It's not going to happen."

"Josie, kiddo, do you think we like this?" Gretchen said. "Do you think we want to be *asking*"—she shot a sharp look at Nancy—"you to do this? I know you have some serious negative associations, but—"

"No, you don't," Josie said. "You don't know."

Her gaze snagged on Kai's.

In a pain-filled rush, it all came back to her: Kai tied up, his fingers broken one-by-one. The sharp crack of his bones, his screams, his tears. Clear as yesterday.

Pain rolled across her chest, sharp slicing blades of it like the gleaming-honed discs of a tiller, cleaving into dirt that was frozen solid and hard as stone.

While Josie knew Lily was the one responsible for torturing Kai, the guilt bowled over her, cutting and suffocating all at once. Lily wouldn't have hurt Kai in the first place if not for Josie. And though his fingers were healed and he was safe at home again, the sense of helplessness haunted her. Nothing her mom had taught her had prepared her for these feelings of guilt and weakness.

She dropped her face into her hands, forcing air into her lungs and the painful memories down into the dark place where she shoved all useless things. If only they'd stay there.

Stay.

"You can't make her do anything."

She lifted her head.

Everyone's attention had shifted—to Judah.

Caroline's tone was full of warning. "Judah—"

"Apparently, impertinence is infectious," Nancy sneered.

Judah's lips pressed, but she could tell he had a few more things he wanted to say. It wasn't surprising he had an opinion on the matter. He always had an opinion and he usually expressed it. Normally though, he was the one enforcing the rules, not breaking them. Speaking out of turn, without the honorifics, to the Eye was against the rules. That he was doing it to back up Josie in defying the Eye was enough to make her wonder if he'd been eating wild mushrooms out in the redwoods.

"Forgive me, Gracious Mothers," Simone said in a small voice, "but I think we should talk about this later? Please?"

"There's nothing to talk about," Nancy said. "The decision has been made. The Triune has agreed."

Caroline bowed her head. Gretchen glared at Nancy.

Josie felt like she'd been hit in the gut with a sledgehammer. "Tessa agreed?"

Nancy stared dully at her. "The Triune assented, and you will comply. If you do not, you will be confined in the detention cells until you do."

"I don't believe this." Judah sat forward. "Josie's right. You're no better than Lily."

"Caroline, deal with your son," Nancy said. "Before I do."

"What are you going to do? Lock me up too? Go ahead," he said. "But you're not going to force Josie to do anything against her will, and if you try—"

Caroline surged to her feet. "Stop right there. I don't know what you're thinking, but you do not come in here and make threats to the Eye. To me."

Judah rose to his feet.

Caroline's nostrils flared.

Simone whimpered.

Josie stared, dumbfounded.

Standing up before the Eye, uninvited, was provocative.

Josie noticed Russell smirking, his eyes dancing, like he hoped Judah would get himself thrown in detention.

Maybe she should've let Judah and Russell fight earlier. Judah seemed to have some pent-up aggression he needed to unleash, and he was about to do it in a big bad way.

"The Eye?" Judah said. "Can you really call yourselves that?"

Caroline's eyes hardened to match Judah's. "What is it you're suggesting, son of mine?"

"I'm suggesting you take your decisions and—"

"Judah, sit down." Caroline slammed her hand flat on the table. "I may not have my powers as Present Eye, but I am still your mother and we are still your elders and you will respect that or you and I are going to have a discussion, at home."

"I'd listen to your mother, Goodwin," Russell said.

"What the hell are you even doing here?" Judah said to him. "This doesn't have anything to do with you."

"Wrong, again," Russell said. "I oversee the tribe's mask collection. If there's a discussion about repairing them, then it has everything to do with me. I'm not sure why you're here. Isn't your girlfriend downstairs? Shouldn't you be with her?"

"There is no discussion," Josie interjected. "I'm not repairing any masks."

Russell put his hand on her leg, leaning towards her. "*Qui desiderat pacem, bellum praeparat.*"

"Pretentious ass," Kai muttered.

The corner of Russell's eye twitched, but he kept his deep-dark gaze locked on Josie. "Think about it."

"You don't really believe that, do you?" she said.

"Don't believe what?" Simone asked. "What did you say?"

"If you desire peace, prepare for war," Josie answered for him.

"We're not at war," Simone said.

"Aren't we?" Russell asked. "Weren't we attacked? Wasn't there a battle at one of your shows, little brother? Weren't you and Josie taken prisoner and held captive? Didn't it take another battle to free you?"

"Not one you were a part of," Judah growled.

Russell's eyes left Josie, turning darker as they fixed on Judah. "Because General Judah didn't think me worthy enough. Or was it that you just wanted all the glory for yourself? Afraid I'd show you up, again?"

"You've never showed me up," Judah said.

"Except at the trials—"

"You cheated—"

"You just can't stand that—"

Josie put her hand over Russell's. "Unleashing the ancient gods into the world isn't going to make it more peaceful."

He clasped her hand. Warmth sank through her skin, slowly.

"Josie, you know, I know, we all know, Lily is not done. She's going to come back. And she's going to keep coming. Even if she doesn't have her mask, even if she doesn't have any masks. She'll come for you. Or for Tessa. And if she can't get either of you, she'll take my brother again or Simone or your dad. There is a war, whether you act or you don't—"

"You don't understand," she said. "The ancient gods . . . they're more powerful. They're too powerful."

"That's right," he said. "That's why Lily wanted them. She wants that power. No one wants her to have that power or any power. She doesn't need you to give her power. She's taking it for herself. She already has sacred tools. Godly devices, Josie. She's blinded the Eyes—"

Nancy sat up straighter. "So now everyone knows, is that it?"

Russell continued, "And she's getting just what she wanted. Look, even Dudley Do-Right over there is defying their authority."

Behind her, she heard Judah mutter threateningly.

Russell plowed ahead. "And that's exactly what she wants. That's why she did it. Insurrection. Chaos."

"He's right, Josie," Caroline said. "We've contacted the sister tribes we trust the most, and we believe that . . . all the Eyes are, in fact, blind. But we've agreed to keep it under wraps for as long as we can. People are scared enough as it is."

"When Lily comes again," Russell said, in his close, convincing voice, "she can face a tribe in chaos, or she can face a tribe armed with the masks of the ancient gods. If your dad were fighting Lily, would you want him to be in possession of the mask he already has, or that ancient mountain god mask you brought back from Lily's collection? Which would give him the best chance of survival?"

As much as she hated it, he made a good point. If her dad were in a fight, she'd want him to have the most powerful mask available.

She glanced back at Kai, at Caroline and Gretchen, at Judah. Kai had suffered because of her. Caroline, Gretchen, and Judah had fought Lily and her minions to save her. If Josie hadn't broken Lily's mask, they might've lost their lives in the attempt. Tessa could've died that day too.

If the Tripartite's breach of the rules earlier had proven anything, it was that the Core still didn't have its Triune. Tessa wasn't ready to assume her proper place as leader. Without her, without their Eyes, the Core was even more vulnerable. Josie knew what that felt like, too well.

"Maybe . . . you're right," she said.

He smiled, squeezing her hand.

"Finally, sense," Nancy said in a tone of *hallelujah*.

Josie turned to the Eye. "But I want some say," she said, "in who gets the masks."

Nancy's face fell. "Now, wait a minute—"

Josie's hand slid away from Russell's as she stood, joining Judah.

"According to the Codes of the Corpora," she said, "the Eye that is blind is corrupted and, therefore, invalidated. Their leadership responsibilities revert back to the Triune. Obviously, Tessa is in no position to take over our tribe, let alone the entire Corpora. But Judah's right. You can't force me to do anything. Technically, you have no power. If Tessa wants to put me in the detention—that's up to her. If you want me to fix the tribe's ancient masks, then I'm setting the terms. I want final say in who takes possession of the masks. In fact, I want first say." She notched her thumb towards Kai. "He gets the first one."

Kai looked up from his phone. "Say what?"

"Kai hasn't even earned a lesser mask," Caroline said.

"Yes, he has," Josie said. "He earned it when Lily broke his fingers. He needs one. The only reason Lily kidnapped Kai was because she couldn't get Simone. And Simone can't summon, so she can't defend herself. Kai's at greater risk."

"He hasn't passed the master-level trials," Caroline said.

"Then he better get on it," Josie said to him.

"I sort of had other plans for the summer," Kai said to her.

"If he passes his trials," Caroline said, "then you can decide which mask he receives."

"Caroline!" Nancy said. "It's not up to her who—"

"She's right, Nancy. The kids are more likely to be—"

"That's right—kids," Nancy interjected. "They're barely adults. We are talking about gods who have not walked the earth in thousands of years, ancient deities by far more powerful than anything you or I have ever been in possession of. He has neither the skills nor the fortitude to possess a god of that caliber. Few do."

Caroline gazed steadily at Nancy. "Then like Josie said, he better get on it."

Kai was grimmer than usual. "I'm not so much liking the sound of this."

Josie stared down at the symbols painted on the floor, symbols for air and fire. "And Judah."

"This is not a game of kickball," Nancy said. "You are in no position to pick and choose—"

"Kai and Judah have faced Lily more than you have," Josie said. "The people closest to me ... closest to Tessa, are the ones in greatest danger. Kai, Judah, my father, they're the ones who need them the most. The only reason I'm considering doing this is because I want to protect them. I want them to be able to protect themselves. So, either you agree to my terms or I'm walking out that door. And there is nothing you can do to stop me."

Gretchen and Caroline both looked at Nancy.

Nancy had her frozen dagger stare fully pointed at Josie. "You may choose a mask for Kai, Judah, and your father, but possession of the rest will be determined by us, as is traditional. We may be blind and we, according to the Covenant, may be invalidated, but we are still the Eye. We are not corrupted. We were deceived and betrayed. Lilith will pay for her crimes. She will be brought to justice, and our powers will be restored. When they are," she said, standing up, "I would hope that all of you recall how to display proper deference to the Eye, or I will not hesitate to take corrective action." She snatched up her tablet and slung her purse over her shoulder. "Russell, walk with me. I want to discuss your report."

Russell stood, gave Josie a warm smile, and then followed Nancy out the door.

Before Josie could catch his gaze, Judah strode out too, not looking back. Caroline's mouth opened, like she might try to stop him, but he was gone before she could speak.

Gretchen pushed out of her chair, clapping her hands together. "That was fun." She came around the Eye's table and placed her hand on Josie's shoulder. "Let's talk art supplies, kiddo."

CHAPTER 5

"**O**H, THIS IS INTERESTING." Simone leafed through Josie's notes. "A speaking stone charm? Wow, this is really cool. Josie, do you realize—?"

Josie frowned up at her.

Simone's face fell. "Sorry." She set the notebook aside on Josie's futon. "Anything?"

Josie ran her thumbs over the hunk of glossy obsidian etched with symbols—one symbol in particular: twin peaks joined by an arc, or a volcano about to erupt. *His* symbol.

On the floor in front of her was a world map. Allegedly, the charm, when held over the map, would shine a light on the location of a specific summoner. The trouble was Josie didn't know the name of the summoner, which was required for the charm to work. She had hoped, since he was becoming manifest, that she could use the god's symbol in place of the summoner's name. After all, they were slowly becoming one and the same.

She peered down at the map.

"Nothing," she said, setting the heavy heart-sized stone down on the map.

"Well, maybe I didn't do it right," Simone said. "The charm is really old . . . maybe we missed something."

Josie glanced towards the French doors. Warm afternoon light pressed against the glass. The long stretch of deck was dull in the summer heat. Spired shadows of the neighbor's cedars stretched long across the yard.

Simone's voice was small and sad. "You thought he'd show?"

"No," Josie said, sagging. "Not really." She peeked up at Simone. "I'm pathetic, right?"

Simone's eyes glimmered with sympathy. "You're not pathetic."

"I feel pathetic. We've drawn his symbol on so many charms . . . he has to know I'm looking for him."

Josie had tried every locating charm she could find. She'd sat in protective circles surrounded by his symbol for hours. She knew he was getting the call. He just wasn't answering. Sometimes she was tempted to draw his symbol on her body again, like she'd done twice in the past, but if she did that, she'd put herself under his power. He could make her do whatever he wanted. The thought of being his slave didn't scare her. What scared her was how tempted she was to do it anyway.

"You know he's struggling with control, Josie," Simone said.

"I know," Josie said. "I wish I could give him the new charm I found." She reached up and grabbed one of the many notebooks off of the futon. They were filled with charms for locating people, grounding and centering, and anything she could find on manifestation. "It's not doing him any good if I can't share it with him."

Simone toyed with her necklace, a leather cord with a cloudy piece of quartz wrapped in blue wire—very Core, but not very Simone. It reminded Josie of Judah.

"I'm sure he's doing research of his own," Simone said.

"I hope so, but he doesn't have access to the Triune's archives like I do. He can't possibly have found the things that I've found."

She held the notebook out to Simone, opened to the page with the grounding charm that she thought might help Fire Guy keep his soul safe from the god.

"I was reading last night," Josie said, gesturing to the stacks of ancient books next to the futon, "and one of the old Latin texts gets very emphatic about a summoner in danger of manifestation needing to undertake a strict regimen of centering. It says if the summoner is even a little bit dishonest with himself, then that place of dishonesty can become an open door for the god."

"You mean like a blind spot?" Simone asked, running a jagged fingernail painted bright pink over the notebook.

"Exactly. No matter how much he cleanses and meditates or how many charms he has, if he's not in tune with his feelings and honest about them, the god will be able to gain a foothold."

"I'm sure he's vigilant."

Josie hooked her arms around her knees. "Maybe I should just ask him."

"Josie, I really don't think it's Russell."

"You keep saying that, but you never say why." She eyed Simone, who'd lately taken up the habit of gnawing on her fingernails. "Is it just because you don't like him?"

"I never said—"

"You've said everything but. Kai hates him. Judah hates him. What is going on with your brother anyway? He was acting weird yesterday."

Simone stiffened. "He wasn't weird."

"He almost got into a fight. He stood up in front of the Eye . . . he basically told your mom to go screw herself. You're telling me that's not weird?"

Simone's freckle-smattered face crumpled. "He was trying to help you."

Josie shook her head, pushing up off the floor. "I knew it."

"Knew what?"

"He thinks he controls the world, doesn't he?" She snagged her cardigan off the hook on the back of the door. "Like if he doesn't step in every time there's trouble, it's all going to fall apart. It's like a sickness."

Simone's voice was bruised. "That's not what he's like—"

"I'm sorry," Josie said. "I just wish he would mind his own business. I don't need him coming to my rescue. I don't need him at all."

"He saved your life," Simone reminded her, "three times."

Josie pulled on her sweater. Though the house was warm, the chill never left her. "I remember."

"You don't act like you remember," Simone said.

"I tried to thank him, and he told me it wasn't good enough and that I didn't really mean it. And then he told me he was done saving ingrates, but of course, no. He had to save me one more time because he's twisted like that. He likes making me feel like I owe him. He likes holding it over my head."

"That's not true."

"Then why wouldn't he accept my gratitude when I offered it? He threw it back in my face, Simone. I know you love your brother. I know he saved my life. I am grateful. But he doesn't want my gratitude. I don't know what he wants and I don't care. I never asked him to save me. I never asked him to help me. I never asked him for anything."

Tears trembled in Simone's eyes. Josie's heart sank. She sat down next to Simone, pushing the stack of notebooks aside.

"I'm sorry. I didn't mean to—"

"I only wish you'd see him for who he really is," Simone said.

"I know you think he's some kind of superhero—"

"No, I don't," Simone said. "I think he's brave and strong and generous and kind. And he is, Josie, if only you'd see it. I know he can come off as full of himself and he can be really blunt sometimes, but you of all people should be able to forgive that. He speaks his mind. Just like you do. Besides, you don't understand . . . if he's acting different it's only because he's—" Her mouth hung open, the words simply stopped.

"Because he's what?"

Simone closed her mouth, sagging and shaking her head. "He's going through . . . stuff."

"Stuff?"

Simone's phone chimed. She dug it out of her pocket. Relief flooded her face. "It's Kai."

"About time," Josie said, standing up. "You've been texting him for hours. I was getting worried."

"Me too," Simone said. "But he's going to be training every day now. I know he wouldn't say it, but it's cool—what you said to the Eye. He wants to prove he can handle one of those masks."

"He can do it," Josie said. "I'm just sorry it means he can't spend as much time with you. Are you going to call him?"

"Is that okay?"

Josie stood up, scooping the hunk of obsidian up off the ground along with the map. She held the stone, bearing the Fire God's symbol, up. "I'd be a hypocrite if I said it wasn't." She went to the door.

"I'm sure it's just as hard for him, Josie."

"I doubt it."

"Why do you think—"

"Because I wouldn't be able to ignore him, Simone," she said. "If he were the one calling me, I would answer."

The tear-shine returned to Simone's eyes. "But the god—"

"I know." She gave Simone as much of a smile as she could manage. "Call Kai. At least we know he'll answer, right?"

She set the stone on the dining room table and started folding the map.

Even before Judah appeared, she heard his footfalls on the stairs—though they were muffled and soft. She scooped up the stone and hurried to find a hiding spot. The last thing she wanted to hear was a Judah-lecture about how searching for a guy who didn't want to be found was sad and desperate. Just as she was stashing the stone in the credenza with the linen napkins, he appeared in the threshold from the kitchen.

She turned to face him, closing the drawer with her backside. "How's Tessa?"

"Better." His eyes narrowed. "What's that?"

"A map." She took the half-folded paper out from under her arm and laid it on the table, smoothing it.

He continued to stand in the threshold—Adonis in destroyed jeans and a fitted T-shirt. The air began to grow stuffy and too warm.

"Just say it," she said finally.

"Say what?"

"Whatever it is you want to say."

His brow slanted sharply. But she was having a hard time deciphering what it was saying. Not that she cared.

"Where's Simone?" he asked, taking a step back. "We have to go."

She finished folding the map. "You're really not going to say anything?"

He crossed his arms.

So Judah, except he wasn't speaking. Very odd. Normally, she wouldn't have been able to pay him to shut up. Instead of enjoying it, she found herself asking,

"What is wrong with you?"

He turned obliquely towards the back door. "Tell Simone I'm waiting in the car."

"Really? After everything that happened yesterday? No critical remarks? No unsolicited opinions? Nothing?"

He gazed at her. Silent.

"Are you sick?"

He rolled his eyes.

"I haven't seen you for . . ."—she searched her memory. When was the last time she'd seen Judah lazing around her sister like an over-proud lion?—"months. Then you reappear yesterday, flip your lid with Russell, freak out on the Eye, on your mom. Simone is worried about you."

"Simone is worried," he repeated flatly.

"Yeah, you're acting weird." She took another step towards him. "Tessa said you turned down a few dozen scholarships. Don't you want to be a doctor? Why aren't you going to college next fall?"

His brow remained fixed in that obstinate, unreadable tilt.

"Well?" she pressed.

His jaw worked for a second, like he was struggling to keep from speaking. Finally, he said, "I don't want you hanging out with Russell."

She dropped the map back on the table. "Are you serious?"

He turned towards her fully, placing his hands on the dark trim of the threshold. "I don't trust him."

"You don't trust anybody."

"And I don't trust him."

"Does this have something to do with that mask you were competing over?" She arched an eyebrow at him. "Are you really holding a grudge about that? Why don't you just get over it?"

"That's not what this is about."

She took another step towards him. "Then what is it about?"

He shook his head, like he might not answer. It was so strange for him to be withholding. Maybe Simone was right to be concerned.

"You're in danger, Josie," he said, spitting out the words as if he were being coerced. "I don't know what your dad, or the Eye, is thinking, letting you have a car—"

"I'm not allowed to go anywhere by myself. I always have to take Tessa and one of—"

"Tessa? She's in as much danger as you are. You saw her yesterday. What have you two been doing for the last two months?"

Bright, hot anger flared up inside of her, the kind that made her back sweat and her toes curl—anger à la Judah. His specialty.

"As much as she's been willing to do, which isn't much," she said. "She's been too busy moping because you've been gone."

"She's been moping," he said in that flat voice again. Flat like a hand slapping her across the face.

"Yes—"

"Are you sure it's not you who's been moping?" His eyebrow reached the heights of its know-it-all cockiness. He folded his arms and leaned against the threshold. "Seen any fire gods around lately?"

Heat like steam churned in her chest.

"Let me guess what you were doing with that." He gestured to the map.

Josie gripped the back of the dining room chair, clenching her teeth and praying to the gods he would shut up. Why had she pressed him into speaking?

"I know you've had Simone making locator charms for you," he said.

"She told—"

"She didn't tell me, it's obvious. I'm not an idiot. I can see," he said, tone abrasive. "Unlike some people."

"What—"

"You should be worried less about some douchebag summoner and more about Lily and her followers. Why don't you spend some of your energy, and Simone's talent, trying to find them? Or how about this? Why don't you do what you're supposed to do and help your sister? We need the Triune. We don't need some rogue hothead thief—"

"He is not—"

"Don't defend him. He's a thief, Josie. He stole that mask—"

"I made it for him—"

"I still don't get that," he said. "How can you make a mask to fit someone and not know who that someone is?"

"Maybe I did know," she said. "Maybe I do know."

Skeptical-slant. Arms crossed.

Her hands fisted. One of these days she was going to clock him. Total *backpfeifengesicht.*

"Oh, yeah? Who?"

"Why would I tell you?"

"Because I'm the one who's here, Josie. He isn't."

"You haven't been here. You've been in California and the Canadian Rockies. I've been here with Tessa, begging and pleading with her to stop pouting about how you're not here and to get up off her butt and train. Why don't you take some of your criticism back upstairs and share it with her? She's the one who needs to hear it, not me."

"That's why, Josie," he said in a barely restrained voice.

She quaked, head to toe. "That's why what?"

"Tessa knows she's not cutting it. I don't have to tell her. She sees it for herself. You're the one who refuses to accept who you are—"

"I do not—"

"You're blind, Josie. You can't see what's right in front of you. You don't want to see the truth, you don't want to hear it—you have the power to shape the faces of the gods and you do the same thing to all of us. If we don't fit the way you think we should, you warp the world around you so we do. If Tessa's failing, it's because of you."

She lifted the back of the chair and slammed it down again. Wood cracked on wood. "How can you say that? How—"

"Because it's true. That's all I've ever done—tell you the truth. You just never want to hear it. Why don't you try it out? Be honest. You never thought Tessa could cut it as the Triune. You still don't."

She shook her head, words stuck in her throat. Why did she always let him get under her skin? No one could turn her from calm and cool to furious and burning the way Judah could. Somehow he'd located her ignite switch, and he couldn't stop himself from pushing it—over and over.

His voice remained low and tense. "I heard what the Other said. I was there. You're the one who was chosen to fix this. Don't whine about it. Do something."

He swept forward and slammed his hand down on the map, crowding into her space.

"You want to look for someone? Look for Lily. Because she's not blind, Josie. You know she's coming for you. You're not the Triune. You're not a summoner. You can't fight her. Your best chance is to find her before she finds you because you can bet when she does come, it'll be when you least expect it, when no one can protect you. And if that happens, there really won't be anything you can do." He leaned in towards her. His blue eyes—usually hard, cool, remote—were bright, close, and hot. "There won't be anything any of us can do. She'll make sure of that."

She glared at him, at his perfect nose and his perfect cheeks and his perfect lips. Why did he have to be so damned perfect?

If only she could find his flaw—like the masks of the gods. All of the gods' masks had flaws—weak points that, if struck just right, could shatter them. That's how she'd broken Lily's mask with nothing more than a well-aimed rock. But even if she could find Judah's flaw and shatter his perfect face, it wouldn't change anything. What she hated about him wasn't his face. What she hated was how he was always right.

As she struggled to come up with a retort, the glow of his golden skin deepened, flushing. His perfect red lips pressed into a thin white line. A bead of sweat rolled down his temple.

She frowned. "Are you . . ."

The heat around him swelled, engulfing her.

Her thoughts turned stammerish and then stopped altogether.

She wanted to step back, but couldn't move.

The doorbell rang.

CHAPTER 6

July 2nd

JUDAH'S GAZE FLICKED TOWARD the door, away from her.

Her breathing resumed suddenly. When had it stopped? Stunned, gathering up her thoughts like discarded clothes, she stared after him as he went to the door.

He lifted one of the slats of the blinds covering the glass panels. He glanced back at her, his brow furrowed.

Then he opened the door.

The slim girl on the other side stepped back when she saw him. Her too-wide smile faltered. She drew the basket in her hands back against her chest, like Red Riding Hood encountering the Big Bad Wolf. "Judah—hi."

"Allison."

She tucked a wave of silvery-blond hair away from her face. Her cheek bones were like a Russian aristocrat's, her eyes Siberian blue. "I heard Tessa wasn't feeling well. I brought this for her." The cellophane around the basket crinkled. "Spa basket and chocolates."

Finally, Josie came back to herself. She rounded the dining room table. "You can come in, Allison."

Judah stepped back, but his brow remained fixed in a suspicious tilt as Allison edged by him, past the invisible protective barriers. He really didn't trust anybody. Allison may have been a material girl and a snob—she'd never gone out of her way to be friendly to Simone or Kai—but as far as sixteen-year-old girls in their tribe went, she wasn't unusual. Shopping and competing over guys was the primary pastime of most girls in their tribe, when they weren't training to wield the powers of the gods.

Josie remembered Simone saying that Allison had pursued Judah around the time he and Tessa had started dating. Relations between Allison and Tessa had been cool for as long as Josie had been around. Not that she was surprised to see Allison making a gesture of friendship. After all, Tessa was the Triune. Nobody could expect to compete with her. Better to be friends than rivals. Allison actually reminded Josie quite a bit of Tessa, slender, blond, beautiful, but Allison's face lacked the openness of Tessa's. Josie could see why Judah had preferred Tessa over Allison. Tessa's smile was easy and natural. Allison's was vaguely predatory.

Judah closed the door and trailed behind Allison as she passed through the living area, looking like he suspected she might be smuggling a bomb in her basket.

When her gaze met Josie's, her smile was wide, but her eyes were cool.

"I don't mean to interrupt," she said, brow arching.

What did that mean?

"How are you, Josie?" she asked. "I heard things have been difficult for you lately." She reached out, giving Josie's arm a squeeze and a rub. Her perfume was over-sweet like melted red candy. "We're all worried about you. If you need to talk, I'm a great listener."

Josie wondered if Allison would be willing to talk about Russell.

Judah hovered behind Allison, his eyes narrowing into slits as she spoke.

Josie leaned back from her. "Thanks, Allison. Do you want to take that up to Tessa yourself? I'm sure she'd love the company. She's bored to death up there. I can show you—"

"Thanks. I know the way. I used to love the slumber parties at the Day house. Your dad makes the best kettle corn." She glanced back at Judah. "I haven't seen you around much lately."

"Stop fishing, Allison."

"Why do you have to be so mean all the time, Judah? Can't you just be friendly like a normal person?"

"Can't you?" he shot back.

"You think you're so much better than everyone else," she said tartly. "But, instant message, you're not. Get over yourself. I am."

She flashed Josie a smile, shook back her hair, and strode away into the kitchen towards the back hall. Josie watched her go.

"I think I like her," she said.

"Nobody likes her," he said. "And if you're going to waste your time with Russell, then you'd better watch out for her.

She's been stalking him almost as long as she stalked me, and she won't pretend to be nice if she thinks you're competition. You're inviting drama. It's not worth the headache, trust me."

"If I'm going to waste my time? But, Judah, you told me not to. Why would you think I would do something against your wishes?"

"Sarcasm. Original. Now you're wasting my time."

He brushed past her into the kitchen. He opened the back door.

"Wait a minute," she said, following him.

He paused. She stopped in the threshold. She gazed at him, trying to provoke the same mystifying sensations she'd experienced moments before. But his eyes were dull and distant as he looked back at her.

"What was that?" she asked finally.

He took his sunglasses from the collar of his T-shirt and put them on. They were big and obscuring.

"What was what?"

Josie knocked on the thin pocket door.

Tessa's voice was choked. "Yeah?"

"Can I come in?"

Tessa sobbed in response.

With a sigh, Josie pushed open the door.

Tessa was up to her chin in cherry-scented bubbles. The clawfoot tub in her private bathroom sat beside a shuttered window. The glass was fogged, though the vent fan was humming softly overhead. In spite of the slanted attic ceiling, the room was bright, airy, and almost double the size of the downstairs bathroom Josie and her dad shared.

Josie sat down on the toilet lid facing Tessa. "What's wrong?"

Tessa wiped her eyes with a towel, shaking her head.

"Did Allison say something—?"

"No, she was very sweet, actually," Tessa said.

"If you're worried about what happened . . . we'll take care of it, Tessa. We'll train harder. We'll—"

Tessa sank deeper. Bubbles obscured her lips. "It's not that."

"Then what?"

Tessa's reddened gaze slid away. "Judah."

Josie wished the wall was closer, so she could bang her head against it. "What about him?"

"I think he's cheating on me."

Josie laughed.

Tessa sat up, scowling. Water sloshed around her. "Josie—"

"I'm sorry," Josie said. "But that's just . . . not possible."

"Why not?"

"Because it's Judah. He's not a cheater. He's a jerk. An arrogant jerk, but he wouldn't cheat. It's not in his programming."

"Something's wrong with him," Tessa insisted. "He barely said anything today."

"Did you give him a chance?"

"He didn't even kiss me."

Josie frowned. A few months ago, Tessa and Judah had been slobbering all over each other every chance they got.

"Not at all?" she asked.

"He patted me on the shoulder."

Josie winced. "Oh."

"Not even a hug!" Tessa covered her face with a hand towel and then flung it away onto the tile. "He's cheating, and I'm going to kill him."

"He might not be cheating. He might just be . . ."

"Losing interest?" Tessa finished for her. "That's even worse."

"So what if he's losing interest? So what if he breaks up with you? You're sixteen. You didn't think your first real boyfriend was going to be your only one, did you?"

Tessa whimpered.

"Tessa, you're the Triune now. Do you know how many men are going to be chasing after you? All of them. You can pretty much have any guy you want."

"I don't want any guy. I want Judah."

"Why?"

"He's . . . he's . . ."

"Perfect?"

"Exactly," Tessa said.

"Exactly," Josie said. "It's annoying."

"He saved your life."

"And was a big jerk about it."

"That's because you were a jerk first."

"Me?"

Tessa rested her chin on the edge of the tub, arm hanging over the side. "Why doesn't he want me anymore? Is it because I'm a terrible Triune? He works so hard at everything. He must think I'm such a slacker."

"What does he work hard at? Being a prick?"

"You don't know. You don't know anything about him. You just hate him."

Josie couldn't help but recall that strange feeling she'd had an hour earlier. The one that had left her speechless and immobilized. Was it just that she hated Judah so much it had dumbfounded her? He made her so angry. Even thinking about their earlier conversation rekindled the creeping burn up the back of her neck. But she didn't want to think about it. She shoved the feeling and the entire conversation into the darkness, refusing to give it any further thought. Useless.

"I love him, Josie," Tessa said.

Josie's stomach sank. "You don't really mean that, do you?"

"Yes, I mean it. He's amazing. You, of all people, should see that."

"Why? Because he saved my life? That doesn't make him amazing. It just makes him ... well trained. He should know how to save someone's life. Simone says he's taken every Red Cross training class they offer."

Tears rolled down Tessa's cheeks. "I feel like I'm dying."

Even though she thought it was frozen, her heart panged. "If he doesn't want you, then ... forget about him. He's not worth it."

Fair advice. If only she could take it herself.

"He is worth it. I'm going to fight for him."

"Fight against what? You can't force someone to ..."

"Be in love with you?" Tessa buried her face in the crook of her arm and sobbed.

Josie felt nauseated. How could she advise her sister to forget about a guy who wasn't interested when she couldn't do the same herself? What a hypocrite. At least Tessa could cry about it. Josie couldn't even do that much.

Watching her sister cling to the edge of the tub, heart breaking, was pulling her down. She'd tried to push her pain into the cellar of feelings-better-forgotten, but it still had a hold on her, dragging her into the darkness with it. Afraid of being sucked into the abyss, she cast out for something, anything, to hold on to—to keep her focused on the here and now.

Ironically, Judah was the first thing that came to her mind. He'd been right. Of course. She and Tessa both had too much work to do to be expending their energies pining for guys who didn't want them.

"Let's talk about yesterday, Tessa."

Tessa lifted her head. "Now?"

"Yes, now." Because if they didn't talk about something else, Josie was going to have to find her own tub and drown herself in it.

Tessa wiped her eyes. "You are so mean—"

"You can sit here and wallow, or we can deal with the fact that the Other took you over to warn us the Covenant is in danger, which means you're in danger."

"We knew that already," Tessa muttered.

True. Lily's original plan had been to destroy the Covenant by systematically killing off each Triune until one came along who would hand over the mask of the Tripartite. If the mask of Life, Death, and the Other were broken, then the Covenant would be destroyed and the gods released back into the mortal realm, no longer controlled by summoners. But as soon as Lily had learned that Josie was a mask-maker, she'd changed her plans, opting to have Josie build her an army—to punish humanity for its crimes against Mother Earth—rather than to destroy the Covenant.

Or so Josie had thought. Maybe Lily hadn't given up on her original plan. Maybe she'd just put it on the back burner.

"I would never give Lily the mask," Tessa said, eyeing Josie like she expected Josie would accuse her otherwise, "no matter what she did to me."

"I know," Josie said, but she was glad to hear Tessa say it. "We have to be prepared for the possibility that she still might try to coerce it from you. And she won't go after you. She'll come after the people you care about,"—Josie's throat clenched—"like she did to me."

Tessa paled. "Gods, why is she such a crazy bitch?" She scrunched her nose. "How did she even think she'd be able to destroy the mask in the first place? She couldn't have known about masks having flaws, could she? Does the mask of the Tripartite have a flaw? Oh gods, do you think that's her new plan? Kidnap you, threaten to kill you in order to get me to give her the mask, and then force you destroy it for her?"

Kuso.

Josie's fingers burrowed into her thighs, but she kept her voice even and calm. "If that's her new plan, then it's not going to work, is it? Because you would never give up the mask of the Tripartite, no matter whom she threatens or kills. Not if it's me or Dad or anybody. And even if she did manage to get hold of the mask, I would never destroy it. I don't know if the mask has a flaw, and I won't be looking for it."

Tessa nodded, but she sank deeper into the tub.

Josie took a steadying breath. "But she might not need me to destroy it."

"What do you mean? You're the only mask-maker in the world. You're the only one who can see a mask's flaws, aren't you?"

"I think so, but I don't know. Besides Lily intended to destroy the mask way before I became a mask-maker. She must've have had another plan."

"Like what? What else can destroy the mask of the Tripartite? Should I ask them?"

"Even if you did, they won't be able to tell you, or they shouldn't be able to. According to the Covenant, they can't tell anyone how the Covenant might be undone. But obviously, they've found ways to bend the rules before so..." She frowned. "Lily was a Past Eye. Maybe one of her visions of the past showed her something that she thought might help her destroy the mask. We know she's been using demons to retrieve godly devices..."

"You think there's a godly device that can destroy the mask of the Tripartite?"

"I don't know." Josie dug her fingers into her forehead. Judah had been right. She'd been wasting too much time searching for Fire Guy. She should've spent the last two months trying to figure out what kind of divine tools Lily might have in her arsenal. She knew there were myths about weapons that had been used to destroy god's masks, but the mask of the Tripartite wasn't just any old mask.

"I don't see what I can do anyway. Didn't the Other tell you to save the Covenant?" Tessa said.

"No. The Other told me that I'll decide the fate of the Covenant, which isn't really telling us anything. Maybe you're right. Maybe that means Lily will try to force me to break the mask at some point. But at the end of the day, Tessa, you're still the Triune. You have to be able to defend yourself and the Covenant and all of us, including me."

Tessa scooped up a handful of bubbles, letting them slide down her arm. "I can't," she said. "We both know I can't."

Josie ground her teeth. Was Judah right about this too? Were Josie's misgivings causing Tessa to doubt herself? Josie didn't want to believe she had that kind of influence over her sister. They hadn't grown up together. Until a few months ago, they hadn't even really known each other. But if there was a chance that he was right about this too, then Josie had to do whatever she could to make her sister, her Triune, believe in herself.

But how?

Josie leaned forward, grasping the end of the tub. "Mom chose you, Tessa. She wouldn't have done that if she didn't think you were capable."

Tessa's brow furrowed. "Don't you mean she chose you to be the mask-maker?"

"And when she did that she chose you to be the Triune. I know you have mixed feelings about Mom, but she always did what she thought was best for the Core. That's what the Triune does, even when it meant sacrificing her personal life, even when it meant that we had to sacrifice too. Even when it meant that you had to grow up without her and I had to grow up without you and Dad."

The dew returned to Tessa's eyes, but the tears didn't fall.

"Mom used to tell me that being a leader wasn't about making yourself or anybody else happy. It's about doing your duty and doing what's right. Mom would never have chosen you if she didn't think it were right, if she didn't think you could handle it. If Mom thought you could do it, then you can. I believe that. I have to. And you should too."

Tessa drew her knees up. "I'm scared, Josie—"

"That's okay," she said. "Courage isn't the absence of fear, Tessa. Courage is taking action in spite of your fear."

"Did Mom tell you that too?"

"Yeah, she did."

"If she chose me, Josie, then why did she train you? Why didn't she tell us?"

"The future is in constant flux. Maybe by the time she had the vision and made the decision, it was too late. She died before she could tell us."

"I wish I had known her better."

"Sometimes I think the same thing."

"So what do we do now?" Tessa asked.

Josie stood up. "We get to work."

CHAPTER 7

JULY 3RD
THE NEXT DAY

"SO WHAT DO YOU THINK?" Gretchen asked, opening the door.

Josie glanced around the familiar room. "It's the art lab."

"I know," Gretchen said, flipping on the lights. "It should work, shouldn't it?"

Josie followed in Gretchen's heady wake of sweet patchouli and charcoal. "But don't you need it to teach classes?"

All the tribe kids were homeschooled. They often took classes from tribal elders, including art classes with Gretchen.

"It's summer. I'm only teaching one class. I hardly have time to teach anymore anyway. With the economy the way it is, ceramic cafés aren't in high demand. I can close shop for a couple hours and teach downstairs. This really is the best place for you to work. There's not much else available—an office suite upstairs, tiny, no light. Nancy thought we should convert the mop closest in the subbasement, next to the archives and the detention cells."

"I'm shocked," Josie said.

The mischievous glint in Gretchen's green eyes reminded Josie of Beech. "Don't worry about her, Josie. Nancy's always been a tight ass."

"You shouldn't talk that way about her," Josie said, surveying the room. Usually, it was full of kids. Without the constant chatter, it seemed much bigger. And lonelier. "You're part of the Eye now, blind or not."

Gretchen smiled. "Consider me chastised."

Josie circled one of the work tables. "Sorry," she said. "It's not my place to reprimand anyone, especially you. Forgive me, Honorable Mother."

"Now I'm the one who feels insulted," Gretchen said. "I'm not sure I'll ever get used to being called that."

Josie looked from one end of the room to the other. The kiln room and Gretchen's office were near the door. Half a dozen tables sat in the middle, cabinets and sinks along the walls. Under the blocks of windows were easels and a couple of kick wheels.

"If it doesn't work, we can find something else—"

"No, it should work fine," Josie said.

Gretchen studied Josie. "I talked to Beech last night. He said to say, 'Hey.'" She mimicked her son's deep, laid-back voice.

Josie and Beech had been involved in an almost relationship that had ended amicably, but awkwardly, after

Josie realized the Fire Guy was the only one she wanted to kiss. Whoever he was . . . wherever he was . . .

"How is Beech?" she asked, fighting through the hollow ache pulling on her again. Gods, why couldn't she forget about the Fire Guy?

"He's . . . Beech," Gretchen said. "He's loving the road, the travels, the experience. You know how he is."

Josie nodded. Beech's carpe diem attitude gave him a breezy view of life Josie envied, especially now. He'd always encouraged her to take charge of her own life, to not be bogged down by the disappointments and the BS. She could've used his peculiar brand of encouragement at the moment. She could pep talk Tessa all day long, but who was going to give her the pep talk?

"I think he misses the tribe," Gretchen said, "his friends, you."

Josie smiled a little. She doubted Beech missed her all that much. One of his philosophies was not to get too attached to anyone. For a while, she'd thought he was Fire Guy—she'd even hoped it was him. But after kissing Fire Guy, she'd known it wasn't Beech behind the guise. Beech kissed her like he wanted her. Fire Guy kissed her like he needed her.

"I miss him too. Tell him I said, 'Hey back.'"

"I will." Gretchen hooked her thumbs in the belt loops of her paint-splattered jeans. "This is sort of a big deal, kiddo, you know?"

"I'm not sure anyone in the tribe is actually prepared for how big."

"Don't think we can handle it?"

Josie didn't answer.

Gretchen played with the wooden spacer in her earlobe. "It's not about what we're ready for, Josie. It's about what you have to give. If every artist waited until the world was ready for them, there wouldn't be any art at all."

"No offense, Gretchen, Honorable Purveyor of the Past, but this is bigger than art."

Gretchen smiled. "Nothing is bigger than art, Josie. Not war, not love, not death, not the gods. Without art, the gods aren't real—they don't exist in the mortal realm."

Gretchen's vivid green eyes seemed to breathe and give off oxygen. "You're an artist, Josie. I know you feel alone because you're the only one doing what you do. You're freaked out by the power of your art. That's okay. That's more than okay. It's not the artist's job to determine how their art will be used. You can't control the world. All you can do is create. If the warriors want to use it to kill, then that's what they'll do. If the philosophers want to deem it good or bad, right or wrong, it doesn't matter. If you stop and think about it, then you'll never do anything, you'll never live. That's our job as artists, Josie. To make life real, to give it power, to live."

Gretchen grinned, wildly. "Look what you did," she said. "I sound nuts, don't I?"

Josie lifted a shoulder. Gretchen sounded passionate. And it made Josie ache. She wanted to feel passion again.

"I am nuts, kiddo," Gretchen said. "We all are. But at least we can be crazy together."

Someone rapped softly on the door. Russell cracked it open.

"Special delivery."

He backed in, pulling a utility cart as tall as he was. Josie's heart began thunder, but she couldn't tell if it was because of Russell or the cart full of masks. Stowed in individual wooden boxes, she didn't have to see the masks to hear them. Already, they were speaking to her.

"Mask-Maker."

"Hear me."

"Restore me."

"Josie?" Gretchen frowned. "You need to sit down? You lost all color, kiddo."

Russell came to her, touching her arm. His cologne was subtle, crisp and cool, a distant, aloof scent. "I can take them out again if you need me to," he said.

Josie leaned against one of the tables, setting her bag down. "I just need a minute."

"Let's move the masks into my office. I told Nancy we'd keep them under lock and key anyway," Gretchen said.

Russell nodded, giving Josie a concerned look. He wheeled the cart into Gretchen's office. The door closed behind him, muffling the gods' demanding voices. Josie took a deep breath, trying to shake off the flood of memories: Lily's overpowering presence, her compost stench, her death-mask guise of dirt and maggots, and her complete control over Josie.

Gretchen sat down on the table next to her. "What did that bitch do to you, Josie?"

"It's not what she did, it's . . ." Josie hung her head.

"What?"

Josie looked up at Gretchen, into her vivacious eyes. "I spent my whole life preparing to be the Triune. I expected a lot, but I never expected to be . . ."

"Powerless?"

"Weak," Josie said.

Gretchen put her arm around Josie's shoulders. "You're not weak, Josie."

"I was weak," she said. "When Lily started breaking Kai's fingers, I gave in. Right away."

"You did the right thing. You couldn't let her hurt an innocent person. If you had, you wouldn't have been able to live with yourself. That's not weakness. It's humanity. You care. That's what makes you different from her. That's why we're the good guys and she's the big bad bitch."

"What happened to her?"

"She lost it," Russell said, closing the door softly behind him, "somewhere in the jungles of South America."

"Didn't Nancy tell you to keep that information to yourself?" Gretchen asked, hopping down from the table.

"Are you going to turn me in?" Russell asked.

Gretchen spun her spacer again. "We're treading dangerous waters here, kiddo."

"Josie has as much right to know as anyone else," Russell said, coming closer. "Don't you think?"

"Know what?" Josie asked.

"Sure," Gretchen said, "but I shouldn't be saying that. After all"—she raised her pierced eyebrow—"I am the Past Eye. I'm supposed to be enforcing the rules, not breaking them." She stuck out her tongue, also pierced. "Sometimes being the adult in the room is no fun at all." She held out a magnetic key card to Josie. "This will open all the doors you need to open. Keep it safe. If there's anything you need, you have my number. Call me."

Josie nodded.

Gretchen headed to the door. "I didn't hear any top-secret secrets being spilled," she said, giving Russell a wink. She closed the door.

"What secrets?" Josie asked.

Russell took Gretchen's place on the table next to Josie.

Dressed in a black T-shirt and jeans, he looked more causal than usual. Sitting next to each other, it appeared they'd coordinated their outfits. She studied his face. She still couldn't tell what he was thinking or feeling. The dramatic planes were less expressive than a mountain god's mask. All she could feel at the moment was cold.

"I've been going on a lot of 'trips' lately, Josie, if you hadn't noticed."

"I noticed."

He smiled a little.

Her face started to warm. "So?"

"So, I and many others have been tracking down all the leads that have been pouring in about Lily. I didn't find much in Asia, but Nancy thinks they've figured out when Lily started her path of mass destruction and when she might've had this mystery son you told us about."

"Fog God."

"The man himself."

"So what did you learn about Lily's son? Did they find out who he might be? Where he might be?"

"Neither," Russell said. "Only that, about twenty years back, Lily spent six years traveling, almost a year of which she was in Brazil. I assume your mom told you about what happened to the tribe there."

"You mean when she had to put the tribe's Eye and its elders to death?"

He nodded, grim-faced.

"That's what you get when you murder an entire village so your gods can drink some blood," she said. "But Lily wasn't there when that happened."

"Not when your mom came and brought down the hammer, but from what we can piece together, she was there right before. Would it surprise you that most of the tribal members who were spared from your mother's justice didn't survive long? A string of unfortunate disasters finished almost all of them off shortly after, leaving very few people alive who knew anything about what actually happened down there."

"Lily?"

"Seems likely."

"How did no one know?"

He shrugged. "No one had any reason to suspect. Back in the day, Lily was a free spirit. Every week she sent home cheery postcards, telling everyone she was having a wonderful globe-trotting adventure, learning so much from our sister tribes—"

"Right, like how to sacrifice humans and summon demons to steal sacred tools from the Beyond—very educational."

"You have to admit, she made herself pretty damned powerful."

"Yeah, I guess I have to admit that. So what about this son of hers? They think he was born in Brazil?"

"Possibly. It's hard to say. She spent some time in China too, both before and after Brazil, but no one there was willing to admit to knowing her."

"What about Fog God's father?"

"Our sources are sketchy. None of them agreed who it was, exactly, but they all agreed that whoever he was, he is dead."

"Was he one of the people my mother executed in Brazil?"

"Hard to say. Rumors are... Lily had a penchant for sacrificing her lovers."

"That is twisted."

"Agreed."

Josie blew out a breath. "I wonder what Fog God would say if he knew his mom had sacrificed his father to increase her own power."

"What makes you think he doesn't know?"

"I have a hard time imagining I would speak to my mom if I knew she'd murdered my father."

"Maybe he's afraid if he doesn't help her, the same thing will happen to him."

She gave it some thought. More than once it had seemed like Fog God would've preferred to handle matters differently than Lily. He'd stopped Lily from torturing Josie, but then he'd kidnapped Kai. So he was savvier than his mom, if nothing else.

"Or maybe he's just as sick and twisted as she is, in his own special way," she said. "He'd have to be. No reasonable person could support her."

"I don't know, Josie. Nancy's allowed me access to the reports. You might be surprised."

"Surprised by what?"

"How many followers she seems to have. Who they are—upstanding types. Elders, matriarchs. We even have intelligence that some of the other Eyes are behind her."

"They're insane."

"They're acolytes," he said. "She's been preaching what people want to hear."

"What? That the world needs to be purged of humanity? Do they know that they are also humans?"

"Not purged entirely, Josie. Cleansed. The world's overpopulated. The march of human progress has left the earth scarred. We're Corpora. The voices of the gods. When the rivers are poisoned, when the air is toxic, when the mountains are razed, what happens to the gods, Josie? You said it yourself—the ancient gods were more powerful. Why are modern gods so much weaker? Does it have anything to do with the fact that we've beaten the planet down to its breaking point? You traveled with your mother. You must've heard the tribes ask her this same question. What was her answer?"

Josie swallowed hard. "She never really had one. Most of the time she let the Other bore everyone to death with its vague non-answers."

"So are you surprised that not everyone was happy with that?" His hand slid over hers. Faint warmth stirred inside of her. "What do you think? Honestly?"

"Honestly?" She shifted, discomfited. "I assumed she was doing the right thing. I assumed the Other knew what it was talking about when it said the fate of the gods was not in the hands of humanity. Except then it risked my sister's life to tell me the Covenant's toast if I don't do something, so I guess the Other's sort of a liar."

He squeezed her hand. "What are you going to do?"

She glanced towards the door of Gretchen's office. "Looks like I'm going to bring back some ancient deities and hope they're used to save humanity, rather than to destroy it."

"Humanity will survive, Josie," he said. "Whatever happens."

"That's not very reassuring."

"Are you afraid of dying?"

"Of dying or of being dead?"

"Is there a difference?"

"When I find out, I'll let you know."

"I don't think anybody wants you dead, Josie. Not even Lily. You're no use to her dead."

"Again, the reassuring skills are less than impressive."

He smiled. More warm flutters.

She'd promised herself she'd stop thinking about Fire Guy and focus only on the work ahead of her, but Russell was right here. His hand was holding hers.

Whenever Fire Guy had touched her, it had felt like he'd lit a hidden layer of jet fuel under her skin. She didn't feel that now. Did the lack of conflagration mean that Russell wasn't her Fire Guy? Or did it mean the summoner wasn't the one who had inspired those fiery feelings after all? Was it just the god she was interested in?

Russell's dark eyes lowered, the fringe of his lashes brushing his cheeks. Once again, she studied his face, searching for similarities between it and the mask she'd created.

"So . . ." he asked, "you and Judah."

She stiffened. "What about us?"

"You're not friends?"

"He's my sister's boyfriend. That's all."

His hand tightened around hers. He smiled. "Good."

She smiled back. "He did tell me not to hang out with you though."

His smile faded. "What did you say?"

Her hand slid out from under his. "We got into an argument."

"Who won?"

"No one ever wins with him."

"That's not true," Russell said, standing up. "I won. I beat him in the trials. You know that's why he hates me. He's a sore loser."

She folded her arms. "Are you bragging?"

"A little. You should've seen his face that day. Priceless."

She tried to imagine how nice it would be to see Judah routed. But the thought of him suffering humiliation and defeat didn't make her feel better. In fact, it made her queasy.

Her phone beeped. She pulled it out of her back pocket.

"Please tell me it's not Judah."

"Unavailable number," she said, frowning. No one called her except Simone, her dad, and rarely, Tessa. "It's a video message."

She opened it.

At first, she thought it was blank. All that came up was a white screen. But then she realized the white was moving... rolling, churning. Fog.

Her heart seized.

The fog thinned. A face emerged: big manga eyes frozen with fear, a black gag over her mouth, spiky hair dyed vivid pink.

Simone.

CHAPTER 8

JULY 3RD

"IS SOMETHING WRONG?" Russell asked.

She slid off the table, struggling to breathe. The video had stopped, locked on Simone's face. Josie called Simone.

No answer.

She called Kai.

No answer.

Russell touched her shoulder. She flinched.

"What is it?" he asked.

She couldn't speak. Her voice felt jammed in her throat, like a cat digging in its claws, refusing to budge. She called Simone again.

Voice mail.

Her hands trembled.

Her contact list was short enough that all of the names fit on the screen at once. She was about to call Kai again, but instead . . .

Judah picked up before the first ring ended.

"What's wrong?" he asked.

Her voice returned in a rush. "Where's Simone?"

"Upstairs," he said. "Why?"

"Check."

She could hear his footfalls thumping on the stairs. "What happened?"

"I got a message."

"From?"

"I don't know."

"What kind of message?"

"Just find Simone."

A few seconds later, she heard Judah call, "Simone?"

And then—

"Judah!" Simone yelped. "I'm in the shower!"

Josie let out a heavy breath, her knees buckled. She leaned against the wall beside the kiln room door and slid to the floor. Russell watched her, face dark and clouded. She covered her eyes, squeezing her temples between her fingers and thumbs.

"She's here," Judah said. "What was the message?"

Her throat was choked again.

"Josie—"

"Fog," she said. "And Simone."

Judah was silent. Josie glanced up at Russell. He was scowling now.

"Where are you?"

"The art lab."

"Where's Tessa?"

"Downstairs at yoga class."

"Your dad?"

"Upstairs in his office."

"Are you alone?"

She looked up at Russell again. "No."

"Who—?"

"It doesn't matter," she said. "It wasn't real. It was just . . ."

A prank? A threat? Psychological warfare?

Judah was silent for a moment. "Are you okay?"

"Not really."

"I'm going to call my mom. Stay where you are. We'll be there in a few minutes."

Russell's gaze was heavy on her. Too heavy. She hid her eyes under her hand again.

Judah's voice was soft in her ear. "Josie?"

"What?"

"I will be right there. Okay?"

"Okay."

"Send me the message," he said. "And tell Russell not to leave you alone."

"It's a fake," Caroline said.

"Obviously, Caroline," Gretchen said, rolling her eyes, "but a good one."

Caroline shrugged. "It's pretty amateurish actually. Whoever did it doctored a photo of Simone, added some CGI fog, and—"

"Mom," Simone cut in, annoyed.

Simone sat beside Josie on the modern leather couch. Josie's dad sat on her other side, his hand rubbing her back. Behind his rimless glasses, his hazel eyes were lit, vehement. He'd taken off his suit coat and loosened his tie, like he was ready for a fight. His cheeks were flush, agitated, even the top of his bald head was pink.

"All I'm saying is that anyone could've done it, it didn't require much skill. I've taught plenty of classes showing kids how to create similar effects," Caroline said, sitting down on the edge the desk.

Stacks of boxes were lined up along the walls, bursting with legal documents. Otherwise, her dad's office was tidy: sleek wood floors, wood walls, minimal décor. She was sure his clients found it reassuring, representative of his well-organized nature and exuding just the right amount of affluence to suggest he'd won a few cases. Josie wished she was comforted.

Surrounded by everyone in the world she cared most about, minus Kai, who was downstairs in the gym, training for his first round of master-level trials, she felt more vulnerable than ever.

Gretchen may not have thought that having family and friends was a weakness, but at the moment, Josie wasn't so sure. Fog God hadn't needed to hire a professional graphic designer like Caroline to get his message across. Josie had gotten it loud and clear: I'm coming for you. I'm coming for everyone you care about. And there's nothing you can do to protect them.

"We'll get you a new number," her dad said, tucking some of her loose hair behind her ear. "I'll get you a new phone if you want."

He glanced over at Judah, who was standing in front of the door like a sentry. Judah nodded. Somehow he'd turned into her dad's go-to guy.

Tessa sat in the chair next to the couch, shooting Judah mixed looks of desperation, anger, and grief. Tessa had been the last person to arrive at their dad's office. When she'd appeared, Judah had barely looked at her. He hadn't kissed her or hugged her. Tessa looked crushed. So much for focusing on her training and putting Judah out of her mind. Josie could tell Tessa was just waiting until they got home so she could fall apart, but at least she was waiting.

"But why?" Tessa asked, finally showing some interest in what had happened. "Does he think you've forgotten him or something?" She gave Judah another pained look, like she might consider sending him threatening videos if it would get his attention.

Judah continued to watch Josie. "He's trying to scare you."

Josie clenched her phone in her hands, gazing up at Judah. "And he knew it would work," she said, "just like when he kidnapped Kai."

"But why?" Tessa asked. "What's the point?"

"To get inside your head," Judah said. "To psych you out."

Her dad sat forward on the couch, looking at Caroline. "When we find this—"

"We will find him," Caroline said.

"Damn straight." Gretchen squatted down on the other side of the coffee table. "Don't let him get to you, Josie. That's just what he wants."

Tessa flopped back. "But I don't get why—"

"Tessa—" Their dad's voice was tired.

"It's a ploy," Caroline said.

"A ploy?"

Judah's brow showed annoyance. He really had lost interest in Tessa if he was giving her that look. There was nothing affectionate or warm in it. "A ploy's a tactic, Tessa."

Tessa's own look simmered. "I know what a ploy is, Judah. I just don't understand what the purpose behind it could possibly be—"

"So I won't fight," Josie said softly. "So when he comes for me, the next time, I'll remember what will happen if I don't do what he wants." Her gaze touched on Simone's trembling eyes and then fell to the floor.

Her dad's arm wrapped around her shoulders. His clean familiar smell, fabric softener and expensive soap, worked in vain against her frayed nerves. "That's not going to happen again, Josie."

She glanced at him and then past him to Russell, who'd been staring out the big block of windows, scowling the entire time. She couldn't tell if he was angry or concerned or confused—she couldn't read him at all.

The tension between him and Judah had returned the second Judah had walked through the art lab door behind Simone, who had thrown her arms around Josie, crushing her, and saying over and over, "I'm sorry."

Even now, a taut energy hung between them, though Russell hadn't looked at anyone since they'd convened in her dad's office. It was like having a panther and a lion locked in a cage together. Add Tessa's fractious energy to the mix and the air was almost too volatile to breathe.

"You don't have a clue where they are, do you?" Josie said.

Caroline and Gretchen exchanged a look.

"We have leads," Caroline said noncommittally.

"I've found a few locating charms in the Triune's archives. I'm not sure if they'll work, but you should try them. It's worth a shot." She set her phone down on the coffee table, clearing her throat. "And . . . we could try to consult the Fates."

Tessa sat upright. "Josie, we talked about this—"

"Not you," Josie said to her. "Me."

The room went dead silent. Finding the Fates was an arduous process. Even if the Triune was able to get them to listen to her question, it didn't mean they would answer. If they did, they would expect the Triune to give up something in return—years off her life.

Finally, Tessa said, "You can't. You're not the Triune."

"No, but I was supposed to be. I was born to be. And I would've been, if the Tripartite hadn't decided we needed a mask-maker instead. I was chosen because I had the Triune's blood. If it's good enough to make me a mask-maker, then it might be good enough to get the Fates to answer my call."

"You haven't been through the trials," Tessa said.

"But I've trained for them my entire life."

"You're not a summoner, Josie," Caroline said. "You can't traverse the pathways."

She pursed her lips and shot Judah a warning look. He seemed to be sending it right back at her.

In fact, she had traversed the pathways once before, but only Simone, Kai, and Judah knew about that. She wasn't sure she could do it again, or if she should, but if it meant finding Lily and ending this for good, then she was willing to try.

"It's not possible, Josie," her dad said. "Besides, I know what's required. It's no simple matter. The Invocation itself could kill you if you don't speak it precisely—"

"I know the Invocation, Dad. Mom made sure of that. I won't mess it up. The worst thing that could happen would be that they ignore me."

"No," Judah said, "the worst thing would be that you'd find them and ask them where Lily is. How many years to do you think they're going to want for that information?"

"It doesn't matter."

"Yes, it does."

"It's worth it."

"No, it's not."

"You said I should do something—"

"Not this."

"Judah's right," her dad interjected. "It's not happening. No one is going to the Fates. We are not that desperate. End of discussion."

"He's right, kiddo," Gretchen said. "The Fates are serious last resort talk. Don't give up on us yet, huh?"

She sat back. "Well, then I have another idea."

Simone whimpered. "Josie—"

"Lily has more than one sacred tool at her disposal. The time bender, plus whatever's allowing her to block the Eye's sight—"

"Josie!" Caroline stood up, face white, like she'd been slapped.

Josie glanced over at her dad. "The Eye's blind, Dad. Not just ours, all of them."

His brow cocked, but otherwise, he had a pretty good poker face. He glanced at Caroline and Gretchen. Tugging at his goatee, he bowed his head a little. His scalp darkened from pink to red. "Oh." He looked around the room. "And everyone else here already knows this?"

"I found out before, and the Other mentioned it—"

"And it's not something we want spread around, kiddo," Gretchen reminded her.

"You can trust me," her dad said, holding up his hands to Caroline. "I would never—"

"I'm making you a secret-keeping charm, young lady," Caroline said, pointing at Josie.

"Fine, whatever. While you're at it, you should think about making a demon-summoning charm too."

More silence.

"What have you been smoking?" Tessa said.

"I'm going to play out a little scenario for you, Tessa," Josie said, locking gazes with her sister. "Fog God kidnaps me again—"

"Josie—" her dad started in a warning tone.

"Lily forces me to fix her mask. She forces me to fix all of the masks she's been hoarding. And then she comes for you, except she's not going to put on a big show like she did the last time when she just wanted to distract you long enough to get to me. She's going to pop in when, you're say, I don't know, called to some run-of-the-mill ceremonial bullshit for some remote tribe in a country you can't even locate on a map. And she's going to trap you in your own personal time disruption, freezing you, so that it won't matter if you can control the Tripartite or not, because you won't have a chance to summon them before she runs you through with a sword. And when time resumes, you'll be dead before you hit the floor."

Her dad placed a heavy hand on her shoulder. His voice was stern. "Josie—"

She shook him off, surging to her feet. "Was that too much for you, Dad? I'm sorry. I didn't want it to happen, but I couldn't stop it. I couldn't do anything." She looked from Gretchen to Caroline. "You say you're looking for her. You asked me to arm you. Are you ready for what that means? Are you actually preparing yourselves? Or is this still not quite real for you? I think you all have this image in your heads of that fidgety little hippie who you thought was Lily. But she played you. She played all of us. Are you asking me to give you the most powerful gods to have walked the earth in a millennium just so you can sit on your butts and wait for her to murder a few more people? Which of your loved ones is she going to have to gut in order for you to take her seriously?"

She snatched her phone off the table. "I can't do anything. He knows that," she said, holding up the phone. "That's all this was. A reminder. When he shows up, I won't be able to fight him. I'll be as helpless as I was the day that Mom was murdered."

Gretchen was kneeling on the floor now. "You're not helpless, Josie."

She leaned down to look Gretchen in the eye. "You don't need to worry about me. You need to worry about yourselves. I've kept my place. I've let the leaders lead. I'm not the Triune,"—she gave Judah a pointed look—"I get that. But you asked for my help, so I'm giving it to you. You'll get your masks. But it won't be enough. Lily has nothing to lose. She doesn't care about anyone. She wants us all dead. That's the plan. What's your plan? She has at least two sacred tools, probably more."

She looked around, hoping to see some flickers of urgency. Instead, all she saw were looks of concern—like they all feared she was having a breakdown.

"Do any of you get the level of craziness we're dealing with here?" she asked. "Consulting the Fates? Procuring a couple divine weapons of our own? All that would do is level the playing field. Right now, she has all the higher ground and we are just down here in the shit, blind and helpless. It's time to stop talking and do something."

She stormed to the door. Judah remained where he was, blocking her way.

"Was that truthful enough for you?" she asked.

She reached behind him and grabbed the handle, opening the door, pushing it into his back so there was enough room for her to squeeze through. He didn't budge.

"Josie, you're acting crazy," Tessa said from behind her. "Where do you think you're going?"

Josie turned. "By the way, Tessa. This little speech I just gave—I hope you paid attention because the next time our leaders need a kick in the ass, it's your job."

CHAPTER 9

"**A**RE YOU ACTUALLY FOLLOWING ME?" she said, stopping in the middle of the stairs and turning to face Judah. "What about my dramatic exit just now made you think I wanted company? Especially yours?"

"Where are you going?" he asked.

"To the art lab. I have weapons of mass destruction to repair." She turned and started down the stairs again.

"How?" he asked.

She stopped on the landing. Why couldn't she just walk away? "How what?"

He came down the stairs after her, slowly. "You suggested my mother make a demon-summoning charm to procure a few sacred tools. I don't guess you meant for her to murder anyone in order to fuel an endeavor like that, did you?"

"No," she said. "Although I can think of one person who might need to bleed a little."

He crossed his arms.

"Tessa can do it," she explained. "She doesn't need to sacrifice anyone. If your mother can produce a charm that will summon a demon, Tessa can control it, assuming she can gain control of the Tripartite. The demons are scared shitless of the Other. They'll do whatever it tells them to do."

His gaze turned away, thoughtful.

The broad stairwell was stuffy and damp, smelling faintly of antiseptic and sweat. Too warm. Drowse-inducing. It was still morning, but she was exhausted. She leaned against the wall, scrubbing her hands over her face. The window above seemed to condense the light rather than spread it. Shadows clung to the corners around them.

"Let me take you home," he said.

"I'm not allowed to be at home by myself."

"I'll stay with you."

She eyed him. "Did they tell you to do this?"

"Who? And what?"

"Your mom. My dad. Follow me. Babysit me. Half of the tribe has already done Josie-duty. Sitting around my house all day, jumping up every time I open my bedroom door, escorting me back and forth between here and home, which is what I tried to tell you the other day. I'm never allowed to leave by myself, not even with Tessa. It's worse than being held prisoner by Lily. At least then I knew what she was up to. This waiting is endless. I'm starting to wish she'd get it over with. Anything would be better than this . . . slow death."

"Stop it," he said.

She scowled up at him. "Stop what?"

"Feeling sorry for yourself."

"You know what I need to stop?" She pushed away from the wall. "I need to stop talking to you."

He caught her arm before she could descend the next flight of stairs.

She tore away. "You are so asking for—"

"You were right," he said.

"That you need to be punched?"

"The Eye, the matriarchs, the elders, they all need a kick in the ass. They're not as afraid as they should be. They're not ready for what's coming, but scolding them isn't going to change that. You're wasting your breath."

"Then what will change it?"

"You know what. You said it yourself. Blood. More people are going to have to die before the Core takes real action."

"I refuse to accept that."

"Refuse all you want, Josie. You're only causing yourself frustration. You're not helping anyone."

The door above them clicked open. A moment later, Tessa appeared on the stairs. She stopped a few steps shy of the landing.

Judah stepped back from Josie.

"What are you two talking about?" she asked, giving them a look like she suspected they'd been talking about her.

"Blood, dying, the apocalypse, what we always talk about," Josie replied.

Tessa recoiled. "That's not funny, Josie."

"You're right, it's not."

Tessa came down the last couple steps to join them.

"You shouldn't have spoken to me like that, not in front of other people," she said.

Josie smiled.

"I'm serious," Tessa said.

"I know you are," Josie said. "You're absolutely right. No one should ever speak to you that way. Don't let them."

Tessa's moment of strength seemed to fade. "How am I supposed to stop them?"

"You can start by commanding the room. When you enter, no one speaks unless you've given them permission, especially in formal situations in front of an audience. If they do . . . Mom used to flash Death at people. That usually shut them up."

"Flash Death?"

"You won't be able to do it until you can control the Tripartite, but imagine another girl shows up to a party wearing the same dress you're wearing, what's the look you give her?"

Tessa's gaze turned cool and sharp.

"Not bad. Keep practicing. In the meantime, I beg your forgiveness, Mother of Mothers. And if I disrespect you again in public, you'd better do more than flash Death at me."

"Like what?"

"I don't know. Put me in detention."

Tessa and Judah looked at her like she was nuts.

Tessa twined her hair around her finger. "I don't want to put you in detention."

"That's very nice of you, but I deserve it. I was out of line. You're the Triune. You don't put up with shit like that, not from anyone. Not even your sister."

"I don't want to be mean to people, Josie."

"You're not a politician, Tessa. You weren't elected. People don't have to like you, but they do have to fear you. You were chosen. Like it or not, you're an autocrat, and sometimes, you have to be a tyrant. If, on the off chance, we capture Lily and she's brought before you, you're going to have to execute her. And you'll have to do it publicly. And not just her. All of her followers. Anyone who had anything to do with Mom's murder. Can you do that?"

Tessa went pale.

"The answer is yes," Josie said. "Practice that too."

"Practice what? Killing people?"

"You don't kill, Tessa. You exact the righteous fury of the Divine, you uphold the sacred tenants of the Covenant, you exercise justice to its ultimate ends. The rules that apply to everyone else, don't apply to you. You are not like anyone else. You are more than a human, more than a summoner. Do you know the gods exist, Tessa?"

"Of course I know that."

"How do you know that?"

"Because . . ."

"Do you know that you exist?"

"Yes."

"How?"

"Because . . ."

"Because you, Tessa. You are the answer to every question, especially the ones that can't be answered. You are the heir to Lu-Ji, the first Triune, Mother of the Covenant. She outwitted Death, defeated Life, and bridled the Other. That's who you are. That's what it means to possess the blood of the Triune.

That's your blood, Tessa. The gods serve you. You command them. You are their god. Be it."

"You're pushing her too far," Judah said.

Josie turned on him. "Shut up. Or better yet, leave. You don't know anything about this."

"I don't want him to leave," Tessa said.

Josie let out a long breath. "Of course not."

"Josie, I know you're trying to help me—"

"No, Tessa, I'm trying to save you. I'm trying to give you a crash course in what it took me seventeen years to learn. The Other violated the terms of Triune's Articles of Possession to warn us that the Covenant is in danger. Do you know what that means?"

Tessa chewed her lip, looking like she might cry. "I know what it means, Josie."

"Of course you do, then I'm just"—she glanced over at Judah—"wasting my breath."

His brow said, *Oh, so you were listening.*

Josie turned away. "If you will excuse me, Light of the World, I'm going to get to work. I believe you decreed that I should repair a few masks for the tribe?"

"Josie, I was going to talk to you about that. I didn't expect the Eye to order you to do it."

"They didn't. They couldn't. They're not really the Eye anyway. I'm going to go. I'm sure you two have things to discuss."

She started down the stairs.

"Josie, you're not going to do it alone, are you?" Tessa called after her. "After what happened with the Fire God's mask, I don't think that's a good idea."

"It won't be like that," she said over her shoulder.

"How do you know?" Tessa asked.

Josie reached the bottom and glanced back. The light rendered Judah and Tessa dark silhouettes above her. "He was different."

She reached for the door, but before she touched the handle, the door swung open. She stepped back.

A broad-shouldered young man with warm eyes came through the door. When he saw her, he smiled and bowed.

His voice was soft, but strong. A voice from another life.

"Josie-san."

CHAPTER 10

July 3rd

SHE STARED, MOUTH OPEN. Finally, she spit out, "Daisuke. I—wha—you cut your hair."

He ran a hand over his close-cropped black hair. His smile widened.

"What are you doing here?" she asked.

He glanced around the stairwell. "I'm looking for Caroline-san."

"No, I mean, what are you doing in Portland?"

"I've been sent as emissary."

"Official?"

He inclined his head.

"Congratulations."

"Thank you, Josie-san."

"You can drop the san, huh? I'm nobody anymore. Why didn't you tell me you were coming?"

"Caroline-san suggested it be a surprise?" he said.

"I'm surprised," she said. The last time she'd seen Daisuke in person was the day her mother had been murdered. She'd video chatted with him after that, but not for months.

"Who's this?" Judah asked.

Josie flinched. How could someone so big move around so quietly? He was practically breathing down her neck. Tessa was right behind him, lingering on the bottom step, smiling shyly.

"This is Daisuke. He's an official emissary from the Osaka tribe," Josie said. "Daisuke, this is the Triune, Supreme Voice of the Divine and my sister, Tessa."

He bowed low. "Mother of Mothers," he said in flawless English. "Forgive my disrespect. I did not realize you were in our presence. On behalf of my father, family and tribe, I beg your forgiveness, Light of the Three-Faces and Song of the Heavenly Presence."

Even in the shadows of the stairwell, Tessa's pink glow was evident. Tessa had met with a couple of official emissaries, but she still had trouble hiding her discomfort whenever she was greeted formally. She glanced at Josie, seeking guidance.

Josie sighed. "The transgression is forgiven, Daisuke. The Mother of Mothers takes no offense. This meeting was incidental, not official. Besides, you're in America now, so . . . forget about it. Remember, we're all boorish brutes here. Our new Triune prefers a casual mode of interaction."

Daisuke stood upright, peeking at Tessa from the corners of his eyes. She toyed with the hem of her skintight, pink tank top. She was still in her yoga gear, which was more than flattering on her.

"You are as I remember you, Josie," he said.

"You mean brash and off-putting. Some things never change."

She noticed Daisuke's eyes touch on Judah, who was still lurking behind her, filling the stairwell with oppressive heat.

"This is..."—she faltered, about to introduce him as Tessa's boyfriend, but she didn't want to bring up that sore subject—"Judah. He's Caroline's son."

"Yes, she has spoken of you," Daisuke said.

Judah was giving Daisuke a visual pat down. He really didn't trust anybody. "You're the house guest we've been expecting," he said.

"Caroline-san offered and I accepted," Daisuke confirmed.

"Yes, I did!" Caroline called. The door above slammed. A moment later, Caroline appeared. She hurried down the stairs, smiling. "Daisuke, my apologies. I meant to meet you downstairs when you arrived. My phone's battery died and I didn't get the alert. I am so sorry."

He bowed to her as she came down the stairs, passing Tessa.

"That's because you always forget to charge it," Judah muttered.

"We are honored by your presence," Caroline said, sparing Judah an irritated look. "Please, come with me. The rest of the Eye is waiting in the sanctum to greet you properly." She gestured back up the stairs.

"I will see you again, Josie?" Daisuke said before following Caroline.

"Of course you will," Josie said. "I haven't had a chance to thank you properly for saving my life."

"Please, no, Josie—"

"Don't pull any of that Japanese humility on me, okay? You saved my ass. I would've gotten myself killed if you hadn't pulled me out of there."

"Pulled you out?" Tessa asked.

"He was the one who put me on the plane to Portland after Mom was murdered," Josie explained. Tessa probably would've known that if she'd paid any attention to the inquiry into their mother's death. But to be fair, in those early days Tessa's entire focus had been on keeping the Tripartite from turning her brain to soup.

"You know," Josie said to Daisuke, "the Fourth of July is in a couple days—"

"Tomorrow," Judah corrected.

"Really? Anyway, please come to our house, as our guest. I know you love the immersive cultural experience. There's nothing more American than a barbecue on the Fourth of July."

Tessa raised her eyebrows at Josie, grinning. If there was anything she loved, it was a good party. To Josie it sounded exhausting, but it was the least she could do after Daisuke had stopped her from throwing herself on Lily's sword and had carried her out before the building had collapsed on top of her. And she knew he would love it.

"I would be honored," he said.

Tessa's smile was broader than it had been in a long time. "Yay. We'll do it up."

"Right," Josie said less enthusiastically. "Of course, you're invited as well, Caroline."

"Thank you, Josie. I'd love that," she said. "Daisuke, shall we?" She started up the stairs. Daisuke hesitated, waiting for Tessa to move.

"Casual, Daisuke," Josie reminded him.

His lips pressed. "I cannot walk before the Voice of the Supreme Divine."

"Oh," Tessa said. "Sorry."

Daisuke's eyes lowered.

"She's a Triune-in-training, Daisuke," Josie said to her subtly shocked friend. "You might be better off if you just think of her as my sister."

He gave her a sidelong look that said such a thing was impossible.

"Give it a shot anyway," she said.

"Tessa, you should come too," Caroline said, gesturing Tessa up the stairs.

Tessa nodded and followed. Daisuke's eyes slid over to Josie once more.

"I'll see you later," she said.

"Later," he said.

"You're avoiding, aren't you?" Judah asked as she gazed up at the contents of the cabinet. This one was filled with every kind of glue imaginable, from fabric glue to ultra-toxic plastics glue.

She closed the cabinet door and frowned at him. "No, I'm not."

His brow said, *Yeah right.*

In fact, she was avoiding.

She'd spent the last twenty minutes taking inventory of the art lab's supplies. Judah stood by the door, watching her, making her neck burn and her skin itch. She would've asked him what he was doing there or told him to leave, but she knew why he was there. Josie-duty. No doubt her dad had sent him to act as bodyguard, even though she was in the heart of the tribal center. If she wasn't safe here, she wasn't safe anywhere.

As irritating as his presence was, what irritated her the most was her relief. Unlike all the other babysitters she'd had, Judah, somehow, made her feel safer. Probably because he'd saved her life three times before. The one person who annoyed her most, the one she worked hardest to pretend didn't exist, was also the only person she trusted to actually protect her. Irony of ironies.

Someone knocked on the door. Simone mushed her freckled nose on the glass, crossing her eyes, sticking out her tongue.

Judah opened the door. Simone stumbled in. Already she was tangling her fingers in her charm bracelets. "Hi. How's it going?" Her gaze bounced back and forth between Judah and Josie. "Okay?"

"It's fine," Judah said, shutting the door. "Josie doesn't want to do this."

"I never said that."

"Yeah, you did," he said.

"Okay, I did, but I am going to do it," she said, marching to Gretchen's office. She swiped the key card and pushed open the door.

She stopped, leaning back as she was assaulted by a myriad of imperious, deafening voices.

"Mask-Maker!"

"You will—"

"You must—"

"I command you—"

"Restore me!"

She jammed the card into her back pocket. "Shut up! Or no one's getting restored."

Silence.

"The masks?" Simone said meekly from behind her.

"Yes—"

They were beginning to rumble and mutter again.

"And they'd better keep quiet, or they will stay in their little wooden coffins and continue to collect dust for another thousand years."

They fell silent again.

Josie shuffled in, surveying the rack of boxes.

Gretchen's office was narrow and cluttered, thick with the scent of dust, black tea, and patchouli. Slotted between a paper-piled desk and an overburdened bookshelf, the cart loomed over her. Half of the plastic drawers were empty. Twenty-six contained wooden boxes. Twenty-six ancient gods who were waiting to be returned to the mortal world.

Most of the masks used by the tribes today were the weaker ones. They either hadn't existed yet or hadn't been considered powerful enough to be of use during the long centuries when the tribes had warred. Most of the ancient masks had been broken during those wars. A series of ineffectual and short-lived Triunes had been unable to quell the bloodshed until one had come along who, through some bloodshedding of her own, ended the wars. She destroyed many more masks after that. The Triune could request that the Tripartite give her the power to destroy masks—the ones she deemed too potent and dangerous to be used by summoners. But the tribes had been allowed to keep many of the shattered remains.

The ancient gods weren't more powerful simply because they were older. They were more powerful because they were drawn from the most obvious sources: the hearts of the oceans, the depths of the jungles, the apex of the skies, and the most active of the volcanos. Not only that, but the sources of the past were nothing like they were today.

Gods of the ancient past were representatives of skies that had been brighter with stars, oceans that had been cleaner and more alive, an earth that had been fecund and untamed, a molten core that had been younger and hotter. Though those things were gone, the gods were not. Their power remained rooted in what had been, not in what was currently.

Standing before them, Josie could sense, without touching a single drawer, which gods were which—fire, earth, air, and water. She could smell the salt, taste the loam, feel the breeze, and see the fire. And she could tell how powerful each mask was by how much her stomach twisted when she looked at each of their boxes.

"You don't have to do this," Judah said.

He leaned against the door, holding it open. Simone stood closer, clacking her bracelets around and around.

He was right. She didn't have to do this. Even if it was what her tribe and the Triune wanted. They couldn't force her. But

Lily was out there. She would come back. Everyone Josie cared about was in danger. If repairing the ancient masks would keep her dad and Kai and Judah safe, then . . .

"What element is Kai most closely tied to?" she asked Simone.

"Water," Simone said.

"Really?"

Water summoners tended to be nurturing and empathetic, not exactly the words that first came to mind when Josie thought of Kai, but there were always exceptions.

"What did you think it was?" Simone asked.

"I honestly never thought about it." She ran her fingers down the boxes, torn between two. One tasted of salt, the other of fish and mud. "Ocean or river?"

"I don't know. He doesn't like the beach very much."

"This god doesn't have anything to do with the beach," Josie said. "It's about as far from the surface as you can get. Think deep, dark . . ."

"That sounds like him," Simone said.

"Are you sure he can handle something like that?" Judah said.

She pulled the ocean god's box from the cart. "No. I'm actually certain he can't. Not yet. But we're all taking on more than we should these days. Why should he get left out when we're all having so much fun?"

She squeezed by him, ignoring his glare—completely.

Taking the box to one of the tables, she slid the cover off. Inside, nestled in curls of wood shavings, were a handful of paper-thin shell shards. Josie leaned over the box, head throbbing, shoulders aching, and heart heavy as a block of ice.

"How are you going to repair that?" Judah asked, leaning over her.

On her other side, Simone peeked around. "Will you have to go to the Beyond?"

"How exactly does that work anyway?" Judah asked. "You're not a summoner. You're not in possession, but you traverse the pathways of the gods?"

"I don't know how it works." She went to one of the cabinets and pulled out a big plastic jar stuffed to the brim with sea shells. "But I'm not going to do it that way."

"Why not? Isn't it faster?" Simone asked.

"Yeah, but—"

"It sounds dangerous," Judah said.

She plunked the jar down on the table. "You think crossing the street sounds dangerous."

"For you, it is."

"It is faster," Josie said to Simone. If she were going to keep from killing her bodyguard, she would have to resume ignoring him as much as she could, which would not be easy considering his big fat mouth full of its big fat opinions. "But I'm not even sure how I did it. I was running a 105 degree temperature at the time. It was an out-of-body thing." She rubbed her forehead. "And if I leave my body right now, I might not want to come back."

Simone's lip stuck out. Judah's brow plunged.

She held up her hands in surrender. "Sorry. I forgot. No dark humor for Josie." She clapped her hands together. "Let's bring back a primordial ocean god. I mean, what's the worst that could happen?"

CHAPTER 11

July 3rd

THREE HOURS LATER, Josie had a table covered in broken seashells. The ocean god was especially annoying. All of the shells for his mask had to be as white as possible. On the drying racks in the kiln room was the clay face she'd carved. Once dry, she would make a mold from it. In the meantime, she sorted through shells, arranging pieces into a mask-shaped mosaic on another table.

Every once in a while, when she picked up a shell to inspect it, a deep, eerily calm voice would murmur, "No, not that one."

"I'm running out of options here," she said to the god.

"You should come to me. Find me in the Beyond," the god said, again.

The invitation chilled her. Panicked memories of facing that endless unknown filled her, pushing her heart into an uncomfortable sprint.

"No, thanks," she muttered.

She glanced over her shoulder at Simone and Judah.

On the long table in front of them, plastic boxes of beads sat open beside spools of wire and thread. For long stretches of time, Simone's electric engraving tool was the only sound in the room. Simone had gone down to the coffee shop for sandwiches and caffeine hours before, but the sandwiches remained untouched. The coffee cups were long empty.

Judah's eyes lifted to meet hers. He seemed to have a sixth sense for when she was going to look in his direction.

In front of him was an open notebook, crammed with tiny black handwriting.

She turned to face them fully. "Is that one of my notebooks?"

Simone pushed her magnifying headset back from her eyes. The engraver continued to buzz in her hand. "Oh, yeah, I borrowed it. I hope that's okay."

Josie turned a piece of shell over in her hands. "Sure. Just felt like reading up on the ancient views of manifestation?"

"No, you copied a charm in here, the spoken initiation charm," Simone said, flipping the pages in search of it. "A speaking stone."

Josie stepped closer. "Yeah. I felt like I had to. The scroll I found it on was falling apart. Mom and I had been working on digitizing the archives, but . . ."

Then she was murdered.

"I'm just about done with one now," Simone said, flipping her magnifying lens down in front of her face again. "Do you know how cool this is?" she said as she etched into the thumb-sized hunk of green agate. "If it works, it could totally change the way charms are made. I just can't believe that something like this could've been forgotten."

"Maybe there was a good reason," Judah said, turning back to the page he'd been reading.

Josie was tempted to snatch it away from him. She wasn't sure why it bothered her that he was reading her notes. Maybe she didn't want him to know just how much time she'd been putting in on Fire Guy's behalf. But if Judah had any snide remarks, he was keeping them to himself for the moment. Thankfully.

"Like the reason masks aren't molded to summoners anymore?" Josie asked.

Brow slant: *Exactly*.

"I can see that," Simone said, "except this is like the reverse."

Josie circled around behind them. "Reverse?"

"In the Age of Manifestation, mask-makers made specific masks for specific summoners. Then they realized, hey, not a good idea, right?" Simone said.

"Understatement," Judah said.

Josie peeked over his shoulder. The notebook was open to another charm—one of the many grounding charms she'd copied for the Fire Guy.

"So instead of couture, they switched to off-the-rack, one-size-fits-all. You just had to find a mask that fit well enough." Simone switched off the engraver. "Charms are just the opposite. Right now, if we want to create a charm with any real oomph, we need an activation stone engraved with the name of the person who the charm's intended for. It has to be specific or the charm won't work. It's clumsy. Like the other day when I had to stop to carve Tessa's name into the sleeping charm? It took forever. She could've died while I was working. And what if my engraver had lost juice? What if I had messed up? We would've been screwed."

She blew on the stone. Fine dust glittered in the air.

"If this works"—Simone strung the stone onto a string already full of beads—"I can make whatever kind of charm I want, even the big daddies, and they'll be ready to go whenever we need them."

"It's the difference between having a cannon and having a hand grenade," Judah said, less than enthused.

Simone wrinkled her nose at him. "Well, I wouldn't put it like that." She glanced over her shoulder at Josie. "But... yeah."

She knotted the string, daubing it with glue.

"The symbology for that charm was really intricate, Simone." Josie couldn't help but think of all the locating charms Simone had made lately, none of which had worked. Besides, charm-making could be as dangerous as summoning. Channeling powerful symbols of the gods, drawing forth magical energy always carried a risk. "Maybe you should wait on it. Let your mom look at it first?"

"Too late." Simone turned in her chair, holding the bracelet strung with polished stones. "Who wants to try it out?"

Josie and Judah exchanged a look.

"What is the charm?" Judah asked, tilting his head to inspect the stones engraved with tribal symbols, most of which would've looked like nonsense to an outsider—squiggles and spirals and clusters of dots.

Simone clutched the bracelet against her chest. "Nothing dangerous. Help your sister out."

His eyes narrowed.

"I'll do it," Josie said, holding out her arm, wanting to show support. How could she not? Simone had been there with her through everything.

Simone gave Judah a peeved-frog look. "Okay," she said. "This"—she touched the largest of the stones, a green agate— "is the activation stone, which I carved with the spoken-initiation charm." She put it to her lips and said, "Josephine Day."

Then she slipped the bracelet around Josie's wrist.

Judah and Simone looked up at her.

"Is something supposed to happen?" Josie asked.

"How do you feel?" Simone asked.

"Tired," Josie said.

Simone's forehead wrinkled. "No, I mean, how do you really feel, Josie? You haven't been yourself lately. You act like everything's okay, but it's not, is it?"

"Simone—" Judah's tone was full of warning.

"Shush it," Simone said to him. "Tell me, Josie. The truth."

Josie had no intention of telling Simone the truth. Simone worried too much as it was. If she knew how bad it was, really, she'd put Josie on suicide watch.

She'd planned on saying she was fine, really, but instead heard herself saying,

"It's like I'm dying, Simone. Every day it's worse—" She clamped her hand over her mouth.

Judah looked away.

Simone's expression turned sad-puppyish. "It'll get better, Josie—"

Her lips moved beneath her stifling hand. "No, it won't."

She snagged the bracelet—a truth charm—ripped it off her wrist, and tossed it onto the table.

"I'm sorry," Simone said, jumping out of her chair and into Josie's path as Josie turned to storm away. "I've been worried about you," she said. "You won't talk to me. You don't talk to anyone."

"That's my choice, Simone," Josie said.

Tears shone in Simone's eyes again. "I know, but I'm your friend, Josie. That's what I'm here for."

Behind her, Josie was all too aware of Judah's presence—a hot swell pressing against her back. Sweat rolled down the curve of her spine. If she and Simone had been alone at that moment, she might've forgiven her best friend, but she was too mortified. She didn't want Judah to know how miserable and weak she felt. He would use the information to make more of his too-right observations.

Instead, he said to Simone,

"You've been sneaking into the tribe's charm book."

"So have you," Simone said.

"The truth-charm, Simone?" he said. "Do you know how much trouble you'd be in if Mom found out?"

"I had to! There's a serious lack of truth telling around here and it sucks!" Simone held her hands out to Josie. "Please, Josie, understand . . ."

Josie shook her head and pushed past Simone. Halfway to the door, there was another knock.

Russell's face appeared on the other side of the glass. She didn't know if she felt like crying because she was relieved or because she was so raw from finally admitting how awful she actually felt.

She went to the door and opened it.

"Hey," Russell said softly as he stepped inside. He frowned. "Something wrong?"

"No. Nothing," she said.

His gaze flicked towards the back of the room, but Josie couldn't look. She didn't want to look at Judah or Simone at the moment.

"I came to tell you I have to leave town tonight," he said. "I didn't want you to think I was just disappearing on you."

Was that a hint? A reference to how guilty he felt for bailing on her as the Fire Guy? She wanted that to be true—and felt pathetic for wanting it so badly.

"Oh. Why?"

"Nothing pressing. I'll try to be back tomorrow night. I thought maybe . . . we could . . . do something when I get back." His voice was low and close, but it carried across the silent room anyway. She could feel the enmity flowing towards them from Judah.

"Do something?" she repeated.

He chuckled. "You don't make this easy on a guy, you know that?"

"I don't?"

"You're pretty intimidating, Josie Day, in case you didn't know."

"I am?" She didn't feel intimidating. She felt awkward and uncertain and muddle-headed. How did that come off as intimidating?

"You're so hard to read. It makes you seem sort of... unattainable." He ran his hand down the front of his shirt. "Or it could just be me. I'll be honest. Usually the girls come to me. I've never actually had to work for it."

The words were on her lips, if you're my Fire Guy, you don't have to work for it. Just tell me the truth and I'm yours. But without breath behind them, the words curled up and died.

"You're probably used to it," he said.

"Used to what?"

"Being chased. Should I put my name on a list or something?" he asked, dark eyes searching her face.

"There's no list," she said, growing warm. If there had been a list, it would've had only one name on it. If only she knew what that name was. "Is that what you're doing? Chasing me?"

"It's starting to feel like it," he said.

"I'm sorry," she said. "I don't mean to make you work so hard. To be honest, I'm not very good at all this social interaction ... stuff. Chalk it up to spending most of my life on an interdimensional island with no one to talk to but my mother and a bunch of crabs. But this whole friendship thing is sort of new to me. Actually, I find it pretty intimidating myself."

His eyebrows rose.

"Are you surprised?" she asked.

"I am surprised, actually," he said. "I sort of had the impression you were unshakeable."

"Like Molly Brown?"

"She was unsinkable."

"I'm definitely not that."

On the contrary, she felt as if she was constantly sinking, deeper and deeper, into the darkness. If Russell was Fire Guy, why go through all this oh-so-ordinary routine of asking her out on a date? Was he testing her?

The Fire Guy had always contended she wasn't really interested in him, but in the god. He'd tried to use it as an excuse to push her away more than once.

In her mind, they were one and the same. The god was a part of him. They could never be separated completely, even if the summoner gained total control and the god never became manifest.

Whenever they'd been together, Josie could sense the summoner's hesitation. She hoped he'd realize it wasn't the god she wanted. The god wasn't real without the summoner. The summoner was real. He was the one she'd been kissing. He was the one she wanted.

If he needed her to show interest in him without the mask, she could do that. She was more than happy to do that.

"We can . . . do something," she said, smiling.

A hiss and crack were followed by Simone's surprised yelp. A fire erupted on the table, orange flame and rancid black smoke. Russell circled his arm around Josie and drew her back.

Judah pushed away from the table and retrieved the fire extinguisher from the wall. He dowsed the flames in a haze of CO_2.

The stink of burnt plastic continued to spread even though the fire was out. Russell opened the door. He started to corral Josie towards it, but she slipped free of him.

"Simone?"

"I'm okay!" Simone said, coming out from behind the corner of the kiln room.

She hurried to Josie's side, waving her hand in front of her face.

Judah plunked the fire extinguisher down on the table. He went to the windows and levered them open, allowing in a hot breeze.

"Does this happen every time you repair a mask?" Russell asked.

"It wasn't the mask," Josie said. "I'm working on an ocean god right now. It was . . ."

"The engraver," Simone said. "It just . . . went up."

Judah strode back towards them, impassive-faced, but brow tilted to furious. Without looking at anyone, he walked right by and kept walking.

Not weird. At all.

CHAPTER 12

A Fog God Interruption

"**N**O ONE CARES. YOU DON'T CARE," she moaned.

Gods, he was sick of listening to this.

"You're right, Mom, no one cares," he said.

His mother shook off her apparent infirmity to bolt upright in her bed, clawing at the silk sheets. "You wouldn't speak to me like that if I still had my mask." Her eyes rolled upwards, and she flopped back into the small mountain of pillows. "My mask..." She stretched her fingers towards the glass box on the bedside table, as if she couldn't reach it.

The mask was broken in two pieces. The halves sat under glass, mounted on wooden pedestals. In the past, he'd rarely seen the mask when it wasn't on his mother's face. Now, displayed like some grotesque reliquary, he wished he could stop seeing it.

Muddy brown, carved with ancient symbols no one but the gods understood anymore, mouth gaping in an almost comic rendition of the mask of tragedy, the remaining eye always seemed to be glowering at him, the same way his mother was always glowering at him—accusingly. Why haven't you brought her to me yet? Where is the mask-maker? Where is Josie Day?

He had a pretty good idea of where Josie Day was. For the moment, he was content to leave her there.

His mother on the other hand ...

"I can't stand this—" She tore at her hair. Once dyed red, the color had faded. Her black and silver roots showed clearly. "I need my mask."

He turned his gaze toward the open balcony doors. A tropical breeze drifted in, trying in vain to warm the room. It may have been 80 degrees outside, the sky almost as turquoise as the ocean, but his mother's room was crypt cold. Even out of possession, she had magical ability. After all, she'd drunk human blood and handled godly devices more than enough to move beyond being a mere summoner, yet she preferred to lie in bed and act like an invalid.

Meanwhile, he spent all his free time reassuring their followers that they weren't completely done for. It was pissing him off. He wasn't a diplomat. He wasn't even a leader. He worked behind the scenes. That's how he liked it. That's how he wanted it to be. If only his mother would stop whining and let him handle things in his own way or get up off her butt and take charge.

"You might be interested to know that Josie's started repairing the tribe's masks."

His mother ceased her self-pitying writhing and eyed him. Her skin was like pastry flour. Why didn't she go outside once in a while?

Finally, he saw something of the woman he knew—the leader. The sagging softness of her face began to tighten and harden as she sat up. "Is that right? And how many despoiled masks would that be?"

"Twenty-six," he said.

"Twenty-six ancient gods returned to us," his mother said, smile growing.

"That's right," he said. "Be patient. Once she's done, I'll bring you the masks and her."

His mother's smile turned demure. He drew back. Whenever the hungry-cat smile came out, it was time to leave.

"I've been thinking about that," she said, smoothing the sheets over her lap. "And I've activated a sleeper."

Behind his insubstantial guise of fog, which clouded the edges of his vision, he stiffened. "A what?"

Her toxic-waste green eyes simmered. She picked up her phone and seemed to send a message. "Just a little insurance."

"Insurance against what? What the hell—?"

The door beside him opened. His chest clenched. A wolf walked through the door. Actually, a tree god, sheathed in sleek gray bark, with the face of a wolf. A god with an animal aspect—very rare. He'd stolen it himself from a small arm of the Frankfurt tribe residing in Gengenbach. It was one of the masks that Josie had repaired before they'd lost her.

And his mother had given it to someone without consulting him. His hands fisted under his guise.

The Wolf moved silently. Yellow eyes aglow, its fangs protruded from its long snout, shiny-wet.

"Who is this?" he asked.

"Be polite," his mother said, smiling. "All you need to know is that she's here to help you"—his mother's sweet tone dissolved like sugar in bitter black coffee—"and to bring Josie Day to us, should you encounter any . . . difficulties."

"You mean if I get caught or killed," he said, eyeing the Wolf. "You're part of the Triune's tribe?"

The Wolf's eyes flashed, but she didn't speak.

"She's close at hand. Should you need her, all you have to do is contact me," his mother said. "I will send her to you."

"Why all the secrecy? I know the identity of everyone working with us," he said, barely holding back his anger. He had to pick and choose his battles with his mother. Even in her weakened state, without her mask, she still had the Sword of Eternity in her stash, along with a time bender. Even though she was his mother, he didn't trust her entirely.

"Everyone?" she repeated thoughtfully. "Hmm."

He burned behind his cool guise. "I'll bring Josie to you, just like I did the last time. All we have to do is wait—"

"All? All?" She leaned forward, her face contorting again. "I've been waiting for months! What have you been doing? Nothing! But the Wolf will remedy that, if you can't. The Wolf has her own plan in action. A back up."

"I told you I'd take care of it," he said. "And I will."

"I believe you, my beautiful boy," she said. "But I serve Goddess Earth, not your pride. While you play in the shadows, my goddess is raped and beaten. We must do all we can to ensure that her torture is brought to an end as swiftly as possible. You do agree . . ."

Now that was a loaded question.

"You know I agree—"

"Then there's nothing more to discuss." She sank back, hand covering her eyes. "I don't know why you don't come more often."

He eyed the Wolf again. Back up? More like usurper. He didn't like this. Not even a little.

He knew exactly what his mother was up to. She thought he needed some competition to motivate him to move faster. But what she didn't understand, what she would never understand, was that a little patience could reap a much more satisfying victory than a headlong rush into battle half-prepared.

The further removed they were from the Triune's murder, the more complacent the Core grew. As for Josie, she was doing just what they wanted her to do, willingly.

"Mothers are never appreciated." She stretched her arm towards the mask, stroking its glass showcase. "Are we?"

He stared down the Wolf. "You were the one, weren't you? You sent that message to Josie—"

"Don't worry about what the Wolf is doing!" his mother interjected. "Worry about what you're supposed to be doing! Bring me Josie Day!"

The Wolf bared her fangs.

"I'll take care of Josie," he said. Then to the Wolf, he said, "Stay away from her."

He thinned the fog of his guise and swept out of the balcony doors in a rolling cloud, chased by shadows and cold.

CHAPTER 13

JULY 4TH
THE NEXT DAY

"DAISUKE?" JOSIE ALMOST dropped the piping-hot marionberry pie she'd been pulling from the oven. "Can I get you something?"

He shook his head. "I was hoping to speak to you."

She set the pie on the cooling rack. "Of course."

Outside on the deck, she could hear the pleasant rise and fall of conversation, Caroline's bright laughter foremost.

They'd decided to keep the party intimate since their backyard wasn't very big. Once they'd set the folding table up on the deck, it was even tighter, but Tessa didn't seem to mind. She'd been basking in Daisuke's unwavering attention since he'd arrived a couple hours before with Caroline, Judah, and Simone. Gretchen, who lived next door, and her girlfriend, Roxy, had also come by. Everyone seemed to be having a good time, except Judah. He'd been scowling at his beer bottles, one after the other.

Josie shook off the oven mitts onto the counter. "What's up?"

Daisuke was dressed casually in a white T-shirt and jeans, American-style, he'd told her with a smile. He looked much less like the teenager she remembered and far more like the twenty-year-old he would be in a few months. Still, he seemed to be having trouble adjusting to the informal manner of her American tribe, especially around Tessa.

When Tessa had insisted he call her by her first name, his neck had gone splotchy red. Josie then had explained to Tessa that in Japan a person would never have referred to the Triune by her first name unless that person was on *extremely* intimate terms with her. Tessa had simply waved Josie off, smiled widely at Daisuke, and said, "Well, you're in America now. And, here, you'll call me Tessa."

Josie could sense Daisuke's continued discomfort. She set the cutting board on the counter next to the bag full of avocados.

"I don't feel like I'm doing enough to thank you," she said as she took up the chef's knife.

He shook his head, refusing her attempts to show any gratitude.

"Simone said there was a fire yesterday," he said.

"Uh-huh." She started slicing the avocados into halves. "Simone's engraver just went up. It was the weirdest thing. We had to clear out because of the smoke. I wasn't anywhere close to finishing the mask I was working on." Her neck ached when she thought about sorting through more shells.

"You were chosen," he said. "You must feel honored."

"Not really." She lofted an eyebrow at him. "Are you shocked?"

"Not really," he said, imitating her with a small smile.

She smiled back. She had known Daisuke for as long as she could remember.

Once, his mother had been his tribe's Future Eye, but she had died when Daisuke was three, while trying to mitigate the ferocity of an oncoming tsunami. Josie had visited his tribe more often than others because her mom and his father had had something going on. Although Josie and Daisuke could never produce any evidence, they were both certain of it.

"The Other came to me. It spoke to me while Tessa was out of possession." She drizzled olive oil over the split avocados.

At this, Daisuke's eyes widened. "In violation of the Triune's Articles?"

"Yup," she said.

"When?"

"Just two days ago," she said. "It was bound by the Covenant to warn me since Tessa's unable to receive visions of the future. The Covenant's in danger. That's why I'm a maskmaker. My mother chose me. Apparently, bringing forth the gods has something to do with saving the Covenant from dissolution. But what that something is, well . . ." She held up her hands.

Daisuke was silent. She knew he was shocked now, even though his face didn't show it.

"You should not be telling me this," he said after a moment.

"Probably not, but... you should know how bad things really are even if everyone else wants to pretend that they're not. You need to prepare yourself."

He gave a curt nod. She had the urge to hug him. She restrained herself. She'd been spending too much time with Simone and Tessa, who were serial-huggers. The look of gravity on his face was such a relief—finally, someone besides Judah who seemed to grasp how dire the situation actually was.

"I would hope to be as prepared as I can be," he said, trailing off.

"But?"

"I have studied the reports of the Earth Goddess—"

"Lily."

"When she abducted you, you repaired masks for her? Ancient masks?"

Josie nodded. "I brought one back with me. I repaired quite a few, many of them tree gods, but they're not the kind of trees you want to meet in a dark alley, if you get my meaning."

"And you are repairing masks now, for your tribe?"

"Uh-huh." She twisted the pepper mill over the avocados.

"In comparison, my own interests are less important."

She set the mill down, wiping her hands on her apron. "What interests?"

He looked around the kitchen as if he expected to find a spy lurking.

With a flick of his wrist, Daisuke retrieved his mask.

Josie's mouth fell open. "Your mask."

The river god mask, with its vivid red tongue and wicked horns, was broken. Three pieces were stacked, one on top of the other, in Daisuke's hand.

"What happened?" she asked, stepping towards him.

"When the air god hit me, when your mother was murdered," he said.

"I didn't notice. I'm sorry."

"I was granted another," he said. "This one is not so important."

"Bullshit," she said, knowing that he wouldn't have mentioned it if it wasn't important.

Already, the thudding of her heart was drowned out by a growing susurration of rushing water. As much as she tried to block it out, the river god's voice murmured in her head,

"Mask-Maker, restore me."

"Give it to me," she said.

He practically pushed it into her hands. "I would not ask—"

"You don't have to ask," she said.

He bowed. "Thank you, Josie-sensei."

"Don't call me that."

"You touch the faces of the gods and bring them to life."

"No, I don't," she said. "I'm fixing something for a friend. That's all."

"Then I am most fortunate in my friends."

"Burgers?" Judah asked.

"Daisuke loves burgers." She glanced over her shoulder to the deck, where Daisuke was hanging on Tessa's every word.

She couldn't tell if he was doing it out of respect or if he was actually interested. "And they're not just burgers. They're adobe avocado bacon burgers."

She turned back to the grill. The patties sizzled and popped. The aroma of smoke and meat was almost dizzying—the perfect incense for another stunning summer day.

As the light began to filter through the trees and the blue sky turned dusky, doves began to coo from the branches, their plaintive calls drawing Josie away from the warm laughter and friendly conversation like a sad love song.

Her dad had been reluctant to give her control of the grill, but she'd insisted. Besides, he was too preoccupied with Caroline. Cheeks flushed, he was fiddling with the buttons on his shirt—a lot. His girlfriend had broken up with him a couple months prior, but he didn't seem terribly heartbroken about it. Josie envied him.

Simone was present too, in close conference with Kai, who looked tired and distracted.

"Daisuke travels a lot," Josie said to Judah. "He likes to experience local culture."

"I can see that." Judah took a drink of his beer. He was only eighteen, but they were all drinking. Imbibing wasn't unusual for Core teenagers. Once a person reached adulthood—fifteen for the Core—they were considered old enough to summon a god, marry, have children, drink. Although the mores of the society around a particular tribe often influenced how much freedom of choice their younger Core members were actually given. Her dad was stricter about drinking than others in their tribe. Today though, Caroline's carefree presence seemed to be affecting him. Josie had never seen her dad smiling the way he was—goofily.

Josie smirked again at Tessa, who was soaking in Daisuke's rapt attention. "Jealous?" She shoveled the burgers off the grill and onto a platter.

"Should I be?" he asked.

"Tessa is," she said, turning off the burners. "She thinks you're cheating." She met his unreadable gaze. Even his brow had gone into blackout mode. "Are you?"

"You're actually asking me that."

"I want to know."

"Just like you want to know where your mysterious fire summoner disappeared to?"

She picked up the platter of burgers and took them inside. For some reason, Judah followed her. He seemed to be doing that a lot lately. She'd been doing her best to blot him out of her mind, but he made it difficult. He made everything difficult. Just when she thought she'd successfully purged her last encounter with him, he'd show up again.

She washed her hands. Laying out the grilled buns, she assembled the burgers. He stood by the table with his back to the door. She didn't know how he could make a blue T-shirt, jeans, and flip-flops look pretentious, but it seemed like no matter what he wore he was showing off.

"When did you become so selfish?" he asked.

How did he know just what to say to make her feel worse?

"You've been sitting around feeling sorry for yourself for months," he said, heedless of the fact that she had many sharp, stabby instruments within reach. "Tessa's nowhere near ready. The Eyes are blind. Lily is out there, waiting for the right moment to get her hands on you, and the only thing you care about is finding some douche of a fire god summoner who ditched you."

Hot tremors jolted through her limbs like shockwaves. "You don't know anything about—"

"I've stayed away, Josie, because I'd hoped you'd get your priorities straight. The unity of the Core is poised for collapse. An ineffectual Triune. Powerless leaders. A half-mad summoner with way too much power is plotting a mass extinction of the human race. And you are the only one who can do anything about any of it."

"Right." She slapped the bacon on top of the burgers. "Build an army."

"Think, Josie. Have you ever considered the possibility that since you can make the gods, you can destroy the gods? We're alive right now because you destroyed Lily's mask."

"I broke it. I didn't destroy it."

"But could you?"

Her mind went blank. "I don't know—"

"If you can reach into the Beyond and bring forth the face of a god, then why can't you send it back?"

She wiped her greasy hands on a towel. "I never considered it."

"You should," he said, tilting his beer bottle back until it was empty.

"In order to do that, I'd have to go back to the Beyond."

He set the bottle down on the table in the corner. "Are you afraid?"

"Yes, I'm afraid," she said, surprised by her own admission. And to Judah, whom she had no intention of admitting anything to.

She glanced at him. He wasn't pouncing. Was there some granule of humanity beneath his chiseled-to-perfection façade?

While she never would have said it—not to his face—Judah was one of the few people she trusted. How could she not? He'd saved her life more than once. He wasn't nice about it, but he'd done it. He'd orchestrated her rescue from Lily too. And why?

The only reason she could come up with was that his overinflated ego seemed to demand he play the hero. He'd flat out told her they weren't friends, and he'd been right. Being around him felt like banging her head against a wall. So it was more than a little frustrating to find herself listening to him, and once again agreeing with him, and worse, about to ask him for help.

But it was time. She knew she'd been putting it off too long already. Like she'd told Simone, traversing the pathways was a faster means of repairing a mask, but it was also anxiety-inducing.

The first and only time she'd gone she hadn't known what to expect—she hadn't even known what she was doing. But now, the thought of crossing into the paths of the gods, to the boundary of the Beyond, of leaving her body behind . . .

Was her heart pounding because she was terrified, or because she was thrilled? Sometimes it seemed the more intense her emotions, the harder it was for her to tell what she was actually feeling.

But what was she waiting for?

She took off her apron, wiping her hands on it. She put the burgers in the warming drawer and turned it on.

"Come with me," she said, slipping into the shadows of the bedroom hall.

She led him into her room. She went straight to the patio doors. Dark wood blinds hung over the glass. Out on the deck, she could hear Caroline's full-belly laughter and Tessa's smiling voice, chattering away.

Josie flipped the latch, locking the doors.

Judah stood in the hall, eyeing the room like it might be a trap.

"I won't bite." She swept a pile of wooden figurines aside with her foot. Animals of Africa, one of the first series she'd started after Fire Guy had left her. "Close the door."

He came inside, shutting the door behind him. He frowned at the carvings cluttering the dresser. He picked up a little bear-like creature with huge ears and big eyes: *Cheburashka.* Part of her foreign cartoon characters series.

"This is what you've been doing?" he asked.

"When I lived on the island with my mom," she said, opening the top drawer of her dresser, "I used to run. I'd run until my legs gave out, if that's what it took. But I can't do that anymore, so—" She gestured to the half dozen cartoon characters, along with the other series she'd done: animals of Australia, trees of Africa, volcanos.

"You could run at the center's gym," he said. "They have treadmills."

"It's not the same," she said, pulling the pieces of Daisuke's mask out from the half-empty drawer. Most of her clothes were stuffed into the overflowing hamper in the corner. She couldn't remember the last time she'd done her laundry.

"I could take you," he said softly.

She laid the fractured pieces of the mask on her futon, shoving aside the rumpled blankets. "Take me?"

"To the beach," he said. "To run. If you want."

She stared. "Why would you … what about keeping Josie locked up and under constant surveillance? The Eye would never let me go someplace that wasn't protected."

He lifted his shoulder, seeming to be more interested in the corners of her room than her. "We don't have to tell them. We could translocate. We'd be gone and back again before anyone noticed."

She almost said, yes, let's go right now. To run and run and run until she collapsed on the sand, staring up at the sky feeling nothing but her pulse racing and her lungs burning. Once there had been a time when doing that would've made all her anxieties vanish, all her thoughts mute, all her pain trivial. She longed for that kind of release again, but a part of her knew that no matter how far she ran, or for how long, this wasn't a pain she could outrun.

Besides, she was stunned. Judah proposing they break big time rules? Just so she could blow off some steam? Why? Because he felt sorry for her? Or was he actually trying to be nice? And if so, why?

She had trouble looking at him, unnerved by the sudden shift in the air. She knew how the air around Judah was supposed to feel, hot and oppressive, like having the sun glaring down on her, shining a beam on every flaw, every mistake.

The heat remained oppressive, but in a way that made her thoughts melt together and the bones in her body feel less than solid.

The silence was stretching on, turning awkward.

When she opened her mouth, all that came out was, "Ah . . ."

"Let me guess—you'd prefer for Russell to take you." His kind tone turned blunt, jarring her. "Maybe that's the 'something' you two could do together once he gets back."

Now she was back on solid ground—and it was covered in hot coals, burning her from the soles up. "You shouldn't eavesdrop."

"He just wants to use you."

"You don't know that—"

"Everyone knows that. Put his name on a list? How about he gives you a list of all the girls he's played in the last ten years? It would have to be printed in annual installments—"

"So you're trying to protect me? Is that it?"

"I'm just trying to get you to open your eyes, Josie."

"My eyes are open. Right now, I see an over-opinionated frat boy wannabe who should mind his own damned business—"

He sneered. "Frat boy—"

"I didn't bring you here to fight, okay? You want to help me?"

His brow remained belligerent, but his mouth stopped moving.

Again, she wondered what she'd been thinking. Every time she engaged with Judah, it ended in an argument. But if she was going to try to fix Daisuke's mask by going to the Beyond, she couldn't think of anyone else she'd want to be there. It was annoying and confusing and she couldn't think about it too much. If she started thinking about any of it too much, she was likely to call the whole thing off.

"I need you to . . ."—she knelt in front of the mask—"watch me."

He took a step towards her. "What am I watching you for?"

"I don't know." The rush of water began to fill her ears as she looked down at the shattered face of the god—the green paint, the wicked white eyes, the lashing red tongue split almost straight down the center. "I'd just feel better if you watched me, in case . . ."

"In case what? You need first aid? You're not planning on letting yourself be burned again, are you?"

"He's a water god."

"I'd prefer if you didn't drown again either," he said.

"Are you sure about that?"

His eyes flashed. "Why do you say shit like—?"

"Are you going to help me or not?"

His eyebrow angled extra sharp: *You're driving me effin' crazy.*

She wiped the cold perspiration from her forehead. The rush of water was turning into a roar. She barely heard Judah when he asked,

"What are you going to do?"

"Just don't . . ." Her fingers reached out towards the pieces of the mask. Already, her voice sounded distant in her ears as her sense of her body was slipping away.

"Don't what?"

"Don't let me go too far," she said as she touched the mask . . . and slipped out of her body.

CHAPTER 14

July 4th

DOWN INTO THE DARKNESS.

Judah, her room, her body became distant echoes. Clawing fingers of panic grasped at her, begging her to return to where there was light and warmth and breath.

The last time she'd traversed the pathways had been to bring back a mountain god. The journey had felt like ascending, straining upwards towards the heavens, climbing to the impossible summit.

In the pathways of the water gods, she plunged. If she hadn't recently drowned, it might not have been quite as disturbing.

Though she was only a spirit, a terrible sense of suffocation overtook her, inflating pressure inside and crushing weight outside. And no light, anywhere.

Just when she thought she couldn't take it, that she had to turn back or she really would be lost for good, she came to the edge of the pathways—the boundary that separated the paths of the gods from the Immortal Realms.

Before her, the vastness, the bottomless void, the Beyond.

"I am here," a voice said to her as its face began to emerge out of the darkness.

The face of Daisuke's river god rippled before her—its true face. The changing face of the raging green river—vortices, calm depths and roaring rapids, temperate currents and wild power. His tongue flicked black like silt, not red as it had been painted on the mask. He didn't have horns or fangs like the mask had either, but he was green—deep, murky green. The nearer the face came, the firmer its shape grew.

She started to reach for it, over the precipice, but then hesitated.

This was Daisuke's god. But the face before her was far more than what the original mask-maker had conceived. She could feel the power rushing over her like a flash flood. The old mask had been a glimpse, a rendition, a shadow. This face was channeling more of the god's power. If she took it now, as it was, it would not be the god's full power, but it would be much closer, maybe as close as was possible. Maybe too close.

This was what she'd been afraid of. The power. More specifically, her ability to bring this kind of power back to the mortal realm. Even in the hands of someone she felt certain she could trust, like Daisuke, it was dangerous. Anyone could take the mask from him, at any time.

The gods were indifferent to the fate of humanity. Like the mountain god had told her before she'd brought him back from the Beyond, life was transient. One day, the world itself would cease to exist. What did he care if humans were around to see that day or not?

He didn't. He was a god.

But she was human. If she was going to bring masks back from the Beyond like this, she had to find a way to control it. And quickly, because the longer she stayed, the more the currents pulled at her, tugging her towards the Beyond. If that happened, she would be dead.

She studied the face. Soon she realized why it was channeling so much power, because it looked very much like Daisuke—the same broad cheekbones, the same full jaw and lips.

The last thing she needed was to doom Daisuke to the same fate as her Fire Guy.

"You can't be manifest," she told the god.

"If that is your will, Mask-Maker," the god replied in its crashing water-full voice.

"How do I prevent it?"

"It is all within your vision," he replied.

"My vision?" she asked.

But the god didn't elaborate.

She frowned, teetering on the edge, not wanting to rush, but anxious to return. Even though she was surrounded by darkness, currents swept around her, pushing and tugging at her, and she had an ominous sense that she wasn't entirely alone.

She focused on the mask. Maybe she was thinking too much about Daisuke. She erased his face from her mind and forced the memory of the old mask forward in her thoughts.

"As I recall," she said to the god, "you were uglier."

Just like that, the face changed: eyes rounding, cheeks plumping, chin pointing, fangs and horns reappearing—more like what the mask had been. Weaker. But still, more powerful than it had been. At least she felt certain it wouldn't put Daisuke's soul in danger.

She reached out, stretching as far as she dared into the emptiness, tottering on the edge of the Beyond, and grasped the face. The ripples and whirlpools froze at her touch, an image of what it would be in the mortal plane. She drew the face out of the Beyond.

A strong surge pushed her, shoving her forward.

Dizzy panic reeled through her as she kissed the barely perceptible skin between mortality and death . . . and almost tumbled over to the other side. But pressure circled her arms, far away and faint, but present. A voice called her—Judah. He'd caught her. He was pulling her back.

She swore she heard a rustling voice like dead, dry leaves caught on a gentle breeze. Was Death out there, watching her? Waiting?

Judah's distant presence pulled at her while the currents continued to shove, growing stronger, keeping her trapped on the precipice. Even though she wanted to return, she wasn't moving. The undertow slammed into her. An icy flood spilled through her—the cold that had been eating away at her for months. Behind her, the chasm opened up, like the mouth of the whale, ready to swallow her.

The empty roar in her ears asked, wouldn't it better? Wouldn't it be easier to just . . . let go?

Before she could answer the question, she heard Judah say,

"Josie, come back now."

And she did.

She gasped.

Her stomach lurched into her throat. Her muscles jerked and then went limp.

Judah held her up on her knees, against him.

As she took a breath and then another, the scent of him flooded her, a mix of clean, expensive sheets and a warmer, resinous sweetness.

Taking another deep breath, she was just about to thank Judah for bringing her back to this world of scents and for smelling so good—really, really good—when he took her chin, roughly, and forced her to look up at him.

"Are you here?" he asked.

She swallowed back the sting of bile and nodded. A giddy kind of rush was shouldering in against the weakness. A warm feeling. It had been so long since she'd felt warm.

"Josie—"

"I'm here," she said with some effort.

Restored, green paint glistening as if wet, the mask slipped from her fingers to the hardwood, clattering softly. The symbol on its forehead glowed for a moment and then vanished.

Judah let out a breath that shuddered against her. "You weren't."

"What?"

"You were here and then for a split second,"—his hand slid from her face, fingerprints of warmth lingered on her cheek. He snapped his fingers—"you weren't. Like that. And the whole time, you were transparent . . . like a ghost."

"Oh," she said, rubbing her forehead.

"Oh?"

"I . . . stumbled."

His eyes flashed. "Stumbled into the Beyond?"

She looked away. "Almost."

"You knew it would happen—" he said accusingly.

"I didn't know it would happen." She gripped the edge of the futon, slipping away from his too-warm grasp. "I was afraid it could happen."

"Afraid. Yeah, I guess," he said. "You almost died. Again."

She started to stand, but her knees buckled. She sank back onto her heels.

He gripped her arm. "Are you sure you're all right?"

She gazed at the river god's face, noting the weak point across the bridge of the nose. If she ever needed to break it, she could.

He grabbed her other arm and turned her towards him. "Josie—"

Her hand pressed to his chest to push him back.

"I'm fi—"

His heart pounded against her palm. In response, her own heart throbbed—a deep painful pulse she felt all the way down in the darkest, coldest depths.

She snatched her hand back and turned away, forcing him to let go. She shoved up to her feet. The heat coming off of him was intoxicating. Nearly dying again, traveling the pathways, it had done something to her. Not only did everything smell amazing—and feel amazing—but it seemed more vivid and alive. Judah's eyes were bluer, his lips redder, his hair more like gold.

"How long did it take?" she asked, unable to look at him and unable to stop looking at him. His skin glowed as if he had his own personal sun inside.

"A couple minutes," he said flatly, still kneeling on the floor.

She scooped up the mask and looked down at him. "I would thank you, but I'm sure you'd just tell me that I don't really mean it."

His bowed his head, brow plunging deeply—angry.

Her unexpectedly revived heart wrenched—guiltily.

"I didn't know that would happen," she said. "I didn't know *what* would happen."

He stood up, slowly. "I hope not."

"Which is why I asked you to be here," she said, feeling like she needed to assuage him for some reason. She'd never felt like that before.

But she was feeling all kinds of things she hadn't felt, not for months anyway.

Not only was she no longer cold, she was flush all over. If only she weren't with Judah, she might actually be able to enjoy this restoration of her senses.

The world was alive again, after months of bleakness and chill, except the only thing in the world she could see was Judah.

A crazy urge came over her to touch him, to feel his heart beating furiously against her palm again, to press her nose against his throat and drown in his smell. She clenched her hands and tried not to breathe too deeply.

What was wrong with her? This was Judah. *Tessa's* Judah.

She shouldn't have been having any kind of feelings about him—let alone *those* kinds of feelings.

Her latest brush with death had done something to her—stricken her with some form of temporary insanity.

Whatever the case, she grappled the feelings and shoved them into the forgetting place of her mind, slamming and bolting the door behind her. Crazy urges, inexplicable emotions, useless thoughts, the oubliette was where all things related to Judah belonged.

Except he was still there, glaring at her.

"You shouldn't go back again," he said. "It's too dangerous."

"What about sending the gods back to the Beyond? What about being the only one who can do anything about Lily and the Covenant and saving all of humanity?"

His arms crossed. "Not like this."

"We don't get to have it both ways, you know?"

The rigidity of his brow faltered. "What—?"

"Are we at war? Or not?"

His lip curled. "Russell said that, not—"

"I know who said it, but he was right. You agree with him, don't you? I know you won't admit it, but you know as well as anyone—better—that we're already fighting for our lives. Do you want me to do everything I can to save us, or would you rather put me in a bunker and have me sit idle while all of human civilization is decimated? Because it seems like you can't quite make up your mind. One minute you're scolding me for not doing enough, and the next you're telling me to stop."

"You don't know that going to the Beyond will help—"

"And I don't know that it won't, but I have to try, don't I? Maybe I can send the gods back to the Beyond. Maybe I can get a hold of Lily's mask and banish it from the mortal realm once and for all. That's worth knowing, isn't it? It's worth trying, but before I attempt something like that, I need to get a grasp on this. Travelling the pathways *is* dangerous. It *is* risky. And I won't feel safe going back unless you're with me—"

She caught her breath, holding it in her throat, but it was too late. The words had rushed out before she'd realized what she was saying.

A look appeared on Judah's face, that same one from the day before, the one that had tripped up her thoughts and left her dumb and immobilized.

For a moment, all the laughter and muffled conversation drifting through the patio doors muted. A bubble had formed around her and Judah. Inside, it was all held-breaths and heart-thrumming silence and heat.

And then he moved, shifting towards her. "Josie—"

The bubble burst.

She stepped back, clutching Daisuke's mask to her chest and breathing too fast.

"I didn't mean—" She circled around him, keeping her distance, and stowed Daisuke's mask back in her drawer. "I just meant—"

What had she meant? Trying to figure it out was making her head ache.

He moved closer. "Will you—"

She slammed the drawer shut. *Cheburashka* teetered on the edge and fell to the floor. "We should get back. They're probably hungry—" She slid past him, not meeting his eyes.

He reached for her. She flinched, bumping into the wall.

His hands drew back, flat and open, appeasing.

She shook away the whispers of thoughts slipping past the barriers in her mind. She would not hear them. She would not feel anything she didn't want to feel.

"All I meant," she said, speaking in a rush, "was that I would feel safer with someone to watch me when I travel the pathways. I didn't mean it had to be you. It could be anyone." She took a deep breath and stepped away from the wall, sneaking a glance up at his face. "In fact I would prefer if it were someone else."

He winced. The expression was so fleeting, so faint, she wasn't sure she'd seen it. Judah never showed distress or pain. He was always Mr. Cool, Mr. Right, Mr. Perfect.

In a second though, his face was impassive again.

A blunt laugh escaped him. "Right." He yanked open the door. "Thanks for reminding me."

CHAPTER 15

July 4th

After dinner and the fireworks from Oaks Park were over, Josie slipped away from the deck to the front porch. She sat on the swing, cardigan wrapped tightly against the damp chill. The chains groaned softly as she swung.

Bars of warm light slid through the window blinds behind her. Every so often she could hear her dad and Caroline chuckling in the living room. They'd left the deck soon after the fireworks, when Tessa had started giving them weird looks. Josie guessed it would be pretty uncomfortable to watch her dad flirting with her boyfriend's mom—that is, if she'd had a boyfriend.

The burning of exhaust and the wetness of loam hung in the air. When the wind blew, a whiff of the river came with it, fishy and brown. Grill smoke clung to her clothes and the faintest breath of Judah's cologne—ode de jackass. She might've stayed on the deck, but the clashing of awkward vibes was too much.

Tessa was giving Judah the cold shoulder. It had become painfully obvious that she was batting her eyelashes at Daisuke to make Judah jealous—with no success.

Judah had lapsed into an uncharacteristic brood, staring into the middle distance, not speaking or looking at anyone. Meanwhile, Kai was even less engaged than ever. He spent most of his time huddled over his phone. Once Gretchen and Roxy had headed home, Simone had nothing to do but shoot Josie and Judah worried looks.

Josie finished the rest of her beer, her head dropping back against the swing. She closed her eyes and tried to lose herself in the swing's rocking rhythm.

Her phone rang.

She sat upright. Her heart stopped. Everyone who would call her was within shouting distance.

She withdrew her phone from her pocket with the tips of her fingers, like it might explode.

The number came up unavailable.

She stood up, clutching her phone in one hand and her beer in the other.

Why was her first instinct to call Judah?

She ground her teeth. She'd let all his acts of heroism get to her. Even if it were Fog God calling to make threats in a more personal manner, so what? Her mother had put her through so much training, Josie's spine was supposed to be steel. She'd been spending too much time around her father and sister and Simone, who all thought that if you weren't sobbing over every stray kitten, you were soulless.

Fear was inevitable, but courage was a choice. Another Triune-ism.

She answered.

"Hello?"

"What'd you think of the fireworks?" Russell asked.

She didn't want to admit how relieved she was to hear his smooth, dusky voice.

She even smiled a little as she asked, "Have you ever been in Sydney on New Year's Eve?"

"I can't say I have."

"If you ever go, wear sunglasses."

"Would you rather be in Sydney right now?"

"They don't celebrate the Fourth of July in Australia."

He chuckled. "I'm aware. You just look like you'd rather be somewhere else."

She leaned against the porch railing, scanning the dark street. "Where are you?"

"Look to your left," he said.

From the darkness in front of Gretchen's house, Russell emerged. She hung up as he approached. Dressed in black jeans and a maroon T-shirt, he easily melted into the shadows of the big trees and car-lined street.

He strolled up the front walk, looking like a part of the night come alive with his dark hair and eyes and shadow-kissed face.

She met him at the bottom step. Since he was a part of her tribe, he could pass through the outer protective circles around the house. Like Allison, he could even knock on the door, but if he wanted to get much further, she would have to invite him.

"You're back," she said.

He smiled.

"What are you doing here?" she asked.

"I was going for a walk."

"Don't you live in Eastmoreland?" she asked, referring to the neighborhood north and one—or two—tax brackets up from hers.

"My parents live in Eastmoreland," he said. "I'm staying there right now, but it's just temporary. My roommate bailed, and I couldn't afford the rent on my own. Since I've been busy helping the Eye, I haven't had time to find a new place. As soon as I started college, I moved out, boldly bucking the ancient Core tradition of mooching off my parents until I'm married."

"Aren't you still in college?"

"Graduate school," he said. "I'm supposed to be working on my thesis, but lately, it seems like all I do is chase down leads on Lily."

"Is that what you were doing last night?"

"No, just tying up a few loose ends," he said. "Party over?"

She drew her sweater tighter around her. "It is for me, but everyone's still out back."

He put the sole of his foot on the edge of the step. "Are you planning on working tomorrow?"

She sighed. "I guess."

"Having trouble?"

She shrugged.

"Anything I can do to make it easier?" He touched her forearm. More warm flutters. "I'll do whatever I can to help."

She chewed her lip.

Did she trust Russell enough to tell him about her ability to traverse the pathways? Being a mask-maker was unusual enough, but having the ability to reach into the Beyond? Not even summoners could do that. Only demons and gods . . . and the dead.

But this was Russell. The Eye trusted him. And he'd trusted her enough to tell her what he'd learned about Lily and the mysterious Fog God.

Since her argument with Judah earlier, she'd become determined to return to the pathways and the Beyond, if for no other reason than to learn how to do so without feeling like she needed him—not that she needed him. All his life-saving had simply made him her go-to safety person, like having a regular fix-it guy.

It was time she branched out and tried trusting someone else, someone who didn't make everything so complicated and infuriating—someone not named Judah.

Russell was the perfect choice. She didn't know why she hadn't thought of it sooner, especially since she suspected he might be the Fire Guy.

To hell with Judah. She didn't need him to protect her, from anything.

"Actually," she said, "there might be something you can do."

His eyes were so dark and deep—a girl could drown in those eyes. "Anything."

"How about I get a couple beers and we can talk about it?"

He smiled. Warm flutters, growing warmer, faster.

"Sounds good."

Under the festoons of twinkling lights strung over the deck, Tessa looked like an angel queen. Her skin seemed to shimmer, even in the shadows. No wonder Daisuke's eyes were glazed and dreamy.

Josie crept along the driveway to the cooler by the garage, hoping to go unnoticed. Tessa was in the middle of recounting the time they'd been attacked by Lily's TemperMentals at the beach.

The lid of the cooler creaked as she lifted it. She winced.

"Josie," Tessa called from across the table, which was cluttered with empty beer bottles and bent caps, "where have you been? Don't be antisocial when Daisuke's here."

Tessa had finally figured out how to pronounce his name correctly, or semi-correctly, more like Dice-k.

Josie pulled two beers from the cool water and stood up.

"I'm not being antisocial," she said.

Her gaze was drawn to Judah's. Half in the shadows, his eyes glowed. She could see the anger lingering in the darkness around his brow. A hot flare shot through her.

How did he do that? How could he piss her off with nothing but a look? Why did he have to be so . . . Judah?

"Thirsty?" Tessa asked, raising her eyebrow at the two beer bottles in Josie's hands.

She moved the bottles slightly behind her. She wasn't going to mention Russell's presence. Unlike her sister, she wasn't interested in provoking Judah—not really. It just seemed to happen whether she wanted it to or not.

A lingering sense of guilt nagged at her. She'd downplayed it, but he'd saved her life earlier—again. If she had fallen into the Beyond . . .

"Come sit with us, Josie," Simone said, pleading.

"I will," she said. "In a minute."

"Why in a minute?" Tessa asked. "Why not now? I was just about to tell Daisuke how the TemperMentals were material enough to grab you and drag you off. You should tell it. It happened to you."

A terrible knot cinched in her gut. "There's really not much to say."

"What are you talking about?" Tessa said. "It was crazy. You drowned. And then you almost died of hypothermia."

Most of the time, Tessa was hyperaware of other people's feelings, but when it came to Josie, she seemed to have permanent blinders on.

Tessa turned back to Daisuke. "It was the first time I went into full possession of the Tripartite . . ."

Josie ground her teeth as her sister continued telling the story. The last thing Josie wanted to do was relive drowning. And she especially didn't want to think about how Judah had saved her—using the powers of an ocean god mask to pull the water from her lungs, carrying her back to his car, stripping off all her clothes, holding her against him to keep her core temperature from dropping into the fatal digits.

Even though she was able to forget about it most of the time, she often had nightmares about drowning. Judah's rescue, on the other hand, she'd managed to stuff deep into the oubliette.

But now that Tessa was sitting there, retelling the story with her particular brand of teenaged dramatic flair, Josie couldn't stop the memories from creeping out from the dark, forgetting depths. As soon as those terrifying moments of near-death gained purchase in her consciousness again, all the other times Judah had been there for her came back too: when he'd treated her burns after she'd repaired the Fire God's mask, when he'd caught her as she plummeted off a cliff during her escape from Lily, and just now, when he'd pulled her back from falling into the Beyond.

She'd never thanked him for any of it.

No wonder he was pissed off.

Was it so impossible for her to say a simple thank you? Maybe she had terrible people skills, but she wasn't soulless.

She slipped the bottle opener from her back pocket and popped the cap off her beer. She took a swig, her heart galloping at derby speed.

She swallowed the beer and cleared her throat.

"Judah, can I talk to you for a minute?"

They all looked at him, showing surprise, except Daisuke, who didn't know how Josie had gone out of her way to avoid Judah and how strange it was for her to be asking to speak to him.

Judah didn't move. He sat there, glaring at her.

Another flare of irritation seared her. What was she thinking? What did it matter if he thought she was an ungrateful—

He set his beer bottle aside and pushed up from his chair.

She backed into the deeper shadows of the driveway around the corner of the house and out of the view of the others. Behind her, parchment yellow light from the kitchen crumbled down the steps. She set the beers down on them. The hose reel was mounted to the house next to her. A slow drip from the spigot left a dark trail across the pavement underfoot, forming an amorphous shade that brought back more memories of Lily's phantom TemperMentals.

Judah approached her warily. When he stopped, he crossed his arms over his chest—so Judah.

She gazed up at him, wondering what the hell she'd been thinking. The first and only time she'd tried to thank him, he'd told her not to bother. Then they'd gotten into an argument. Why did she feel like she needed to try again? Maybe she'd had too much to drink. Now that he was standing in front of her, she wasn't sure she could do it. The thought of being honest with him, bare . . . It scared her. And she didn't know why.

"You saved my life," she said in a whisper. "Tonight. You know that."

He stood there, gazing down at her with those glowing blue eyes, like twin cobalt stars. They'd always been so distant and cool, but lately, they seemed closer and hotter.

She fought through the tightness in her throat. "Say something."

He looked away, towards the darkness crouched beside them, inching closer as the night grew deeper. "Do you know how my dad died, Josie?"

Her mind went blank, baffled by his redirect. "Um . . . he died fighting a fire, didn't he?"

Judah nodded. His tone was matter-of-fact. "Three-story apartment building on Glisan. Someone left a candle burning, the curtains caught. No sprinklers. None of the smoke detectors worked. He was carrying out a ten-year-old girl. The ceiling collapsed. They both died."

"I remember," she said. "You were . . ."

"Seven." He continued to gaze away from her, his voice husky, pained.

Another terrible ache was emerging from that crowded place of things-better-forgotten within her. It wrapped round her throat and brought tears to her eyes. Grief.

Grief she hadn't been allowing herself to feel for the loss of her mother, swearing that she wouldn't until Lily was brought to justice. But Judah had dredged it up somehow. How did he do that? How did he make all those years of training, of learning how to control her emotions, just disappear?

She wanted to be angry at him, but how could she? The pain in his voice was so raw. It called down into the depths of her, evoking a response that she didn't want to feel, yet she couldn't stop him. She didn't even try as he continued to speak in that same ache-inspiring voice.

"After he died, Mom sent me to a psychologist. I reduced all her red and orange crayons to nubs, drawing pictures of fire. I'd always wanted to be a firefighter, just like my dad. When she asked if I still wanted to be a firefighter, I told her I didn't. She asked me what I wanted to do instead. I told her I wanted to be a god, so I could stop fires from happening in the first place."

Josie cleared her throat. "Was she Core?"

He shook his head. "She told me it wasn't possible. I asked if she'd gone to college. She said she had. I told her it must've been a college for idiots. After that session, she and my mom had a long talk."

"What happened?"

"I never went back. Then I learned how to summon the gods, and I realized that even a god can't stop every fire." He continued to gaze into the darkness. "But I keep trying."

"Is that what I am? A fire that needs to be put out?"

He looked at her, finally.

"Why don't you see it, Josie?"

Her voice came out weak. "See what?"

The pained expression glanced off his face again. "Exactly."

"Just tell me—"

"Josie?" Russell's voice made her wince.

Judah's expression shifted in an instant, from breath-thieving to fear-inspiring. Josie put a quelling hand on his chest and turned towards Russell. He halted a few steps shy of them. Thin scraps of light brushed his face, darkening the hollows under his cheeks and brow, giving him a skeletal appearance.

Judah seemed to get taller. His chest felt like stone under her palm. "What are you doing here?"

Russell slid his hands into his pockets. "Is this how it's going to be now, Goodwin? I'll forget the tire thing. We really don't want to throw our long-standing truce out the window now, do we? After all, we're on the same side."

"The only side you're on is your own. Why don't you get out of here before—"

Josie pushed against Judah, but he was immoveable. "Because I don't want him to," she said.

Judah glowered at her. His eyes seemed to be shooting off arcs, like solar flares.

"Josie told me what you said, about not wanting her to see me." Russell took an aggressive step forward. "You've got a lot of nerve—"

"Leave. Now," Judah said.

Russell planted his feet. "I don't think Josie wants me to leave."

"No, I don't," she said. "And no one is going to fight either. Got it? That's just stupid."

But Judah ignored her.

"She doesn't know you like I do," Judah said.

"No, I'm hoping she'll get to know me much better."

Judah let out a disdainful snort.

"In fact," Russell went on, "she was just about to tell me how I can help her repair the tribe's masks."

She cringed, shooting Russell an annoyed look.

Judah hooked her under the arm and hauled her around, turning his back to Russell.

"What do you think you're doing?" she said.

For a second, it seemed like he was so furious he couldn't get his teeth unclenched long enough to speak.

"No way—" he said.

"I'm not asking permission." She pried at his fingers. "Let me go."

"She asked nicely, Goodwin." Russell said. "You heard her."

Josie tried to look over Judah's shoulder at Russell. "It's fine, Russell. I will take—"

Judah seized her face between his hands, forcing her eyes back on him. The heat of his touch stunned her. The pained look was back on his face, so clear she could feel it down in her chest. Deep down.

"Why don't you trust me, Josie?"

"She said to let her go, Goodwin." Russell's hand clamped down on Judah's shoulder.

The blue stars went supernova.

Josie grabbed for Judah. "Wait—"

Too late. Judah spun and shoved Russell.

Russell staggered a couple of steps and then sprung back. His fist slammed across Judah's face.

Judah's head whipped to the side, but he rebounded and barreled into Russell, driving him all the way back into the garage.

Josie stared after them, dumbfounded.

From the backyard, she heard Tessa call, "Judah?"

Josie couldn't say who went into possession first. One second they were grappling, and the next they were both in god form.

Judah vanished. In his air god guise, he was invisible.

Russell, on the other hand, blazed to life. Orange flames licked over his body.

Josie's heart stumbled. Russell was in possession of a fire god.

Russell rushed forward, a hulking figure shrouded in dancing flames. And then he was lifted off the ground and rocketed straight up into the air—Judah.

Josie rushed back to the deck.

Everyone had left the table. They stood on the steps, craning their necks. Tessa pushed Josie.

"What did you do?"

"Me?" Josie said. "Your boyfriend started it."

"Yeah." Kai wore a rare whole smile. "I hope he kicks Russell's ass."

Simone's hands were over her mouth, her eyes wavering like she might cry. "We have to stop them."

"They are in so much trouble," Tessa growled, glaring upwards. Against the pale city night was a distant pinprick of fire—Russell.

His orange light grew smaller and smaller as Judah pushed him farther into the atmosphere.

As much as she knew she should be trying to find a way to stop them, she kept getting sidetracked by the fact that Russell had a fire god mask. It wasn't her Fire God, she could tell that right away. Her Fire Guy had possession of an ancient volcanic god. His form was black smoke. When fire rippled over his body, if it was any one color, which it rarely was, it was almost always blue.

But few summoners were allowed to possess fire masks. The gods of fire were volatile and difficult to control. If the Eye had granted Russell a fire god mask, he must've shown a great aptitude for the element and proven his control through numerous trials.

If he could control one fire god, then it was all the more likely that he could control another.

Daisuke came and stood next to her, gazing upwards with everyone else.

"Portland is proving very interesting," he said conversationally, like he often witnessed two summoners breaking a dozen codes of conduct by brawling in possession, and right in front of the Triune.

"Your gift for understatement is stunning," she said.

"This is"—Tessa was turning whiter by the second—"unacceptable!"

Josie agreed. Judah and Russell would both be punished for going into possession during a fight. If she'd been Triune, she would've put a stop to it long before it had started, but . . . she wasn't.

She glanced over at Simone, who was clutching Kai's arm and squinting up at the faint orange streaks. She'd been right. Something was very wrong with Judah. This erratic hothead was not the cool, controlled Judah that Josie had known for the last six months. She didn't know who this Judah was.

"I'm going to get them," Tessa said.

"Wait a minute," Josie said, shaking off her shock and taking her sister's arm before she assumed the mask of the Tripartite and made the situation worse. "You don't have to do that."

Tessa's hand was poised—a split second from reaching into her sanctuary and summoning the Tripartite's mask.

Tessa shook off Josie's hand. "I can do this, Josie. I've summoned the Tripartite's powers plenty. I'm not going to lose control if that's what you're afraid of."

That's exactly what she was afraid of, but she wasn't about to say it out loud.

"I know you won't, Supreme Divine. You're the Triune, Mother of Mothers, Voice of the Three-Faces, Eyes of Life, Hand of Death, Will of the Other, do you really think this little scuffle is worthy of your intervention?"

Actually, it was worthy of her intervention, but not worth the risk to Tessa's life if the Tripartite overwhelmed her.

Tessa didn't look entirely convinced. Her hand was still poised in the air, ready to grab her mask.

"A drunken testosterone-fueled brawl on the Fourth of July?" Josie persisted. "They're probably happening all over the country right now. Really, Light of the Divine, this is not worth the effort. Once they're done you'll mete out the punishment without having to break a sweat."

Slowly, Tessa's hand fell to her side.

Simone and Daisuke crowded around. Simone touched Josie's arm.

"You have to do something," she pleaded softly.

Josie's eyes turned up again.

Fire lanced the sky in a violent orange streak. They were lucky terrae couldn't see the works of the gods, although there were always a few exceptionally perceptive types. Hopefully, they would assume it was just illegal fireworks.

Josie went to the patio doors that led into her bedroom, digging the key from her pocket. She unlocked the doors and retrieved Daisuke's mask.

She returned it to him in both hands, bowing low. "My friend, thank you."

He took the mask from her, bowing in return. "Josie-sensei, I do not deserve—"

"Enough of that," she said, taking his arm and guiding him back down the deck. She pointed upwards to the spiraling coil of flame. "They're going to come down soon. When they do, I need you—the Triune needs you—to cool them off. So she can deal with them."

The corners of Daisuke's eyes crinkled. He bowed again to Tessa. "It would be an honor to assist the Triune."

Tessa tucked her hair behind her ear, smiling a little.

Daisuke ran his thumbs over his newly repaired mask, seeming to study its glossy green surface. The mask appeared much like it had been but was, in fact, so much more. Could Daisuke tell by looking at it? Was he able to sense the increased power the mask was channeling?

Josie leaned close to him, her voice soft. "If you don't think you can handle it, be honest."

His face remained serene but offense shone on the dark surface of his eyes.

She inclined her head and stepped back.

"We have incoming," Kai reported.

Overhead, a ball of fire plummeted towards them like a meteor.

Daisuke placed the river god's mask to his face. Green water swirled around him, molding to his body at first. Then he began to grow—larger and larger.

Kai and Simone backed up onto the deck. Daisuke's whirlpool of a guise doubled in size. The top of his head leveled off with the gutters.

The ball of fire hurtled towards them.

Simone buried her face in Kai's chest.

Josie watched. Her certainty that Judah and Russell wouldn't really hurt each other wavered as the fiery figure plunged towards the earth at terrifying speed.

While in possession, Russell was protected from most injury. Still summoners fighting in possession could hurt each other, even kill each other. If one god weakened the other enough, the weaker god's guise could fail. In that case, if he were to fall from a few hundred feet, then he would be just as dead as anyone else.

Josie's heart clenched as she watched.

Daisuke's godly arms shot out. The two rushing streams formed a pool to catch Russell before he hit the small patch of grass between the deck and the fence.

But the ball of fire was slowing. Five feet above Daisuke's pool, Russell jerked to a halt and dangled. His flames sputtered and almost went out, but then rippled back to life.

He writhed in the air, body of lion-orange fire lighting up the towering cedars and glinting off the churning water below.

Ropes of flame coiled around Judah's invisible form, revealing his shape as they wound over his torso and neck. Judah twisted and thrashed against the fire, still hovering above Russell.

Judah's struggling caused Russell to fall another couple of feet. Then he stopped again, hanging like a marionette by the lashes of flame twined around Judah.

The pool of water retreated back into Daisuke's guise with a soft whoosh. He strode forward, guise murmuring and rushing like a river full of rapids.

Then with a roar, his guise trebled. The river giant towered over them, over the deck and the garage, as tall as the peak of the roof and the tops of the cedars. Two gushing streams whipped out from his body. One wrapped around Russell with a sizzle. The other around Judah. Both hung suspended in capsules of murky water.

Daisuke lowered and then released them, letting them fall the last few feet to the ground in a crumple. Russell's fire went out. Judah, once again, was invisible.

Daisuke's guise shrank to more closely match his true size as he stepped back.

Russell lay in the grass, groaning—unmasked.

Simone hurried down the deck. Tessa started towards Russell too, muttering under her breath how much trouble they were in. Josie was close behind until she hit an invisible wall and was shoved back.

Simone and Tessa knelt over Russell, who seemed only semiconscious. Kai and Daisuke stood nearby.

Tessa turned her face up to the sky. "Judah! Show yourself right now!"

Josie started to call for Tessa but her words were muffled by an invisible hand clamping over her mouth. An arm hooked around her waist. In a breathless whoosh, Judah translocated with her, taking her away.

CHAPTER 16

THE PROTECTION CIRCLES AROUND THE HOUSE prevented him from taking her off the property, so they reappeared on the front porch.

She tore free from him, spun, and shoved him as hard as she could.

"What the hell do you think you're doing?"

He took off his mask, making it disappear with a flick of his wrist.

She recoiled.

His chest heaved. Blood smeared his face. A gash on the bridge of his nose and his lower lip were both clotting dark. Another wound sliced right through his brow, trickling blood over his eye.

Apparently, the fight hadn't been limited to godly powers. Judah looked awful.

At the sight of all the blood, her rage wavered. She couldn't stop herself from thinking he might need a doctor, but she stomped down her concern.

Judah had started the fight. If he was hurt, it was his own damned fault.

"Have you lost your mind?" she said. "Do you know what you just did?"

His tongue ran over the blood on his lip. His words were punctuated by heavy breaths. "Stay—away—from him."

She stared, not sure she'd heard him right.

"What?"

He wiped the blood from his mouth with his hand. His eyes were blistering blue. Waves of fury continued to roll off of him.

She took a deep breath. "How many times do I have to tell you to mind your own damned business?"

Even cut, bleeding, and swelling, she could tell by the rigid set of his brow that nothing she was saying was getting through.

She ground her teeth, half-tempted to leave. Talking to him was pointless. When he thought he was right, there was no arguing with him.

Blood coated his teeth as he spoke, "Did you tell him? About the pathways, about—"

"No."

"Don't."

"What can I say to make you understand?" she said. "You don't have any control over me. If I want to traverse the pathways, I will. And if I want Russell to help me—"

Judah's eyes flashed, his mouth opened, his whole body flinched as it tensed.

"No!" Her hand flew up, halting him. "This is my power, my life, and my decision."

He continued to glare at her, blood running in slow streams down his face, dripping dark splotches onto the porch.

"Look at you." She shook her head, still baffled by his total loss of control. "You know there's going to be an inquiry. You know they could strip you of your summoning privileges. They could exile you both if they wanted to—"

"I won't—" he said thickly.

"It's not up to you," she said. "Why can't you grasp that concept? If the matriarchs want you to leave, then you'll leave. Not even Tessa could stop them. I know you think you're indispensable, but you're not. Our tribe managed to survive long before you came around, and it'll continue to do so long after you're gone."

"What about you?" he said. "How long will you survive if I'm gone?"

Punch. Gut.

As battered as he was, she was sorely tempted to hit him, just one more time. Complete *backpfeifengesicht.*

"You think I need you to be here?" she said. "You think Josie will drop dead the second Judah's gone? You've been away for months and I'm still here. It's not your responsibility to protect me. It never was. I mean—"

She jammed the heel of her hand against her forehead, trying to reconcile the image of the distant, cool Judah she'd known for the last few months with the bloodied, fire-eyed Judah standing in front of her now. The two wouldn't mesh.

She dropped her hand.

"What is this?" she said, gesturing to his bloodied face and torn clothes. "Who are you?"

The front door opened.

Her dad stopped dead. His eyes bulged behind his glasses. He flipped on the porch light.

Judah turned his face away as the light struck him.

Josie's stomach clenched. In the light he looked much worse—more cuts, more swelling, more blood.

"Marc, what is it?" Caroline appeared next to Josie's dad. Her mouth dropped open. "Judah?" She pushed open the screen door and grabbed Judah's arm, circling around him so she could look at his face. "Oh my gods, what happened to you?"

"Nothing," Judah muttered, leaning away from his mom's hands.

Caroline's face hardened. "Like hell. You're going to tell me what happened right this instant." She glanced over at Josie, eyes lit almost as bright as Judah's. "Were you attacked?"

Josie looked at Judah, but his blood-reddened lips were sealed.

"No," she said. "He got into a fight."

Caroline stared at her like she thought Josie was lying.

Her dad came around, took one look at Judah, and stepped back again. He ran a hand over his smooth scalp. "A fight with whom? A heavyweight boxer?"

"Russell," Josie said.

Caroline's incredulity disappeared. "Damn it, Judah. I thought we'd settled this."

"You mean they've done this before?" Josie asked.

Caroline was grim as she tried to inspect Judah's face, but he kept turning away. "A couple of times, when they were younger, but nothing like this." Caroline sighed. "We're going to the hospital."

"I'm not going anywhere," he said.

"There you are!" Tessa cried, storming towards them. She slowed when she saw Judah's battered face. All the color leeched from her cheeks. "Gods . . . Judah, are you okay?" She joined Caroline in crowding him, seeming to forget her anger.

"How's Russell?" Josie asked.

Tessa frowned at her. "He's conscious. Daisuke thinks he might have a couple of broken ribs."

"Hell," her dad said. "Where is he?"

"Out back," Tessa said.

Dad touched Caroline's shoulder as he passed. She gave him an exasperated look before he hurried down the steps. Then her gaze locked onto Josie again, searchingly. For some reason, Josie felt a pang of guilt.

"What happened?" Caroline asked her.

Josie glanced at Judah and Tessa. They were both giving her sidelong looks. She knew what they were thinking, even though, as Triune, Tessa shouldn't have been thinking it. They wanted her to lie. Getting into a fight was one thing, but using their godly powers was a big-time no-no.

"Judah's drunk," she said.

A flash of rage blazed across Judah's eyes, but he kept his mouth shut.

"Russell stopped by," Josie went on, "and Judah started shooting his mouth off. They got into it and it just . . . got out of control."

Out of control. Words she never thought she'd use to describe Judah. But it was true—he'd snapped. Maybe he really was drunk. He hadn't done much through dinner besides glower and drink, except that didn't explain why he and Russell had almost fought days earlier. Maybe she didn't know Judah as well as she thought she did.

Caroline's hands smacked against her thighs. "Well, I've had too much to drink to drive. I'll go next door and see if Gretchen's sobered up. Maybe she can take us to the hospital."

Judah opened his mouth, but Caroline pointed a stern finger at him.

"No arguments," she said. "You've done enough fighting."

She gave Josie one more scrutinizing look, like she knew she wasn't hearing the whole truth. Then she strode down the steps and across the driveway towards Gretchen's house.

Tessa fixed Judah with a hard stare. "Give me your mask," she said.

He gazed down at her like he hadn't heard.

She held out her hand. "Give it to me, or I will take it."

Instead of giving her his mask, he took off his ring—the key to his stash. His knuckles were busted and bloody. He winced as he tugged the ring off. He dropped it into Tessa's hand like he didn't care if he ever got it back.

Tessa slid his stash ring onto her thumb. "I already took Russell's mask. I might give them back if one of you will explain to me what really happened. Gods, I know you think he's a douche, but…" Tessa raked back the long ribbons of her hair, looking as confused as Josie felt. "Are you really drunk?"

"I don't trust him," Judah said, more to Josie than Tessa.

"That's obvious," Tessa said.

"You think he's working for Lily?" Josie asked. "Do you have any proof?"

He looked away.

"Josie's right," Tessa said. "That's a serious accusation—"

"I'm not accusing him."

"No, you're just threatened by him," Josie said.

Judah snorted, shaking his head. "You're unbelievable."

"Me? You're the one covered in blood."

He sucked in a breath and spit into the yard.

Tessa made a face, pulling back from him. "Judah, what's happened to you? This is just . . . look at your face."

His fingers grazed the bloody swell of his bottom lip. He grimaced. Josie ignored the twinge of sympathy in her chest. Why should she feel sorry for him? He'd done this to himself.

Tessa reached for him, but he flinched away from her.

A wet, pained gleam shone in Tessa's eyes.

"It's like I don't even know you anymore," she said.

"I tried," he said seemingly to himself. "But I can't." His voice was disbelieving—and defeated. Josie's chest hurt hearing it.

Josie found herself wanting to ask him what he meant. Before she could, he started down the steps and the front walk.

"Where are you going?" Tessa chased after him. At the end of the walk, she caught up with him, touching his arm. He jerked back like she'd stung him.

"I can't do this anymore," he said.

Josie moved to the top of the steps, not sure why she didn't just go inside or out back to check on Russell.

"You can't leave," Tessa said. "You're hurt. Your mom—"

He let out a derisive puff and turned away again.

"If you walk away . . ."—Tessa's voice was tear-torn—"don't come back."

Though he was thick in the shadows, Josie was sure his eyes flicked up to her.

"I'm sure you'll survive."

He stalked away.

CHAPTER 17

JULY 9TH
FOUR DAYS LATER

"ARE YOU SURE YOU WANT TO DO THIS?" Simone asked again as they rode the elevator up to the second floor.

"Do you want to help me or not?" Josie asked.

Simone wound her necklace around her finger, worry-faced.

"What is that anyway?" Josie asked, trying to get a better look at the necklace. "Did Judah make that for you?"

Simone's hand closed around the pendant of quartz wrapped in blue wire. "Why do you ask that?"

"It looks like the necklace he used to wear."

"He still does wear it," Simone said. "He remade it into a bracelet. Speaking of which." She tugged a couple of the bracelets off her own wrist and held them out. Unlike most of her others, these weren't made with plastic beads, but with stones.

Josie eyed the etched stones, remembering Simone's bout of truth-robbing. "What are they?"

The elevator binged. The doors slid open. Josie stepped off. Simone hurried to her side.

They passed the upstairs lobby with its flat screen and lots of modern black leather couches. A few of the tribe kids were lazing around, playing video games or staring at their computers. Across from it, a red door sang out against the white of the walls—Caroline's graphic design office. Inside, the lights were off. All the other offices were lit. Through narrow windows running alongside the doors, Josie caught glimpses of people at their desks, huddled over computers, talking on their phones. Someone's sad-eyed beagle peered up at Josie and Simone as they walked by. Another subdued Monday morning at the tribal center—business as usual.

"They're sleeping charms," Simone said, "like the one you used on Tessa. I figured if the Tripartite tries to take her over again . . ."

Josie took the bracelets, feeling bad for her suspicions. "You used the speaking stone charm?"

"The big green ones are the initiation stones. Just put it to your lips, say Tessa's name, and the charm should be activated," she said. "I'm sorry about that, Josie. The other day . . . the truth-charm, it wasn't fair."

Josie slipped the bracelets on. "I know you were worried. And I appreciate your concern, but it was sneaky."

"I know. I'm sorry," Simone said, "but I'm still worried about you."

They came to the art lab's door which was decorated with a psychedelic mini-mural. Hidden within the vibrant swirls and saturated scapes—people dancing, the sun shining down on a field of tulips, the moon lulling over a conifer forest— were dozens of protective symbols, charms in their own right, very magical and very powerful.

Josie swiped her card and pushed open the door. She flipped on the lights.

Gretchen had cleaned up after the fire. But even six days gone the stink of burnt plastic lingered.

"How is Tessa?" Simone asked.

"She cried for three days straight," Josie said with a heavy sigh. "Allison was there all day Saturday. She baked cookies. They invited me up to watch sappy movies, but I passed."

She didn't mention that she'd spent the day researching divine tools and whittling. She'd started a new series: famous statues of Adonis. Last night she'd begun a basswood rendition of Rodin's *Death of Adonis*.

"And then yesterday," she went on, "Tessa finally decided to go to the island and consult with her guides. She's still there."

Josie circled the table covered in shattered shells. Four squat boxes had been stacked on the corner. She opened the top box. Big plastic bags full of shells. Days ago she'd told Gretchen she'd need more, but that was before everything had happened.

"Aren't you going to ask me how Judah is?" Simone said, looking sadder than the beagle they'd passed.

Josie closed the box. "Do I have to?"

"Josie—"

"He's alive, isn't he?"

"Yes, he's alive." Simone dropped into one of the molded plastic chairs on the other side of the table. "And he's miserable."

"He should be miserable. He almost killed Russell. Four of Russell's ribs are fractured, his shoulder was dislocated, and his kidneys are bruised. He was in the hospital until yesterday. They were afraid he had internal bleeding."

Simone hung her head. "Kai told me."

"Has your mom decided when the inquiry will be?"

Simone shook her head. "Nancy's still out of town. They'll have to wait for her to come back." She lifted her pierced brow at Josie. "What are you going to tell them?"

Josie frowned. "What do you mean?"

"What really happened, Josie?"

Josie removed her messenger bag and dropped it on the ground. "Judah freaked and beat the crap out of Russell. That's what happened."

"Why?"

"Why don't you ask him?"

"I'm asking you. And the Eye is going to ask you too. They're going to want to know everything that happened."

The memory of Judah's hands on her face came back to her—the heat.

"They were fighting because of you, weren't they?" Simone said.

Josie pushed the phantom pulses of Judah's thought-consuming heat away. "What do you mean?"

Simone rolled her eyes. "Come on, Josie."

"Come on what? Judah hates Russell. Everyone knows that. Just because he won the mask and Judah didn't—"

"Russell didn't beat Judah in the trials," Simone said, vehement. "Russell cheated."

Josie folded her arms. "How did he cheat?"

"In one of the trials, they had to carry a lit candle through the forest and keep it burning—"

"A fire element trial."

"Right. It was a clear day. No wind, no clouds, nothing. Perfect. Russell went in the morning. No problems. In the afternoon, it was Judah's turn. The moment he stepped onto the path, this crazy storm came out of nowhere. One minute it was dead calm, and the next like a monsoon."

"So Judah's flame went out?"

"No. He kept it burning all the way through the forest, except someone moved the trail signs. He got lost. By the time he found his way out, the wick had burned down to nothing. Lily was the presiding judge. Even though they proved that the trail signs had been tampered with and he'd kept the fire going longer than Russell, because it wasn't lit when he finally found his way out, he lost."

Josie frowned. "That doesn't mean Russell cheated or that he had anything to do with the storm or the trail signs. Did you ever think Judah might've lied about what happened? Maybe he just got lost and was too ashamed to admit it."

"Everyone who saw it thought a summoner had interfered, but Lily said the results were final and that was the end of it."

"That seems really unfair to Russell," Josie said. "You don't have any evidence. You don't know it was him."

"Who else would it have been?" Simone's face was a stubborn pucker. "That fire god mask should've been Judah's. Instead, he got the air god mask."

"That's still pretty impressive. That air god mask is nothing to sniff at. And I'm surprised that he was even allowed to compete for any mask, especially considering he was . . . what? Thirteen?"

"He was twelve. His birthday is tomorrow, you know. He'll be nineteen."

"That's nice," Josie said dully. "Are you having a party?"

"We don't celebrate."

"Why not?"

"Because Judah won't let us. The anniversary of Dad's death is the next day." Tears perched in the corners of her eyes.

Josie squatted down, peering across the table at her. "I'm sorry—"

Simone leaned towards Josie. "Call him."

"Who?"

"Judah."

Josie stood up. "Why?"

"Because . . . you need to talk to him."

"About what? How he broke my sister's heart? Or how he sent the guy I like to the hospital?" She held up her hands. "I think it's better that I don't talk to him right now. Besides, the last time I tried to talk to him, things didn't end so well."

"Josie, do you know where he is right now?"

"You know I don't—"

"He and my mom are on their way to Eugene. They're going to talk to the admissions director. The track scholarship they offered him is long gone, but she's hoping she can still get him in for next fall."

"Eugene? He struck me as more of a Reed type."

Then again, he was some kind of all-state athlete, so maybe the Division I athletic program outweighed his desire to brag about being part of the West Coast Ivy League.

"He was accepted at Reed. He turned them down, along with all the other schools."

"Well, whatever. He should go."

"No, he shouldn't. We need him here."

"Eugene's not that far away. You want him to sacrifice his education so he can stick around and play guard dog? I can understand why he'd want to leave. After everything that's happened, it's probably for the best."

"It is not for the best, Josie. He doesn't want to leave. He only thinks he does."

"Huh?"

"He's a warrior, Josie."

Josie grimaced. Simone had never resorted to old-school Corpora labels before. Few people did, even in the more orthodox tribes. Josie only used them when she wanted to startle people.

Warriors, scribes, artisans were titles that no longer held the meaning they once did. Her father was an elder and a scribe, but if someone outside of the Eye were to call him those names to his face, he probably would've wondered what he'd done to piss them off. Only the Triune, the Eye, and the matriarchs were referred to traditionally on a regular basis.

But Simone had achieved her desired reaction. Josie was temporarily left speechless.

"That's right," Simone said. "And he takes it seriously. He takes everything seriously. That's why he didn't want to go to school this fall. He knew he wouldn't be able to focus on his classes when Lily's out there plotting against us. The tribe needs him right now. We need him. You need him, but everyone's acting like nothing's wrong. Even my mom. She's the one who decided to call the admissions director. He's just . . . given up. And it's not like him. He needs someone to remind him who he is. He's forgetting, Josie. He's not being honest with himself and it's . . . changing him."

Josie stared at her pink-haired, manga-eyed best friend. "And you think *I'm* the person who needs to talk to him?"

Simone flattened her hands on the table, seeming to struggle to speak. In the end, all that came out was, "Yes."

Josie shook her head. "Why would he listen to me? He didn't the other night when I told him not to fight with Russell. And why should he? I'm a drudge artisan, Simone."

Simone squeaked. "Don't say that."

"You want to use Core terms? Then let's do it. We're both drudges. Neither of us can summon a god to save our lives."

Simone's eyes quavered.

Josie leveled her gaze at Simone. "No tears. Let's face it. We can't summon gods, can we?"

"No," Simone said in a small voice.

"That's right. Most people in the tribe look down on us."

"No one looks down on you, Josie."

"Oh yes, they do. It's even worse for me because I was supposed to be the Triune. Even Judah gave me flak about it. Once, he said I might be defective and that's why the Triune had sent me a rejection letter. He called me Miss Nobody."

Simone's lip stuck out. "That was months ago, Josie. Before—"

"Who cares when it was? He said it. The point is I'm tired of it. I'm tired of being powerless, I'm tired of being judged, I'm tired of your brother and everyone thinking that I'm a waif. I am not a damsel in distress, Simone. I don't want to be locked up in a tower. I don't want to . . . feel like this anymore."

She whipped out her keycard and pointed it towards the office door that was painted with its own mural full of protective symbols.

"I am going to fix those masks. I am going to traverse the pathways and find the faces of the gods and bring them back from the Beyond. And I don't need anyone to watch me or protect me or save me. I can do this on my own, without anyone. I don't need"—Judah—"anyone."

She marched to the office door.

"Josie, just because you need help, it doesn't mean you're a waif," Simone called after her.

Josie swiped the keycard and whipped open the door, flipping on the light. She yanked the ocean god's box from the rack. She brought it out to one of the empty tables.

"I'm not leaving you," Simone said as Josie sat down.

"I'm not asking you to," she said. "I'm not asking for anything."

She pushed the lid off the box.

A few seconds later, she plunged into the darkness.

Once more, she gazed into the abyss of the Beyond.

The ocean god's eerie white face appeared out of the pitch, smooth as porcelain, glowing with unearthly light.

Currents pulled and shoved at her, but she held tight to her purpose. She could do this on her own. The tribe needed masks and they would get masks.

Reaching into the emptiness, she withdrew the ocean god's face from the Beyond.

She turned, focusing on the faint tug of her body to guide her back. She started forward. An icy current swept by, shoving her back.

She reeled on the edge, with nothing to hold onto but the god's mask and her own horror. Knowledge of herself, her memories, her face, her name, flickered in and out of her awareness, like a light flipping on and off within her. One moment, she was. The next, she was Beyond. She fought to regain her balance, to remain, to live.

"Josephine," a seductive whisper murmured all around her. Death. "Careful, dear daughter."

Finally, she flung herself away from the edge, stumbling back, but the Beyond kept tugging her forward, as if it had a rope lashed around her middle.

"Didn't I tell you to piss off?" she said to Death—wherever he was.

"Is that any way to speak to me?" Death said. "After I've gone to all this trouble?"

Her hands clenched around the mask. "What trouble?"

Death's laugh was like a candle flame softly *whick-whicking* in the wind. "You are too much like your mother sometimes, I fear. That's what you are, afraid. Fear can be blinding, wouldn't you agree, dear daughter?"

"I'm not afraid," she said, putting her head down and focusing all her energy on returning to her body. Slowly, she began to move.

"Oh yes, you are," Death said.

As sense of her body grew stronger, she felt as though she was falling again—falling forward.

"Afraid of being..." Death's voice grew distant as she hurtled back to the mortal realm and into her body.

She toppled out of her chair.

Simone clutched her arm, kneeling beside her.

"Are you okay?" Simone asked. "Oh my gods, Josie, that was so freaky. You were gone. You disappeared."

Josie dropped the ocean god's mask. She sucked heavy breaths. Her lungs burned as if she'd been running for hours.

Death's last word echoed in her ears, hardening the chill within her.

"...unmasked."

CHAPTER 18

July 10th
The Next Day

THE FIRST THING SHE DID when she woke up was pick up her pocket knife and the half-finished carving of *Death of Adonis.*

The naked figures of Adonis, sprawled on a plinth, and Aphrodite, clinging to his dead body, were rounded and smooth. The trickiest part was getting her knife under Aphrodite to carve the small portion of Adonis's face that was visible, which wasn't much—the line of his eye, a bit of his hair.

She liked the sparse detail. Unlike the first carving she'd done, Thorvaldsen's *Adonis*, Rodin's was all emotion. Adonis seemed to be disappearing, lost under Aphrodite's grieving body, his fingers melting into the ground under him.

Checking against the image on her phone, she worked the edge of her knife lightly against Aphrodite's arm. There were finer tools she could've used, but she preferred her pocketknife.

Finally, sitting up, she blew away the shavings. They fluttered through the streams of morning light slipping between the blinds over the French doors.

She ran her thumb over Adonis's arm, thinking how smart it had been not to show his face. Adonis was supposed to be the mortal god of beauty, the epitome of desire. None of the other statues struck her as particularly beautiful or made her feel any desire. How could they? They were someone else's version of beauty. Not hers. Rodin had known better. He focused on the emotion, Aphrodite's grief, not the faces. As Josie studied her own rough-hewn copy of the master's, she could feel that grief like it was her own.

She lowered the carving. Her room was such a mess. Wood shavings everywhere, clothes, books, notebooks in heaps along the walls, some kind of wet stain by the patio doors . . .

Her hand clenched around her pocketknife, breath catching.

A wet red stain like blood.

It oozed under the doors from outside.

She reached for her phone. Then stopped herself, annoyed.

What was wrong with her? She didn't need to call Judah. Her dad was home. Gretchen was right next door.

She didn't need any of them. Was she really going to cry for help because of a little puddle of crimson?

Knife in the one hand and the carving of Adonis clutched in the other, she stood.

Heart thundering, she went to the French doors, grasped the blind's cord, and pulled.

She stared. Her stomach heaved into her throat.

Red paw prints. They covered the glass, up and down, like a giant bleeding dog had been clawing at her doors. She opened the blinds over the other door. More paw prints, smeared and still dripping.

She backed up, tripping over her own dirty laundry, and opened her bedroom door.

"Dad?" she called as calmly as she could. "Dad?"

"Yeah? What is it?" Her dad peeked into the hall from the kitchen, coffee mug in hand.

"Can you come in here, please?" she asked.

Her dad came in, wearing his skintight cycling gear, showing off his lean physique. "I was thinking I'd ride to work today. Gretchen said she'd take you to the—" His face fell. "What's wrong?"

But she didn't have to tell him. He'd spotted it even as he was asking.

He grasped her arm and drew her to him. "What is that?"

She shook her head.

He moved towards the doors warily. She trailed behind him.

He peered through the glass, frowning, pushing his glasses back on the bridge of his nose. He grasped the handle and opened the door.

The warm air was metallic. She knew the scent of blood. Her guts roiled.

"What the hell?" He squatted down to inspect three bloody lumps on the deck.

Josie took a step closer. Tufts of white could still be seen under the matting slick of blood.

"Paws," she said.

Severed paws. Canine maybe.

He covered his mouth. Then he stood up and closed the door. Grasping her arm, he hurried her out of her room.

"It'll be all right," he kept saying. "Everything's all right."

He shut her bedroom door and flicked his wrist. His sea god mask appeared in his hand—a long sedate face, painted with curls of white and pale blue.

"I'm taking you to the center now."

He brought the mask to his face. Two white-capped waves crashed together on either side of him, swirling and engulfing his body. He wrapped his arms around her and drew her into the cool susurrations of his guise.

"Everything's all right."

"Here, Josie, I found this for you," Gretchen said, handing Josie a sweater.

Josie took it. "Thanks."

She pulled the sweater on. She hadn't stopped shivering since her dad had translocated her to the center. All she'd worn to bed was a tank top and a pair of cotton pajama pants. She didn't even have socks or shoes. She drew her knees up, hugging them. Tucked in her lap were her pocketknife and the carving of a dead Adonis.

Gretchen sat down next to her, resting her arm on the back of Josie's chair. She handed Josie a mug of coffee too. Josie held it close to her face, letting the steam warm her cheeks.

A second later, her father and Caroline reappeared. Both were water gods. Her father's usually tranquil guise churned with frothy white irritation. Caroline's guise was blue like her eyes, calmer, but deeper.

Both of them removed their masks, their guises vanishing. Their faces were strained and concerned.

The door opened. Tessa strode in, Daisuke not far behind her.

Her sister looked thinner and paler, but fiercer. No trace of tear stains on her cheeks or redness in her eyes. Her hair was pulled back in a plain ponytail, her jeans were sandy, her T-shirt rumpled. She looked like she'd been camping on the beach or running. Josie ignored a pang of jealousy.

Tessa put her hand on Josie's shoulder, giving it a squeeze.

"When I find them, Josie," she said, "they are so going to pay."

"Find who is the question." Caroline said, leaning against the Eye's table.

"It had to be that fog jerk again, right?" Tessa said. "He's the one who sent the last message."

Her dad brought Josie's messenger bag over to her, along with her sneakers.

"There's a change of clothes in there," he said, "and a few other things."

She took the bag. "Can't I just go home?"

"Not yet," Caroline said. "Not until we clean up that mess and reestablish all of the protective circles. Please think. Have any of you invited any strangers through the outer protective circles? A pizza guy? A girl scout? Anyone? Please say yes."

The Day family looked at each other, transmitting the same message. None of them had invited anyone from outside the tribe into the house.

Josie stowed Adonis and her knife in her bag and put on her shoes.

Her dad took off his glasses, rubbing the bridge of his nose. "Damn."

"I don't believe this," Tessa said. "Another traitor in the tribe? How many can there possibly be?"

"That's not necessarily the case," Gretchen said, clearing her throat and giving Caroline a significant look. Josie knew just what they were thinking.

"It's not Daisuke," Josie said. "I trust him more than I trust either of you . . . sorry."

Daisuke bowed. "If I should leave—"

"Daisuke couldn't have done it," Tessa said. "He's been with me on the island."

Both Josie and her dad frowned at Tessa.

Tessa held up her chin. "I underwent the first trial. I needed someone to come with me."

Josie turned in her chair, looking up at her sister. "You underwent the first trial?"

Tessa nodded.

"And?"

Tessa smiled a little. "I completed it."

Josie smiled. "I knew you could."

Tessa's smile broadened. "I would've taken you, but I needed someone who could bring me back in case I couldn't do it myself."

Josie understood. The Triune's initiation trials could result in injury and, in the later stages, death. The first trial was fairly simple, but still required Tessa to maintain control over the Tripartite for an extended period of time—hours, not something she'd ever been able to do before. Josie wanted to be annoyed that her sister had gone without even telling her, but she was too relieved that Tessa had passed. No wonder Tessa looked so tired.

"And I know you're super busy at work, Dad," Tessa said. "Daisuke knows so much about it, and I knew Josie trusted him—"

"You don't have to explain, Tessa," Josie said. "I mean, Mother Triune."

"Ugh, do you really have to call me that?"

"It is proper, Mistress of the Three," Daisuke said.

"Okay, that's enough. I'm the Triune, and I am decreeing that no one in this room is going to call me any of those weird old names." She gave Daisuke a sharp look. "It's Tessa, okay? That's it."

He bowed.

"And stop that too," she said.

"We still have to face the fact that someone in our tribe is terrorizing Josie," Caroline said. "I mean, for an outsider to get through those protective circles . . ." She shook her head in a way that reminded Josie all too much of Judah. "I laid those circles myself."

Josie didn't question the strength of Caroline's protective charms. No one in the room seemed to be, except Caroline.

"Were they real?" Josie asked. "The paws?"

"It looked like it," her dad said, "but it's hard to say. I've contacted a friend I have in forensics. Once I send them what we found, we'll know for sure."

Josie shook her head. "It's not like him."

"Fog God?" Tessa asked.

"It's not his style," Josie said. "The blood and the dismemberment. It's all too . . . messy."

"Could be he's entering a new creative period," Gretchen said. "Carmine and fur."

"Maybe, but something about it just seems—"

A knock on the door interrupted her.

Caroline stood up. "Enter."

Simone's faded pink hair appeared, followed by her big worried eyes.

Caroline sank back onto the table. She waved her daughter in.

Simone hurried across the room. She bent behind Josie's chair and wrapped her arms around Josie's shoulders. "Are you okay?"

"Not really," Josie answered, gazing over Simone's shoulder.

Judah slid in and stationed himself beside the door, not coming any closer.

She hadn't seen him since the fight.

His face was a mask of fading bruises ranging from egg-yellow to midnight-purple. A thick scab crusted his lower lip and the bridge of his nose. A hash-work of stitches sliced through the slant of his left eyebrow. He didn't look at Josie or at Tessa, who was glaring at him, not disguising her anger or pain.

"Judah, close the door," Caroline said.

"Not quite yet, please," Nancy said, pushing the door open wider. She gave Judah a scowl as she passed him. Her heels clicked on the tile.

"Nancy, when did you get back?" Caroline asked.

"Early this morning," she said, stopping close in front of Caroline, her shoulders rigid beneath her silk blouse. "We have matters to discuss." She turned and examined the rest of them.

"Did you get the pictures I sent you?" Caroline asked.

Nancy turned obliquely towards Caroline. "The bloody paw prints? I did." Her gaze turned to Josie, steely and cutting like straight razors. "You're becoming quite an artist, young lady."

Rage bubbled up inside of Josie, but before she could speak, Tessa stepped forward.

"I don't like what you're implying," Tessa said.

Gretchen crossed her ankle on her knee, leaning back. "Hear, hear."

Nancy's eyes flicked over to Tessa, like she was sizing her up for a fight. Then her gaze moved to Daisuke.

"Does this matter involve the Osaka tribe?" she asked.

"He's here because I want him here," Tessa said.

Josie glanced at Simone, lifting her eyebrows. Simone, sitting in the row of chairs behind, gave Josie a pursed-lip smile in return. Apparently, passing her first trial had given Tessa some Triune-style confidence. About time.

Josie stole another look at Judah. He was staring at Nancy dully, like a bailiff watching a nasty exchange in a courtroom. Then she remembered—today was his birthday, and tomorrow was the anniversary of his father's death. She tried to imagine how awful that was for him. It wasn't hard. All she had to do was think of her mother.

A lump formed in her throat.

"We have another traitor in our tribe," Tessa said. "What are we going to do about it?"

"Hunt him down, cut his hands off, and use his fingers to paint with his blood?" Gretchen asked.

Nancy's face went white. Tessa's nose scrunched. Even Josie's dad turned a little green.

"I like it," Josie said.

Gretchen grinned.

"Short of bringing all five hundred and forty-one members of our tribe in for questioning," Nancy said, "I'm not certain what we can be expected to do about it."

"We should question them," Tessa said, riding her new-found confidence right into a wall.

Nancy smirked. "If you have the time and inclination to do so, Mother of Mothers, then that is your will. But might I suggest that you consider the other obligations which have been sorely in need of your attention these last few months."

Tessa's shoulders fell. The Triune's duties had been stacking up around Tessa. On top of everything happening with Lily, there were all the usual fires to put out: trials for crimes, disputes in need of mediation, induction ceremonies, death rites, naming rituals, a whole host of minor duties, and her introduction tour. She was expected to visit every tribe and every Eye and soon. She needed to establish herself as a force to be reckoned with and respected.

"As for us," Nancy said to Gretchen and Caroline, "I have information that we need to discuss. And I believe we also have... an inquiry?" She turned towards Judah and clucked her tongue. "Well, that is unfortunate."

Tessa caught Josie's eye. She knew what her sister was thinking. Tessa had already covered for Judah, but now that they'd broken up, she was less inclined to lie for him. Unfortunately, she'd already done it. If she changed her story now, it would undermine what little respect the tribe had for her.

"No inquiry," Tessa said. "So he got into a fight—"

"So he put Russell Vale in the hospital," Nancy said. "I spoke to Russell's parents. The doctors said it looked like someone had tried to kill him."

Every gaze turned to Judah. He didn't blink.

"When you began your training," Nancy said to him, "you swore an oath to protect your tribe. Not to use those skills against your own brother—"

"He's not my brother," Judah said in a low voice.

"He is a member of your tribe."

Judah looked away towards the windows. "If you say so."

Nancy held up her hands, as if to say, *You see?*

"Judah, Russell may have been a foster child," Caroline said, eyes matching her son's for intensity, "but he is a part of our tribe. You will acknowledge that."

Josie frowned. She hadn't realized that Russell was a foster child, not that it mattered. Simone and Kai were foster kids too—orphaned children from other tribes. Fostering was common in the Core, a way to keep the bloodlines strong and strengthen the ties between the tribes. Kai had a chip on his shoulder about it, but he'd never said that Russell was a foster kid too. He always made it seem like he suffered alone.

Simone, on the other hand, loved Caroline and Judah as fiercely as Josie loved her dad and sister, maybe more. And for all his faults, Judah had treated Simone better than most brothers treated their sisters. He'd never displayed any kind of bigotry against foster kids, not even subtly, like many tribal members did.

Then again, they weren't talking about just any foster kid. They were talking about Russell.

"I acknowledge that he is a part of this tribe," Judah said mechanically.

"I want to know just what it was that triggered this incident," Nancy said. "Russell said you attacked him without provocation."

"That's not true," Josie said.

Now everyone was staring at her.

"Russell grabbed Judah. Judah shoved him back. That's how the fight started," she said.

"Grabbed him?" Nancy said, incredulous. "Why would he do that?"

"They'd been arguing," Josie said.

"Arguing about what?" Nancy asked.

"Judah told him to leave," she said. "Russell didn't want to go."

"I thought you said Judah was drunk," Nancy said.

Josie shrugged. "He'd been drinking all afternoon."

"And why were you there?"

"I live there."

Nancy's eyes narrowed. "Russell told me he came to see you," she said. "He said that Judah grabbed you and he merely came to your defense."

Josie cursed inwardly. When she'd spoken to Russell on the phone, she'd told him how Tessa was covering up the involvement of the masks and not to mention it, which he'd agreed to for his own sake. But they hadn't discussed what had led up to the fight.

"I didn't need to be defended," she said.

"But Judah put his hands on you. You told him to let go of you, did you not?"

"Yes," she stated. "But I didn't ask Russell to—"

"Why did Judah put his hands on you?"

"He wanted to talk to me—"

"And he needed to physically grab you?"

"He *really* wanted to talk to me."

"Did he hurt you?"

"No—"

"But you were afraid he might?"

"No."

"What did he want to talk to you about?"

Josie's tongue stuck to the roof of her mouth. Her silence lasted a second too long, she knew. Nancy's eyes turned bright, Caroline's frown deepened, her dad pushed his glasses back, and Tessa's gaze narrowed.

"He doesn't like Russell," she said finally, knowing how weak it sounded.

Nancy's gaze cooled. "He had to grab you to tell you that he doesn't like someone?"

"He *really* doesn't like Russell."

Before Nancy could fire off another question, Caroline stepped forward.

"I don't see how this is getting us anywhere," she said. "Judah and Russell have always . . . disliked each other. We all know that."

Nancy turned towards Caroline. "Are you condoning—?"

"I'm not condoning anything, but I think we have enough on our plates without adding a full inquiry. Wouldn't you agree, Sister?"

Nancy plunked her purse down on the table. For the first time since Josie had met her, weariness showed on her taut face. "Just because he is your son does not mean that he can go unpunished—"

"I'm not suggesting he go unpunished," Caroline said, sagging back onto the table. "Both of them should be punished."

"Punitive measures are well and good," Nancy said, "but my primary concern is that it doesn't happen again. Russell has proven invaluable these last few months. We can ill afford to have our people in the hospital at times like these."

"Agreed," Caroline said.

Nancy turned to Judah, who was still by the doors. "Russell claimed not to have any idea why you attacked him so viciously. Do you have an explanation?"

Judah didn't answer.

"How can we be certain that it won't happen again?" Nancy asked.

"It won't," Judah said.

"You expect me to take your word for it? Your behavior has been deeply concerning as of late, young man. I'm afraid you've come under some less than exemplar influences."

Josie scowled, but held her tongue. She knew just who Nancy considered to be a bad influence. Maybe Josie had inadvertently been the trigger for the fight, but she hadn't expected Judah to send Russell to the hospital. Judah appeared to have taken his share of pummeling too. Once his face was healed it wouldn't be as perfect as it had been. The cuts on his eyebrow and his nose would definitely scar.

A scrap of paper appeared in Tessa's hand. She unfolded it. She scanned the message. Her lips flattened into a thin line, but otherwise, she remained expressionless.

"I thought you had all the messages diverted to the island," Josie said.

"I did," Tessa said flatly, "except for ones like these." She held the paper out towards Nancy and Caroline. Nancy took it. As her eyes moved over the message, her face tightened until it looked like it might split down the center. She handed the note off to Caroline.

"What is it?" Josie asked.

"That's none of your concern," Nancy said before Tessa could reply. "You're excused," she said. "The Triune and the Eye have business to discuss."

"Did something happen?" Josie asked.

Tessa's gaze met Josie's. The surface of her eyes trembled, but she didn't say anything.

"We'll leave you," her dad said, starting towards Josie.

"Actually, Marc, stay," Caroline said, looking pale as she passed the note to Gretchen. "We're going to need a scribe."

"Daisuke should stay too," Tessa said.

Daisuke frowned a little. No one argued.

Something had happened, probably concerning the Osaka tribe since Daisuke was being invited to remain. The only reason they'd call for a scribe was if they were going to have a formal meeting. The only time they had formal meetings was at the monthly full-tribal council or when something bad had happened.

"Is it Lily?" Josie asked. "You have to tell me."

"No, we don't," Nancy said. "You haven't remembered yourself since you've returned to us. You are not the Triune, you are not part of the Eye, you are not even a matriarch or an elder. You will leave, now."

Her dad stepped towards her. "Go to the café. Get some breakfast. All right?"

Simone took Josie's arm and pulled her up to her feet. "Come on."

"Judah, stay with them," Caroline said, raising her brow significantly.

"I don't need a bodyguard," Josie said, slipping her arm away from Simone. "Or an escort." She turned and left.

CHAPTER 19

July 10th

"AREN'T YOU GOING TO EAT?" Simone asked.

"Aren't you?" Josie asked.

Simone's vegan bran muffin sat untouched on the plate in front of her.

Judah slouched on the bench seat next to his sister. He hadn't ordered anything, not even coffee. He hadn't spoken to or looked at her once either. She was starting to find it as annoying as when he ran his mouth.

Around them, most of the tables were empty. Over the door, a bell jingled every few minutes as the morning commuters picked up their coffees to go. The whirr and hiss of the espresso machine failed to drown out Josie's pestering thoughts. Blood on her door, video message threats . . . Judah ignoring her.

Simone dropped her chin into her hand and gazed down at her phone. "I still haven't heard from Kai."

"You know how busy he is," Josie said, pushing her own blueberry muffin away. "The master-level trials are a lot of work."

Work Judah had completed when he was twelve. Russell must've been around seventeen when he'd competed against Judah in the fire element trial. Josie had to admit, it was impressive.

"I guess," Simone said listlessly. "He's just been . . ." Simone shrugged.

"Been what?"

"Distant."

"Kai? How can you tell?"

Simone made a face at her.

"Sorry." Josie stirred her mocha. Not even the ambrosia scent of espresso and chocolate was awakening her appetite.

"Don't worry about Kai," Judah said, startling Josie with his sudden participation in their conversation. "He's not blowing you off. Training for the trials is intense."

"I know," Simone said with a sigh.

Yet, somehow, Judah's reassurances seemed to work on her, even though he hadn't said anything different from Josie. Simone peeled off a hunk of her muffin and popped it into her mouth.

"So?" she asked Josie after a moment.

"So what?"

"So what do you think it meant? The blood and the paws?"

Josie sank deeper into her chair. "Honestly, I've been trying not to think about it." She dug into her bag and pulled out Adonis and her pocket knife.

"It's awful," Simone said. "Who would do that to a poor defenseless animal?"

"Lily's murdered people, Simone. Killing a dog isn't going to make her shed any tears."

"You don't think Lily did it—"

"Not Lily herself, but someone loyal to her. I can't think of any other reason someone would want to smear blood on my window."

She ran the edge of the knife between the back of Adonis and the pitted block of stone on which he was sprawled, lifeless.

"It's scary," Simone said. "They were right outside your door."

Josie concentrated on cutting in the fine lines of Aphrodite's hair.

"You're not even wearing half of the protective bracelets I've made for you," Simone said.

"They won't make a difference," she said.

"Josie—"

"Well, they won't." She held up one of her forearms as evidence.

A thin scar ran from her wrist to her elbow, left there by Fog God when he'd cut away her protective bracelets the second time he'd tried to kidnap her.

"We're just fooling ourselves into thinking we're safe. If there is a traitor in the tribe, it could be anyone. I'm not safe anywhere. Not even here. None of the center's circles or charms will protect me from a member of our own tribe."

"Maybe Tessa should take you to the island," Simone said. "You'd be safe there."

Josie brushed away the fine dust from Adonis. "No."

"But—"

"I told you. I'm not going to be locked up in some tower or trapped on an interdimensional island listening to the primordial gods bitch all day. Besides, if something happened to Tessa, then I'd be stuck there until the next Triune figured out how to translocate to the island. There's no food. No water. You have to bring everything in."

"I thought you said there were crabs."

"Yeah, but they're not quite real. Nothing is. It's like living in a bleak impressionist painting. Everything's shifting all the time and running together. There's no day, no night, no sun, no stars. It's gray, it's empty, it's depressing. Perfect training ground for life as the Triune."

"You always seemed like you liked it there."

"Nobody likes it there," she said, turning Adonis around, deepening the pitted texture of the ground beneath him—like he'd washed up on a rocky beach. "My mom didn't stay because she liked it. She stayed because my dad was here and she couldn't stand to be around him—and she didn't know where else to go."

"Weren't they happy they split?"

"He was happier. Tessa was happier. That's why we left. He wanted a wife. She was the Triune. She couldn't attend all the fancy dinners with his lawyer friends when she had to go execute people for performing human sacrifices. You want to be with the Triune, you'd better be prepared to take a backseat."

She glanced at Judah again, but he still wasn't looking at her.

Was that why he'd broken up with Tessa? Because he'd realized that to be with her, he'd have to give up his own plans and dreams? If so, then he'd actually been pretty smart. Better to do it now than ten years and two kids later. Whatever the case, she was having trouble not thinking of him as Tessa's boyfriend. She kept expecting Tessa to appear and wrap herself around him.

"Oh, don't look," Simone said, huddling over her almond milk chai latte.

Josie glanced over her shoulder.

Allison had just come in. When she saw Josie, she rushed over.

"I told you not to look," Simone whispered across the table.

Flushed streaks of pink sat high on Allison's cheeks. Her ice-blue eyes glittered. Her long hair hung wet around her shoulders, shower-fresh. She clutched the strap of her red leather bag.

"Did you hear?" she asked Josie breathlessly.

Josie straightened up. "Hear what?"

Allison's gaze skimmed Simone and Judah and then settled back on Josie again. "Where's Tessa? Did she go?"

"Go where?"

"To Japan. I hope not. It's way too dangerous after what happened."

"What happened?"

Allison glanced around the café, but no one was close enough to overhear.

"Their Eye," she said in a whisper. "They're all dead."

Josie stared at her, dumbstruck.

Simone's mouth hung open too.

Judah was the only one who seemed to be capable of speech. Strange, since he'd barely spoken for the last hour.

"Where'd you hear that?" he asked skeptically.

Allison's gaze frosted over. "I have a friend in the Hong Kong tribe. He just texted me. Everyone over there is talking about it." Allison leaned in towards Josie. "He said it looked like they'd been torn apart, like by wild dogs."

Josie's heart plunged into her stomach.

"How would he know that?" Judah asked.

"Because the bodies were found out on the street. Someone took pictures and posted them online. It's causing a huge uproar. Apparently, the Japanese find it extra offensive, but you can see the pictures yourself if you want. I'd be happy to forward them to you." Allison gave him a glare to rival his own. "Gods, you look terrible. Russell really beat the shit out of you, didn't he? What are you even doing out? Shouldn't you be in detention after what you did? I heard you started the whole thing. And how could you break up with Tessa? Are you stupid? Where is Tessa anyway?"

Josie rubbed her forehead. "She's in the sanctum with the Eye."

"Is that Japanese guy around still? What's his name? Dice?"

"Daisuke," Josie said.

"He was your friend, right?" Allison said. "You trust him? He's been hanging around Tessa, a lot."

"Yes, I trust him."

"Well, I don't trust anyone outside of our tribe," Allison said. Then looking at Judah she added, "I don't even trust everyone in our tribe." Her eyes returned to Josie. "You look awful. Did you not sleep well?"

"I never sleep well," Josie said.

Simone's phone chimed. She picked it up, reading the screen.

"Maybe you should take something. I have pills. You can have some. I sleep like a baby." Allison wrinkled her nose at the carving on the table. "What's that?" She picked it up before Josie could answer. "I didn't know you did other kinds of art, besides the mask kind, I mean. What is it?"

"It's Rodin."

"Huh?"

"It's Aphrodite and Adonis."

"Are they kissing?"

"No, he's dead. She's grieving."

"Isn't Adonis supposed to be hot? This guy doesn't even have any abs. And that's Aphrodite? That doesn't look like Aphrodite to me. You made her butt way too big."

"Thanks for the input," Josie said, holding out her hand.

Allison put the carving in Josie's palm. Josie slid it to the far corner of the table, as far from Allison as she could.

"I'd stick to the mask thing if I were you." She eyed Josie more critically. "Are you sure you're okay? You look paler than usual."

"You just told me that the Eye of the Osaka tribe was murdered. How am I supposed to look?"

Allison put her hand lightly on Josie's shoulder. Candy-sweet perfume coated Josie's throat and stuck, thick and gag-inducing. "You know I'm always around if there's anything you want to talk about."

The door jingled and a tall young man in red suspenders and horn-rimmed glasses walked in, looking neat and professional in his quirky fashion. Josie knew him best as Kai's bandmate.

"Oh, there's Ty," Allison said. "I wonder if he's heard yet. See you later." She rushed over to Ty.

Josie stared after her. "I don't like her."

"Nobody likes her," Simone said, sliding off the bench. "I have to go." She held up her phone. "That was my mom. She wants me to meet her in her office."

"Why?"

"I made the Eye some of those locating charms, you know . . ."—Simone's gaze slid over to Judah, who was studying Adonis and Aphrodite—"the ones you found on the island."

"They didn't work before," Josie said.

"It's worth a shot though," Simone said with a shrug. "I finished them last night. I haven't had much to do since you and Kai have been . . . Anyway, Mom wants to go get them and bring them back. I guess they're willing to try anything at this point."

Josie wrapped her hands around her coffee cup.

"Um . . ." Simone hovered by the table, strangling her wrists with her bracelets. "I'll come right back as soon as I can." She started to walk away, but stopped, turning back. "Don't fight, okay?"

They both stared at her until she turned and hurried to the nearby door that led back into the tribal center.

Josie gazed down at her barely sipped mocha. On the other side of the table, Judah had the carving in his hand, tilting it back so he could look at it.

"Do you think it's true?" she asked, peeking up at him.

The warm morning light streaming through the windows behind him made the bruises on his face all the more sour and ugly. The scabs were thick and black, painful to look at.

For a moment, she wasn't sure if he'd answer. He just kept studying the carving.

"Allison doesn't have enough imagination to make up something like that," he said finally.

She let out a heavy breath. "I can't believe it. That must've been the message Tessa received." She took a sip of her coffee. Her stomach turned unhappily. She set the mug down. "I knew those women. Hisa was like a second mother to Daisuke…" She slumped back in her chair, running her fingers over her lips. "It had to be Lily, right?"

Judah didn't answer. He still wasn't looking at her.

"But why?"

"Another message," he said.

"That's one hell of a message all of a sudden."

"It might not be so all of a sudden."

"What do you mean?"

His thumb grazed the top of Aphrodite's head. "I overheard my mother and Daisuke talking, right after he arrived. About you. About the Osaka tribe's ancient masks. They wanted you to repair them. That's why he came here. Tessa told me that the Osaka Eye was willing to take the Tripartite's mark as a sign of their loyalty."

Josie dropped her elbow onto the table, shielding her face from the rest of the café. Not that anyone was eavesdropping on them. The nearest patron was a girl with dreads down to her waist wearing big white headphones and bopping on her stool as she typed nonstop on her laptop.

"They were willing to become her slaves?" She dug her finger into her forehead. "Is that what we've come to?"

"No one trusts anyone anymore. And with good reason."

She covered her face. "Please don't make this about Russell."

When her hand left her eyes, he was still staring at the carving.

Why wouldn't he look at her? Was he angry? About what? Tessa? Russell? He must've been really angry, because he'd never avoided eye contact before. Usually, glaring at her was one of his favorite ways to express his anger. And why did his refusal to make eye contact make her stomachache worse?

She sat back. "Okay. So somehow Lily found out that Osaka's Eye was about to make a big declaration of loyalty to the Triune, and she had them killed to send a message. I guess that makes sense. If you're completely crazy, which she is."

Judah's phone buzzed. He pulled it out of his pocket. His thumb tapped the screen. His brow turned sharp. His gaze snapped up—over Josie's head. Josie followed it. Allison smiled, waggling her fingers at him as she left the café. The bell jingled pleasantly.

"Did she send you the pictures?" Josie asked him.

He put his phone away. "I don't know how she got my new number."

She held out her hand. "Let me see."

He looked at her for the first time since that night on the porch, when he'd been fire-eyed and dripping with blood.

Pain. Chest.

"You knew those women?" he asked.

Her throat tightened. "Yes."

"You don't want to see."

Josie drew back her hand. "Was it like she said? Like wild dogs?"

His gaze turned away again, back to the carving. He frowned, thoughtful.

"You think it was the same person, don't you?" she asked. "Did you see what happened at my house last night?"

"My mom sent me the photos," he said.

"Three," she said. "I get it now. Three paws. Three dead members of the Osaka Eye."

"You don't know—"

"Come on," she said softly. "Coincidence? You don't think that. And you don't need to pretend like you do to make me feel better. Nothing is going to make me feel better right now."

"Nothing?" he said in a low voice. "Not even if your fire summoner reappeared right now to rescue you?"

"Rescue me from what? Threats? Besides, you've rescued me more times than he has."

In truth, she'd barely thought about Fire Guy this last week. Not since before the fight. Yet that cold ache that was eating her up inside had only spread, deepening. She'd thought that once she managed to put the Fire Guy out of her mind, she would start to feel better. Instead, she felt worse than ever.

She slung her bag over head, across her chest. "Has Tessa given your mask back yet?"

He still wasn't looking at her. "No."

She stood up. "Well, you won't need it, because I'm going to make you a new one."

"You don't have to do that."

"I'm not just doing it for you. That crazy bitch just murdered the Eye of Daisuke's tribe. I'm pissed off. I have to do something. I can't just sit here. I'm a mask-maker. This is what I can do."

His fingers tapped the edge of the carving. "Are you taking the pathways?"

"Yes."

His brow hardened, but he didn't say anything.

"You're not going to try to stop me?" she asked. "You're not going to argue at all?"

"What's the point?"

She stood there for a moment, chewing on her words, trying to stop them, but they came out despite her efforts to swallow them back. "You're not coming with me? Aren't you supposed to be on Josie-duty?"

His jaw flexed. He stared hard at the carving. No response.

Why did she feel like her chest was being gored by a wild boar?

"Fine." Her gaze went to the door, but her feet didn't move. "Did you get in?"

"Get in?" he repeated.

"The university. Are you going?"

"I could if I wanted to."

"I think you should."

He snorted. "Of course you do."

He still wasn't looking at her. He just kept staring at the carving of Adonis and Aphrodite. The desire to punch him returned, but it wasn't quite the same as before. She didn't want to hit him so he'd shut up, she wanted to hit him so he'd look at her.

Whatever that was about, she couldn't think about it. She wouldn't. This was still Judah—the arrogant jerk who'd broken her sister's heart and who'd beaten Russell bloody. The Judah who had told her they'd never be friends, that she was Miss Nobody. The Judah who deserved to be banished to the oubliette and forgotten.

Still . . .

"Do you know why Aphrodite is crying?" she asked. "It's not just because Adonis is dead."

He didn't answer.

"It's because it was her fault. Adonis was killed to punish her."

His gaze rolled up to meet hers. All she'd wanted was for him to look at her, and now that he was, she had to look away.

"You should go to the university," she said. "Get away from here, away from . . ."

Me.

Before Lily shows up again and you're the one who's dead on a stone plinth.

"Anyway," she said, wringing the strap of her bag, "I have work to do."

She started towards the door.

"Don't you want to take this with you?" he asked.

She glanced back. He held the carving out towards her.

"Keep it," she said, pulling open the door. "Happy birthday."

CHAPTER 20

July 19th
Nine Days Later

Clashing winds buffeted her.

At times, she had the sense of falling. Then she'd be whipped upwards again, as if she'd hit a trampoline and had bounced effortlessly into the air. As often as it was dark, it was light. The pathways of the air gods shifted from pitch black to cloudy white to robin's egg blue to blush pink streaked with purple and orange—all the hues of the sky. Sometimes the clouds swirled close around her and she was assaulted by panic-filled memories of Fog God stealing her away.

But then he came to her.

Death.

For the last ten days, she'd travelled the pathways. Air, water, earth. Every time, Death had been waiting for her. Each time he was more solid than the last, transforming from a voice, to a phantom-wisp of darkness, to a full-fledged figure, broad-shouldered and lean.

This time, he looked like one of those street performers in a full-body sock. Contours of a muscled physique—and a face and a mouth—hidden under a thin layer of black. She expected that by the time she was finished fixing the tribe's masks, he'd have a fully visible body with eyes she could look into. What would Death's face look like? The question both terrified and thrilled her.

"So much pain," he said sympathetically. "You should not be in such pain."

Clutched in her hands was the mask of an air god. All around her, the wind swirled and nipped. The pathways were mute and gray.

"You must face your fear," he said. "You must be honest with yourself. You, the Triune's daughter, the daughter of Death, my daughter, you should not feel this misery."

His voice tugged at her, soothing the ache inside of her. As much as she hated him, as much as she wanted to run back to mortality, she wanted to stay and let his reassurances spread like icy balm over that pain.

"Why do you keep meeting me here?" she asked. "Why are you being so nice? What do you really want from me?"

"Why should I want anything but for you to be happy?" he asked. "Why should you want anything but that as well?"

"I don't know what you're saying."

"I think you do. Allow me to give you a bit of advice, dearest. Follow your heart, wherever it leads, even if it is to my door."

She shifted back. "You want me dead? Is that what this is about? Maybe you think if I'm dead, the Covenant will be destroyed and you'll be free. Is that it?"

Death's shadow hands went up in protest. "You could not be more wrong. I want you to live, Josie. I want you to live fully, not this half-life. Why do you deny yourself? Why do you deny your feelings? Why do you deny your own happiness?"

"I'm not denying—"

"You can lie to yourself, but you cannot lie to me. I know your life, Josie, from beginning to end. I've seen it in all of its infinite possibilities. I've sifted those possibilities through my fingers. You are so close, so close to realizing your full potential. But you're holding yourself back by holding on to what you *think* is right instead of doing what you *feel* is right."

As he spoke, his face seemed to grow more detailed. The nose and brow sharpened, the eyes showed lashes, the outline of teeth and a tongue appeared behind his lips. Around them, the pathways stirred like the wind-gusted clouds in the winter sky over St. Petersburg.

"What do you mean my full potential?"

"That I cannot tell you. I have bent the rules already, coming here, speaking with you, encouraging you."

"Encouraging me?"

"That's right. Encouraging you to find your courage."

"Courage for what? To face Lily again?"

"Her? You think she is any match for you? You are *my* daughter. If she knew what you were truly capable of, she would drop to her knees and beg your forgiveness and your mercy. The only weakness you possess is the weakness you create for yourself. Weakness is not a state of being, it is a state of mind. You allow your mind to rule you too much. That is your mother's doing. That was her path, but your path is not hers. You make the same mistake with your beautiful sister as your mother did with you. You teach her the way you were taught, instead of the way she needs to be taught. Lovely Tessa was quite lost until that young . . . Daisuke came to her aid."

Josie inspected his face. Had she seen a flash of color touch his lips? They were definitely becoming more defined as he spoke. The peaks of the top lip showed, the swell of the bottom sharpened. Something about them seemed familiar.

"Are you jealous?" she asked. "Of Daisuke?"

"Why would I be jealous of a mortal?"

"Or maybe you don't like him, because you're afraid he'll actually help Tessa take full control of your power."

"If sweet Tessa wanted my power, all she'd have to do is ask. At her command, I would bleed the world."

She'd been lingering in the pathways too long, she could tell. Sense of her body was becoming patchy like a bad connection on a phone, the signal cutting out the longer she stayed.

"I have to go," she said.

Death's shadow hand reached towards her, skimming her essence. She was actually chilled. When she'd translocated with other summoners through the pathways, she'd experienced heat and cold—because she'd physically moved through the paths—but never when she'd traversed them on her own in spirit. Her body wasn't here to feel heat or cold and yet . . .

She drew back from him.

"Before you go," he said, "look at me. What do you see?"

She gazed at his shadow face. Again, a flash of color. His lips appeared for a second, red and real. So familiar.

"I—"

"I'll tell you what you see," he said, "what you want to see, dear heart. I am as you wish me to be. That is your power. I will tell you something more, because I feel I may not be given another opportunity. Do you know the stories of my traitorous daughter?"

"Lu-Ji?"

"The first Triune. She betrayed me and banished me to this existence of emptiness and loneliness."

"I know her story."

"Do you? I suggest you look again. In fact, I suggest you look again at everything and everyone you thought you knew. Once you find what you've been missing, don't let it go, even if it seems irrevocably lost. Don't stop looking. It will be returned to you, I promise."

"What is this?" Nancy's voice cut into Josie's consciousness. Josie opened her eyes.

"Gods, Josie, are you okay?" Caroline knelt next to Josie, who was lying on a blanket spread on the floor.

After repairing the first few masks, she'd decided that since she was going to fall on the floor every time, it'd be easier to start out there.

As she sat up, Josie struggled to shake off the frost of Death's touch. In her hand, the air god's mask was sharp-edged and gray, light as a handful of down, but oddly, made of metal. Most air gods' masks were crafted of wood. But this wasn't just any air god.

"You're freezing." Caroline gathered the blanket up and wrapped it around Josie, who was shivering, teeth chattering. "Your lips are blue."

"I'm fine," Josie said.

"Don't look fine, kiddo." Gretchen squatted down in front of Josie, inspecting her face.

"What were you doing?" Caroline rubbed warmth into Josie's arms.

Nancy stood over them, frown-pucker in full effect. "Taking a nap?"

"Here." Josie held the mask up towards Nancy. "This one is yours."

Nancy snapped up the mask. As she inspected it, her frown diminished until her face was smooth, unreadable. The metal was light-weight—polished tin, punched with swirling designs. Josie pushed to her feet with some help from Caroline.

"It's the North Wind," Josie said, wrapping the fleece blanket tighter around her.

Nancy's frown returned for a second. "You don't mean—"

"Yes, I do," she said. "*The* North Wind. Not just some northerly gust. Who knew we had it in our archives all this time? It definitely belongs with you."

Nancy's lips parted, apparently surprised—maybe impressed? But then her face hardened again. "What were you doing on the floor?"

"This isn't all tea and cakes, you know?" Josie said without bite.

She didn't have the energy to tangle with Nancy. All she wanted to do was go home, huddle in bed, do some more research into divine weaponry, and then end the night whittling until her hands went numb. "The others are in here."

On trembling legs, she led them back to Gretchen's office.

"Josie, I had no idea this took so much out of you," Caroline said, arm still wrapped around Josie's shoulders. "You should've told us—"

"So you could stop me?"

"Well—"

"Maybe we could help you, kiddo. Did you think of that?" Gretchen asked from behind Caroline.

"I don't need help."

Josie swiped her key card. The door lock clicked. She met Caroline's worried eyes, but had to look away. They were too similar to Judah's—the same plunging brow and vivid blue hue. Josie was trying not to think about Judah. Every time she did, she got this strange feeling in her gut, like she'd eaten a box of razors.

She hadn't seen him since that day in the café. She should've been happy to have him off her back. Instead, she too often found herself wondering what he was doing, why he hadn't come to check on her, and if he'd been thinking about her at all. When she caught herself thinking these things, it made her want to run straight back to Death.

"You've kept this place really clean," Gretchen said, scanning the art lab.

Josie went into the office. Caroline and Gretchen hovered behind her.

"I told you not to worry about clean up," Gretchen said. "I told you I'd take care of it."

"You're too busy," Josie said, stacking up the boxes.

She handed half of them to Caroline and carried the other half herself. The worst of the shivering was subsiding. "You should've told me you were coming."

"Why? So you could set your alarm clock?" Nancy asked, one hand on her hip and the other holding the mask of the North Wind to her chest possessively.

Josie shuffled back to the work tables. She set her stack of boxes next to Caroline's. She took the top one down and slid open the lid. The white face of the ocean god shone.

"This one's Kai's," she said. "How is Kai? How are his trials?"

Caroline took the box from Josie's hand, tracing the mask lightly with her fingers. "He passed the last round of trials with flying colors. If he keeps it up, I wouldn't be surprised if he knocks out the next three rounds before the equinox."

"I hope Lily gives us that kind of time."

Gretchen and Nancy stood on the other side of the table. Nancy took another box and opened it. The god channeled into the rough clay mask rumbled in Josie's ears.

"Earthquakes," Josie said. "Whoever has that one should be very, very grounded." She looked at Gretchen. "I haven't found one that would suit you yet."

Gretchen smiled. "I already have one. The one you lifted from Lily."

"The mountain god?"

Gretchen nodded. "He was a bit more than Baby Bear could handle. So Mama Bear took possession of it." She gave Josie a wink.

The first mask Josie had brought back from the Beyond, a mountain god mask, had temporarily been in Beech's possession during the fight with Lily, but Josie hadn't been told what had happened to it afterwards. She was glad Gretchen had a mask with some real punch to it.

"How do you like him?" Josie asked, meaning the mountain god.

"He's a bit of a hardass, isn't he?" Gretchen said.

Josie smiled a little. "Yeah."

"Don't worry. I know how to handle the holier-than-thou types." Gretchen arched an eyebrow, tilting her head towards Nancy, who was gazing down at the North Wind mask again.

"Twelve masks," Caroline said. "That's almost half. You've been busy."

"No more so than you," Josie said. "Is there any word about who killed the Osaka Eye?"

The mood darkened. Nancy flicked her wrist. The North Wind mask disappeared into her stash.

"That's privileged information."

Josie ground her teeth. "What about their masks? Are they sending them?"

Caroline pulled out a chair. "Why don't you sit down?"

"I don't need to—"

"Sit your butt down, lady," Gretchen said, pulling out a chair for herself, flipping it around, and sitting with her bare, tattooed arms folded across the back.

Josie sank into her chair, turning a thick silver ring around her thumb—Judah's summoning ring.

Before Tessa had left for her next round of trials, she'd given Josie the ring. She'd returned Russell's personally. Josie had been planning on passing Judah's onto Simone, but she hadn't seen her best friend for a while.

Caroline sat down too, heavily. "We're not certain that we want to repair any of the other tribes' masks."

"You don't trust them," Josie said, again reminded of Judah.

"Why should we?" Nancy said.

"The Osaka Eye died. I think that proves they were on our side, don't you?" Josie asked.

"Too bad they're dead," Nancy said.

"And the new Eye . . ." Caroline sighed, running her hands over her abnormally pale face. When she frowned, her expression was just like Judah's. The shapes of their mouths were completely different though. Judah's was wider, his bottom lip fuller, redder.

"Well,"—Caroline sat back in her chair—"we just don't know them."

"I probably do," Josie said. "I know almost everyone in the Osaka tribe, more or less. If you're going to take a chance on trusting any tribe, I'd trust them."

"Tessa seems to feel the same way," Caroline said.

"Only because of her new . . ."—Nancy ran her thumb along the edges of her French-tipped fingernails distractedly—"friend."

Daisuke. He'd gone back to the island with Tessa again.

Last week, Simone had gently hinted that the tribe was starting to talk. Tessa had hardly been seen without Daisuke shadowing her the last two weeks. Josie didn't mind. In fact, she was relieved. Daisuke had effectively taken over Tessa's training, and Tessa actually seemed to listen to him. No surprise. Daisuke was warm, gentle, and attentive. He was also unfailingly patient. Virtues Josie lacked across the board. Death's words haunted her. Maybe she had failed Tessa, but the only thing Josie knew about being Triune was what her mother had taught her, in the way her mother had taught her.

The rest of what Death had said was needling at her as well, especially what he'd said about Lu-Ji. Why had he suggested that Josie go back and read the stories about the first Triune? For some reason it felt like a trick, but Death had seemed so genuine in his concern, which was probably why she was suspicious. Whether or not the gods were really as emotionless as her mom had always claimed, Josie was certain they would play off a human's emotions to get what they wanted. No doubt, Death was up to something. But what?

She sighed, sinking back in her chair.

"If you're asking me," Josie said pointedly to Nancy, "then I'm more than willing to fix Osaka's masks. It's a risk, I know, but if we're preparing for war, then we're going to need to choose our allies."

"Don't you think you should take a break?" Caroline asked. "You look ..."

"Exhausted," Gretchen said.

Josie looked at each of them—from Nancy's gray on gray pallor, to the bluish bags under Gretchen's green eyes, to the deep lines marring Caroline's forehead under her careless fringe of blond hair.

"I can't look any worse than any of you," she said.

"Thanks a lot," Gretchen said, rubbing her eyes, "but you're right. We could all use a break." She shot a look at Nancy, like the Future Eye was the one who'd been driving them all so hard—not that Josie would've been surprised if that were true.

"Did any of the locating charms help?" Josie asked.

Nancy's stern look seemed to indicate she was about to tell Josie that wasn't any of her business either, but Caroline beat her to the punch.

"Actually, they did. They didn't show us Lily's location, but they did help us locate some of the people we suspect might be her followers."

Josie sat up straighter. "I can't believe they worked."

"We were hoping they'd lead us to her, but so far... bupkis," Gretchen said.

"But that's good though," Josie said, "right? I mean, that's something at least."

"It is something," Nancy said sternly. "Something we shouldn't be discussing at this moment."

"Well..."—Josie sat back—"why are you here? Did you just come to check on the masks or—?"

"We're all headed out," Caroline said. "Nancy and Gretchen and I have official business to attend to and, as you know, your father has depositions in San Francisco."

"And?"

"And we have to figure out what to do with you in the meantime," Gretchen said.

"Do with me? Can't you just post the goon squad on me until one of you gets back?"

"We could, but . . ." Caroline said, biting her lip.

"But nobody wants Josie-duty," she finished.

"It's not that no one wants it, it's just that the logistics are difficult," Caroline said. "None of us are certain when we'll be back, and frankly, Josie, we don't know who we can trust anymore. We don't want to risk putting you in the hands of whoever it is that's been terrorizing you."

Josie hated that she agreed. "So what do you want me to do?"

"I want to put you in the detention center," Nancy said, smiling as if it were a friendly suggestion.

Caroline placed her warm hand on Josie's icy forearm. "I want you to stay at my house."

Josie's heart convulsed. "Judah's okay with that?"

Caroline's gaze combed Josie's face so closely that Josie had to look away. "Actually, Judah's out of town."

"He is? Where?"

"Camping near Crater Lake."

Josie frowned. A fresh chill broke out over her body, and she huddled deeper in her blanket. "So who's going to—?"

"A few of our most trusted friends will check in on you."

"But why your house? Why couldn't I just—?"

"I've created some very special protective circles," Caroline replied, "but due to their unusual nature, they could only be drawn around my own home. The first will prevent anyone but a few, select people from translocating within a one block radius."

Josie's eyebrows shot up. "No wonder you look beat."

Caroline nodded. "It was . . . trying. But we tested it and it seems to be working. Only myself, Judah, and your father can translocate into the house, and Tessa, of course. No one except Nancy, Gretchen, and Kai can cross onto the property, whether they're in possession or not. I've also been working on a few other circles . . ." She bit her lip. "Suffice it to say, there should be no safer place for you in the world. For a while. I don't expect them to hold for very long. I had to use triangulation charms, and you know how tricky those can be."

Josie nodded. Triangulation charms were used in lieu of painting the entire neighborhood with protective symbols. Invisible ink didn't have enough staying power outside, and people tended to get a little freaked out when crazy symbols appeared in their yards—even in Portland. Triangulation charms could be disguised as bird houses, wind chimes, lawn ornaments, just about anything.

"So instead of being a prisoner here, I'll be a prisoner at your house?"

"You won't be a prisoner, Josie," Caroline said. "You'll be my guest. We can't tell you not to leave the house, but . . . it really is for your safety, until someone we trust, who is fully capable of protecting you, is back in town. Your father and I will leave on Monday. We plan to be back Friday. Gretchen intends to be back before then too."

"As soon as I can," Gretchen said.

"And Judah has promised he'll be back on Friday, just in case any of us are delayed."

"What about the masks? You want me to just stop working for five days?"

"No. You can take the masks with you and whatever you think you'll need. They'll be as safe as you are."

Caroline gave Nancy a warning look, curtailing any argument. But Nancy didn't seem to have any. She was watching Josie coolly.

Caroline continued, "I have a list of volunteers who've offered to bring anything you and Simone need. They'll leave it in the driveway—that's as close as they can get."

"So we both get to be locked in the craftsman-style tower," Josie said.

"It's only for a few days," Caroline said.

Five days, actually. Josie didn't bother pointing it out. She couldn't think of any way to argue without sounding like a whiny teenager. And an ingrate. Clearly, Caroline had gone to a tremendous amount of trouble to set this up and . . . it was only for five days.

Once, Josie had been trapped on the Triune's Island for almost two weeks. She'd nearly had a breakdown when the last of the batteries had died, and she couldn't drown out the primordial gods' constant complaining. Her mom hadn't left her there exactly. She'd gone on one of her spirit-guided trips through the pathways. She'd apologized profusely when she'd finally returned and had taken Josie to a five-star resort in the Turks & Caicos for the next month. It had been a nice thought, but after a week, it became just another island she was trapped on.

It seemed like Josie couldn't escape a life of perimeters. At least on the Triune's Island she could leave the ruins she'd called home and move around. Being stuck in Caroline's house, nice as it was, felt like a transfer from solitary to a shared cell. The sad part was, at the moment, she might've preferred to be in solitary. She'd been avoiding Simone lately. Mostly, she'd been avoiding all the worried looks.

"I guess I don't have much choice, do I?" she said.

"No one is forcing you, Josie," Caroline said.

Except someone *was* forcing her. Lily. Even without her mask, even missing in action for the last three months, Lily had found a way to put Josie behind locked doors.

"Is that all?" Nancy said, checking her watch. "I'm leaving early tomorrow. I have a lot to do."

"Yes, Nan," Caroline said wearily.

"What about these?" Nancy asked, gesturing to the other masks. "Back in the vaults?"

Caroline chewed her nails. "Do you think it's safe?"

"We could put them in our sanctuaries," Gretchen said. "We could split them up between us."

"I'm not sure that's any safer," Nancy said. "Besides, my sanctuary won't hold another."

"I have plenty of room," Gretchen said, "for these anyway. My trip isn't as ... perilous as yours, Nancy. They'll be safe with me for a week, safe as anywhere."

"Gretchen's right," Caroline said. "I'd feel better if they were with her since we don't know who the collaborator might be, and we don't know what kind of access they might have here." Caroline shook her head. "Gods, I can't believe our own center is compromised ..."

"Let's do this," Gretchen said, starting to open the boxes.

"Why don't you take them to my office, Gretchen?" Caroline said. "I'd like to speak to Josie privately for a moment."

Gretchen slid the lids back on the boxes and started to stack them. "No problem." She gave Josie an encouraging smile. Josie didn't feel encouraged. A private talk with a member of the Eye rarely bode well.

Nancy helped Gretchen with the boxes.

When the door had closed behind them, Caroline turned to Josie.

"What did you do to my son?"

CHAPTER 21

JULY 19TH

JOSIE STAMMERED, GENUINELY THROWN. "What . . . what do you mean?"

Caroline sighed heavily and sank back in her chair, looking thoughtful.

"Your mother and I were never very good friends, Josie. Did you know that?"

"She wasn't very good at making friends," Josie replied, not sure what this had to do with Judah or why Caroline would think that Josie had done something to him.

"She never was," Caroline said, "not even when we were kids. But it wasn't really her fault, you know. She was the Triune-to-be. We all treated her differently. Looking back, I'd say that many of us girls were fairly cruel to her."

"She never said—"

Caroline's smile was melancholy. "Of course not. Your mother was an excellent Triune. She would never have allowed the past or her personal feelings to interfere with her duties to the Core. It's only now that I'm beginning to understand the kind of pressure she must've felt, and at such a young age. She was truly remarkable, which is probably why I was jealous of her for so long."

Josie stared at Caroline, who, even exhausted, was beautiful—her face golden and expressive, her physique lean, her smile genuine.

"Why would you be jealous?"

"Why do you think? She was the Triune. The boys followed her around like a pack of starving puppies, but it wasn't just her power. She was so smart and controlled. And just . . . gorgeous. Even when we were young, it always seemed like she had the world by the tail. No matter how many rumors we girls spread, or how many times we snubbed her, she never acted like it bothered her. It drove us crazy."

"You probably remember yourself being meaner than you were," Josie said.

"We were always nice to her face, Josie. We had to be. But she was never invited to our parties. She was never asked to sit with us when we were at the center or to go to the movies or the beach with us. And the things we said about her behind her back . . . they really were terrible. I'm ashamed of the way I behaved back then."

Caroline hung her head for a moment, looking even more tired than she had minutes before.

"But like I said, if your mother was ever hurt by any of it, she never showed it. She perfected the façade of the Triune. And she wore it. You never knew what she was really thinking or feeling. Sometimes, it was frightening. You could look her right in the eyes knowing that she possessed all this incredible power, the power over life and death, and you could never feel quite sure where you stood with her." Caroline's eyes touched Josie's face lightly. "When I look at you, Josie, you remind me so much of her."

Josie shifted, uncomfortable. She wasn't sure what Caroline was implying, and she wasn't sure she wanted to find out.

"That beautiful dark hair," Caroline said, catching a stray strand gently, like a mom. She grasped Josie's chin. "This face . . . those gray eyes. Just like your mother." Her hand fell away onto her crossed knee. "And just like your mother, you picked up that Triune façade."

Josie was reminded of what Russell had said to her before. "Hard to read, is that it?"

"Very."

Josie nodded.

"My daughter loves you. She thinks that you are the most amazing person in the world," Caroline said. "Josie's so strong, she says. Josie's so passionate. So fierce. Josie kicks ass."

Josie smiled a little and then felt badly that she'd been avoiding Simone so much. But she guessed she'd have five days to make up for it starting Monday.

"I really don't," Josie said. "I'm not really that strong—"

"Yes, you are, Josie. To knock my son down the way you have, you'd have to be."

Josie's stomach clenched. "Knock him . . . What do you mean?" Sure, she'd fantasized about knocking Judah down plenty, but she'd never actually done it.

Caroline gazed steadily at her and then down at the floor as if considering her words carefully. "I admit Judah's gotten pretty full of himself these last few years. Once he started dating Tessa—even I found him obnoxious. But he had always been my perfect boy. He really strove to live up to that, and he succeeded. For so long, he was, in so many ways, perfect. I knew it couldn't last forever, but... I honestly didn't expect him to change as much as he has since..."

"Since?"

"Since you came back."

Josie tapped her foot, struggling to work through the tightening pain in her throat. "I don't understand what you're saying. What? You think I hurt his feelings?"

"I know that the two of you have had... a tense relationship. I don't think Judah was prepared for the kind of challenge you would present."

"You mean because I don't do what he says when he says to do it?"

Caroline smiled. "That might be part of it." Her smile faded. "Josie, I don't want to step on your toes or force you to..." Her lips pursed. "I'm his mom. I'm worried about him. Last fall all he could talk about was going to college, when he wasn't talking about Tessa. Now, not only did he break up with *the* girl, but he turned down schools that people would sell their souls to get into. He's been so distant and edgy. I can't say anything without setting him off. One minute all he wants to do is get away from Portland, and the next he refuses to even discuss it."

"I'm sorry, Caroline. I just... I really think it has more to do with Tessa becoming the Triune than anything else." She slumped back, folding her arms over her chest. "I'm sure it threw a pretty big wrench in his ten-year plan, not to mention Lily turning psycho on us. I know it messed up my plans."

"I guess... I don't honestly know what it was that precipitated this change in him, but I do have a strong feeling that it has more to do with you than you realize."

"I don't see how. He doesn't care about me," Josie said. "He told me we weren't ever going to be friends, and he's right. We're not."

Caroline touched Josie's knee. "I don't know when he told you that or why, but he does care about you, Josie. A great deal."

"I'm sorry, Caroline. I don't want to be disrespectful, but... Judah... we're just... we don't get along. It's okay. I don't think it bothers him. The last time I talked to him... if anything it seems like he cares less about me than he ever did, if that's possible. Whatever is going on with him, I don't think it has much to do with me."

Caroline pressed her hands together at her lips, studying Josie like a chess board.

"When you look in the mirror, Josie, what do you see?"

Death's words came back to her. *Only what you want to see.*

"See?"

"Do you see a fierce, passionate, beautiful woman? Do you see a powerful, intelligent, fearless human being? Do you see how people want to know you? How they want to be accepted and acknowledged by you? How they want to be close to you? Because if you don't see those things, Josie, then you're not seeing yourself. Not fully. Few of us do. We all see ourselves weaker, uglier, lesser than others do." She leaned in. "What do you see when you look at my son?"

A *backpfeifengesicht?*

"I don't know," Josie said after a moment. She hated this. She'd been trying so hard not to think about Judah at all. "Like you said, he's . . . perfect."

The fine lines around Caroline's eyes deepened as she smiled. "You were never around for the braces, were you?"

"Braces?"

"You think those teeth came in that straight? I wish. The orthodontist sent *his* kids to college on Judah's teeth. And the acne? Total nightmare. When he was thirteen, he'd refuse to leave the house for whole weeks. Prescription acne medication? Also not cheap. You'd think there'd be a charm for that. He's fortunate that my father was a ruthless bastard who invested all his money in all the right places and left it all to me. And the physique? Hours of training, Josie, every day, for years. The amount of time he spends working out? It's almost unhealthy. I finally put my foot down and told him to start washing his own clothes. Teenage boy sweat-stink?"

Caroline stuck out her tongue, crossing her eyes in a silly way that made her seem much younger. "I guess when I was your age I might not have minded a sweaty boy so much, but when it's your own son?" Caroline shook her head, wrinkling her nose. "His laundry hamper really should have toxic waste warnings on it. Every Christmas, I buy him cologne."

Josie almost smiled, though she still had trouble imagining Judah spotty with crooked teeth.

"The point is, Josie. Judah's not as perfect as he seems. And honestly, he's worked for it. Hard. He was smart, but he pushed himself to excel. That is something he was born with—tenacity. When he goes after something, he usually achieves it. Not because he's perfect, but because he's pig-headed. He refuses to give up. This whole thing with Russell? After Russell beat him in the trials, Judah spent two weeks in his room. He didn't talk, he wouldn't eat . . . I'd never seen him so depressed. But then one day, he laced up his shoes and went out the door and started running. And he hasn't stopped . . . until now."

Caroline gazed at Josie again for a long moment.

"I know Judah can be cocky and . . . judgmental," she said finally. "It's not uncommon for someone who's worked so hard to achieve, and has succeeded, to fall into the trap of thinking that everyone else is just lazy, either mentally or physically. They have this distorted idea in their head that if they push others the way they push themselves, all will be right with the world. So when someone comes along who seems so strong and so passionate—someone who pushes back just as hard as she gets pushed—it tends to throw those overachieving, perfect-seeming people for a loop. It might make them seem defensive or arrogant or just downright mean."

Josie looked away, towards the windows. Even though she knew Caroline was talking about Judah, she realized she'd been guilty of the same type of arrogance, just like Death had said.

She'd been pushing Tessa and had been failing miserably. She'd thought that if Tessa just toughened up, tried harder, focused more, then she might finally get it. But Tessa hadn't been the poor student. Josie's teaching methods were what had fallen short.

Caroline stood up.

"Do me a favor, Josie. The next time you see Judah, the next time you talk to him, give him a break, huh? Try to remember, he's not perfect. Even if he wants you to think he is. And believe me, he wants you to think he is."

CHAPTER 22

JULY 20TH
THE NEXT DAY

JOSIE SWITCHED OFF THE TREADMILL. She hung on the bars, panting. Her legs wobbled like over-cooked spaghetti. Her heart slammed against her chest. Sweat dripped off her face and drenched her clothes.

"So that's what they mean by fun run."

She flinched, almost falling off the machine. She hadn't realized anyone else was in the gym. She'd come early. The windows over the pool were still dark.

Kai stood behind her, bare-chested, in skintight swimming shorts, a towel slung over his shoulder. He was slim, but all lean muscle. She wondered if he'd always been that way and hidden it beneath the black T-shirts or if it was the product of his recent training. On his chest over his heart was a tattooed *S*.

Her own chest continued to heave as she squirted water into her mouth and forced herself to swallow.

"You're here early," she said after catching her breath.

"Usually." He looked strange without his eyeliner, his black hair wet and shoved back by his goggles. Normal. Cute. She might not have recognized him if not for that half-smirk he always wore. "Whatcha running from?"

"Take a wild guess," she said grimly, mopping her face with a towel. "Simone never told me about the tattoo."

Kai glanced down at the black cursive letter. "Inside I'm fluffy marshmallow goo," he said, smile growing. "Didn't you know?"

She stepped off the machine. Her legs continued to vibrate with the motor's thrum. Grimacing, she massaged the sensation out of her thighs. Running on the treadmill felt like having electricity pumped into her body—not the feeling she'd been looking for. But since she couldn't run outside, it was the best she was going to get.

"Speaking of Simone," she said, "I think she misses you."

"That's funny. She said the same thing to me about you last night," he said. "She thinks you're avoiding her, which reminds me . . ." He turned away. "Stay put, huh?"

She took another swig of water. He left the gym floor, heading back through the equipment towards the locker rooms. She stretched and wiped the sweat off the machine. A wall of glass separated the treadmills from the pool, but chlorine tainted the air anyway. That, mixed with the stale scent of sweat and disinfectant, made it difficult for her to take a deep breath. An older woman was swimming laps. Another young woman came in and moved down to the far end of the long room to the ellipticals. Otherwise, the gym was empty and quiet.

Finally, Kai returned. In his hand was a plastic bag stuffed with beaded bracelets. He held it out to her. "Guess I don't have to tell you who these are from."

She took them. "Guess not."

"Be a pal and wear them."

Josie shifted the bag around. At least Simone hadn't done them in rainbow colors like the last batch. The beads were mostly purple and black. "Why didn't she just give them to me herself?"

"Like I said, avoiding. Are you?"

Josie sighed. "Maybe . . . a little."

Kai looked towards the pool. "She makes it hard, doesn't she?"

"Makes what hard?"

"Being self-absorbed and miserable," he said. "It's hard to be around Simone and feel sorry for yourself. No one can feel sorrier for you than she does."

Josie smiled a little. "How's training?"

He shrugged. "I'll be taking over the world any day now."

"Gods help us."

"How's the Beyond these days?" he asked.

She choked on her water. "How did you know I was . . . Simone told you."

"She thinks you're taking an unnecessary risk."

"Did she tell you to ask me to stop?"

"Even if she did, I wouldn't. Besides, why would she tell me that? If you're not going to listen to her or Judah, why would you listen to me?"

"Maybe you're the voice of reason."

"Then we're in real trouble."

She smiled again.

"I don't blame you," Kai said. "I'd do it too. Why waste all your time with Popsicle sticks and a glue gun when you can hop over to the Beyond and snag a godly face off the shelf? But you know those Goodwins. They've never ridden a bicycle without a helmet."

"Caroline talked to me yesterday."

"Oh yeah, told you about the lockdown, did she?"

"How did you . . ." She shook her head. Simone, again. She really couldn't keep anything to herself. It was a miracle she hadn't told the whole tribe about Josie and the Fire Guy. "Actually, she mostly wanted to talk about Judah."

"Oh yeah? Is he planning round two with Russell? I'd pay good money for ringside seats to that bout."

"I wouldn't know. I haven't seen him."

"Right. Simone said he was off scaling the mountain or something. Guy needs to try some Prozac, you know? Maybe toke the old ganj from time to time. Take it down a notch."

Though her heart was no longer pounding, her chest started to hurt again. "I think he's already done that with me."

"Don't tell me you're missing his overbearing, alpha-male bit." Kai shook his head. "That's typical."

She frowned. "What do you mean by that?"

"You'd think that in a matriarchal society like the Core we'd be ahead of the curve when it comes to sexual politics, but it seems like every woman still wants to be a princess and every guy wants to be the knight. The women in the Core are the most powerful summoners, but they all want to be rescued from their tower and swept off their feet."

Her teeth set. "I don't want to be a princess."

"Whatever you say, your highness."

She slung her own towel over her shoulder. "Thanks for the bracelets." She started past him.

"Wait," Kai said, catching her arm with the tips of his fingers. "Don't be pissed."

"I'm not," she said. "I'm just..."

"I wasn't trying to say anything personal," he said. "I just get sick of the status quo around here."

He shot a dark look towards the pretty young woman sweating away on the elliptical. Her gaze was locked on the ceiling-mounted TV, even though she had ear buds jammed into her ears. Kai looked back at Josie. The girl's eyes flicked over to him, like she'd been waiting for him to look away. Once she saw Josie watching her, her gaze jumped back up to the screen.

Josie wondered if Kai had any idea of how often girls were sneaking looks at him when he wasn't paying attention. They'd been practically drooling over him at his concert... before Lily had crashed it and destroyed the club and most of the street. But Kai acted as if everyone, except Simone, had ignored him his entire life.

"You don't need Sheriff Judah questioning you every time you step out your door," he said. "I figured you, of all people, would be glad he was out of town. Simone acts like it's the end of the world if Judah isn't on duty 24-7."

Josie didn't want to admit that she felt safer when Judah was around. Or that when she'd received the threatening messages, he was the first one she'd wanted to run to. She didn't even want to admit it to herself. The whole reason she'd caved and come to the gym was to run away from the pestering thoughts of Judah.

"I know you're not like the other girls around here," he said. "Occasionally, you seem to think about someone other than yourself. Believe me, that's rare."

"Occasionally?"

He bumped her chin with his fist. "That's why I like you, but you've been blowing off my lady and that ain't cool."

"I just don't want her to worry."

He smirked. "Asking Simone not to worry is like asking the sun not to rise. Besides, what does she have to worry about?"

Josie chewed her lip a little. "I've seen Death."

"Say what?"

"Don't tell anyone, especially Simone. She'll freak out."

"No shit, I guess, huh?" He glanced over at the girl again. Her eyes flicked back to the screen. "How can you see Death when he's locked up in the Tripartite?"

"It's just an aspect of him that's locked into the Tripartite. He's like any other god. A part of him is in the mask, a part of him is in the Beyond, another—"

"I get it," he interjected. "So Death is what . . . trying to lure you over to the other side?"

"I don't know. He won't tell me."

"The better supervillains keep their evil plans to themselves," he said. "Is he stopping you from fixing the masks?"

"No. I've already repaired almost half. The Eye came and took them yesterday."

"I hope they put them in a safe place. After the blood tagging on your window—"

"Gretchen put them in her stash," she said.

Kai's black eyes, somehow, darkened. "Simone said the paws were real. She bawled about it for almost an hour." He took the towel off his shoulder, strangling it. "Even I think that's twisted."

"Agreed."

"You think it was Fog Dude again?"

"I don't know," she said. "It doesn't really seem like his MO, but regardless, it still means there's another traitor in the tribe."

"Have any suspects in that lineup?" he asked.

"I wish."

"How about Russell?"

"Seriously? You too? He's your brother."

"Foster brother, and please don't remind me. Dude has evil prick written on his CV. He spent most of his childhood inventing new ways to torment me. Have you ever woken up to a bed full of mouse traps? Let me tell you, not fun. If Lily is going to take out humanity, I'd put his name first on the list."

"That's not funny."

"Do I look like I'm joking?"

"What would Simone say if she heard you?"

"Well, I'm not talking to Simone, am I? Come on, Josie. You're not really falling for that douche, are you? A pus-filled genital wart on a syphilitic leper has more charm—"

"Gross."

"Exactly. As someone who was saved from torture by your goodwill, I feel obliged to warn you that he's only after one thing, princess, and it ain't your pretty brain."

"Thanks for the warning."

"But you're not going to listen, are you?"

"You sound just like Judah."

"The enemy of my enemy is my friend or at least... temporary ally."

"You think everyone is your enemy."

"Allow me to give you another piece of unsolicited advice—trust no one."

"Now you really sound like Judah."

"I'm sure there are a lot of people who underestimate Judah because he looks like a Hollister poster boy, but don't be fooled. Appearances are deceptive. Just because someone's good-looking doesn't mean they're brainless. Judah's like a metal stick-up-the-ass, but he's smart and he's deadly. I know that. Don't be fooled by the way I look either, Josie. I know what everyone thinks. Guy who wears the eyeliner and doesn't like to play all their reindeer games. But they don't know me. Not even a little."

She glanced over at elliptical girl again, who was still ogling Kai from afar. "Are we talking about the gooey marshmallow again?"

His sideswiped grin returned. "You tell me."

"Do I strike you as someone who trusts people easily? I hate to break this to you, Kai, but I trust you. Are you telling me not to?"

"I'm just curious why. I don't recall doing anything to earn a place on your kickball team. Nancy was pretty pissed when you told her you wanted to give me one of those masks."

"You earned it," she said, "when Fog God kidnapped you. When Granite God broke your fingers. When you stood up for me when I was feverish and delirious and on the verge of . . . you earned it."

"Now who's full of marshmallow goo?"

"In every tyrant's heart there springs in the end this poison, that he cannot trust a friend."

"Ooo, quotey."

She smiled. "Thank Aeschylus and my mom. She was full of that kind of stuff. Of course, that was all geared towards making me a better ruler of the Core, but it's probably still true. Simone might be the only person in the world who trusts everyone completely without question. The rest of us have to pick and choose whom to trust and with what. Right now, I choose you."

"You must be feeling pretty desperate."

"Probably."

"But you don't trust me enough to steer clear of Russell."

"I honestly haven't been thinking about him."

"And after he nearly died defending you from Big Bad Judah? What really happened that night anyway?"

"Good question."

"Vale!" The older woman who'd been swimming laps pushed open the door from the pool. "We're wasting daylight here. Those trials aren't going to pass themselves. Move it."

"I hate it when she calls me that," Kai muttered.

"Sorry I got you into this."

The woman blew her whistle. They both flinched. Even the girl on the elliptical jerked, interrupting her smooth bobbing rhythm.

"On the double!"

"Yes, ma'am," Kai said, heading towards the door.

The woman strode back across the pool deck.

"Oh, Kai," Josie called after him. "Core girls don't want to be princesses. They want to be Triune. Big difference."

"Maybe, but they forget," he said, "the Triune doesn't need a knight. She's the knight, the queen, the bishop, the whole chess set all in one. She doesn't need anyone."

He let the door close. Josie watched him toss aside his towel, pull on his goggles, and dive in. All the while, the older woman barked at him.

He was wrong.

Her mom could've used a knight, a bishop, a pawn, anybody. In the end, she'd needed somebody. All she'd had was Josie and Josie couldn't save her. Maybe if her mom had trusted a few more people, someone might've been there to be her knight.

CHAPTER 23

July 20th

When someone knocked on the art lab door, startling her out of her brood, she was surprised to see Russell's dark eyes peering through the glass at her.

She glanced down at the sketchpad she'd been doodling on and was horrified to see Judah's eyes glaring up at her. She slammed it shut and hurried to the door.

"What are you doing here?" she asked as he stepped in. "Aren't you supposed to be resting?"

"It's been more than two weeks, Josie," he said. "There's only so much convalescence a man can stand before he starts to get twitchy." He ran his hand over his silky red button-down, frowning. "That's not the reception I was hoping to receive."

Josie shut the door. "I'm sorry. I'm just...surprised. Of course, I'm glad to see you." She forced a smile. "You look good. How do you feel?"

"Good. I mean, I've felt worse." He returned her smile with a flirtatious one of his own. "How are you?" He glanced around, searching the bare tables and counters. "How's progress on the masks? Everything all right?"

"Everything's fine," she said. "I've completed thirteen. I just finished one this morning."

His eyebrows shot up. "You have been busy. So I guess I won't be as put out about you not returning my last...few calls."

Josie winced. She had meant to call Russell back, but she just...hadn't. "Sorry about that."

He waved her off. "Like I said, you've been working. My ego is only slightly bruised. Much less than my kidneys." He smiled again.

"You seem like you're in a good mood," she said.

"Why shouldn't I be? I'm with you."

Faint warmth crept up through her. She wasn't sure what to do with this strange sensation he was provoking. She was actually surprised he was able to provoke anything at this point.

"I have to say. I was disappointed you never made it over to see me."

"I wanted to," she said sincerely, "but no one would take me. Since the bloody paw print incident, I'm not allowed to drive myself around anymore."

Russell's face darkened. "Whoever did that—"

"Thanks," she said, wandering back to the table. "But I'm not really looking for vengeance. I'm much more interested in justice."

"Two sides of the same coin," Russell said. "Where are the masks?" he asked conversationally.

"Gretchen took them."

"Took them where?"

"She's holding onto them until the Eye reconvenes."

"Nancy said she was headed out of town," he said. "How long do you think it will take you to finish the rest?"

"I've been doing one a day," she said. "So, two weeks? I could do more, I think, but . . ."

"But what?"

But Death. She knew his comfort and encouragement was a ploy, and since she didn't actually know his ultimate plan, her interactions with him were all the more dangerous.

She leaned against the table. "It's not easy."

Russell came to her, running his hands down her arms and taking her hands. Long-quiet flutters stirred in her stomach. "I'm sorry I haven't been here to help you. I wanted to be."

"It's all right," she said. "Actually, it turns out I don't need help like I thought."

He squeezed her hands, gazing into her eyes steadily. "Too bad." He let go of her hands and reached into the pocket of his slacks. "I have something for you." He pulled out a small velvet bag and put it in her hand. "Open it."

She unknotted the top of the bag. Inside was a silver chain. She hooked the delicate chain with her finger and pulled it from the bag. On it hung a flat quarter-sized pendant. One side held a faceted piece of clear quartz, on the other a mirror—both were etched with tribal symbols.

He pulled up his sleeve to show her the black leather bracelet around his wrist, with a matching pendant.

"It's a locating charm," he said. "I know you probably already have one or two—or a dozen—but probably not one like this. I met a charm-maker in Burma. He might be the only one in the world who knows this charm." He took the necklace from her and slipped it around her neck. "It will allow me not only to translocate directly to wherever you are, but also to see whatever you're seeing." He turned the pendant around so the mirror was against her chest. "But only if the mirror is turned out. Otherwise, just keep it to your skin."

She lifted the pendant and inspected the etched symbols.

She was torn. On the one hand, she didn't know Russell that well and accepting a charm like this from him definitely made her uncomfortable. On the other hand, she'd felt so vulnerable lately. After being kidnapped, beaten up, held prisoner . . . she actually didn't mind having someone else—besides Judah—watching out for her. In a way, she was relieved not to have to ask for it either. Admitting that she needed others to protect her from Lily was almost as hard for her as saying thank you to Judah for saving her. But the brutal fact was she did need to be watched. Russell's necklace wasn't really any different than Simone's locating charm bracelets or her dad tracking her cell phone. At least Russell wanted to help. Everyone else just seemed to be obliged to do so.

"That's very thoughtful," she said.

"I just want you to be safe, Josie," he said. The back of his fingers brushed her cheek. A fresh bout of goose bumps broke out over her.

The tightness in her chest told her that a kiss was imminent. But before he'd even leaned in, there was another knock on the door. He turned.

Josie stood. Allison smiled, holding up a paper bag from the café and a cup of coffee. She'd been bringing Josie lunch every day, not because anyone asked her to. She'd simply taken it on herself.

Josie went to the door, opening it.

Allison sidled in, made-up like she was on her way to a photo shoot—bright pink lipstick; a very short, very white skirt; and sandal wedges with a heel that made her a couple of inches taller than Josie, though Josie knew she was the taller one.

"Thanks, Allison," Josie said, taking the bag and coffee.

"My pleasure," Allison said. As always, her smile never quite reached her eyes. They cooled even more when they touched on Russell. The tension was evident. Josie wondered if the rumors were true. If Allison and Russell had slept together, but she found she really didn't care.

Allison's tone didn't carry any hostility in spite of the rumors. "Hi, Russell. How are you?"

His hands slid into his pockets. "Fine. Thanks for asking."

Allison toyed with a lock of hair, highlighted platinum blond. "It's good to see you up and around. I can't believe the Eye hasn't done anything about Judah. I thought they were going to have an inquiry."

Josie took the food back to the table where her bag and sketchpad sat. "They have more important things to deal with at the moment."

"I guess." Allison's gaze bounced back and forth between Josie and Russell. "I'm sorry. Am I interrupting something?"

Russell wasn't showing any interest in Allison. He turned to Josie's sketchbook and started to open it.

"Don't!" Josie slammed her hand down on the cover.

He lifted his hand, looking surprised and maybe a little hurt. "Sorry, I didn't realize it was private."

"It's not private," Josie said, sliding the sketchbook away from him. "It's just that it's embarrassing—just doodles. I may be a mask-maker, but I'm a terrible artist."

"Yeah, you should've seen this carving she did, of like Apollo," Allison said. "Atrocious."

"Adonis," Josie corrected.

"How could you tell? You couldn't even see his face," Allison said. "That chick with the fat butt was in the way."

"Aphrodite." Josie's hand curled around her pen, but she fought back the stabby thoughts.

"Rodin's *Death of Adonis*?" Russell asked.

"Yeah," Josie said. "You know it?"

"I was an art history major," he said. "I wrote a paper on Rodin. You did a carving of it? I'd love to see it."

Josie turned Judah's ring around her thumb. "I sort of... got rid of it."

"Good thing," Allison chimed in. "Like I said, you should just stick to the mask-making thing. I thought I saw Gretchen and Nancy carrying a bunch of boxes into Caroline's office earlier. Were those the masks?"

"Maybe."

"I heard they've been putting people through tests and stuff," Allison said. "Serious trials. Truth-charms. I guess they're right to be so paranoid. You don't know who you can trust these days." Her eyes flicked over to Russell, narrowing, and then back to Josie, widening, innocent. "Who do you think I should talk to about trying out?"

"Trying out?" Josie repeated.

"Yeah, for one of the masks. I mean, I'm like Tessa's best friend now. And since we're such good friends too, I figure I'm much more likely to be in the line of fire. I've passed the first round of master-level trials. I could totally handle it, and then you'd have one more person who can protect you."

Josie wanted to ask when she and Allison had become friends. Just because Allison had been bringing her lunch for the last two weeks, it was hardly enough to constitute friendship in Josie's book. But in spite of her tactlessness, Allison had been very sweet to her. And she and Tessa had become better friends in the little time Tessa had for anyone besides Daisuke.

"I don't know who you should talk to," Josie said finally. "Gretchen, I guess. Or Caroline."

"They put all those masks in Caroline's office?" Allison asked. "That doesn't seem like a very safe place."

"They're safe, Allison."

"Yeah, but I didn't see them carrying any of them out again—"

"Don't worry about it—"

"I just thought they'd be a bit more careful," Allison said. "I mean, that one mask you made got stolen, right? The fire god mask? They never found out what happened to it, did they? I know the summoner helped you out that one time, but where's he been since then?"

"Good question," Josie said, folding her arms.

Russell settled back against the table. "You ask a lot of questions, Allison," he said. "Have you always been such a busybody?"

Allison's nostrils flared. "I'm just curious. There's nothing wrong with that, is there?"

"Not unless you're a cat."

Allison's eyes narrowed. "Did you think that was clever?"

"Clever enough for you," Russell said, face hard and shadowed even under the bright humming fluorescents.

Allison's lip curled. "If you wanted me to leave, you should've just said so. You don't have to be mean about it. I thought we were friends."

Russell gazed at her for a long moment. "Did you?

Another knock on the door cut into the tension building between Allison and Russell. Simone waved frantically. Tears glistened on her cheeks.

Josie rushed forward, past Allison, who stood there staring.

Josie pulled open the door.

"Simone, what's—?"

Simone grabbed Josie's arm and dragged her down the hall to the lobby.

"Simone, what is it?" Simone stopped abruptly behind one of the couches. Josie bumped into her. Simone shook her head, too choked with tears to speak, and pointed at the TV.

Images of smoke filled the screen. Below read the caption: Forest Fire Ravaging Crater Lake National Park. The video flashed to billowing pillars of smoke over the green peaks of trees, police setting up road blocks, and fire fighters gearing up. The reporter spoke in a tense, grave voice.

"The fire appears to be spreading rapidly, fueled by fierce winds. Evacuations are taking place throughout the area, but a number of campers and hikers, taken unawares by the sudden conflagration, are still unaccounted for . . ."

Simone clutched Josie's arm.

Josie stared at Simone's pale face and red-rimmed eyes.

"Judah?"

Simone threw her arms around Josie's neck, sobbing.

The building felt like it was collapsing around them, the floors giving way.

Josie held up Simone's shaking body. She glanced back at the TV.

"Rangers and rescuers are combing the area, but the ferocity of this fire is hampering efforts to locate the missing."

CHAPTER 24

July 20th

J OSIE PACED THE GOODWIN'S FAMILY ROOM. "It didn't work the last time."

"It will work," Simone said, grinding away at the obsidian with her etcher.

Caroline stood on the other side of the breakfast table, chewing her nails. Josie's dad had his arm around her as if for support, but Caroline looked tense enough to hold up the ceiling and the entire second floor by herself.

In the background, the twenty-four hour news networks had the fire on continuous coverage. They were already declaring it one of the worst wildfires in state history, even though it had only started eight hours before. The fire was spreading far and fast. Drought conditions in the southern part of the state, along with wicked winds, were feeding the flames, sweeping them westward with terrifying speed. Voluntary evacuations were already being called for along I-5.

"I can't believe Tessa would confiscate Judah's ring without telling the Eye," Caroline said for the dozenth time. She looked down at her phone again, like it might've rung without her noticing.

Josie spun Judah's ring around her thumb, biting her tongue. As Triune, Tessa could confiscate anyone's mask at any time without explanation. It was unusual, but within her purview. Josie knew that Caroline's complaint had less to do with Tessa and more to do with her concern for Judah.

No one had heard from him for three days. When called, his phone went straight to voicemail. Her dad had been on the phone with everyone he could think to call, but the rescue workers were scrambling and no one could give them any answers. Caroline had wanted to translocate down there right away, but Simone had convinced her to wait until she tried the locating charm. That had been two hours ago, and Caroline's face was so tight it looked like she'd had a facelift.

"Okay, done," Simone said, switching off the etcher. "Map?"

"Right here," Josie's dad said, pulling the map from the back pocket of his slacks. He'd gone down to the store and picked up a map while Caroline had gnawed her nails down to nubs, and Josie rubbed her thumb raw spinning Judah's ring.

He laid it out on the breakfast table. Simone pushed the stone towards Josie.

"You do it," she said. "I feel like I'm going to pass out."

Josie pushed one of the chairs aside and took the stone. It was as big as a paperweight and twice as heavy.

Before, when she'd tried to use this charm to find the Fire Guy, she'd gone into a state of deep meditation beforehand. She'd followed the instructions to the letter, clearing her mind, centering herself, releasing her turmoil of emotions, so that she could focus entirely on the god's symbol and nothing else.

This time, she didn't even close her eyes. At the center of the stone was Judah's name, written in Core symbols. Immediately, his face appeared in her mind.

Where the hell are you?

"Look," Simone said. "There."

She pointed to the map. A brilliant blue light shone on it like a laser beam.

"Wait," her dad said, taking a photo of the map with his phone. He tapped at the screen and then turned it towards Caroline. "Right near Prospect."

"Send it to me," Caroline said.

Her dad tapped his phone again. Caroline's buzzed a moment later.

"Josie, give me his ring." Caroline said.

Josie handed it over.

"You two stay here," she said. "Marc."

He nodded. They both went into possession. Two gods of water, one gray, one blue. Then they vanished.

Josie set down the stone. The blue light faded.

"It worked," Josie said to Simone.

Simone just stared up at her, brow wrinkled, coiling her necklace around and around her finger.

When Josie's dad reappeared and removed his mask, sweat was dripping down his face. His shirt was soaked through and the acrid scent of smoke clung to him.

Simone jumped up from her chair.

He wiped his forehead with his rolled up sleeve. Twigs stuck to his shirt and his pants were wet and muddy.

"He's fine," he said to Simone.

Simone dropped back into her chair and started crying again.

Josie remained where she'd been, near the window. "Where is he?"

"He's at one of the firefighters' temporary bases," her dad said. "He's fine."

Josie's heart started beating again tentatively. "Why didn't he answer his phone?"

"He lost it. Fell out of his pocket I guess. He had to move fast. He lost a lot of his gear actually, but he's all right. Caroline chewed his ear off for not calling her, but he's been busy. He's assisting the rescue workers. Seems he knows a few of them from all those wilderness training courses he's taken." Her dad pulled out a chair and sat down with a heavy breath. "He plans to stay on for as long as they'll have him. Caroline's trying to talk him out of it, but I know a losing argument when I hear one."

"That's so great." Simone stood up and hugged Josie and then hugged Josie's dad too. "I'll get you something to drink."

"Thank you, Simone," he said. "We translocated in outside of town and walked in a ways." He gave Josie a weak smile. "Italian shoes, not the best for humping alongside the roads of southern Oregon." His smile faltered. "What's wrong?"

Josie blinked. "Nothing."

Her dad leveled his gaze at her. "He's fine, Josie. I saw him with my own eyes."

"Good," she said.

He frowned at her.

Simone came back with a glass of iced tea.

Josie turned towards the window. The panic gripping her dissolved slowly, allowing her to breathe again, but as it let go she felt herself emptying out, feeling hollow again. What was wrong with her?

"Can you take me back to the center, Dad?" she asked.

His frown deepened. "Now?"

"You need to go back to the office anyway, don't you?"

"Well ... I guess, but wouldn't you rather stay here with Simone?"

Josie didn't look at Simone. She could feel Simone's worry from across the room.

"I'd rather get some more work done myself," she said.

"Let me go home and change first," he said, taking another drink of iced tea. He set it back down on the table. "I'll be back shortly."

He retrieved his mask again, went into possession, and translocated.

Finally, Josie looked at Simone. "Did you call Kai?"

"I sent him a message," Simone said. "We haven't been talking much lately, actually."

"He said he saw you last night."

"Oh, he did. But he couldn't stay long and ... I don't know. He was acting weird."

"Weird how?"

Simone shrugged.

"Well, he gave me the bracelets." Josie held up her arm so Simone could see the half dozen bracelets on her arm.

"Good," Simone said weakly.

Josie's arm dropped to her side. "Isn't your anniversary coming up?"

Simone nodded, eyes down. "Next Friday."

"Have you made plans?"

Simone shook her head and then shrugged. "No big deal. He's so busy. Training for the trials is way more important."

"You think he forgot?"

Simone wiped the lingering tears off her face. "Judah's okay. That's all that matters, right?"

Josie looked back out the window. The afternoon light was bright across the back yard. The sky was endless blue. Hard to believe that just a few hours away, smoke was filling up the horizon.

"Josie—"

"Right," Josie said. "Of course."

"You were hoping to see him, weren't you?" Simone asked softly.

"What? No."

"Your carving. The one of Adonis and Aphrodite," Simone said. "He kept it. It's on his nightstand. Next to his bed."

Pain dug deeper into her already hollowed chest. She wondered how deep it would dig before it found what it was looking for or gave up.

Images of fire licked across the TV screen.

When Josie had seen Russell today, it had startled her. When she'd told Kai she hadn't been thinking about him, she'd meant it. She hadn't thought about him, because she hadn't been thinking about the Fire Guy.

The sudden shift might've signaled that she was moving on, but if that were the case, then why did she still feel like she was oh-so-slowly dying?

She knew she was sick of feeling like this all the time, so weak, so desperate, so . . . rejected. She hated it. She had to find a way to make it stop.

She couldn't stop thinking about what Death had said either. How she needed to look at everything she'd thought she'd known again. How she needed to do what she felt what was right, instead of what she thought was right. But all she felt was empty and aching.

"This fire," Simone said softly, staring at the screen with Josie. "Have you thought that maybe . . ."

"Someone started it? A godly someone?"

Simone nodded.

"Of course I have, Simone. I'm sure we're all thinking it. We've all been waiting for Lily to start her age of destruction—"

"I don't mean Lily."

"Then who did you mean?"

Simone raised her eyebrows.

Josie scowled. "You don't think the Fire Guy did this."

"Not on purpose," Simone said, "but maybe accidently. If he's struggling to control the god . . . you know how stuff like this happens, Josie. All the time, even with summoners who aren't becoming manifest."

"Sure," Josie acknowledged, "but this wasn't him."

"Why not?"

"Why would it be?"

"Why couldn't it be?"

"Well, I guess it could've been, but it could've been a lot of things."

Simone crossed her arms, scowling.

Josie sighed. "Russell hasn't been in any shape to start any fires—"

Simone threw her hands in the air. "It's not Russell!"

"Why are you so sure? Do you know who it is?"

Simone took a step back. "No."

"But you're sure it's not Russell."

"Yes."

Josie rubbed her forehead. "You know, I'm not even sure I care who it is anymore."

"What do you mean?"

"I mean . . . he doesn't want to be with me, Simone. He has good reasons, and you know . . . that's fine."

"Josie, don't quit," Simone said. "You'll find him, just . . ."

"What Simone?"

"Don't stop looking," Simone said, echoing Death's words.

Was it a coincidence? She doubted it. Is that what Death had been implying? That she shouldn't give up looking for her Fire Guy? Why would he care?

"He doesn't want to be found, Simone. Or, at least, he doesn't want me to know who he really is."

"Or it might be he just wants you to find him. Maybe he wants you to realize who he is—to unmask him."

Simone's words hit Josie in the gut—more echoes of Death. He'd said Josie was afraid—afraid of being unmasked.

She touched the pendant Russell had given her. A locator charm. Maybe it was a subtle hint. Maybe Russell wanted her to realize he was the Fire Guy after all—to find him. A few weeks ago, all she'd wanted to do was find him, to unmask him, but she'd gotten distracted by . . .

Her gaze flicked again to the TV. It was so like Judah to turn a camping trip into an opportunity to play the hero. She could just imagine him evacuating campers, manning the first aid station, putting up road blocks. It wouldn't have surprised her if he tried to get out there and fight the fire himself, just like he'd always wanted to do.

And he hadn't thought once about his mom or Simone or anyone back home who might've been so worried her heart had gone into seizures thinking that something had happened to him. He'd been too busy saving the world.

"What about you?" Josie asked. "Are you going to remind Kai about your anniversary?"

Simone's face fell even further. "Maybe I won't have to. He still has a week."

CHAPTER 25

JULY 22ND
TWO DAYS LATER

JOSIE STARED AT THE COMPUTER SCREEN, sipping coffee. Gretchen's office was windowless, but she could hear the thunder rumbling outside.

Earlier in the café, everyone who hadn't been talking about the fires had been making chit-chatty remarks about the unprecedented storms. For people who lived with rain month after month, they seemed completely awestruck by the thunderstorms. Sustained thunder and lightning were, apparently, uncommon in Portland. Two days of it had people throwing around words like Armageddon.

If they'd only known the truth, they might not have joked about the end of the world.

The storms were part of the plan to extinguish the flames scouring the southern half of the state. It wasn't often that a tribe took such large scale action to avert a "natural" disaster.

Apparently, Judah had made a pretty convincing case to his mother that the tribe needed to intervene.

But Josie tried not to think about the fires or the storms or Judah. She kept herself occupied with repairing masks, researching, and whittling as much as she could.

On the computer she pulled up another story about Lu-Ji from the archives. Even though Lu-Ji had lived so long ago no one was sure how long it really had been, Death was still holding a grudge over what she'd done.

Josie wasn't at all convinced that his meetings with Josie had been solely for her benefit.

Over the last two days, she'd repaired two more masks. Each time she'd lingered, waiting for Death to appear, but he never had.

Still, she decided that it couldn't hurt to look again at Lu-Ji, the first Triune, like he'd suggested. The story on the screen was one she'd read a hundred times before.

Lu-Ji, sick of the gods' insane interference in the lives of mortals, outwitted Death and stole his Gauntlet, the symbol of his power. Then she conquered Life in battle and won Life's Chalice, the Cup of Immortality. Finally, she confronted the Other and engaged in a philosophical debate that ended in the Other agreeing to trade Death's Gauntlet and Life's Chalice for the mask of the Tripartite. Gods could no longer walk the mortal realm; thus, the Triune and the Corpora Deorum were born—though they didn't come to be named such for many more centuries.

She read it again and again. She pulled up every version available, but didn't see anything new. Why had Death wanted her to look again? What had he wanted her to find?

When the door opened, she started. Tepid coffee splashed over her hand.

"Oops, sorry, kiddo," Gretchen said, smiling wearily. "Didn't mean to freak you out."

Josie wiped the coffee away with a tissue. "No problem. How's firefighting?"

Gretchen plopped down on the edge of the desk. Her rain jacket shed water onto the messy stacks of sketchbooks piled haphazardly next to the computer.

"Water's not my element." She ran her hand over the wet black spikes of her hair. "I admit, even the wimpy little river god I've been summoning has been kicking my ass, but I think we're finally turning back the tide, so to speak."

Josie nodded. "How are my dad and Caroline?"

"They're fine," Gretchen said. "Between Caroline's work off the coast and Nancy's work up in the air, we're feeling pretty confident that the terrae can take over again soon and manage. But it is one wicked stubborn blaze. You'd think two days of icy rain would snuff it—no such luck. Got to say, I was pretty lucky myself. Came out of possession by this creek to take a break, had a tree limb fall right on me, used up all my charms against physical injury." She pushed back her sleeves. Only a couple of bracelets circled her wrists, where there had been a dozen or so. "Good thing Simone's a little worker bee. I'll need more before I head out again. What about you? Been busy?"

Josie picked up the newest mountain god mask. The slate-blue face, with its white-tipped nose and chilly demeanor, would have been another good match for Nancy—if she'd been an earth summoner.

Josie handed it to Gretchen. Then she reached back and retrieved another box from the cart and held it out to Gretchen. A sea god.

"This one's for my dad," she said.

"Two more, huh?" Gretchen took the masks.

"Have enough room in your stash?"

"I'll manage." Gretchen removed the sea god mask from its box—the face was painted indigo and had a vicious set of fangs and a hungry kind of voice. Not the personality Josie would've matched up to her dad if she'd had a choice, but of all the water god masks she'd fixed it was the most powerful. She wanted her dad to have as much protection as she could give him.

Gretchen took both masks in her right hand and with a twitch of her wrist, they were gone.

"Fourteen," Gretchen said, sliding the lid back on the box. "Pushing yourself a bit?"

"I want to have the last of them done by the time I'm released," Josie said.

Beginning tomorrow morning, she would be confined to Caroline's house for the week. Nancy had postponed her plans to leave on Saturday in order to help with the firefight. But, otherwise, nothing had changed. Everyone was headed out first thing in the morning.

A crew of tribe members had already gathered up a host of supplies and hauled them over to Caroline's house. Simone was left to sort them out since no one was allowed to come closer to the house than the end of her driveway.

Gretchen leaned her arm on her thigh. "What's going on with you, kiddo?"

Josie stared down at the murky brown depths of her coffee. "Nothing."

"Bullshit," Gretchen said. "What is it? Your mom's death? A guy? Please tell me it's not on Beech's account."

"It's not Beech or my mom."

Of course, she would've given anything to see her mom again, to hear one of her quit-your-whining-and-get-back-to-work speeches. She often found herself wondering what her mother would've said or done if she'd been in Josie's place now. But Josie couldn't imagine her mother as anything other than the Triune. Josie felt like she knew what a Triune would have been doing at this moment—hunting Lily—but Josie wasn't the Triune. When she wasn't repairing masks or researching, she found herself falling into darker and darker places within herself.

Gretchen's gaze felt like a gentle hand on her shoulder. "Heartbreak?"

"I really don't—"

"Who?"

"It doesn't—"

"You going to let it drive you to the nuthouse, *mi amor*? Huh? You don't look good, Josie. When was the last time you ate?"

Josie rubbed her forehead. The ache in her skull expanded at her touch. "Last night."

Her dad had ordered pizza, exhausted after a day of swelling the creeks and rivers. Flooding a few houses had been deemed better than allowing whole towns to burn down.

Gretchen bowed her head. "Feels like dying, doesn't it?"

A sharp pain cut through Josie's chest.

"I remember," Gretchen said. "The first time I fell in love . . . it was terrible. The drama." Gretchen chuckled a little. "We were awful to each other. We made it so much harder than it had to be. I know it won't do any good to tell you that it does get better, but it does. It will. You just have to give it . . ."

Josie ran her thumbs over the rim of her coffee cup.

"Or maybe that's bullshit," Gretchen said.

Josie looked up, surprised.

Gretchen's tongue stud slid over her lower lip as she studied Josie. "When Beech started seeing you," she said finally, "I warned him. I told him, I don't think you want to get involved with Josie Day."

Josie frowned. "Why?"

"My son gave you the upfront talk, didn't he? The one about how he's polyamorous and doesn't adhere to all these ridiculous, unnatural notions about monogamy?"

Josie nodded.

"Of course he did. He may be the bad boy, but he's really a good guy. He likes to play it straight with people."

"You don't believe in monogamy either, do you?"

Gretchen's gaze rolled up to the ceiling. "There have been times when it hasn't worked for me, when other arrangements have seemed more appropriate. But . . ."

"You love Roxy, don't you?"

"Very much."

"You're monogamous with her?"

"Very much."

"And you don't want to be with anyone else?"

"I don't, and I don't want her to be with anyone else. When I think about it, I get this awful feeling, like if I see her touch another woman, I might just forget I'm a pacifist." Gretchen smiled, seemingly to herself. "I haven't admitted that, not even to her, but it's true. It doesn't really meld with my philosophies, and I've been pretty vocal about my philosophies. If anyone knew that I felt this way, there would more than a few of them who'd call me a hypocrite. I don't believe in jealousy or possessiveness. I don't think they're healthy emotions, Josie. You can't possess another person, you can't control them, and you shouldn't try. At the same time, if Roxy left me right now . . . I feel like I might just open myself a nice hole in the ground and let it swallow me up."

Josie's hands tightened around her coffee cup, like it might anchor her against the feelings of emptiness.

"I told Beech you weren't the trifling kind of girl," Gretchen said. "I think he realized that. I think that's part of the reason he left."

Josie looked back up at Gretchen. "You think he left because of me?"

"I think he left because he was afraid he might be starting to have the same kind of revelation that I've been having these days," she said. "Sometimes you can live by principles. You can state what you think is true, what you believe to be right, but then someone comes along and turns you into a stuttering, hypocritical hole-digger."

Josie squinted, not sure she was following.

Gretchen smiled. "What I mean is, we change, Josie. We all change. Sometimes even our most deeply held beliefs change. It doesn't have to drive us to the nearest bridge for the big jump. I know that if Roxy left me, I'd want to die, but I wouldn't. I'd survive. I'd be changed, but I'd live. Of course, I hope she stays. I will do whatever it takes to make her want to stay. But who knows? Maybe I'll feel differently in ten years or twenty. I don't know. I'm the Eye of the Past, not the Eye of the Future, but . . . right now, I can't imagine living without her. I don't want to. And for me that is a really big change."

"Beech didn't love me," Josie said.

"No, but I think you made him want to love you," Gretchen said. "You haven't noticed, but you do have this thing about you, *chica.*"

"What thing?"

"This . . . I'm complex and beautiful, and I dare you to conquer me kind of thing."

"I don't want to be conquered."

Gretchen smiled. "I hate to break it to you, but yes, you do. In so many ways. You're like . . . the remote summit. You're withholding and unwilling and begging to be won over. Conquered. It's exactly what you want. That's okay. That's who are you. We're all on our own paths. We have to be who we are in order to get where we need to go. My only concern is that you don't seem to realize the effect you have on . . . certain people. But more than that, lately, it looks like you've been defeated. You are dealing with some heady forces of godly power, Josie. You've got a majorly f'd up B conspiring to put you in chains—again. Your mom's death . . . and now I've got this inkling that there's some Romeo out there causing my Juliet to have thoughts of plunging a dagger into her tender breast, like you don't have enough problems. I know you're tough, but we all have our breaking points. Most of the artists I know, if they'd had to deal with a fraction of the craziness you've faced lately, would've driven down some dark, dark streets a long time ago. I've seen a lot of friends lose their lives over the years. Call it the artistic temperament, call it human nature, call it human frailty, call it whatever you want, but don't do it, Josie."

Josie ignored the lump in her throat. "The only thing I'm doing is fixing masks."

"Yeah, but how? I've noticed that none of the supplies I've left you have been touched, and this place is always spotless at the end of the day. You're hiding things, Josie. Not just from me, but from yourself, I think." Gretchen slid off the desk and crouched next to Josie. "I am here to help you battle the darkness, kiddo. Let me."

Josie fought within herself. One part of her wanted to spill out everything to Gretchen, but another part of her just... couldn't. When she finally spoke, her voice sounded strangled, "You can't."

"Talk to me. Tell me what's going on."

"I don't know."

In the corner of her eye, she saw a troubled crinkle on Gretchen's face.

After a moment, Gretchen said, "You can't talk to me—"

"It's not that—"

Gretchen held up her hand. "You can't talk to me. That's okay. But promise me, you will talk to someone. The biggest mistake you can make when you're hurting is to think that you're alone. You're not alone, Josie. When you're ready, I am here for you. Please come to me, okay?"

"I'm not—"

"Okay?"

Josie bit her lip and nodded.

"Okay," Gretchen said, standing up. She dug into her jacket pocket and pulled out a pack of cigarettes.

"I didn't know you smoked," Josie said.

"We all have our faults, kiddo. What can I say? I've been smoke free for almost ten years but then all this . . . Like I said, human frailty." She plucked a cigarette from the pack. "I'm supposed to take the rest of these masks"—she gestured to the masks still waiting to be repaired—"over to Caroline's this afternoon. I can take you home afterwards if you want. I'll wait with you until your dad gets back."

"Okay," Josie said.

Gretchen gave Josie a wink and left.

Josie sat there for a few minutes, staring blankly at the computer screen.

After a moment, she stood up, pulled on her jacket, and followed Gretchen.

All the smokers hung out in the back lot by the receiving door for the commissary kitchen.

She descended the stairs, trying to keep hold of her courage. She could tell Gretchen about Fire Guy, about traveling the pathways and reaching into the Beyond, about Death. Gretchen would understand. She might not be able to help, but maybe she'd been right. Maybe part of Josie's problem was that she'd been carrying all of this on her own. It was something her mom had taught her. A Triune stands alone. But Josie wasn't the Triune. She didn't need to stand alone.

She walked quickly down the long hall. The center had once been an old auto manufacturer. The building was huge. The halls were wide and, on a Sunday afternoon, eerily empty.

The commissary was at the far end, next to the gym and the pool. The scent of chlorine hung in the damp air. More thunder grumbled.

She turned down a dim hallway adjacent to the commissary towards the exit door. Bitter tobacco smoke bit at her nostrils. A deafening crack of lightning made her flinch. The lights flickered.

Pulling up her hood, she pushed open the door.

She stepped outside into a puddle.

A red puddle.

Blood.

CHAPTER 26

JULY 22ND

GRETCHEN WAS SPRAWLED UNDER THE OVERHANG—face pale as bleached paper, her jacket open. Blood pooled on her chest and soaked her tank top. Red ran off of her in streams, diluted by the rain.

"Gretchen!" Josie took another step into the downpour.

The door shut behind her.

A growl stopped her cold.

She turned and came face-to-face with a wolf.

Amber eyes flashed at her. Fangs shone, dripping wet.

Josie stumbled back, heart dizzy, head pounding.

She knew this god. She'd repaired its mask for Lily. A tree god. The Wolf.

The god let out a snicking snarl. Josie flew back, hit by a godly blow that brought blood to her mouth. She felt the charms around her wrists vanishing.

Smashing against the slick pavement, her shoulder crunched. Pain doubled her vision.

She rolled over, groaning.

The Wolf crouched over Gretchen, its slender sliver-hued back to Josie. The head was all animal, but the body was humanoid, covered in shifting patterns of coarse fur and rough bark.

"Stay away from her," Josie said, picking herself up.

She searched her pockets for something she could throw. She knew where the weak point was on this mask—the snout. If she could hit it like she'd hit Lily's mask, it would shatter. All she had was her phone. She hesitated. If she threw it, she might miss and break the phone. She needed to call for help, not just for herself, but for Gretchen. And soon.

She tapped her contacts list.

The Wolf growled and swiped its hand across the air like it was tearing through an invisible sheet.

Josie screamed. Another blow ripped across her arm, spinning her around. She landed flat on her stomach. Her phone skittered across the empty parking lot. Thunder rolled. The rain stung as it pelted her.

Her arm was on fire. The sleeve of her coat was shredded, blood running freely. She gritted her teeth and pushed up, scrambling for her phone.

"Mask-Maker," the Wolf growled. The god's voice was low and deadly, deep as thunder. The summoner's voice was female, light and sensuous.

Josie scooped up her phone and turned to face the Wolf.

"If you come willingly, I won't bite," the Wolf said.

The Wolf was inside the center's protective circles, which most likely meant the Wolf was part of Josie's tribe, although there were other possible explanations, but that was the most obvious one.

"Why don't you just kill me?" Josie said, backing up.

She could bolt for one of the side doors, but the Wolf would have more than enough time to catch her while she fumbled around for her key card. She could run for the street, but the gates were locked too. Besides, if she left the protective circles, the Wolf wouldn't have any trouble translocating with her. And the Wolf had powers unlike any other god Josie had encountered. The Wolf had inflicted wounds without even touching Josie, without summoning and drawing on the elements.

There was no way out of this. She needed help. And time.

She ran her thumb over her phone, not looking at it—not wanting to draw attention to it.

"Mother Goddess wouldn't like for me to kill you," the Wolf said, stalking closer.

"She's not Mother Earth. She's just some trumped-up earth goddess who's high on human blood."

The Wolf growled.

"And right now, she's not even that. You're more powerful than she is," Josie said, stealing a glance at her phone, making sure she had her contacts pulled up. Then her eyes flicked back up to the Wolf. She pressed the screen on her phone at random, hoping that she was dialing someone. Anyone.

"I am more powerful," the Wolf said. "The Osaka Eye could attest to that."

"You're the one who murdered them."

"And drank their blood. Which is how I gained the power to do this."

The Wolf swiped her hand across the air again.

Josie cried out, stumbling. Burning pain seared across her upper thigh. Blood ran down her leg. She kept her feet though, eyes watering with each limping backward step, pain ringing in her ears. She bumped into the parking lot fence. The iron bars pressed against her shoulder blades, like they were pushing her back towards the Wolf.

"Nowhere to run," the Wolf said, a smile in her voice. "Too bad. I like it when they run."

Josie glanced down at her phone. The screen read: Judah. Call Failed.

Kuso.

The Wolf continued to stalk her. "Let's take care of the last of the those pesky charms, and then we can be on our—"

A blazing column of fire spun to life between Josie and the Wolf.

Josie threw her arm up against the sudden blaze, squinting.

If there was a fight, it didn't last long.

A snarl and howl were all she heard. Then the glare of flames extinguished.

She dropped her arm.

Russell rushed to her. Rain ran over his face and soaked through his red T-shirt.

He grasped her elbow. "Are you okay?"

She sucked air.

"You're hurt," he said, lifting her arm.

"It's nothing," she said, gently removing his hand. "Gretchen." She pointed across the parking lot.

Russell raced to Gretchen's side. Josie followed, limping.

A red-tinged stream rushed under Josie's feet, towards the storm drains.

When she finally reached Gretchen, she fell to her knees.

She searched Gretchen's neck for a pulse.

"I'm calling an ambulance," Russell said, phone already at his ear.

Josie's frozen fingers prodded Gretchen's throat. The thin skin was frost-white, chilled.

The shadows seemed to darken in those seconds, every one like Death's shadow. She leaned over Gretchen, shielding her face from the rain.

Russell was talking to the dispatcher, his tone urgent and irritated.

"She's not conscious. She's bleeding all over the godsdamned place. Just get here," Russell snapped.

Finally Josie felt it—a faint, slow throb against her fingertips.

"She has a pulse," Josie said to him.

Russell relayed the information to the dispatcher.

Josie peeled off her jacket and then her sweater underneath. She pressed the sweater to the seeping wounds on Gretchen's chest.

"Stay here," Josie whispered. "Don't forget Roxy. Stay for her. She needs you . . . we all need you."

Russell crouched down again on Gretchen's other side. He was still on the phone with 911, but he caught Josie's eye. He lifted Gretchen's limp hand.

White bands showed on her fingers. All of her rings were gone. The key to her stash was gone. The masks—fourteen of the tribe's most powerful ancient gods—were gone.

On their way to Lily.

JULY 24TH
TWO DAYS LATER

"How are you?" Tessa asked, sitting down on the edge of the Goodwin's guest bed. She'd aged in the last few days. Her eyes had a hard gleam in them that Josie had never seen before.

"Alive," Josie said. "Did you see Gretchen?"

Tessa nodded. Her hair was pulled back in a severe ponytail and looked like it hadn't been washed lately. She smelled too, of sweat and salt and sand.

"She's better," Tessa said.

"That's what Dad said before he left."

The lamp next to the bed was dim. The curtains were drawn against the night. The clock by the bed glowed red, 4:34, but Tessa's soft knock hadn't woken Josie. She hadn't been sleeping. She'd hardly slept for days.

"He couldn't cancel," Tessa said.

"I know. He said that too," Josie said with a weary sigh. "Life goes on, huh?"

Her left arm and leg still ached under their bandages, no matter how many pain relievers she took. The Wolf's special powers had left deep wounds. Between her arm and her thigh, she had over a hundred stitches.

"How are you?" she asked.

Tessa bowed her head, spinning her rings around her slender fingers.

"Surviving. The trials are . . ." She glanced away to a dark corner, her lips pressing tight. "Daisuke thinks I need to wait to start the next round, but I've already waited too long. I guess you knew that though, didn't you?"

"You took as long as you needed."

"I wasted time," Tessa said more strongly. "I see that now. I've seen . . . a lot of things."

Her breath seemed to hitch and a tear-shine appeared in her eyes.

"You're getting the visions now?" Josie asked.

Tessa nodded.

"Bad things?"

"It's all so confusing," Tessa said. "I can't make sense of them, but . . ."—she met Josie's gaze—"yeah. Really bad."

Josie kept her face neutral, though her heart kicked into a gallop. "The future changes—"

"I know—"

"All the time—"

"I know—"

"How bad?"

Tessa's voice was a whisper. "Bad."

Josie reached out. Tessa took her hand.

"Don't be afraid," Josie said.

"I was about to say the same thing to you," Tessa replied with a small smile.

"Did you . . . see me?"

Tessa nodded, her gaze probing Josie's face.

Josie almost didn't want to ask, but . . .

"What did you see?"

Tessa shook her head. "The visions don't make sense," she said. "Daisuke says they're not like watching TV. They're more . . . interpretative, like dreams. His mom was an Eye of the Future."

"I know." Josie squeezed her sister's hand. The skin felt rough, dry. Their mom's hands had always been dry too, no matter how much lotion or how many creams she'd used.

"What did you see?" Josie asked again.

"Death," Tessa murmured, "walking the earth."

Josie's stomach sank. The only way Death could walk the earth was if the Covenant were destroyed. The only way Josie knew of to destroy the Covenant was to murder the Triune and all her heirs.

"That won't happen," Josie said.

Tessa turned her face away.

"It won't," Josie said. "Believe me, please."

"I want to," Tessa said, giving Josie a weak smile.

Josie's heart ached. She knew that smile too. The smile a reassuring adult gives to a scared child, the smile a fatalist gives to the hopeful, the smile her mother had given to Josie, so many times. The smile that said, I wish you were right, but I know you're not.

Tessa snorted, humorlessly. "You know the funny thing? In my visions, Death looks like Judah."

Josie tensed. "What?"

"Daisuke says it's just a metaphor or symbol or something, because of all the negative emotions I've felt towards Judah lately. Some part of my mind associates Judah with Death.

Except..." Tessa's hand slid away from Josie's. She ran her fingers over the nails. The polish was chipped, the once manicured tips rough and jagged-looking. "Have you seen him?"

Josie barely heard Tessa's question. She was recalling the shape of Death's lips the last time she'd seen him. She'd only caught a glimpse, but his mouth had looked familiar—the width, the curve, the color. Had they looked like Judah's lips? Was that why they'd seemed so familiar? But that couldn't have been, could it?

"Caroline said that he's still down south. The fires seem to be under control now." Tessa dug her finger into a hole in her jeans. Not a trendy store-bought rip, but an honest-to-goddess hard-won tear. "Don't think I'm pathetic or anything, but... I still miss him. Sometimes. I don't think he misses me though."

Josie fought to speak through the noose tightening around her neck. "Why do you say that?"

Tessa shrugged. "I don't think he's missed me for a long time."

Josie almost didn't ask, but she felt like she had to, like she needed to.

"Do you still love him?"

The sheen glossing Tessa's eyes cracked like a thin layer of ice over a springtime puddle. It was answer enough.

The noose cinched.

"I keep thinking he'll send me a message," Tessa said, "or call, you know, to apologize. To say he wants me back."

Josie cleared her throat. "What about Daisuke?"

Tessa smiled a little. "I know what everybody's saying, but we're just friends."

"Maybe you should talk to—"

Gods, she couldn't even say his name. When she tried, the noose cut off her breath.

"I can't," Tessa said with a sigh. "Not right now. Everything's too crazy. I need to go back to the island. I have to complete the next round."

"You should listen to Daisuke. If he thinks you're pushing yourself too hard—"

"If you were me, what would you do?" Tessa asked.

Josie pursed her lips.

Tessa nodded. "I'm going. Do you want to come?"

Josie frowned. "To the island?"

"I can take you. Daisuke's there. You can both wait for me."

"For my own protection?"

"I want you to be safe."

"And I want you to be safe too," Josie said. "But we both have work to do, don't we?"

"You can still repair the rest of the tribe's masks on the island. And there are the others, Josie. The ones in the Triune's vaults—"

"Don't mention those, Tessa. We're not touching those."

"But if Lily attacks—"

"Those masks were destroyed and locked up for a reason."

Tessa fixed her gaze on Josie's, showing none of the emotion that had been there seconds before. Tessa really was becoming the Triune.

"If I ask you to fix those masks, will you?"

"If you tell me to repair those masks, Divine Mother, then I will because you're the Triune. But if you ask me, Tessa, I'd say that it's not worth the risk. The tribe's masks are powerful, but the ones in the Triune's vaults? One of your predecessors decided the world would be better off without them, and I think we'd be wise to heed that decision."

"You might not feel that way, Josie, if you'd had some of the visions I've had."

Josie ran her hand over the gauze wrapped around her wounded arm.

"Maybe you're right. Like I said, the decision is yours, Voice of the Supreme Divine. Whatever you decide, I'll do."

Tessa's back straightened. "Thank you, Josie."

She leaned across the bed and hugged Josie. Josie wrapped her good arm around her sister. She could feel the sharp edges of Tessa's shoulders under her T-shirt. Days spent in possession meant days without eating. Josie wanted to scold her sister, but couldn't. If she'd been in Tessa's place, she would've been pushing herself through the trials as fast as she could too.

Tessa pulled back. "I'll be back as soon as I can." She stood up and started to turn away, but then turned back. "If you do see Judah . . ." She hugged herself, seeming to reconsider her words. "Sometimes I wish I could just forget about him, you know?"

"I know," Josie said softly.

Tessa regarded her for a second. "I was a little surprised."

"Surprised by what?"

"That he wasn't here. That he didn't come when you and Gretchen were attacked."

Josie drew her knee close to her chest. "Why would he? Russell had already saved the day. There was nothing for Judah to do."

"He didn't even call you?"

Pain. Heart.

"Why would he?"

Tessa lifted a nonchalant shoulder. "I don't know. Sometimes it seemed like . . ."

"Like what?"

Tessa looked at her again, that Triune façade working its way down from her eyes across her face. It was strange to look at Tessa wearing the mask that Josie had practiced wearing for so many years, the mask she'd thought she'd have to wear for the rest of her life.

"Nothing," Tessa said, touching the doorknob. "Get some rest." She opened the door.

"Tessa?"

Tessa glanced back.

"Thanks for coming."

Tessa smiled a little. "Of course I came. You're my sister. I love you."

"I love you too."

Shadows crowded Tessa's face. "Watch out for Dad, okay?"

"That's all I can do from my tower," Josie said. "Watch."

"I'll be in touch," Tessa said. "Have fun at the party."

"Tessa—"

The door closed.

Josie frowned after her. "What party?"

CHAPTER 27

DEATH WAS NOWHERE to be found.

Josie lingered in the air pathways.

The wind whipped and bullied around her. The light was ethereal blue, clear—no shadows anywhere.

Josie glanced down at the mask. The last one.

She'd repaired the remaining ten in the week she'd been held "guest" at Caroline's house. And Death hadn't showed up—not once. Without a broken mask to guide her, she wouldn't be able to access the pathways. She wouldn't be able to return again until another mask needed to be fixed.

She cursed softly.

Tessa's words had been haunting her.

Death had walked the earth. Death had looked like Judah.

Josie had to confirm that Death's lips didn't look like Judah's. So long as they didn't, then maybe Tessa's vision had been wrong or like Daisuke had said, figurative.

She needed that to be true.

But in ten trips through the pathways, no Death.

"Are you there?" she called out to the endless blue above. She turned back towards the wall of blackness—the Beyond. "Do you hear me?"

No answer. The wind shoved her forward, sweeping her towards the Beyond again. She planted herself, straining against the force of the wind. Time to go back.

Her eyes opened. Back in her body.

The afternoon light was soft on the vaulted ceiling. Through the window, she could see clouds sheeting the sky, forming a thin veil over the sun.

She remained in bed, the weight inside her chest sinking her.

Sometimes she wondered just how far it was to the bottom. How could she possibly feel worse than she had the day before? Yet every morning when she opened her eyes, she felt like she had fallen deeper into the darkness. She wasn't sure why she couldn't shake this chilled ache.

Every day she woke up and repaired a mask or two, first thing, hoping to see Death. Then she forced herself to shower and rebandage her wounds. As she ate, she watched the news coverage of the fires, but since the worst was over, the coverage had been falling off, limited to thirty-second updates sandwiched between the latest political scandal and the celebrity gossip. She dedicated most of her day to reading up on Lu-Ji.

She read different versions of the first Triune's story, in different languages, from the digital archives of other tribes all around the world, over and over again. But whatever Death had been trying to point her towards, she didn't see it.

She also poured over the stories about the sacred devices of the gods. She'd found a very old story about the time-bender, how it had been created by Life to try to freeze one of her favorite demigods and preserve him like a doll under glass. She didn't find anything about what Lily might've been using to blind the Eyes, so she'd moved on to the sword. She suspected Lily's sword was also created by the gods, but there were so many swords. Every god and demigod seemed to have one.

At least once a day during the long hours of research, she would find herself doodling absentmindedly. And, at least once a day, she was furious with herself because what appeared in her notebook was always Judah. Judah's brow, Judah's eyes, Judah's mouth.

She couldn't help but think that the lips that had appeared on Death's shadow face were *exactly* like Judah's.

Every time she caught herself drawing Judah, she tore the page out and threw it away. Then she texted Russell or called him.

He would distract her with flirtatious fantasies about being able take her on an actual date someday—seeing the latest modernist exhibition at the art museum or touring the Japanese Garden or rafting on the Clackamas River. She would wonder again if he were the Fire Guy and if she should ask him. While they talked, for a few minutes, she could almost forget about Lily, about Death, about Judah.

But then the conversation ended and she was still sinking, still confused, still infuriated.

She closed her eyes for a second, steeling herself for another day of the same routine. At least it was Friday, and the last day she'd be trapped in Caroline's house.

Finally, she pushed out of bed.

She placed the mask back in its box on the dresser. All the boxes were stacked neatly there, waiting for Caroline to return and retrieve them.

Josie went to the bathroom and cleaned up. Her wounds were healing, but still sore and ugly looking. Eight gashes, four on her upper arm, four on her thigh, stitched and black scabbed, edged taut pink.

As she stepped out of the bathroom, she heard a faint whimper coming from the other end of the hall—Simone's room.

For the last week, all Josie had heard from Simone's part of the house was the continuous electric buzz of the etcher. Since Gretchen's attack, Simone had been working relentlessly, arming the tribe in her own way.

The door was cracked open, but Josie knocked lightly anyway.

More whimpering.

She pushed the door open the rest of the way.

Simone didn't even look up. She sat on the floor, head buried in her arms, shoulders shaking.

Josie knelt beside her. "What's wrong? Did something happen?"

Simone lifted her head, shaking it. Her roots were ruddy brown, almost an inch now, they'd grown out so much. The pink dye was faded, except at the ends, the rest was yellowish white. Her freckled cheeks were pale and wet, her hazel eyes reddened and spilling over.

"Nothing's happened," Simone said, holding up her phone, like evidence. "Nothing at all."

"I don't understand—"

"It's today, Josie," Simone said. "Our two year anniversary and he hasn't even called."

Josie's mouth opened and closed. She was genuinely shocked.

Simone and Kai had the kind of relationship most people envied. It seemed effortless and perfect. Josie had lost count of the number of times she'd wished someone would look at her the way Kai looked at Simone.

"Are you sure he's okay? You should call him."

"He's fine," Simone said darkly. "Ty sent out an update that he was at Apizza Scholls with Kai a couple hours ago." Her second of anger quickly dissolved into more tears. She dropped her head back onto her arm. "He hasn't called me for three days."

Josie wrapped her arms tightly around Simone. "I'll find him," she said, "and I'll kill him. Okay?"

"Okay." The tears came harder then, sobs racking Simone's petite frame.

Josie held her until Simone lifted her head again.

"I just don't get it. Is it something I did?"

"Don't say that—"

"We didn't have a fight or anything. I thought the reason he hadn't been calling as much was because he was too busy with training and his trials, but . . . three days?"

Josie stood up and retrieved a box of tissue from the nightstand. The bed was crammed against the far wall. Most of the room was taken up by Simone's crafting table and her charm supplies. A rust-patched, red tool chest full of beads and stones loomed next to her closet, bigger than her dresser. The fluorescent magnifying lamp over her table was on, humming softly, casting bone-white light over half-finished charms.

Josie handed Simone a tissue. "Call him."

Simone wiped her nose and shook her head.

"Maybe he just forgot," Josie said.

Simone's lip started to tremble.

"This is how you've been feeling," Simone said finally, sniffing back her tears, "isn't it? Like you're dying. That's what you said. I was a big fat jerk, Josie. I told you it would get better. I'm sorry. I didn't really understand."

Josie knelt again on the rainbow-colored shag rug beside Simone's bed.

"I'm glad you didn't understand, Simone."

Honestly, she still didn't think Simone understood. Simone was crying. Josie wished she could cry. She wished she could have that kind of release.

Simone clutched her phone, glaring at screen like it had betrayed her. "What am I going to do?"

Josie sighed. "I guess you're going to spend your Friday night with me," she said. "Sorry."

"I won't be any fun."

"Neither will I."

Simone smiled a little. "Pizza?"

"And ice cream." Josie forced a smile of her own—for Simone. "And maybe we should take care of this." She plucked at Simone's sad, shaggy locks. "I'm sorry I haven't been here for you, Simone. If I had known—"

"Don't apologize, Josie." She twisted her necklace around her finger. "I don't blame you. I really don't. I just wish I could've helped you, somehow, especially now that I know how . . . awful this feeling is."

"Let's forget about all that, okay? Or try?" Josie stood up.

Her phone buzzed and Simone's chimed. They each looked down. The message was from Caroline. She was meeting Josie's dad in San Francisco. They were going to stay until Sunday. She hoped that was okay and that Josie and Simone understood.

Josie would've been angry if she'd had the energy for it.

"At least someone's happy in love," she muttered. She glanced down at Simone. "How do you feel about it?"

"I'm glad they've found each other. Mom's been really lonely for a long time," Simone said. "I think that's why she's always running off on her crazy adventures. She's been trying to escape . . . this feeling."

Josie slid her phone back into her pocket. "I'm going to go downstairs and see what kind of ice cream's in the freezer. If it doesn't have chocolate in it, I shall be forced to call Allison and have her buy us some."

Simone made a face. "Good thing she can't come any closer than the driveway."

"But she has been extra super helpful, hasn't she?"

Simone hugged her knees. "I know I'm usually the soft sell around here, but the nicer Allison is, the less I like her."

"Well, she's practically been begging me to let her bring us something. Every morning she sends me a message asking how I am and if there's anything she can do."

"Am I a blue meanie if I find that annoying?"

"Yes, you are."

Simone smiled a little more.

Josie did too.

"Okay," she said. "Ice cream inventory. Get your hair dye stuff together and let's get you fixed up." She smirked. "How about blue this time?"

"Because I'm depressing?"

"Because you're a blue meanie."

Simone's smile widened.

Fortunately, the ice cream was well-stocked at the Goodwin household. There were no fewer than five different pints, three of which contained chocolate. No calls to Allison required.

While Josie was in the kitchen, she received a second message. This one from her dad. Basically, he said the same thing Caroline had. Josie didn't begrudge them a chance to have a weekend getaway, she just wished she didn't have be held prisoner for them to do it.

She leaned against the granite countertop and typed in a message: It's OK.

The back door clicked and whished.

Josie flinched, almost dropping her phone. She stared down the length of the kitchen towards the family room.

A moment later, Judah appeared.

He stopped when he saw her, freezing in the wide threshold.

He looked older, his face leaner, like he hadn't been eating much lately either. His gray T-shirt was dirt-smudged and rumpled. His jeans looked like they'd been washed in ash and beaten against a rock. His hair was shorter, almost shorn. The scars across the bridge of his nose and through the peak of his eyebrow were visible, even from ten feet away. Somehow, the thin white marks didn't mar the perfection of his face, but seemed to call even more attention to it. How was that possible?

Her gaze fixed on his lips, studying their shape and color. Had Death's been that full? Or was it just the way Judah held them, poised like he was on the verge of saying something harsh and annoying and right?

She noticed when his gaze tracked down her body and up again, lingering on the gauze wrapped around her arm.

She tugged up the thin strap of her tank top and tucked her hair behind her ear.

All she could think about was what Tessa had said. Not about her visions of Death walking the earth, but about how she still loved Judah.

The silence stretched on for a solid minute, maybe more. Were things so bad between them that she couldn't even say hello?

"Where's Simone?" he asked finally.

"Upstairs. She's upset."

He frowned. "Why?"

"Kai hasn't called her for three days."

Judah's brow lifted. She could still read its tilt, even with the scar—*Is that all?*

"It's their anniversary," she said, irritated on Simone's behalf.

"I know," he said, hefting his metal-framed backpack farther up on his shoulder.

"You remembered Simone and Kai's anniversary?" she asked.

His gaze slid down her again. "Is that what you're wearing?"

Heat crept up her back. "I'm sorry I didn't get a chance to buy a welcome-home-Judah outfit. I've sort of been stuck here for the last week."

"Take a shower, get dressed," he said, striding towards her.

She turned her back to the counter as he approached.

"Make sure Simone does the same," he said.

He paused in front of her, close enough that she could smell him. He didn't stink, but his scent was strong—fire smoke and boy musk. Unlike what Caroline had said about being toxic, Josie had to grip the counter to keep from moving closer to him.

What was wrong with her?

"We're going out," he said. Then he turned, walking through the doorway towards the basement stairs.

She let go of the counter. "We're not allowed to leave," she said after him.

But he had already disappeared down the stairs.

CHAPTER 28

"Where are we going?" Simone asked—again.

Judah didn't answer—again.

He started his CUV.

Simone gripped the dashboard. "Wait. We're really not supposed to leave."

"I told you—"

"I know. Maybe I should just call Mom myself and double check," Simone said, digging into her bag for her phone.

"You don't trust me?" Judah asked darkly.

Simone had her phone in her hand. "It's not that, but . . ." She twisted around in her seat, peering at Josie, looking for backup. "We're not supposed to leave."

Josie glanced at the sharp silhouette of Judah's face, but he wasn't looking at her. He hadn't looked at her since he'd left her in the kitchen.

After they'd dyed Simone's hair electric blue, showered, and dressed, Judah had sent Simone back upstairs to put on something less casual, though he hadn't looked once, let alone twice, at Josie's jeans and T-shirt. Then he'd practically pushed Simone out the door and into the driveway.

The light was turning dusky. The air was calm and too warm. Sweat beaded on Josie's back.

"If he says it's okay, I'm sure he's right," Josie said finally. "He usually is."

The edge of Judah's jaw seemed to sharpen, but he didn't say anything. He put the car into reverse and backed them out of the driveway—out of the protective circles.

"Judah—" Simone squeaked, clutching her necklace. "Are you sure you're okay?"

He shot her a warning look.

"It's just that . . . Josie."

Josie frowned, though Simone couldn't see it as she sat in front of Josie. "What about me?"

"You're in danger."

"So are you. So is everybody."

"You think I don't know that?" Judah asked. He added with a sigh, "This isn't my idea, Simone. I agree with you. If it were up to me, I'd put you both in lockdown."

"Then whose idea was it?" Simone asked.

He didn't reply.

"But Mom said it was okay?" Simone asked again.

He gave her a dull look.

For a few seconds, as they navigated northward through their neighborhood, Simone was quiet.

Then she said, "I'm glad you're back."

Judah seemed to glance at her, but didn't say anything.

Simone turned in her seat again, peeking back at Josie. "Aren't you glad he's back?"

Josie gave her a why-the-hell-would-you-ask-me-that-kind-of-question face. Besides, she wasn't sure who this person was, with his short hair and silent tongue. And the longer he didn't look at her and didn't speak to her, the more irritated she felt that he was here at all, whoever he was.

Instead of agreeing, Josie asked him, "When are you leaving?"

Simone frowned at her.

"Well, you're going to Eugene, aren't you? When do classes start?" she asked.

"He's not leaving. You're not leaving, are you?" Simone asked. "You can't. Not after what happened. You should see Josie's arm and her leg. That wolf god clawed her." Simone held up her bent fingers to demonstrate, slashing them through the air. "I didn't even know a god could do that."

"Most can't," Josie said. "Most don't have animal aspects either. This one's special—and evil. So lucky us."

She turned her face away and glared out the window at the shadow-limned streets. She wasn't sure what was irritating her more, the fact that he wasn't looking at her or the fact that it bothered her so much.

Warm light issued through the windows of the houses they passed. She caught glimpses of people as they moved around their living rooms, their TVs flickering across their faces. Nice, normal people, living nice, normal lives, with no clue that a crazed earth goddess summoner was hell-bent on wiping them all from the face of the planet. Or that she now had sixteen more masks in her arsenal—the fourteen Josie had repaired, plus Gretchen's old mask and the mountain god mask. Gods capable of tearing the earth asunder and swallowing up the entire city.

"I have to leave, Simone," Judah said in a soft voice.

Pain. Wrenching. Gut.

Josie kept her eyes locked outside the car. They took the overpass along the tree-lined boulevard, towards the golf course.

"But Judah—"

"I have to," he repeated with finality. "But I'm not going to Eugene."

This drew Josie's attention back to him.

"What do you mean?" Simone asked, voice high and anxious.

"We'll talk about it later."

He turned off the main road onto a smaller one that wound up a hill. Big, full trees loomed on either side of the street. Through the sunroof, she could see their branches reaching towards each other over the road, blocking out the sky.

For a heart-stopping moment, Josie was back in Lily's sanctum—an old ruin of a building in the middle of Idaho where the walls had been replaced by trees and the roof by branches and leaves, and where Lily had taken naps in a compost pile full of human remains. After they'd rescued Josie, the tribe had uncovered half a dozen victims that Lily had sacrificed to feed her god. They'd been able to identify two and send what was left back to their tribes. The others appeared to be hapless terrae. Since the Core couldn't risk getting outsiders involved, they'd performed quiet burials and then burned the whole place to the ground.

Even now, the stench of damp earth and heady rot filled Josie's nostrils. Josie closed her eyes, like that could shut out the ghost of a scent.

The car stopped.

"This isn't . . ." Simone was saying. "Why are we here?"

Josie opened her eyes. A stately white colonial sat before them, the brass lantern above the red front door glowing warmly in the twilight.

Judah got out of the car, came around, and opened Simone's door.

"Judah . . ." she said in a perplexed but warning tone.

He held out his hand and she took it. He led her up the driveway. Josie opened her own door and followed, not sure if she should. None of the lights were on and it didn't seem like anyone was home.

Then, as they came around to the back gate between the garage and the huge swath of the backyard, lights blazed up around them—the house lights, the yard lights, strings of lights wound around every tree. Josie stopped, stunned.

"Surprise!" A huge crowd of tribe members cried, each of them grinning broadly at Simone.

Judah gave Simone a nudge. She took a shuffling step forward.

On a stage at the far end of the yard, Kai, dressed in a slim black suit, stood behind a microphone. He smiled—a full, real smile.

"Simone, I wrote this song for you. I love you. Happy Anniversary."

Simone's hands covered her mouth. Roxy wrapped her arm around Simone's shoulders and guided her through the crowd to the stage as Kai started to sing.

Josie remained by the gate, watching as Simone was serenaded in a pop-punk fashion.

Tears gathered in her eyes, warm and aching, but didn't fall.

She was happy. For Simone. Really happy.

Instead of making her feel better, it only made her realize how truly miserable she'd been.

Then she noticed Judah watching her while everyone else was gazing at Simone as she joined Kai on stage.

The moment Josie's eyes met Judah's, he stepped back and turned away. He started down the driveway.

"You're leaving?"

He slowed to a stop. He glanced back at her.

"What about Simone?" Josie said, sure that if there was going to be a party, Simone would want Judah there.

He seemed to give this question consideration. Then he started down the driveway again. He got into his car and drove away.

Josie watched him go. More tears formed in her eyes.

"Josie?" someone said from behind her.

She turned.

Russell smiled at her. "Hey there stranger, can I buy you a drink?"

Later in the evening during a break when one of the numerous bands in the night's lineup was moving out their equipment while another set up, Gretchen beckoned Josie over to her. Josie extracted herself from Russell, who'd had his arm around her waist the whole night, and waded through the crowd towards Gretchen.

All around them, the party-goers swarmed. There must've been two hundred. Russell had told her that Caroline and Kai had set up some special charms around the house—distortive, so that none of the neighbors would have a clue there was a party going on. If anyone looked out their window, they'd see a dark house and empty yard. Josie was impressed. Caroline had been busy lately. Apparently, Kai had been too. He'd been planning this for months.

When she finally reached Gretchen, Roxy—cat-faced and curvy, with almost as many tattoos as Gretchen—smiled and stood up from the chair next to Gretchen's.

"I'll go get us some more drinks," she said to Gretchen, planting a quick kiss on her temple. "Don't let her get up," Roxy said to Josie.

Josie held up her hands in concession and then took Roxy's chair as Roxy slipped through the throngs.

"You look like shit, kiddo," Gretchen said.

"Thanks a lot."

"How are the wounds?"

Josie ran her hand lightly over her leg. "Sore, but better. Yours?"

"The same." Gretchen took a swig off her beer. "Roxy's going to translocate you back to Caroline's tonight. She's DS." Gretchen grinned. "Designated Summoner."

Josie scanned the crowd. She'd noticed that quite a few of the older folks in the crowd weren't partaking, though the alcohol was flowing freely. The sour aroma of beer coated the air.

Gretchen leaned in towards Josie, her green eyes bright and intense. "You okay?"

Josie lifted her shoulder.

Gretchen touched the charm around Josie's neck, flipping it over on her fingers. "I guess we're both lucky that Russell gave you this," she said, eyebrow raised, as if she was asking, rather than stating.

Josie nodded. Russell had just happened to glance at his bracelet's charm that day. He'd seen the Wolf reflected in the charm's mirror. That's how he'd known Josie was in trouble. That's why he'd come to her rescue.

Gretchen laid the charm back against Josie's chest. "I didn't realize you and Russell were involved."

"We're not really…"—Josie caught a glimpse of Russell through the crowd, sexy in a fitted white button-up and dark jeans. The moment she looked in his direction, he met her eye. He'd been watching her the whole night—"involved."

"Then why do you let him spy on you?" Gretchen asked.

Josie turned back to Gretchen. "He's not—"

Gretchen pointed to the charm. "So long as you're wearing this, he can see you whenever he wants. He can find you wherever you are."

Josie closed her hand around the pendant. "Only if the mirror is facing out."

"And how often do you pay attention to whether it's out or not?" Gretchen asked.

"He saved me thanks to this. He saved both of us."

Gretchen pressed her hands together around her beer bottle, inclining her head in Russell's direction. "For which I am eternally grateful, but that doesn't mean I'm going to let him set up a webcam in my bedroom."

Josie slid the pendant under her shirt, out of Gretchen's view.

Gretchen tilted her bottle towards Russell. "He's not the guy that's giving you fits, is he?"

Josie ran her fingers over the woven cords of the white wicker chair.

For months, she'd been telling herself that Russell was the Fire Guy. She'd wanted to believe it was him.

Tonight, as he held her close and smiled at her and murmured in her ear, something just wasn't clicking. The warm flutters he inspired were nothing like the heat that she'd been missing, and they never would be. She guessed she wasn't surprised, really.

The question she was wrestling with now was whether or not those flutters were enough. Could she be satisfied with tepid showers when she'd experienced the steaming deluge?

She didn't know.

She did know she was sick of aching and sinking. She wanted it to end, all of it. She hated not being able to control her feelings like this. Russell's attention, if nothing else, distracted her from it. Everyone had warned her that Russell used girls, but it turned out she was the one using him. Had anyone warned him about her?

"I hate to say this to you, kiddo, 'cause I know you've been stressed lately," Gretchen said, leaning in confidentially, though the noise of the surrounding party forced her to raise her voice, "but I know people born blind who can see better than you."

"What—?"

"You need to open your inner eye, and I mean pronto. We may have a traitor in our midst, someone sporting some vicious canine powers." Gretchen's fingers gestured to her chest. The wounds that had almost killed her were hidden under her shirt. "We have to be able to see everyone around us as clearly as we can, but we can't afford to mistrust people either. You especially."

"Because I'm powerless—"

"Because you're too powerful," Gretchen said, face stern. "Do you think the worst thing you could do is to trust the wrong person?"

"I guess."

"Wrong," Gretchen cut in. "The worst thing you could do is not trust. Don't push your friends away. Don't be blind to how much you need them. Don't shut them out because it makes you feel weak to need them. You're only making yourself weaker and more vulnerable."

Gretchen straightened up in her chair. "Look at me. If you hadn't come outside when you did, I'd be dead. And to be completely humble, I'm one wicked-ass summoner. So were the women in the Osaka Eye. Did being summoners save them? Did it help me? No. You helped me. At the end of the day, Josie, we're the difference. Not the gods. Not the masks. But the faces behind them. Us. Those masks Lily stole will work just as well for her as they would have for us, which is what you were afraid of before you started restoring them, I know. But just because she scored a point against us doesn't mean we can give up. We don't have that option. We're the only ones who stand in her way."

Gretchen took Josie's chin in her hand. "I see this look on your face that scares me sometimes. I feel like you're walking that line between here and there . . . anyway, stick with us, huh? You have more than you realize. Your dad, Tessa, and Simone, Caroline, Roxy, and me, we're all here with you, for you."

"I'm trying," Josie said. "I really am."

Gretchen released Josie's chin. "I know this whole mask-theft thing sucks, but I have a secret to tell you that might make you feel better." She curled her finger, beckoning Josie closer. "I gave Kai his mask."

Josie's eyes widened. "When?"

"After he completed the third round of master-level trials last week. My stash was getting crowded and . . . he's going to pass the rest. He's much more controlled than I think anyone expected. Even Nancy admitted that he's the most controlled summoner she's seen since Judah. He promised me that he wouldn't use the mask until he's passed all of his trials, but if he needs it, he has it. And . . . I think he can handle it."

"I'm glad," Josie said, and she was.

She searched for Simone and Kai, who had been inseparable since he'd left the stage, but she didn't spot them. The crowd was too thick. Simone had been smiling so widely, Josie could almost feel the happiness like it was her own—but it wasn't.

Gretchen gazed at her for a long second. "I heard Judah's back in town."

Josie winced. She looked back towards Russell, who was not far off, standing near the back steps of the house and chatting. He met her eye and smiled a little. She forced a smile back at him

"Caroline's worried about him," Gretchen said softly.

Josie gritted her teeth. She didn't want to talk about Judah or think about him. She'd been doing her best to forget about him all night. She wished Gretchen would drop it.

Gretchen clacked her steel tongue stud against her top teeth. "Caroline thinks it has something to do with you."

"I didn't do anything—"

"Be honest, *mi amor*. What were Russell and Judah really fighting about that night?"

"Who has the most testosterone?"

Gretchen smirked. "Well, obviously, but what else?"

"They hate each other—"

"Josie, we need Judah. I know Caroline thinks it would be better for him to go to school. Ultimately, she's right, but not now."

Josie slumped back in the chair. "He's not going to Eugene."

"Oh, really?"

"But he said he's still leaving."

"Where?"

"He didn't say."

Gretchen frowned. "I admit I haven't always been Judah's biggest fan. He's a bit too straight and narrow for me, but he's loyal as hell and one fierce summoner. And he's Caroline's. And we need everyone we can trust close at hand. In fact, Baby

Bear's on his way back as we speak. Of course, he's taking his time about it."

"Beech is coming back?"

Gretchen nodded, grinning. The expression was just like her son's. Josie looked forward to seeing it on Beech's face again.

Roxy returned, smiling. Her make-up was heavy on the eyes and red on the lipstick. She had the look of one of those Parisian cabaret singers, like she'd taken every dare ever put to her—with gusto.

"Are we done extolling our well-aged wisdom?" she asked, sitting on the arm of Gretchen's chair and sliding her arm around Gretchen's shoulder. She put her fingers to her lips. "Oops. I meant to say well-earned." She winked at Josie.

"Yes, I'm old," Gretchen said, "and getting older with every breath. And crankier too."

Josie stood up. The next band was starting to assemble on the stage at the back of the yard. "I'm surprised the Eye let Kai do this and let me attend."

"You mean you're surprised Nancy allowed it. She didn't like it, but we convinced her. If you hadn't noticed,"—Gretchen gestured to the drunken crowd of tribe members, mostly people older than Josie, many older than Nancy—"morale's been low lately. We needed this, kiddo. Don't forget that either. Unwind a little. Laugh, smile, enjoy yourself."

"That's what I've been telling her all night," Russell said, stepping up behind Josie.

His hand slid around her waist again.

"I could use a drink," she said.

He smiled. "Follow me."

CHAPTER 29

JULY 27TH

"I'LL ADMIT IT," RUSSELL YELLED as he wove through the crowd towards the back porch, taking care not to bump anyone or be bumped by them. Whenever someone jostled him, he grimaced. His ribs were still healing. He held the porch door open for her. "I'm impressed. Kai's a pain in the ass, but he knows how to throw a party."

Behind them, a couple of DJs were blasting dance music across the yard. Lights flashed and strobed. On the porch, he grabbed two more beers from a cooler and then led her inside the house. A few people were lounging in the living room, mostly the older members of the tribe. The furniture had been covered in plastic. The walls were bare. The décor appeared to have been removed.

"Are your parents here?" she asked, modulating her voice halfway through her sentence. Her ears still thundered with the bass beat of the music, but inside she could barely hear it.

"They're at a bed and breakfast in Breitenbush."

He led her down the hall to a closed door with a paper sign taped to it: Off Limits, Enter at Own Risk. Below that was the tribal symbol denoting disembowelment.

She smiled, tapping the sign. "That's not a symbol you see every day."

"Didn't you know? In addition to being one of the top realtors in the greater PDX area, my mom is also an avid tribal symbologist."

He pushed open the door, flipping on the lights. The room was dark and cozy—a study. Built-ins lined two of the walls from floor to ceiling, packed with books. A crimson leather sofa sat next to the door and a desk under the front window. Russell eased himself onto the couch.

"Peace at last," he said with a grin.

She left the door open a crack, but the study must've had some serious soundproofing, because she could barely hear the thumping bass or even the conversation in the next room.

She leaned against the desk and took a long drink from her beer. She wasn't sure how many she'd had, but she was starting to feel disconnected from her body, not unlike the way she felt when she traveled the pathways.

"How's the mask repair business?" he asked.

"Booming," she said.

"How many have you repaired?"

"All of them. I finished the last one today."

"You look tired," he said.

"Thanks."

He grinned. "You don't need to fish for compliments, Josie. Even tired you look better than any of the other girls here."

"Thanks again," she said, standing up and perusing the books, "but I wasn't looking for a compliment."

She pulled a slim brown volume from the shelf. The binding creaked. The pages were smooth and delicate—vellum. The language, Latin. A copy of an older copy, the first page explained. The title: *The Life of Lu-Ji, and Other Stories of the Demigods.*

She flipped through the pages.

"You like history?" Russell asked.

"I'd hardly call this history," she said.

She scanned the stories about Lu-Ji: her birth; her life; conquering Life, Death, and the Other. The story was the same. Nothing new, nothing different.

She flipped through the book, feeling irritated. Maybe Death had just been messing with her. It shouldn't have been surprising. The gods could be such jerks.

"I like that one," Russell was saying. "Most of the mythology focuses too heavily on Lu-Ji, I think. That one has some good stories about the other demigods. Si-Fa, especially."

Si-Fa, Lu-Ji's consort. He had also been a demigod, the son of the Primal Ocean Goddess.

"You're interested in mythology?" She glanced over Si-Fa's story.

"Only passingly," he said. "But Si-Fa had to be one interesting guy, don't you think? Did you know that early on, right after the Covenant was established, Death found a loophole and seized total control of Lu-Ji? Death almost destroyed the mask of the Tripartite. Si-Fa saved her."

Josie leaned against the book shelves. "I remember that story. I read it a long time ago, but . . . it's not included in most of the texts about Lu-Ji."

"I know," he said. "Strange, don't you think? I mean, without Si-Fa's Chain, Death would've killed Lu-Ji, ended the Covenant, and the gods would still be walking the earth today. Can you imagine?"

Her heart skipped a beat. "Si-Fa's Chain."

"Now there's a sacred device I'd like to get my hands on," Russell said. "A necklace that can control the gods, even Death? We could give it to our current Mother Triune, and she wouldn't have to worry about losing control ever again." He stood. "You said that Tessa might be able to summon some demons to procure godly instruments. Maybe that's the one that should go on the top of her list."

"Or maybe I could bring it back," she said under her breath. But not for Tessa.

"What?"

If Josie could bring back the Chain, the same way she brought forth the faces of the gods, then she could give it to the Fire Guy. Maybe it could give him control over the god, and he'd no longer be in danger of losing his soul.

Her head started to spin thinking about it. Or maybe that was alcohol.

She gazed up at him, searching his face. "I need to ask you something."

"Okay . . ."

"You may not want to answer it, but it's important."

"Sounds serious."

"I need to know if you took the fire god mask last winter."

He raised an eyebrow at her.

After a moment, he leaned a shoulder against the bookshelf. He had a light, earthy scent that reminded her of the high elevations of the Himalayas, breath-shortening.

"You think I'm the mysterious fire god thief?" he asked.

Not really anymore. But she still needed to ask. Just to be sure. Especially now when she might've finally figured out how to fix her mistake and save Fire Guy's soul. She owed that to him, even if nothing ever happened between them again, which she wasn't sure she even wanted anymore.

"Are you?"

His dark eyes continued to comb over her, glittering in the dim lights. "Do you want me to be?"

She felt her face flush—probably just the alcohol.

"You have a thing for him, don't you?" he asked. "But then, if I were him, I'd know that, wouldn't I?"

"You're not answering my question."

"Sorry," he said. "I didn't take the mask, Josie. I wish I had. Are you disappointed?"

She closed the book and slipped it onto the shelf. "I'm not disappointed."

In fact, she was relieved. If Russell had been her Fire Guy, it would've complicated things more than they already were. Her feelings for the Fire Guy hadn't exactly died, but she was starting to see them for what they'd been—reckless and dangerous. Maybe that was the reason she'd been so happy to be with him. So long as she didn't know who was behind the mask, so long as he stayed hidden in the guise, then nothing they did together was quite real. And she could allow herself to feel things that controlled, duty-driven Josie would never have allowed herself to feel . . . except for . . .

She picked up her beer bottle and downed the last of it. Distracting.

First thing in the morning, she would start more research on the Chain. Regardless of what she did or didn't feel for the Fire Guy, she needed to try to help him. Of course, there was still the matter of finding him.

She lifted the beer to her lips again, only then remembering it was empty.

"Need another?" Russell asked.

"Actually,"—she put the bottle aside—"do you have anything stronger?"

He set the beer bottle on one of the shelves and then squatted down. From a low cabinet, he withdrew a square crystal decanter filled with amber colored liquor and two glasses.

"Will this do?" he asked.

"Whiskey?"

"Bourbon," he said as he poured.

"What's the difference?"

"All bourbons are whiskeys, but not all whiskeys are bourbons."

"Who knew this evening would turn out to be so enlightening?" she said as she took the glass.

He smiled. "Ah, so you're finally flirting with me."

"Is that what I'm doing?" she said from behind the glass. She knew the smell of whiskey, honey and smoke. It had been one of her mom's favorites. Two fingers, two cubes of ice.

"I hope so."

"Maybe I am, but . . ." She let the whiskey touch her tongue. A smooth burn rolled down her throat, light and woody, sweet at the back. She took another drink.

"Is it Judah?" he asked, his eyes growing, somehow, darker.

Her grip tightened around the glass. "Judah?"

"He's jealous," Russell said, sipping his whiskey, "always has been."

The freezing ache in her chest stung as it was filled up with prickling alcohol warmth—false heat. She downed the rest of the whiskey in a quick gulp.

Russell held up the bottle. She held out her glass. He poured her another.

"I have other things on my mind besides Judah right now," she said. Half-truth? Quarter? She took another drink. She wondered how drunk she would have to get to forget Judah's name, his face, the way he'd been acting . . . like he really didn't care.

"I'm glad to hear it," he said. "But you know, it's okay, Josie."

"What?"

"Whatever you want. I'm okay with it. And if it pisses off Goodwin, all the better."

"Judah doesn't care about me."

Russell smiled a bit behind his glass but didn't say anything as he took another drink.

"But . . . just so you know," she said, "I'm not looking for anything . . ."

"Serious?"

"I just need a distraction," she said.

"Like I said, Josie, whatever you want. No strings. Your will is my command." He leaned against the shelf next to her, his arm brushing hers. "I know how you feel. I've been working my ass off to track down Lily and her little minions. Shit's serious right now. You've been repairing masks nonstop, and after that attack . . ."—he brushed her hair back from her face—"we could all use a distraction. Why do you think they let Kai throw this party?"

"Because everyone loves Simone as much as he does?"

Russell chuckled. "Before my brother started dating Simone I wasn't sure he was capable of love."

She gazed down at the copper-colored liquid, swirling it in her glass. "People have probably said the same thing about me."

"Who gives a shit what people say?" he said. "I know what people say about me. They all think I'm a player because I've slept with a few girls. But I never forced them. I never drugged them. I never got them drunk and messed with them when they were too wasted to say no. But somehow I'm the bad guy. Did I pretend like we were more than what we were? No. Maybe I should have, but why? Just for the charade of it? Just to drag things out? More often than not, I'm the one who ends up regretting it. People warned me Allison was a psycho, but did I listen? No, because I don't put stock in rumors."

"I'm not going to have sex with you," she said. "Just so you know."

"Fair enough." He shifted, grimacing, touching his side. "To be honest, I'm not sure I could right now even if I wanted to."

She laughed.

He smiled. "Seriously, Josie. I'm not that kind of guy. I've never done anything a girl hasn't given me permission to do. I'm sure Judah has told—"

"All I really need right now," she said, "is to not hear the name Judah again."

"My pleasure," he said. "I just want you to trust me, Josie. I'm not going to mess with you. I'm on your side. I'll help you in whatever ways you'll let me."

"I appreciate that," she said.

"So what were you going to tell me?"

"Huh?"

"The night of the Fourth. You were going to tell me how I could actually help you."

"Oh, that." She finished off the bourbon. "I don't actually need—"

He poured more into her glass. Her head was already swimmy. Her thoughts echoed inside her skull.

"You trust me, don't you?"

She swallowed another gulp and said, "I've been fixing the masks."

"Yeah—"

"By travelling through the pathways and reaching into the Beyond," she finished.

He choked on his whiskey, clutching his broken ribs as he coughed.

She touched his arm. Tingling heat flickered through her, faint, weak. But better than sinking, better than aching, better than being ignored.

"Are you okay?"

He nodded, clearing his throat and straightening up.

A slow smile spread across his face. His dark eyes seemed to swirl and flash, like black lightning-filled clouds.

"Tell me more."

CHAPTER 30

A Simone Interlude

"**T**HIS IS THE BEST EVER," Simone said, standing up from the bed. "I can't believe you did this."

Outside, the party was still thumping.

Kai pulled on his shirt. "Never underestimate a man in eyeliner."

She laughed. "How did you keep it a secret? Everybody is here."

"Threats, blackmail, you know, the usual," he said, combing his hair over his eye with his fingers. He looked up at her—that look that made her tummy do somersaults. "Actually, I would've preferred to kidnap you off to some remote tropical island, but . . ."—he shrugged—"I knew you'd like this better."

She leaned down and kissed him. "You were right."

"But you would go with me, wouldn't you?" he asked, lifting an eyebrow. "To that tropical island?"

"I'd go anywhere with you," she said.

He smiled. "I am sorry I've been MIA the last few days. I didn't want to let anything slip. I didn't even tell Josie 'cause I was afraid she might let on. So now you know my secret," he said, "what's yours?"

The happy post-sex tingle fluttered away like frightened butterflies. "What? Huh? I don't have—"

He stood up and crowded her, she was jelly. He plucked the cord of her necklace and held it up. "Secret-keeping charm? Spill it, Goodwin."

She snatched the charm back. "If you know what this is, then you know I can't spill anything, that's the point."

"It's your brother, right?" Kai asked, taking a step back. "What's his big secret? He's a dick? But no . . ."—Kai tapped his chin and sat back down on his mess of a bed—"that's not a secret."

Kai's room was a disaster area, gray walls plastered with posters and stickers, clothes piled everywhere, band fliers, comics, guitar picks littering the floor. And it reeked of him. She loved it. But she was prepared to rip open the door and run away as fast as she could if he pushed her too far.

She sidled towards the door. "Shouldn't we get back to the party?"

He slipped on his boots. "Let's see, what's the secret . . . Judah's been acting especially dick-ish lately."

"Kai—"

"Hmm . . ." Kai yanked the laces tight. "He broke up with Tessa, which I'm fairly neutral about. He almost killed my 'brother'—better luck next time."

"Not funny."

"He's been awfully moody, which I can usually get behind, but in Judah's case, it's not so much working for him. He's been going on every mission available, which is overkill even for Judah the Eagle Scout. It's like he's been avoiding something or . . . someone." His face scrunched in exaggerated concentration.

"Drop it okay?" she pleaded.

"He has a secret major enough that he needed to muzzle you with a charm so you'd keep your big mouth shut," he said, seeming to think aloud.

"Hey!"

"Big beautiful mouth," he clarified.

She rolled her eyes. "Thanks."

"I'd say he was torn up over Tessa, except he ditched her."

"That's not exactly—"

"Right after he gave Russell the pummeling of a lifetime, which in and of itself was weird. Russell deserved it, but Judah likes to play it cool and above all that. Russell's been asking for it for years, so what changed . . ."

"I'm leaving now," she said, pulling open the door.

He jumped up. He slammed his hand against the door, shutting it and leaning over her, grinning.

"Josie."

She shrank against the door. "What about her?"

"Oh, it's so obvious," he said, gorgeous black eyes glinting. "Am I right? Or am I right?" He pinched at her sides.

She wriggled away from him, tripping over a stack of records and into the middle of the room.

He leaned against the door with that evil grin of his that she usually loved, but at the moment it was giving her sick-inducing caterpillar crawlies in her belly.

"It explains so much . . . all the fighting and the . . . oh." He straightened up, eyes widening. "Oh, shit. I know what it is. I know what it *really* is."

She held up her finger. "No, you don't. You don't know anything."

"He is busted," Kai said, face lighting up with excitement. "He stole that fire god mask. Straitlaced, rule-sucking, Dudley Always-Do-Right ripped off that mask, which means he's becoming manifest, which means he's all fiery internal conflict and on the verge of going Kilimanjaro. No wonder he flipped out on Russell. This is too good."

She stamped her foot. "This is not good!"

But Kai wasn't done. "And Josie doesn't have a clue. She's been on suicide watch for months because the mystery fire dude dumped her—"

"How did you know—?"

"Obvious?" he said, dismissing her half-asked question. "But it was Judah all along. She hates Judah. Or she thinks she hates him, but she's really in love with him. And he was dating Tessa the whole time. That's messed up. I'm going to write a song about this . . . a whole album. Double album. Epic."

He knelt by the bed and dug out a notebook from under an empty pizza box.

"Kai!"

He held up a finger as he started scribbling lyrics across the paper, muttering as he did. "Carved your face, didn't know your name, when you came, I couldn't see, you, set fire, to me . . ."

She ripped the notebook away from him and tossed it over her shoulder.

"Hey! Inspiration! Stroke of genius happening here. Uninterrupted, please?" He stood up like he was going to retrieve the notebook, but she put her hand to his chest, stopping him.

"Okay, so now you know the truth," she said. "So you have to help me."

He bobbled his head. "You know how I feel about helping."

"Josie's travelling the pathways, messing around at the edge of the Beyond, by herself, to fix those masks and it's doing something to her. I saw her disappear. She nearly died and she didn't even care. Judah is miserable. He says he's in control, but I don't think he is. What he did to Russell was—"

"Awesome?"

"Crazy," she said. "That's not Judah."

"Yeah, but it's not like Judah to steal a mask either."

"Josie made that mask for him."

"And she doesn't even know it," Kai said, shaking his head. "Do you think she really doesn't know it or she's just in denial?"

Simone ran her hands over her face. "I don't know. She thinks Russell is her Fire Guy."

Kai chuckled. "Well, there you go. That would piss any guy off, especially one who's all repressed emotion like Judah. He has to stand by while the girl he wants gets cozy with his archenemy? He's like Clark Kent, Josie's like Lois Lane, and

Russell is totally Lex Luthor." Kai crossed his arms. "I knew he was evil."

She refrained from giving him a sharp poke to the gut. "This is not a comic book. This is real. My brother is losing himself to a fire god. My best friend is trying to lose herself to the Beyond, and my boyfriend is too busy writing songs about it to help me help them."

Kai wrapped his arms around her. "It's okay, kitten. I know what to do."

She leaned against him, wanting to cry again. "You do?"

"Sure, tell Josie the truth."

She pulled back. "No!"

"Why not?"

"Because Judah will kill you and as unpredictable as he is right now, he might actually do it." She shuffled over to the bed and flopped down on it. "He says it's the Fire God who wants Josie, not him—"

Kai sat down next to her, bouncing the mattress. "Bullshit."

"I know, but he says when he's with Josie, he can't tell the difference between himself and the god. He says it's too risky for him to be with her."

"Sounds hot."

She smacked his arm.

"Hey, I overheard some of those conversations you had with Josie about everything she and the fire dude were doing, you know, when you thought I was sleeping—"

She propped up on her elbows. "Eavesdropper!"

"Hardly. You knew I was there."

She smacked him again. "You were supposed to be asleep."

"I was asleep until you started gabbing. Are you going to let me finish or are you going to keep hitting me, because if you're going to hit me, I'll take my clothes off again and we can do it properly—"

She dropped back, covering her face with her hands. "It's hopeless."

He leaned on his elbow beside her. "I don't suppose I could convince you to forget about it and let them deal with their own drama?"

She took her hands away to frown at him.

He sighed. "Didn't think so. Look, it's not hopeless. Judah wants Josie. He says he doesn't because he's pissed off she doesn't see he's the dude behind the mask. Once she does, you can bet he'll forget all this 'I don't want her' stuff—"

Simone pressed her hands back over her face, wishing she could crush the thought, but it came out anyway. "I think he started the wildfire."

"Say what?"

She let her arms flop down on the bed. "I think he was the one who blew Russell's tires and started my etcher on fire—"

"But he wasn't in possession—"

"Exactly. The god is taking him over. He's losing control. And his soul." She sat up again. "That's why he's been going on all those missions. He's trying to stay centered. He says it's easier when he's away—"

"From Josie."

"That's part of it. But . . . Josie's research said if he isn't completely honest with himself it will open up a door for the god to slip in. I think he wants Josie and he just won't admit it. If I'm right, then staying away from her is actually what's causing him to lose control. I keep trying to tell him, but he won't listen."

"All the more reason to tell Josie the truth."

"I can't. We can't. I don't know what she'll do once she realizes it's him. She acts like she hates Judah. What if she finds out the truth and rejects him?"

Kai gazed at her for a moment. "What would you do?"

"Huh?"

"If you found out the guy you loved was actually someone you thought you hated, what would you do?"

"You mean if you and I were in the same position? We wouldn't be. We're not like Josie and Judah, at all."

"Thank the gods."

"I would forgive you, no matter what," Simone said. "You know that. But Josie's different. She's so guarded. She doesn't want to let anyone in, which is part of the reason I think Judah didn't tell her the truth. No matter what, she's going to be angry with him. And what if Judah is right? What if he really doesn't have feelings for her? What if it is the god? It's such a mess."

"He wants her. Now that I know he's the fire dude, it's super obvious. He wouldn't have beaten the shit out of Russell if he didn't."

"But that's just it. What if that wasn't him? What if that was the god too?"

Kai looked even grimmer than usual.

"I'm so scared for him. I'm scared for all of us. And I don't know what to do and it's ..." She dropped her face into her hands again.

Kai wrapped his arm around her shoulders. "Don't stress. We'll figure it out."

"Judah told me he's leaving. But not to Eugene. I think he's running away—"

"Yeah, because that's been working so well for him."

"What do you mean?"

"He's been running for months. Mission after mission? He's avoiding. Josie's denying. And look at them. Judah burned down half the state—"

"I don't know for sure—"

"And Josie's been having heart-to-hearts with Death. I don't see how forcing them to confront their issues could make things any worse—"

She opened her mouth, but he held up his hand.

"But I get what you're saying. The direct approach may not be the best tactic—too much possibility of friendly fire. But it's going to happen, one way or the other. If he did set off those fires, then he's already losing control, in a major way. Whatever he's been doing isn't working. And what happens if he loses his soul? The god wants Josie? Then he's bound to show up on her doorstep in Judah's body, right? By then it'll be too late. If Judah's denial is the god's backstage pass into his soul, then he needs to deal. The sooner the better. So what we have to do is . . . nudge them."

"I've been trying—"

"By yourself," Kai said, taking her hand. "But now you have my diabolical mind at your disposal. I'll think of something. Until then,"—he stood up, pulling her up to her feet with him—"this is your party and I want you to have a good time. I didn't do all of this for my benefit."

"I love you so much."

He pulled her towards him. They kissed.

He opened the door, starting forward, but then stopped, shutting the door again.

"What's wrong?"

"We might not be able to able to wait until tomorrow," he said.

"Why not?"

Kai rubbed his chest in that way that meant he was uncomfortable or anxious. "I just saw Josie. I'm pretty sure it was Josie. At the end of the hall."

"Saw her?"

Kai cringed. "With Russell."

"What do you mean with Russell?" She reached for the door handle. He stopped her.

"They went into his room."

"What? We have to stop them."

"Let's think about this."

"No thinking." She stomped her foot. "She does not belong with Russell. She belongs with Judah. I don't care if they're willing to admit it or not, I know it's true. And if she does something with Russell—if Judah finds out . . . he *will* lose it. We live way too close to too many volcanoes to let that happen."

She ripped open the door and charged down the hall.

She knocked on Russell's door. Her heart hopscotched from her stomach to her throat and back again.

No one answered. She knocked again.

"Go away!" Russell called.

"Russell, it's Simone, I need to talk to Josie right now!"

Through the door she heard Josie say, "Simone?"

Kai leaned against the wall, mouthing the words, *What's the plan?*

Simone shook her head, wringing her hands. *I don't know,* she mouthed back. Then something came to her. She pushed Kai backwards.

"Go to the bathroom, go, go," she said.

"Why?"

"Just do it."

She bit her hand. Tears sprung into her eyes. She worked them up by thinking about Judah losing his soul. By the time Josie had opened the door, her cheeks were burning with tears.

The astringent scent of liquor wafted off Josie. Her eyes were half open, her hair disheveled, she leaned heavily on the doorframe. Drunk.

Russell lurked behind Josie in the darkened bedroom. Simone resisted the urge to axe kick the jerk right in the face. What a skeeve.

"What's wrong?" Josie asked.

"Kai and I had a fight," Simone said, throwing her arms around Josie.

Josie stumbled. They both nearly toppled to the floor.

"Simone, I'm so sorry." Josie's words came out slurred and overemphatic. If Josie sounded like she was on the brink of tears too, then she was majorly drunk. "What happened?"

Simone gave Russell the biggest, saddest eyes she could muster.

He sighed. "I'll be downstairs," he said, edging by them. He paused to push Josie's hair back from her shoulder. "I'll tell Roxy she doesn't need to take you home."

"Wait? What?" Simone said, wiping her tears.

"Your mom made this house almost as safe as yours. And I'm here. I'll take care of her," Russell said, looking far less drunk than Josie.

I'll bet, Simone wanted to say, but held her tongue.

"I'll be back in a few," Russell said, leaving them.

Josie touched Simone's cheek. "What happened?"

Simone took Josie's hand and pulled her into the dim hall, making sure that Russell was gone first. Then she dragged Josie into the bathroom.

Kai was leaning against the vanity.

"Well?" he asked when they came in.

Josie pulled her hand away from Simone's and stalked up to Kai. "What did you do?"

Kai held his hands up, leaning away from her. "What the hell?"

"He didn't do anything, Josie," Simone said, locking the door behind them. "We didn't get into a fight."

Josie frowned at Simone, swaying.

"Wow, you're really wasted," Kai said to her.

"No, I'm not," Josie said, staggering back a step. Simone caught her and lowered her down to the floor.

The mirror around Josie's neck flashed.

"We have to take this thing off," Simone said, reaching around Josie's neck. "I don't want Russell spying on us."

Josie leaned against the shower doors, her eyes lulling. "I'm not drunk," she said again.

"Uh-huh." Simone removed the necklace and then stuffed it into Josie's pocket. "I can't believe you'd even wear this thing. It's creepy."

"He's just watching out for me," Josie said.

"Stalking you, you mean," Kai said, crouching down in front of her.

"Russell said he'd be right back. We have to get her out of here."

"I'll message Roxy."

"He just went downstairs to tell her that he's going to take care of Josie."

"I'll bet."

Simone smiled. "That's what I thought."

Kai pushed his hair out of his eye. "You know what we have to do."

"Wha—" But then she saw the thought prowling in Kai's eyes. "Oh, no. I don't think that's a good idea."

"It's a perfect idea," he said. "They're never going to face facts if they never face each other. Call him."

"He won't come."

"Superman always comes when Lois Lane is in trouble. That's why he's Superman."

"What am I supposed to tell him?"

"Tell him Josie's drunk and she's about to do something really stupid, like sleep with Russell. That should do it."

"I can't say that."

He rolled his eyes. "Then tell him she's drunk and she needs to go home. She might have alcohol poisoning." He tilted his head, inspecting Josie. "Which might be true."

"I do not," Josie said, eyes opening. "And I can hear everything you're saying. And I don't know why you brought me in here to talk about Superman, but I'm going to go find Russell—"

"Wait a minute, Josie," Kai said. "We need to talk about . . . some stuff."

Josie plunked down again, glaring at Kai through swimming eyes. "What?"

Kai searched around the room. "Uh . . ." He waved his hand at Simone, urging her on.

Reluctantly, she pulled out her phone.

"I have to go—" Josie said, groping at the tub behind her for support.

"My trials," Kai said, putting his hand on her shoulder, keeping her on the floor. "I need to talk to you about my trials."

"What about them?"

"Tell me everything you know about the fourth round. I'm supposed to take it next week and I'm . . . scared shitless." He frowned at Simone, mouthing, *Call him.*

Simone let out a heavy breath and stood up. She retreated to the corner of the room as Josie started to ramble about the fourth round of the master-level for water summoners. Josie was good like that. She remembered all kinds of obscure tribal things.

Simone's thumb hovered over the screen for a moment. Judah's name glowed at the top.

The only thing that mattered was saving her brother. He'd always been there for her. She wanted to be there for him too.

But would she be putting Judah's soul at risk if she tried to force Josie on him?

What if she was wrong? What if Judah didn't really love Josie?

A little voice inside her whispered,

You're not wrong.

Gods, she hoped that little voice was right.

She pressed Call.

CHAPTER 31

July 28th
Early

T HE WORLD WAS SPINNING. And Josie could feel it, except her head was spinning in one direction and her feet in another. Her stomach was trapped somewhere in between—twisting.

Some part of her was aware enough to know that she was drunk and that she was at Russell's house. Or she had been. She didn't quite know where she was at the moment or how she'd gotten there. Everything was white, too bright, and seemed to be glaring at her.

"Thanks for coming." Simone's voice sounded like she was trapped inside a fish tank, or was Josie the one trapped under water and behind glass? Was that why the room seemed warped and watery?

"Why couldn't I bring the car again?" a deeper voice said.

Simone appeared above Josie. Her hair looked like a blue porcupine. Josie started to giggle.

"It's just . . . better this way," Simone said to the air.

"Better why?"

"Because my brother's looking for his new girlfriend—" Kai said from the far side of the room.

"Kai! Seriously?"

"What's wrong, Simone? Superman doesn't care if some willing drunk girl decides to molest Lex Luthor in his lair, does he? Do you, Superman?"

"What the hell is wrong with you?" the other voice said.

Simone held up her hands. "It's not that he cares. It's that it's not true. Even though she is drunk, thou shall not speak ill of my bestie in mine presence, got it?"

"Simone, you're wonderful." Josie squinted around the room, trying to focus. Kai and Simone gazed down at her. Otherwise, the bathroom was empty. "Who are you talking to?"

Simone knelt next to her. "How do you feel?"

Josie closed her eyes as the room tilted and spun. "Stupid."

"Ah, the regret begins," Kai said. "Just wait until tomorrow."

"Where's Russell?" Josie said, groping for Simone's shoulder so she could push herself up to her feet. "I have to tell him. I meant to tell him—" She rose, stumbling.

Simone held her arm, steadying her. "Just tell me, Josie. I'll tell him."

Josie leaned against Simone. "Simone, I'm sorry. I've been so terrible, so selfish. Judah was right. He's always right. Gods, why he is always right? It's so annoying."

"I second that," Kai said.

Josie's thoughts were tripping over each other, jumbling together. She put her hands on Simone's face until it became clear in front of her. "Where's Russell? I have to ask him, or did I already ask him?" She tried to think back, but couldn't. When she tried, her legs got dizzy.

"Ask him what, Josie?"

She blinked, refocusing. "He kissed me, Simone."

Simone's eyes popped. "I don't think we should talk about this right now."

"I can't tell what's real anymore. I can't feel anything. This isn't real. Nothing is real." She slid down the glass of the shower door, landing on the plush rug again. "I'm not real."

"Sweet angst," Kai said. "How the mighty have fallen."

"Shut up," the third voice grumbled.

Josie dropped her head to her knees. Now she was hearing voices even when there weren't any masks around. "I'm losing my mind."

Someone knocked on the door.

Kai swore softly.

"Just take her home," Simone murmured.

"Josie?" The knock sounded again. "Are you in there?"

She lifted her head. "Russell?"

"Occupied!" Simone said.

"Josie's charm isn't working." The door knob rattled. "What's going on?"

"She took it off." Simone stepped over Josie, flipped open the toilet lid, grabbed a bottle of mouthwash, and unscrewed the cap. "She didn't want to puke on it!" Simone made a retching sound and splashed the mouthwash into the toilet.

Josie covered her mouth, turning away. "Don't do that."

"She's puking all over the place," Simone said.

"Let me in."

"She doesn't want you to see her like this!" Simone called, making another puking noise and slopping more mouthwash into the toilet.

"Josie, are you okay?" Russell called.

"Not really," Josie said, her stomach clenching and unclenching.

"She'll be fine," Simone said. "She just needs to get it all out. I'll stay with her. I'll let you know when she's feeling better." Simone made more heaving noises. More mouthwash went into the toilet.

"Oh gods," Josie groaned, curling into the corner.

"Take her to my room. She can crash there," Russell said. "Come find me."

"I will! Thanks!" Simone called.

The room went silent. Josie's stomach started to settle, but her head was still spinning.

Simone went to the door and cracked it open. She shut it again. "He's gone."

"Simone, what is going on?" the third voice asked. The duel voice of a summoner in possession. The god's voice was soft, breathy, whispering like a faint breeze through dry leaves. The summoner's voice was deeper, warmer . . .

Josie sat up. "Judah?" She squinted at the empty air between Kai and Simone.

"Just take her home, please?" Simone said. "Look at her."

Josie frowned. "What's wrong with me?"

"You're wasted," Kai said. "And you're about to be taken advantage of by my brother. Or maybe it was the other way around—"

"Kai, you're not being very helpful," Simone said, stomping her foot.

"At least he wants me," Josie said, slouching deeper. "Not like some people."

"Ah, I see, you got this drunk so you could take advantage of him in order to stick it to some other guy," Kai said. "Devious. And who is this other guy, and when exactly were you planning on revealing your evil scheme to him?"

"That's enough," Judah said, closer to her.

"It is you," Josie said, reaching out. Her hand slipped through the air god guise—a sensation like passing in front of a low-speed fan—and touched his neck. "I can't see you. No fair."

"What should we tell Russell?" Simone asked.

"How about telling him to go screw himself?" Kai suggested.

Judah put his arm under her shoulders and hauled her to her feet.

"Sounds like a good idea," Judah said.

She leaned against him. He was warm and familiar and smelled like expensive sheets that had been slept in for a couple weeks—musk and wood smoke and sun-warmed skin. It made her dizzy and sleepy and flushed.

"Why do you smell so good?" She pressed her nose into his chest, her voice muffled. "No fair."

His hands gripped her arms and moved her back a step. "Simone, I don't think I can—"

"Please, Judah. She can't stay here. She's going to do something stupid."

"So what's new?" Judah grumbled.

Josie scowled in the general vicinity of his voice. "Hey. Do I go around calling you names and being invisible and smelling really good, no ..." The room swayed. "Ugh. I think I drank too much."

"Ya think?" Kai said.

"Just take her back to the house and let her pass out," Simone said. She added emphatically, "Somewhere that's not Russell's bed. She's safest at our house."

Judah let out a low sound that might've been a sigh or a groan. "Fine."

He pulled Josie towards him, roughly, jarring her. Her stomach lurched.

"I think I'm going to be—"

In a swish of buffeting air, they translocated.

A second later, they reappeared in a dark, tiny room.

"Sick," she finished, covering her mouth.

Judah flipped on the light. She stumbled to the toilet and vomited.

Sometime later, she flushed away the last of the sour bile and alcohol and sank back against the tub.

Judah was leaning in the doorway, watching her coolly.

Her head sloshed like a bowl of warm Jell-O, but she was able to focus on him. His rumpled blue T-shirt matched his eyes—blue, blue, blue. Brow was set to disappointed and annoyed.

"I know what you're thinking," she said, pushing up off the floor.

Her stomach rolled again, but she leaned against the wall until it passed. She then shuffled to the sink. Thankfully, a bottle of mouthwash sat out on a shelf above the hand towels. She rinsed her mouth, letting the burn of mint scour away the burn of bile. After splashing icy water onto her face and cupping it into her mouth, rinsing it out again, she turned off the faucet.

She pulled the hand towel from the rack and dried her face. A faint resinous musk filled her nose. Pin prickles broke out across her skin, stinging faintly like warm drops of rain.

"Are you going to pass out?" he asked.

"What?" she said, opening her eyes.

"You don't know your limits," he said.

She dropped the towel on the edge of the sink.

"New record," she said. "What was it? Two minutes, three? Longest time Judah has gone before criticizing Josie. Congratulations."

He turned away. She followed him into the dimly lit family room. The basement of Simone's house. The overstuffed sofa called to her from across the room. She fell onto it, but then sat up again, stomach flip-flopping.

"Lying down, not good," she said.

"Drink this," he said, holding out a bottle of water over the coffee table.

She took it, cradling it between her chest and her knees. She pulled the fleece blanket from the back of the couch and draped it over her knees.

Judah had circled to the far end of the coffee table. "Are you cold?" he asked, like he didn't really want to be talking to her.

"I'm always cold," she muttered.

"What?"

"It's not hypothermia," she snapped.

He plucked a trash can from behind one of the side tables and set it down in front of her. "Puke in this." He gazed at her, probing her eyes.

"What are you looking for?" she asked. "Am I dying, Dr. Goodwin?"

He straightened up and turned away, heading towards his room.

She frowned after him, sitting up straighter. "Why do you keep doing that?"

He pushed open his bedroom door.

She shoved the blanket away. "Judah!"

He stopped, half in his room. "What?"

"That's it?"

He turned his face away.

She slumped back. Everything had a blurry edge, her thoughts more than anything. In her chest, she felt that sinking again. She ran the heel of her hand over her forehead, unable to get his musky scent out of her lungs or off her tongue.

"Nothing," she said finally. "I'm drunk."

He started to turn away again.

"It's just—" She couldn't help herself. She really was drunk. "Where have you been?"

He stayed where he was, half in his room, half out, arms crossed. But at least he was looking at her.

"You know where I've been," he said.

"No, that's not what I mean," she said, not sure she knew what she meant. "Why haven't you been … I don't know, around?" She shook her head. "I mean, I know why you haven't been around, Tessa, but …" She took a sip of water, staring down at the mouth of the bottle. She wished she were sober so she could figure out what she was trying to get at.

From the far back recesses of her mind, in the shadowy places where she shoved thoughts that were of no use and better off ignored, issued a whisper.

"I've missed you."

She blinked, stunned. Had she just thought that? Had she said it? Out loud?

She looked back at him, but he was far away and the half of his face she could see was unreadable. Stumbling over her own words, she tried to explain herself and not just to him.

"I know it's crazy because it's not like we're friends, but …"—her voice caught in her chest as another unwanted thought pushed itself out into the open—"I've needed you and you haven't been here."

His face remained too shadowed to see.

She sat up straighter. "Is it because of Tessa or because I've been seeing Russell? I don't care about him. I'll stop seeing him."

"I don't care what you do."

"Don't say that."

"What do you want me to say?"

"I want you to yell at me, to argue with me—I don't care. Just don't ignore me anymore. Gods, Judah, I'm barely holding on. And then you bail on me, just like—" She shook her head. "It's hard enough."

His voice was taut. "You're only thinking about yourself."

"I know," she said. "And I hate it. I don't want to be like this. I don't want to feel like this, but I don't know how to stop it."

"I can't help you, Josie," he said. "I just … can't."

"Judah, wait."

She shoved off the couch and rushed across the room to his door. He shied away from her, stepping back into the shadows of his bedroom. The smell inside stopped her in her tracks. She grabbed the threshold, swaying.

"What do you want?" he asked.

"I want you … to be here." She leaned against the door frame. Her head was spinning. "I need you to be here with me, Judah. I can't do this without you."

"You're drunk," he said. "You don't know what you're saying."

Sweat rolled down her spine. A dizzy warm rush wove up through her, muddying her thoughts even more. Her breath quickened in time with her heart.

"You're right, I'm drunk," she said, losing focus.

Shadows wrapped around him. His blue eyes caught the faintest flickers of light, amplifying them. He looked just like …

"I don't know what I'm thinking," she breathed.

Her head spun. She sagged and passed out.

CHAPTER 32

JULY 28TH
AFTER DAWN

HER EYES ROLLED OPEN, DRY AND PAINFUL, like they were full of gravel and sand. Headache was a kind word for the hammering pain between her temples. Head-agony would've been a better word.

Where was she?

She searched the dark room for a clue. Weak light spilled down a staircase on the far side. She rubbed her eyes and pushed up on her elbow. As her eyes adjusted, she took in the bookshelves, the TV, the pictures on the walls—pictures of Judah and Simone.

She dropped back on the couch and pulled the blanket over her head. Memories of the night before pounced on her— the surprise party, talking to Russell, drinking with Russell, kissing Russell, beyond that all she could recall were fragments. She'd been in a bathroom with Simone—she thought. And then . . . Judah.

She pushed the blanket back again, bolting upright. Her head protested painfully. Her stomach groaned.

She grabbed the water bottle off the table and chugged it, hoping to wash away the recollections that were piling up on her, but they didn't go away. The pain in her head redoubled.

She'd told Judah she missed him. She'd told him she needed him.

But she'd been drunk. He hadn't taken her seriously, had he?

Because she didn't miss him. She didn't need him . . .

Did she?

Heart in seizure, she swept the blanket away and found her shoes, placed neatly at the end of the couch. She shoved them on and started towards the stairs, intent on making a quick escape upstairs and hiding in the guest room before Judah woke up.

But as she approached the stairs and his room, another memory came back to her.

A memory that stopped her. Stopped everything. Her heart, her breath, thought, time.

A shadow with blue eyes. Fire blue. And the smell, the resinous musk, dry sand heat, the faintest whiff of smoke.

She knew those eyes. She knew that smell.

But it couldn't be. It wasn't.

It seemed like she stood outside his door for a long time, trying to convince herself that she'd been drunk, she'd been dreaming, she'd been hallucinating. Nothing held up against the memory of those eyes and that smell.

Out-of-body, she saw her hand close around the door handle. With a soft click, the door swung open.

The smell hit her, assaulted her, rushed out and grabbed her. Her eyes closed against it, but it was already in her lungs, staining every breath.

Her legs carried her into the room. Pale light bled around the curtains over two egress windows, one on the opposite wall and one above the bed.

Inside his room, the scent was smothering, undeniable.

But it couldn't be.

The bed was high off the floor, taking up most of the room. On it, sprawled on his back, arm flung over his face, the sheets pushed down around his waist, Judah was sleeping. His bare chest rose and fell, slow and steady.

Her eyes traced the lines of his torso. Lean and athletic, broad shouldered. Just like . . .

But it wasn't.

Moving closer, her shoes whispered over the wood and onto a rug at his bedside.

Her carving of Aphrodite and Adonis was on the nightstand, just like Simone had said. She didn't know how to feel, seeing it there in such a personal place.

Her gaze slid back over to him.

Even asleep, the edge of his jaw was hard, the angle of his cheekbones, sharp.

In her mind's eye, she compared them.

Her fingers touching a jaw—hard—sliding along cheekbones—sharp—hidden behind a guise of smoke.

But that didn't mean they were the same.

Her gaze skipped up to his wrist. A bracelet.

She leaned closer. She recognized the stone on the bracelet—a blue spear of quartz—even though he'd etched symbols into it that hadn't been there before. She could tell it was the same one he'd used to wear on a necklace, because at the stone's heart was a sliver of light.

The first day she'd met him, she'd used the quartz to help Tessa quiet the Tripartite.

From all those months ago, her voice came back to her, as she'd held the stone in front of her sister's eyes, she'd asked, "Do you see the fire?"

But had Josie seen the fire? Had it been right in front of her all along? And she hadn't noticed? Because she hadn't wanted to see it. Not in Judah. Not in Tessa's Judah.

Her eyes moved, unbidden, to his mouth and traced his lips—the peaks, the swell.

The ache inside her deepened. Suddenly, she was in free fall.

She had to know. No matter what the answer was. Even if it was . . . yes. There was only one way she could be absolutely, without-a-doubt, certain.

Holding back her hair, she leaned over him.

Her lips brushed his, skimming the soft burning skin.

Her heart shuddered in her chest. Dying? Reviving? She couldn't tell.

As she drew back, his arm slid away from his eyes.

She saw the fire in them.

Judah was the Fire Guy. *Her* Fire Guy.

He didn't speak. He just lay there, watching her.

She moved in to kiss him again.

He turned his face away.

"I can't—" he started.

"Don't say that—"

"Josie—"

Her lips grazed the corner of his mouth. "Just kiss me."

He hesitated for a moment longer and then, suddenly, his lips were against hers.

All the missing heat, all the missing emotion, all the missing him, flooded back.

He gathered her to him. Her mouth moved into his. Her fingers slid along his jaw, up his cheekbones—all the same. Her body melded against his. He smelled the same, he tasted the same, his mouth, his body, his heat—same, same, same.

He rolled her over, pressing his weight down on her. His heart pounded against hers until they were caught up in the same desperate rhythm.

Her thoughts raced to catch up. All the pieces started to fall into place. Everything that had happened from the very first moment she'd collided with him outside the Eye's sanctum to this moment now. Questions started to pile up too, and anger.

She tore her mouth away from his.

"You left me," she said, breathless.

He panted, eyes alight. Blue flames. How had she missed it? How had she not seen it?

"I had to—"

"You lied to me. You lied to Tessa." Her stomach dropped, a chill undercut the heat of his body against hers. "She thought you were cheating. And you were. With me. Son of a bitch."

She shoved him away and he let her. She wiped her mouth, like she could wipe away the brand of his lips, but she couldn't.

All the times Judah had saved her, had fought with her, had derided her, told her flat out she was wasting her time with the Fire Guy. And all along it had been him. He'd come to her, hidden behind his mask. He'd kissed her and let her kiss him. He'd touched her and held her, so many times.

"Where is it?" she asked.

He moved off the bed.

"I want to see the mask," she demanded.

"Why?" he asked, rounding on her. "Still don't believe it's me?"

She shoved her hair back as she slid to the edge of the bed. "Don't ask me why. You stole it."

"You made it for me," he said through his teeth. "It's my face, Josie. And you couldn't see it. You want the mask?"

He flicked his wrist—the wrist with the quartz bracelet—and the mask appeared. That's why he'd moved the stone from his neck to his wrist. Somehow, he'd made the stone into a key for a secret stash. A stash for the Fire God's mask.

He brought the mask to his face before she could stop him. In a cloud of black smoke, Fire Guy appeared. Again. Finally.

"Is this who you want?" he asked, his voice blending seamlessly with the god's, rumbling and crackling, deep-chested and derisive.

He swooped in, blue fire dancing over his guise, but she rolled away from him, choking on . . . everything.

She scrambled off the bed. She'd made a mistake. A huge mistake.

"I have to get out of here," she said, starting for the door.

Judah grabbed her arm. "No way."

She yanked against him. "Let me go."

"I've been waiting too long for this," he said, releasing her with a shove.

Her back hit the edge of the bed. "You've been waiting?"

He flipped on the lights and took off the mask.

"I want you to explain it," he said, eyes still ablaze.

He tossed the mask to her. She caught it, fumbling.

She gazed down at the blackened clay. The surface had a glazed sheen. She hadn't seen it since she'd put it in the kiln at the tribal center, when it had set the art lab on fire. Judah had carried her out of the smoke. But he'd gone back, for the mask.

He crowded her. "Now tell me again how you didn't know what you were doing."

She looked up at him, and then back down at the mask.

No mistake. It was Judah's face. And still, she was having trouble reconciling the two. How could it have been Judah all along?

"Do you still want to tell me you didn't know?" he said.

"You should've told me."

"I did tell you. I told you the mask looked just like me." He grabbed it from her and held it up next to his face. Then he tossed it to the floor, disdainfully. "You just didn't want to see it. You didn't want it to be me."

"Of course not! You were Tessa's boyfriend! And you were a jerk. Why would I want to have anything to do with you?"

"I didn't want this, Josie. You did this to me."

"What the hell does that mean?"

"It means that since you made that mask, I've been fighting a losing battle with an ancient volcanic god whose primary objective, besides unseating my soul and taking possession of my body, is to be with you."

He seized her around the waist and kissed her again.

Inwardly, she fought, not sure who she was kissing, hating herself for starting this and hating that he was right. She had done this to him. Worse, she'd come here, selfishly, and demanded that he kiss her. Now that he was, she didn't want him to stop. What if she was making it worse for him? What if being with her really did endanger his soul? But then she remembered—the Chain. If she could bring it back from the Beyond, then Judah would be able to control the god.

She tore away from him, putting her hand to his chest and creating a painful space between them. He caught her elbow, hand still on her waist, not letting go.

"You told me before, you weren't the one who wanted to be with me. It was the god." She forced the words out. They resisted, dragging razor-clawed fingers up her throat. She didn't want to be talking. "Is that true? Is it you, or is it him?"

Brow working, he seemed unsure how to answer. Or maybe he just wasn't interested in talking either. She wanted that to be the case. It surprised her, how much she wanted that. Not from the fire god, but from Judah.

"I can't tell," he said finally.

Bruise. Heart.

"And that night, when you fought Russell, was that the god too? Even though you were in air god form? Is that possible?"

His hands fell away from her. "He's always with me. Even when I'm in possession of the air god. He's insidious. I thought I could control him . . . Simone made that charm. The one you found in the Triune's archives. The barrier charm—"

Her mouth fell open. "Simone knew?"

"I made her promise not to tell. I made her a secret-keeping charm—"

"That was the last time we..." She swallowed back a resurgence of pain and desire. "You took the barrier charm and you left," she said. "It was supposed to help you separate yourself from the god. Did it work?"

"It helped," he said. "It was helping."

"And once you had it, you realized that you weren't the one who wanted me—" More painful shredding in her chest. Tears seared the surface of her eyes, burning away before they could fall. "It was the god who was making you come to me, making you—"

"That's not what I'm—"

She held up her hand. "Don't lie just because you feel sorry for me."

His brow plunged. "When have I ever done that?"

"But you left."

"I knew that if I took his form and saw you again ..." The back of his hand pressed to his lips, like he was staunching a wound. "I haven't touched the mask until just now. I've spent every minute trying to keep him in his place. But ..."

"But what?"

"But you, Josie. I couldn't stop thinking about you. I try. I can't. I don't know if it's because I'm losing control, or if it's—"

He seemed to sway where he stood. His hands curled at his sides. Heat swelled off of him, breaking over her like waves. As they receded, she felt pulled towards him. She wanted to go.

Not to the Fire God. To Judah.

She sank back onto the bed, weak from the revelation and the kissing.

This was Judah. Tessa's Judah.

Being near him was painful because she wanted him. She needed him. Now she understood why he'd left and why he'd been avoiding her all these months, really understood. Proximity only added to the agony of the slow death—dying to be closer, to be touching, to be kissing.

Even now, he was moving towards her. She'd pushed him away twice already. She didn't think she could do it again.

His fingers slid onto her cheek. She leaned into his touch.

This was so bad.

"Last night you said you missed me." His breath was on her forehead.

"I was drunk."

His lips grazed her temple. "Did you mean it?"

"Maybe."

Her eyes slid close as he lifted her face to kiss her, gently, briefly. Then they opened again, meeting his.

"You said you needed me," he said.

"I remember."

"You thought it was just me," he said. "Didn't you?"

"Is that what you want to hear?" she said. "That you're the one I want? That won't change anything. The god is still becoming manifest. He's still trying to take you over. You're right. That is my fault—"

He kissed her again. She didn't push him away. She couldn't. Instead, she pulled him to her. They fell back onto the bed. She needed to feel him again, just for a few more minutes.

His mouth moved down her neck. She held him to her. "I'm sorry, Judah. I'm sorry I did this to you. I'm sorry for being so selfish."

"Don't say that," he said, attacking the hollow behind her ear, running his tongue over the delicate skin, sending shockwaves through her body. "I don't want to hear that right now."

"What do you want to hear?"

His finger slid down her shirt, between her breasts. A faint hiss was followed by the stink of burnt cotton. She winced a little, as the heat touched her skin and her shirt fell open.

And then he kissed her again. Fingers, hot, almost scorching, ran over her bared skin. A wavering sound issued from her throat, a wavering feeling trembled through her.

"That's what I want to hear," he murmured close to her ear.

She kissed his jaw, then his neck. He tasted like salt and sweet smoke.

"Gods, I missed that sound, Josie. I've missed you so much. I've missed this so much."

Her hands ran down the curve of his back, into the dimples, grasping for him.

"You used his powers," she said, tears coming to her eyes again. "Just now."

"I know." His mouth moved down her throat, across her chest.

Her hands were in his hair. "You were right to leave," she said, not believing her own words even as she said them.

"No, I wasn't. No, I wasn't," he said, coming back to kiss her mouth again.

She kissed him, not wanting to do what she knew needed to be done. Not yet. Not when his skin was finally against hers again and his hands were sliding over her and they were together, again. Finally. Not now.

"Say it again, Josie."

"What?" she said, breathless.

"You need me."

"I need you," she said. He sank deep against her as he kissed her. The Wolf wounds stung, but she hardly noticed. "I need you . . . Judah."

But then, her hands planted against chest, holding him at bay.

He growled. "No, Josie, don't—"

"We have to," she said. Saying it took all her willpower. "You were right. You were right to leave. You were right not to come to me, not to do this anymore."

"Shut up, Josie, please."

She shifted, trying to move out from under him, but he pressed down on her, pinning her hips with his.

He cupped her face. "You want me."

"Yes," she said, trembling, aching.

"I want you too, Josie. I don't care about anything else." He kissed her again.

"Yes, you do," she said as quickly as she could when they finally broke for air. "You're not yourself. You used the god's powers out-of-possession. I can't let this happen. You're not—"

His thumb pressed against her lips. "Stop talking."

She pushed against his shoulders, sliding out from under him. He grabbed her again, pulling her back.

"You're not in control," she said as he gathered her to him again.

"Yes, I am," he said. "Otherwise, we wouldn't be talking right now."

"This can wait."

"We've been waiting."

"Then we can wait a little longer," she said, staring into the inferno of his eyes and wondering who she was really speaking to. The thought was enough to quell her, just barely.

She couldn't let Judah lose his soul just because she wanted to be with him, not when there was a chance that she could save him.

He seized her again and kissed her in that way he did, like he needed her, like he loved her.

"I never should've released you." His lips brushed hers as he spoke.

"You don't have to make me your slave," she said.

He kissed her neck again.

She brought one of Simone's bracelets to her lips, finding the largest stone and pressing her lips to it.

"I want you, Judah Goodwin."

"Then be with me," he said. "Now."

"Not now," she said, slipping the bracelet off her wrist and stretching it over her fingers. She slid her palm up his arm, over his hand. She moved her other hand over her head too. "Later. After."

"After what?"

"After I chain up that god inside you and save your soul." She grabbed his wrist and slid the bracelet over his hand.

His eyes lulled. He collapsed on top of her.

CHAPTER 33

July 28th

S HE GRUNTED.

"Gods. Who knew you were so heavy?"

She heaved him up off of her and rolled him onto his back.

She sat up and took a minute to let everything settle within her.

Around his ankles were the charms he'd been wearing to fend off the Fire God's assault on his soul.

She collected the tousled sheet and laid it over him. Her hand skimmed his chest and his cheek. He had other scars on his face besides the ones from his fight with Russell. Small, but clear pock marks on his forehead and a few on his cheeks—old acne scars. How had she never noticed them before? But now that she did, somehow, he looked even more perfect.

She kissed the side of his mouth, just like the first time when he'd been in the Fire God's guise, after he'd saved her from being kidnapped by Fog God.

"I should've kissed you after you saved me from drowning. That's what you wanted. That's why it wasn't enough for me to just say thank you."

She pressed her forehead to his, squeezing her eyes shut.

Everything was becoming clear now. Too clear.

She'd been denying her feelings for Judah for a long time. It hadn't been hard. Her mom had trained her to put aside inconvenient emotions, bury them down in the darkness. Being attracted to Judah had been worse than inconvenient; it had been unacceptable. So she'd hated him. That had been easier. At least that way, she wasn't betraying her sister.

Tessa still loved Judah, and he'd broken up with her because of Josie.

Everyone had been trying to tell her. Simone. Caroline. Gretchen. They'd all hinted at it. Judah most of all. He'd been trying to get her to see him, the real him, all along.

She pushed off the bed. Russell's necklace fell out of her pocket. She picked it up. After a moment's consideration, she put it back on, making sure to turn the mirror to her skin.

Since her shirt had been flayed, she pulled one of Judah's from a laundry basket by the closet. Looking at it she couldn't tell if it was clean or dirty, but it didn't matter. She only needed it until she got upstairs to her own things in the guest room. As she tugged it over her head, his scent enveloped her. She grew flush again.

She dug her phone out of her pocket. While she'd had it on silent, half a dozen messages had accumulated—all from Russell.

How could she have ever thought he was her Fire Guy?

She didn't read the messages. She just sent him a quick text back: I'm fine.

Then she texted Simone, telling her to get her butt home.

She was going to the edge of the Beyond to search for Si-Fa's Chain, and she wasn't going to risk slipping over the edge this time.

She scooped up the Fire God's mask.

She glanced again at Judah, sprawled on the bed asleep.

She was coming back. For sure.

She found a hammer in one of the kitchen drawers.

She laid a dish towel on the table and placed the Fire God's mask on it.

Afternoon light streamed through the windows and slid over the mask's glossy surface in gold ripples.

Tying her hair back, she took a deep breath.

She lifted the hammer. Small and light, it was made for penny nails and picture hangers, not for destroying the face of a god. But it would do.

On the mask of the Fire God, the weak point sat between the nose and the top lip.

Judah's nose, Judah's lips.

She hesitated, studying the mask, marveling at her own willful blindness.

The face was clearly Judah. No wonder he'd been so angry. No wonder he'd been resistant to telling her the truth. It should've been obvious. In hindsight, it was.

If not for Tessa ...

Josie shoved the thought aside.

Her first priority was to find the Chain and bring it back. Not that she was sure she was even capable of retrieving a sacred tool from the Beyond, but she had to try.

The Fire God's mask seemed to be watching her, waiting. If only destroying the mask would destroy the connection between the Fire God and Judah, but it was too late for that. The moment Judah had put the mask on, the god had started to become manifest. The god was a part of Judah now, mask or not.

But if the Chain could keep the god in check, if it could save Judah's soul, then she would do whatever it took to find it.

"See you in the Beyond," she said and swung the hammer.

The hammer cracked against the clay. The mask fell into three clean pieces. The gold light fled from its surface.

She set the hammer aside and sat down. Now all she had to do was wait for Simone. She wasn't going to traverse the pathways again without back up. Even as confident as she felt that she wouldn't slip, she wasn't going to take the chance, not when Judah's soul was on the line.

She checked her phone again. Russell had stopped messaging her after she'd told him she was feeling sick and was going back to bed. She kept his necklace on, but tucked under her shirt. More insurance, just in case. She would tell him that their "relationship" was done later, in person, not over the phone.

She picked up her pencil and shaded in the drawing of the necklace. She'd done multiple perspectives of it, trying to fix the image in her mind.

There were no images of Si-Fa's Chain, at least none she remembered seeing. And she hadn't found any in the tribe's digital archives either. Not that she was surprised. Most people considered Lu-Ji and everything associated with her to be more myth than fact. But Death had told her himself that Lu-Ji had existed. If she'd existed, then it was possible the Chain had once existed too.

She hoped that if she went into the pathways with an image of the Chain in her mind, even if it was an image she'd created entirely on her own, she'd be able to make it appear. But she didn't know if was actually possible. Still, she had to try.

She tapped the pencil on the sketch pad and took a sip of her coffee. Her stomach rumbled, greedily. She'd already devoured a plate of scrambled eggs and four pieces of buttered toast. After the abuse she'd put her stomach through the night before, she was surprised she was hungry at all.

She set down her coffee mug and was about to go back into the kitchen to forage when she heard footfalls thumping up the steps. The basement steps.

Judah was awake.

She swore softly, checking her phone. Two hours.

Simone had said she'd be back as soon as she could, but she had to stay until Roxy came and picked her up.

Josie had hoped Judah would be out long enough for her to make a trip into the pathways at least once. She had a room upstairs full of masks. She'd break all of them, over and over, until she could figure out how to find the Chain, if that's what it took. But she feared Judah would try to stop her—or that the Fire God would.

And in truth, she wasn't quite prepared to see him again.

Her fingers tightened around the pencil. From where she sat, she had a clear view into the kitchen. She watched and waited.

He came around the corner. He paused when he saw her, fingertips poised on the countertop, like he was considering whether or not he wanted to come any closer. Then his gaze fell on the broken mask.

Brow switched from tentative to stunned. Then, pissed.

"Judah—" She gripped her last sleep charm bracelet, prepared to use it, though she knew it would be next to impossible to trick him again.

After her shower she'd only put on a handful of her charm bracelets. Unlike Simone, she didn't really like wearing bracelets up to her elbows. Charms weren't of any real use in the pathways anyway.

She'd put the locator charms back on, along with a couple of the grounding and centering charms.

Right now, she needed to stay grounded and centered, but looking at Judah, she wasn't sure the charms were actually working. She felt about as grounded as a feather and as centered as a melting puddle of slush.

"What did you do?" He crossed the kitchen quickly, no longer hesitant.

Gingerly, he picked up the two top halves of the mask, anger shifting to pain.

"You don't need it," she said.

Back to anger. "I know that—"

"I'm going to repair it."

"What are you—?"

She searched his face, his fire-filled eyes. "Are you . . . you?"

He laid down the broken pieces of black clay. "What do you think?"

She gripped the pencil between her forefingers and thumbs, about to snap it in two. She was looking right into his eyes, but all she could think was how she'd been looking at him for months and hadn't seen the truth.

How could she have been so blind? Even considering Tessa, how could she have ignored the heat flowing from him, reaching out to her, shortening her breath, and making her sweat?

He came around the table, brow softening. Her stomach finally started to feel queasy, but not due to what she'd eaten. She knew this look he was giving her. She'd seen it before. For months, she'd ignored it, pretending she didn't understand what it meant. But now it was so clear.

Her fingertips ached, wanting to touch him again.

He pulled out a chair, turned it towards her, and sat down. Elbows on his knees, his hands rubbed together. He seemed about to touch her, but then his fingers interlaced and went to his chin.

"What are you planning?" he asked.

She eyed him. She thought it was Judah, but it didn't really make a difference. Everything she said to Judah, the god would hear.

"Josie, it's me," he said.

She tapped the pencil against her palm.

"It's more than me," he said. "I feel more like myself than I have in . . . months."

"Good," she said softly.

"I mean it, Josie."

"So do I."

He frowned. "Don't do this. Not now."

"Do what?"

"Shut me out."

She shifted in her chair. "I'm not shutting you out, Judah. I'm glad you feel in control. Overjoyed. Elated. Relieved. But . . ."

"But what?"

"But he's still in there. He's still trying to take you over."

"You don't think I know that?"

She leaned towards him. "I know you know that. And now, I know it too."

His eyes narrowed. "You're up to something. What you said before . . . about chaining the god." He gripped the back of her chair, leaning towards her. "What did you mean?"

"I'm not going to let him take you over, Judah. I am not going to let you lose your soul. And I hope he hears me because I'm serious."

"He hears you."

"Good."

"What are you going to do?"

"You can't stop me. Neither of you can stop me, so please don't try."

She knew it was coming, but she still wasn't prepared.

His hand moved from the back of the chair to her cheek.

"Josie, I meant it. I feel more in control than I have since I first put on the mask."

She wanted to move away from his hand—his thumb gently stroking her cheekbone—but she couldn't.

"I'm sorry I did this to you, Judah. You don't know how sorry."

His hand dropped from her face. The absence of his touch left a chilled pain on her skin.

"I made a mistake, Josie," he said, bowing his head. "A big one."

"No, it was my mistake. As soon as I realized what I could do, that I was a mask-maker, I should've studied. I shouldn't have made any masks or repaired them, before I'd—"

"Not that," he interjected. He took a deep breath and leveled his gaze at her. "I mean..." He ran his hands over his jeans and then sat back, crossing his arms. "I didn't want you, Josie."

Pain. Chest.

His arms fell open again. "I mean, I didn't *want* to want you, but I did." He leaned towards her again. "I do." He looked over at the light-filled windows. "I told myself I didn't because..."—his jaw hardened—"you made everything so difficult."

"Me?"

He looked back at her. Classic Judah brow—slanted, challenging, obdurate.

"Yes, you. You don't know what you're like." His hands rose on either side of her face, like he might kiss her or strangle her. He surged to his feet and paced away. "Nothing I did was ever good enough for you. You threw yourself at me when I was him." He gestured at the broken mask on the table. "But when it was just me? You ignored me, Josie. We'd be together at night and then, when I'd see you the next day, you'd look right through me."

She bowed over the table, hanging her head. "Maybe I shouldn't be saying this right now, but you could've told me the truth."

His gaze tugged at her until she finally looked at him. His brow was pained.

"I tried," he said. "I wanted to. So many times, but... I thought you hated me. I thought if I told you the truth, you'd hate me more."

"So you left me."

"By then I'd convinced myself that I didn't want you and that you didn't want me, that it was him on both accounts." He flipped his fingers towards the mask again. "I was wrong."

She lifted her phone. "Should I get that on the record?"

He sat down once more, closer than he had been, his knee brushed her leg. "Simone told me that I wasn't being honest with myself."

Josie nodded. "And it was allowing the god access."

"That's why I feel more in control now. When I woke up— and by the way, not cool—"

She opened her mouth.

He cut off her apology before she'd gotten it out. "I knew it," he said. "I knew I'd been doing this to myself. I could feel it.

Here." He touched his chest. "I'd been telling myself that you were the problem, that I needed to stay away from you, when in truth, you were the solution. Staying away from you was what was causing me to lose control." He ran his hand over his lips. "In a serious way."

"How serious?"

He hung his head.

"Judah—"

"He started those fires, Josie." The agony in his voice cut through her.

"The wildfires?"

He nodded. "That's why I convinced my mother to enlist the tribe to fight them. They were my fault. I had to do something to stop them."

Josie sank back in her chair. "Gods, Judah. How?"

"That's the worst part. I don't even remember. I was meditating, and then . . . I was staggering out of the smoke and the whole forest was up in flames behind me."

"Then how do you even know—?"

His brow was guilt ridden. "I know."

"It's okay."

"No, it's not," he said.

"No, it's not," she conceded, "but it's not entirely your fault. None of this would be happening to you if it weren't for me."

Then he noticed the notebook. His gaze ran over the drawings. "That's my necklace."

"I know."

He frowned at her. "I know that look."

"Do you?"

"Whatever you're about to do—"

She touched his knee. His words stopped dead.

If only she'd known months ago that all she had to do to shut him up was to touch him. The trouble was, now that she was touching him, she wasn't sure she'd be able to take her hand away.

"I'm glad you're in control—"

His hand slid over hers. "I am."

"But you're still in danger."

"I'm not the only one. There's enough danger to go around at the moment, don't you think?"

"Everything I said last night? I meant it. I've missed you, and I need you. And now that I know it's you, now that you're here with me, I'm not going to lose you. I . . . can't."

Even though she'd promised herself she wouldn't let it happen again, he kissed her.

She didn't try to stop him. There was something desperate and urgent inside her, stomping down all her rational and pleading thoughts. She had to kiss him. She had to touch his face and his hair and feel his heart pounding against her chest and through his palms, which were sliding under her shirt, pressing to the small of her back, pulling her onto his lap.

She'd banished her attraction to Judah because she'd thought it was wrong. Wrong to betray her sister, even just by feeling something. But now that she was allowing herself to feel it, she knew it was right.

"Um . . . hi?"

She and Judah broke apart.

Simone stood just inside the back door, cheeks turning pink. "Sorry to interrupt."

CHAPTER 34

"**Y**OU DON'T KNOW IT WILL WORK," Judah said.

At least the Fire God hadn't seized control of him and incinerated her for suggesting they harness him with the Chain. Judah really did seem to have a handle on the god, for the time being.

"I'm going to try," she said. "I have to."

"No, you don't—"

"You're taking an unnecessary risk." Irritation showed on his brow. "Just like you have been for the last three weeks."

Josie darkened the lines on her sketches. "I suppose Simone told you about that too." She gave Simone a sharp glance.

Simone's lip protruded.

"She didn't have to." Judah put his phone on the table. "I've been tracking you."

She dropped her pencil. "Say what?"

"Every time you went to the Beyond, I lost your signal," Judah said, glowering at her. "Every time, I wondered if it was going to come back."

"How are you tracking me?"

"I bought your phone for you, remember? I set up the tracking account for your dad," he said.

She sagged. She did remember, now. Her dad had always trusted Judah, even after he'd found out that Judah had been spending the night up in Tessa's room. After a few weeks, he'd even let Judah back in the house.

Another thought Josie had to push aside. She'd never asked Tessa how far her relationship with Judah had gone. She pacified herself for the moment by telling herself that just because Judah had been spending the night didn't mean he'd had sex with Tessa. Weak, she knew. The thought he might've slept with her sister not only complicated things more than they already were, but it also made her sick with fury.

"Well, I am coming back," she said, using her anger to dig her heels in against him.

Her phone buzzed. She pulled it out. Another message from Russell. She put her phone back in her pocket.

"It's him again, isn't it?" Judah asked.

"Yeah, he was pretty unhappy this morning," Simone said. "I told him Ty took you home. He didn't like that. Kai wanted to tell him the truth." She rolled her eyes. "Sometimes I don't know what he's thinking, like we need any more trouble with Russell—"

"Where's Kai now?"

"At home. He promised his folks the house would be immaculate when they got back." Simone reached towards Josie. "You know I'm sorry—"

"It's not Simone's fault," Judah said to Josie. "I gave her the secret-keeping charm to keep her quiet."

Simone touched the necklace. "Can you release me now?"

Judah shook his head. "I still don't need the Eye finding out I stole a mask or Mom learning that I'm becoming manifest."

"You should tell her," Simone said. "She's worried about you."

"She is worried," Josie confirmed. "She even talked to me about it. She asked me to give you a break."

His face darkened. "What else did she say?"

"Look, we're just wasting time," Josie said. "I'm going to the Beyond, right now. I'm going to try to find the Chain and bring it back."

"You don't know if that's even possible," Judah said.

"Point noted and ignored."

Simone picked up the sketchpad. "Will it work if it looks like Judah's necklace?"

"I don't know. But since there are no depictions of it, I'm hoping it won't matter. Besides, if I can bring it back, it'd be better if it weren't some bizarre antiquated thing that will draw attention."

Simone pointed at the drawing where the pendant of quartz met the leather braided cord. "What's that?"

"It's a clip. I added it," Josie said. "The stories said the pendant could be removed. Whoever holds the pendant controls the god. So long as the summoner is wearing the necklace and the pendant, the summoner remains in control of the god . . . I think."

Judah's scowl was getting deeper by the second. "You're about to do it again."

"Do what?"

"The same thing you did that got us into this situation in the first place," he said. "Taking action without any preparation. When did you get this idea?"

She ground her teeth.

"You don't have to do this right now," he said. "I told you I'm in control—"

"And did you think you were in control when you nearly died igniting the biggest wildfire in state history?"

He looked like he'd been punched. She hated herself the moment she'd said it, but it was true. They'd already ignored the truth for too long.

Simone paled. "That was you?"

Judah's glare turned deadly.

Josie slid the towel holding the broken pieces of the mask towards her. "I'm not arguing right now. I'm just taking a quick trip through the pathways, like I've been doing for weeks"—she raised her eyebrow at Judah—"and if I can't make the Chain appear, then I'm going to come right back."

She gazed down at the mask and the drawing. She hadn't told anyone about Death, besides Kai.

Even though Death hadn't been around for the last week, it was possible he'd show up. She shuddered, thinking again about Tessa's vision of the future.

What if Death appeared in the pathways, looking like Judah? He'd said that she saw only what she wanted to see.

Was that why his lips had looked like Judah's? Because she'd wanted them to be? All this time, some part of her had been dreaming about Judah, wishing for him, shaping every face into his. She'd been subconsciously giving Death Judah's form. That also explained why she had shaped the Fire God's mask to match Judah's face. If only she'd acknowledged her feelings for him right away, all of this might've been avoided.

She looked over at him. "I'm doing this for you."

"I don't want you to."

"You'll let the god take you over before you'll ask for help," she said.

He pressed his lips together.

"If you've got a better idea, I'm ready to hear it," she said. "But you're wrong. I have been preparing. I did nothing for months but search for a way to help you. This is the only thing I've discovered that offers any real chance for you to keep your soul. Everything else is just stopgap. Saving your soul can't wait, Judah. I don't want to spend another month or day or minute translating ancient tribal BS while the Fire God eats away at you. I have to try this. Look, if it doesn't work this time, then . . . I will wait, for a little while, before I try again. I'll look for more information about my abilities, about the Chain, but I won't wait long, and I am going to do this now."

"If something happens to you—"

"Nothing's going to happen."

"You don't know—"

"But I do know that if I don't do something, you are going to lose your soul. I don't need to know anything else. Nothing else matters."

"What about your life?"

"You think I could live with myself if you lost your soul?"

He looked away. "I'd still be here."

"You mean the Fire God would be here, in your body. No, thanks."

She looked down at the drawing again, but was distracted by Simone's sniffling.

"Simone, I'll be okay—"

"That's not it," Simone said, sinking back into her chair. "I'm just so glad you two are finally . . . you know."

"I'm sorry I didn't listen to you, Simone," she said. "I know you've been trying to get me to see the truth for a long time. It must've driven you crazy. And I haven't been a very good friend lately either. I've been way too caught up in my own drama."

"I forgive you," Simone said easily.

Josie envied Simone's ability to give so freely and never think twice about it.

"Let's get this over with," Simone said. "I hate watching you travel the pathways. You get all ghostly. It's creepy." She shivered visibly.

Josie set the sketchpad aside and placed her hands on either side of the Fire God's mask.

Judah's hand closed around her wrist. The look on his face was almost enough to stop her.

"I am coming back," she said again.

His hand slid away. "You'd better."

She focused again on the mask. The crackle of fire filled her ears.

Fire. Everywhere.

Polychromatic flames whirled around her like little dust devils and Oklahoma-sized tornadoes. Rivers of it ran under her feet in molten orange flows. Blue and purple flames etched above her in broken streaks, mimicking lightning against a smoke-black sky.

The pathways of the fire gods. She'd never seen them. None of the other masks had been fire gods. She had traveled through them with Judah when he was disguised as Fire Guy, but translocation only took a split second. And frankly, when she'd been in Judah's arms, she hadn't noticed anything but the feel of him against her.

Already, she missed him.

"This is so bad," she murmured, wondering how she'd convinced herself that she hated Judah all this time. All she wanted to do was get back to him.

Her mother had taught her too well to put aside her own feelings in favor of doing the right thing. Was that what Death had been trying to tell her when he'd said she needed to stop doing what she thought was right and do what she felt was right? Was that what he'd meant when he'd told her that she was denying herself happiness? Had he been talking about Judah? And had he pointed her towards Lu-Ji stories so that she could learn about the Chain and find a way to save Judah's soul?

Was it possible that Death had actually been trying to help her?

Josie put the question aside. She couldn't lose focus.

She approached the wall of darkness—the Beyond.

Fire tumbled over the edge, a firefall. Phantom flames swirled up her legs, around her waist, as if trying to keep her from plunging over the edge or to take her along for the ride. She held her ground.

She searched the impenetrable murk.

"Looking for something?"

Josie tensed, but it wasn't Death's smooth, cold voice she'd heard. This voice was deep and warm. Whirling dervishes of fire spun around her whipping flames like silk veils—red, blue, yellow, green.

"It's nothing personal," she said.

She searched the darkness of the Beyond for his face, but it didn't appear. She guessed the mask wasn't important. The power that would've been in it was already being channeled into Judah.

"You broke my face," the Fire God said. "I take that rather personally."

Was it her imagination, or did he sound like Judah? The inflection, the derision, the provocative tone that struck straight at her core, for better or worse.

"You can't have him," she said.

"I already have him. You gave him to me."

She stared down at her toes that were perched on the edge between the rivers of fire and the vast black emptiness. "It was a mistake."

The Fire God's laugh moved through her, infuriating and intoxicating.

"If you say so." His mirth came to an abrupt halt. "I should be infuriated by what you're attempting, but I've grown too fond of you. It's not every day that a daughter of Death, a mask-maker, comes into your life."

"If you like me so much, help me find the Chain. Or better yet, just leave Judah altogether."

"Ah-ah, you know that's not how it works. Once manifestation has begun, I am as helpless to stop it as you are."

"Then help me find the Chain."

"Help you make me a slave? I rather preferred it the other way around, but the boy chose to release you. He's a righteous fool. I will take over his body, and I will have you, in ways the boy has only dreamt of."

"Very romantic."

"Call it that if you want."

"You're only trying to distract me." She took a deep breath and refocused, bringing the image of Judah's necklace forward in her mind. "It won't work."

"Do you know why we all want you?" the Fire God's voice was a steamy murmur. "Because you're beautiful? You are, but there are greater beauties. Your sister, the Master Slaveholder herself, she is something. I do believe Death has a bit of a crush on her. But the boy lost interest in her the moment you appeared."

"I'm not listening to you," she said, trying to tune out his voice and focus on the Chain. But he kept talking, and the Chain remained fuzzy in her mind, out-of-reach.

"The very first time he saw you, the day you returned, he wanted you. Not because you were beautiful, but because he felt you, deep down. You moved him. He thought he understood the world, but when you appeared, you changed it.

You reshaped it. You recreated it. It's not an illusion or a trick. It's a real power, as real as the wind or the water or the fire. A divine gift."

"Because I'm a mask-maker, you mean," she said.

"Ask yourself why you were chosen. You are striding the worlds, standing between mortality and immortality as easily as you might cross a bridge. Does that strike you as . . . usual?"

"Why are you telling me this?"

"I like you."

"You want to use me."

"Call it what you want."

She re-gathered her focus and tried to visualize the Chain again, but the Fire God's question kept resurfacing in her mind, distracting her. Why had she been chosen? Why could she travel the pathways?

After a moment, she swore softly, opening her eyes. Before her, nothing. In the corners of her eyes, flames.

The Fire God chuckled. "The boy's growing anxious. He really is wound tight."

"He has to be to keep you in check."

"I am a god of the deep fire. I am a master of patience and control. I go dormant for centuries, and you'd never know I was only biding my time."

"Until what?"

"Until I'm ready."

"Ready for what?"

"I didn't like all those things you said to him. About wanting him over me."

"Are you jealous?"

"He is nothing—a puny soul in a mortal body. When I assume possession of him—"

Her fists curled. "That's not going to happen."

"If you're going to grasp the full breadth of your power, you must first learn to accept that which is inevitable. Only then will you be able to assume your right—"

He kept talking, but she tuned him out. His voice faded to a distant whisper. She concentrated on the black wall before her. For Judah.

A faint image appeared before her. A tiny speck of light that she wasn't entirely sure she'd seen, until it started to grow larger and clearer.

She reached out. Her hand closed around the spear of quartz, coiled in metal wire. She drew it out of the Beyond. The cord fell against her forearm, shimmering in the firelight, not quite leather like she'd imagined it, but still supple and soft. A material she'd never seen before but, somehow, had brought forth.

The Chain.

"Bravo," the Fire God murmured. "Watch out."

"Wha—"

Arms closed around her. Real arms. An all too familiar voice said,

"Salutations, Lady Day."

Then she was gone.

CHAPTER 35

TAKE A DEEP BREATH WITH SIMONE

WHEN JOSIE WAS IN THE PATHWAYS, she became transparent.

Poised on the chair, frozen, trance-like, she was like a photograph projected onto a backdrop of their world. Simone could see right through her to the sofa and chairs on the other side of the room. It made her tummy ache.

Worse was the expression on Judah's face. Simone could tell watching Josie ghost-out was killing him. His hands were locked together so tightly at his lips that it looked like he might break his own fingers.

"How long do you think it'll take?" she asked when she couldn't hold her breath anymore.

Judah didn't respond.

A few more seconds passed.

"I never should've let her do this," he said.

"We couldn't have stopped her," she said. "You know that."

Another couple of seconds dragged on, feeling more like minutes.

He dropped his hands. "I'm pulling her out."

Simone glanced over at his phone, lit up on the table. A little dot was blinking on a map of Portland, directly over their house, flashing the words in red: Signal Lost. Searching.

"It hasn't even been two minutes," she said. "If you pull her out too soon, she'll just go right back."

Judah slid back in his chair, pressing his fist to his mouth.

Simone studied him. For the first time since he'd told her he had taken possession of the Fire God, he looked like himself. His eyes weren't quite so bright and flickering. His voice sounded more even too, not strained and full of pain like it had been lately.

He glanced at her.

"I was right, wasn't I?" she said. "About Josie. That's why you're in control right now. You just had to be honest with yourself."

Judah frowned. She knew that frown, though she didn't see it very often. It was the grudging-acknowledgment-that-you-were-right-and-I-was-wrong frown.

He shoved out of his chair. "I'm going to lose control if she doesn't come back."

Simone twisted her fingers up in her bracelets, watching Josie intently. After another minute she said, "I have the worst feeling—"

"I'm pulling her out." Judah took a step towards Josie.

And then she was gone.

Just like that.

Vanished.

Simone's breath was sucked from her lungs. She stared at the empty chair, willing Josie to reappear.

But she didn't.

"No . . ." She stood up. "She's coming back. She said she'd be back."

Tears started to run down her face. She swiped at them fiercely, not ready to cry.

This wasn't happening. It couldn't be happening.

"We just have to wait," she said. "She'll be back."

She backpedalled from Josie's empty chair until she bumped into the window. The glass was hot from the afternoon sun. The heat burned through her shirt, but she didn't move.

"She'll be back. She said she was coming back."

They stood there for another few breaths. Neither of them moved.

Judah seemed to have turned to stone.

They stared at the empty chair. Nothing happened. No Josie.

She slid to the floor, twisting the elastic of her bracelet around her fingers until they went numb.

"She's coming back." She glanced up at her brother. "Judah?"

His eyes slid shut. A ragged breath left his lips, tearing at Simone's chest like nasty, murderous wolf claws.

He went very white like he might pass out. His shoulders sagged, and he stumbled a few steps. Catching himself on Josie's vacant chair, he dropped to his knee.

"Judah." She shoved up from the floor and knelt beside him, gripping his shoulder.

The window glass had been hot, but he was scorching. She snatched her hand back. Her palm stung.

Judah lifted his head. His eyes opened and rolled over her. They were full of fire.

"Judah, no—"

The blue flames swirled in his eyes, spilling out of his irises and over into the whites. Heat built in the room, the acrid scent of smoke, soured by sulfur.

Judah rose to his feet. In his hand, Josie's chair burst into flames.

She yelped and threw herself back. "Judah, you have to fight this—"

The voice that answered her wasn't her brother's, though it came from his mouth—it rumbled, shaking her insides like the sub-bass at a dance club.

"He's gone, Charm-Maker." The smile wasn't Judah's smile either. Judah's smile was like the sun, this was like falling into a fiery pit. "For good."

"You're lying!"

The eyes of flames seemed to reach out for her. She cowered, grimacing from the heat.

"He believed her dead," the Fire God said. "He went to find her." He peered down at Judah's phone. "Foolish, impulsive boy. If only he'd waited . . . but that's what love does to you mortals. Makes you blind and impetuous."

The heat around Judah was oppressive. Any second she expected his clothes to burn to ash like the chair, but she moved closer anyway. She glanced down at the phone. The screen read: Acquiring Signal.

Her shattering heart hit pause for a moment. "Josie's not dead?"

"No," the Fire God said, gazing down at the phone.

He held Judah's body unnaturally still. His clothes ruffled as if by a breeze. Shadows played under his skin, like pulsing flames.

"But Judah—"

"What does this mean?" The god pressed his finger to the phone.

Under his finger was a blinking green dot. On the screen, the words: Signal Found.

And then the phone started to smoke.

"No!" She grabbed for the phone too late.

A flame spurted up, burning through the table. The phone turned to goo. She staggered back, gagging on the foul stench of melted plastic. Then she raced into the kitchen, snagged the fire extinguisher from under the sink and ran back just as the fire alarm started to beep. The Fire God frowned up at the blaring alarm. A moment later, the alarm began to drip off the ceiling in clotted clumps. The shrill beep died away.

She pulled the pin and aimed the hose first at the table, dowsing the flames, then up at the ceiling.

Smoke and CO2 vapor clouded the air. When it started to clear, the Fire God was still standing there, staring down at the blackened table where the phone had been.

"Hmm," he said, looking down at his hand—Judah's hand. "This will require . . . practice."

Simone flung the fire extinguisher at him. He caught it with one hand, before it cracked against his temple. The fires in his eyes brightened.

"Where is my brother?" she screamed, choking on the fumes and smoke and her own tears.

"His body is right here," the Fire God replied, dropping the fire extinguisher to the floor with disinterest. "As for his soul, I assume it's traveling the paths of Death, searching in vain for Josie, but I don't know for certain. The souls of mortals are Death's domain. Ask him."

"That's not true! That can't be—"

"Where can I locate another of those . . . devices?" the Fire God asked, pointing towards the smoldering hole in the middle of the table where the phone had been.

Simone choked on her tears, quieting her sobs. "Josie. You're going to find her?"

"I tried to warn her," the Fire God said, glancing around the smoke-filled room like the conversation was boring him.

"Where is she?"

"How would I know? Some lowly little air god appeared and abducted her. Transgressing into the fire pathways, for that alone, I should kill him. Give me your device. What's it . . . a phone. Give me your phone, and it will show me where she is. Then I will retrieve her. And then she will submit to me and become my slave and do as I command."

She took a deep breath. "You mean it? She's really alive? You're really going to find her again?"

"And when I find that air god, I'll render him a blackened husk of human waste."

"The tracking app doesn't work on just any phone. We need Judah's password."

"I know the password," the Fire God said, as if surprised. "JDay127."

Simone's heart started breaking again, in slow motion. "The day Josie came back to the tribe. January 27th." A sob caught in her throat, but she shook away the grief. She needed to save Josie. "I'll go get Judah's computer. He probably has the app loaded on it."

Smoke swirled around the Fire God like exotic dancers, and those eyes full of blue fire, nothing like Judah's . . .

She looked away again, throat raw from smoke and unshed tears. "Just find her."

The Fire God smiled.

CHAPTER 36

Josie dropped face-first onto a floor of coral-pink tile.

Scrambling upright, Chain clutched in her hand, she backed up to the wall.

A wide bed sat before her, swags of netting draped above it. To her right, veranda doors opened to a white beach and, beyond that, a turquoise sea.

Mist wafted around her in thin currents, but if Fog God was still there, he wasn't showing himself.

She took a step towards the doors. The moment she did, a figure came strolling up the concrete path outside, stopping in the threshold.

Dressed in flowing white like a Greek goddess, Josie almost didn't recognize Lily for all the weight she'd lost. Her face was gaunt. Purple shadows circled her eyes. No longer dyed red, the ends of her hair were dark, hanging almost to the backs of her knees. Her skin was white as plaster.

"Josephine." She smiled, but her voice was cold.

The whole room was cold, making the view outside seem like a trick. Maybe it was.

Josie pressed against the wall again, tucking her hands under her arms and gathering up the cord of the Chain. She worked it through the short sleeve of her shirt and into her bra.

Lily stepped into the room. Her skirts dragged behind her, ragged, like a torn shroud.

"How have you been?" Lily asked.

Josie swallowed hard, shivering.

"Very good," Lily said as if Josie had answered. Her eyes were muddy green and bulging. "How have I been? So nice of you to ask. Not very well I'm afraid."

As she approached, a pungent, unwashed smell filled Josie's nostrils.

Lily stopped a few feet from her. With a flick of her wrist, a sword appeared in her hand. She pointed the long blade at Josie. Josie flattened. The tip whispered at the hollow of her throat.

"Not very well at all," Lily said. "But I'm sure you want to make me feel better, don't you? You want to apologize to me for your disrespect, don't you?"

Josie glanced down at the sword. The surface of the metal rippled like waves. She knew this sword. It was the sword that had killed her mother.

"Ah, yes, the Sword of Eternity," Lily said. "Quite an interesting history, this sword. The God-Slayer, it's been called. You do want to apologize, don't you?"

She looked back at Lily, down at her actually, since Lily was shorter. So tiny and so evil.

"Not really."

Lily bared her teeth. A sound like tires squealing issued from her throat.

Josie's eyes squeezed shut, bracing herself to see Death one more time.

Then Lily began to snort and snicker. Josie's eyes cracked open.

"I see what you think of me, Josie. I suppose I can't blame you after everything. I had hoped you would come around to see our side of things eventually. My son thought so. But one must be prepared for disappointment. And I am prepared, Josephine, far better than I was prior to our last meeting."

She stepped back. The sword vanished, replaced by a broken mask of dark clay. She held it out to Josie.

"Repair it, now."

Josie glanced around the room again. The bedroom furniture was rattan. Ruby-hued accent pillows were studded with beads and mirrors, making Josie wonder if they were in the vicinity of the Subcontinent.

She wasn't about to draw attention to the fact that her phone was still in her back pocket. Wherever they were, she hoped there was cell service. Judah could track her. She also hoped that Judah would be smart like he had been the last time and call the cavalry. The thought of him charging in here by himself made her nauseated.

"There aren't any tools—"

Lily smacked Josie.

Stinging pain swelled across her face. Her eyes watered.

Lily shoved her broken mask against Josie. One of its sharp corners jabbed into her chest. The fetid stink of rot and blood filled her nostrils. A low groan called to her—the voice of the Earth Goddess.

"You don't need any tools," Lily said, smiling knowingly. "Just reach your pretty little fingers into the Beyond and bring back my mask."

"How—?"

Lily didn't let her get the question out. "If you insist on playing this tedious game again, I am prepared to provide you with motivation."

She spun around, still holding her mask. On cue, the double doors to Josie's left opened.

A hulking god of gray granite entered. Ahead of him, he pushed a bound and bleeding Russell.

Josie's heart plummeted. Not this again.

Granite God shoved Russell down to his knees.

Russell's eye was swelling from a fresh blow. A rivulet of blood trickled out of his nose and soaked into the gag tied between his teeth. His good eye widened when he saw Josie, and he thrashed against his captor. Granite God kicked him in the back. Russell landed hard on his face, a stifled howl of pain tearing through him.

Josie winced, knowing that Russell's ribs hadn't yet healed from his fight with Judah.

Another god entered. A lithe god covered in silverish fur, who moved like glycerin over marble. The Wolf. Granite God stepped back, seeming to defer to the smaller, sleeker god or to be afraid of her.

"Pick him up," Lily said.

The Wolf seized Russell's hair and yanked him back up to his knees. Another pained sound issued through the gag.

"The Wolf can rip out his throat and feast on his blood, or you can repair my mask."

The Wolf leaned down. Its crimson tongue ran up Russell's neck.

Russell cringed. The Wolf's eyes flashed gold-hued amusement at Josie. The corners of its mouth tugged upwards in a wolfish grin—all fangs.

"If you want to save your friend here," Lily said, "you will do it now. Or I will let the Wolf play with him until you—"

Josie snatched the two halves of the mask from Lily's outstretched hand.

Lily's smile returned. Her lips were thin and violet hued, like a corpse's. "The Wolf isn't known for her patience."

Russell's dark eyes were pleading. Next to him, the Wolf salivated. A thin strand of drool dripped from its tongue and puddled on the floor. Lily wasn't making idle threats about the Wolf killing Russell. The Wolf had murdered the Osaka Eye. Josie wasn't about to let Russell become her next victim.

"Be quick," Lily said with a tiny smile.

Backpfeifengesicht.

Down into the pit.

The cavernous hole reminded Josie of the Beyond—no light.

Rustling snake-skin murmurs and deep, earth-creaking groans echoed around her. Of all the earth god pathways she'd travelled, this one was the darkest, the most unsettling.

When she hit the bottom she found she was already at the edge of the Beyond.

She teetered on the balls of her feet. The pathways around her were so dark they were virtually indistinguishable from the Beyond. Only the faintest unsettled sensation in her gut told her that if she tottered too far forward she would be in danger of never returning.

The face appeared before her, ready.

In the Beyond, Lily's goddess was even more gruesome than Josie remembered. Churning black clods of soil rolled across the forehead, cheeks, and chin, only to be swallowed by the gaping pit at the center. A sinkhole. She seemed to be consuming herself.

Josie paused only long enough to make it clear in her mind that the Earth Goddess would not be manifest, and then she grabbed the mask from the Beyond. When she pulled it into the pathways, the sinkhole vanished. The mask became drab, brown, and uninteresting—deceptive.

Josie was about to turn her attention back towards her body when she heard a faint whisper. In the pathways, disembodied whispers were common. But something about this one stopped her. It pulled at her, almost as much as her own body was pulling at her.

The mask remained inert in her hands. It hadn't been the goddess whispering.

The cave-like echoes continued around her, water dripping, wind murmuring, a faint scratching noise, like an animal, or a person, trapped and trying to escape.

She started to shift her focus back to her mortal body, but then heard it again, more clearly: a distant whisper.

"Josie."

She searched the darkness of the pathways around her. "Death?"

No response.

She turned back towards the Beyond.

A pale glimmer caught her eye, stopping her.

A wisp of rippling bluish light appeared in the black of the Beyond—a ghost of a ghost.

She halted, finding herself perched on the precipice again.

"Who are you?" she called to the far-off flicker. "What do you want?"

She willed the shade to take shape, to come closer, to answer her. Instead, the flickering light was eclipsed, as if someone had stepped in front of the movie projector.

And then she was shoved back.

Sprawling, she stared at the darkness of the Beyond, stunned.

In all the time she'd been traversing the pathways, forces always seemed to be pushing her towards the Beyond. Never once had they pushed her away.

She picked herself up, frowning at the wall of emptiness. "Make up your mind. Either you want me or you don't."

No response. No light. Nothing.

She lingered for a moment longer.

Then she returned to her body, Lily's mask in hand and a terrible sinking feeling in her gut.

CHAPTER 37

JULY 28TH

LILY RIPPED THE MASK OUT OF JOSIE'S HANDS.

Josie slid to the floor.

"I've missed you." Lily cradled the mask. Then she brought it to her face.

Josie pressed against the wall, hating herself, hating her power. Why had her mother done this to her? Nothing good was coming from her ability to bring forth the faces of the gods. Instead of protecting the Covenant, she only seemed to be hastening its destruction.

The Earth Goddess's guise sheathed Lily.

Branches sprouted, spiraling down over her head and up around her feet, lacing together in the middle. Leaves and flowers sprouted in her hair and then died. The wilted petals were gathered up by a trailing gown of writhing roots at her feet. And the stench—a jungle outhouse, ozonic, rotting, puke-inducing.

Josie's head swam with it. The perfume of her nightmares.

TemperMentals appeared in a crow's cloud above Lily's head. Phantom entities, semitransparent, hued decayed brown and rust red, with the ability to menace, injure, and abduct.

Lily's goddess shadow fell over Josie, now towering nearly eight feet tall. Her death mask of wet black earth gaped down at Josie in a facsimile of a smile.

Russell let out a pitiful fear-filled sound, cowering now from Lily and the Wolf.

"You have what you want," Josie said. "Please, release him."

In possession, Lily's voice was buried under the deep rumble of the goddess's.

"Well, since you asked so nicely," Lily said. "Take him back."

The Wolf's smile seemed to droop, but she hauled Russell to his feet and carted him out of the room. His dark eyes were fear flattened. Through his gag, he tried to say something to Josie as he stumbled through the doors, but whatever it was, she didn't understand.

"Now I've shown mercy, wrath deserves its turn as well," Lily said, her gaping hole of a smile widening. "Let us taste the blood of the mask-maker."

The Sword of Eternity appeared in her hand.

The tendrils of Lily's guise slithered across the floor, laying snares. Josie shouldn't have been surprised that Lily was going to kill her outright, but she was, a little. She knew Lily still had a sizable cache of masks waiting for repair. Either her plans had changed or she just didn't care anymore.

Josie's fingers dug against the wall behind her. Her eyes darted, searching for an escape, even though she knew there wasn't one. A nest of vines covered the floor between her and the open veranda doors. Granite God stood like a boulder in front of the other doors. Lily inched closer, filling Josie's nostrils with her decaying stench, making it hard for her to breathe.

Though her legs shook, she pushed up to her feet.

"Going to run?" Lily asked.

"No," Josie said, forcing the word out though her lungs were panic drowned.

"Care to beg?" Lily asked, lifting the sword.

"No."

"Oh, I see, you're being brave now, is that it?"

Josie pushed herself away from the wall. She prayed that Judah wouldn't come, that no one would come. Maybe Death would do her a favor and tell Tessa there was no point. No reason to send a rescue party after a corpse.

She wished desperately that she hadn't stopped Judah earlier in his room. She wished that she could get that moment back and relive it one more time—differently. She wished she could tell him she loved him. Because she did.

And she wished she could tell Tessa she was sorry for betraying her.

As Lily lifted the sword, flourishing it, Josie was taken back to that moment when her mom had been frozen in time and Lily had plunged the sword into her mom's stomach.

She wondered what she would say to her mother when they met again.

I know you did the best you could.

I'm sorry I failed.

"Just like a daughter of a Triune," Lily said, irritated, "to play the stoic. They say the blood of the gods lives in the line of the Triune. I missed the opportunity with your mother, but now I have another. What power do you think drinking the blood of the gods would grant me? I'm sorry you won't be alive to find out."

The sword hissed through the air towards Josie.

Arms wrapped around her. A cool mist brushed her skin. The Fog God. The sword sliced through the mist of his guise, so close to Josie's neck that she grabbed at her throat to make sure there wasn't blood.

He'd translocated her to other side of the room.

He let her go, pushing her to the floor. Lily screamed in fury. The sound beat against Josie's eardrums. Her vines writhed and thrashed.

Josie scrambled to her feet. The vines caught her ankles, almost toppling her again. Behind her, the veranda opened up to the sparkling blue sea and clear blue sky. Between her and Lily, Fog God.

Okay. She was surprised.

"How dare you!" Lily screamed.

"Not part of the plan," he said calmly.

Josie tore at the vines, trying to loosen their hold, but they slithered further up her legs and nipped at her fingers.

"Plans change," Lily said. "She's caused enough trouble. I've decided to be rid of her before she causes any more."

"You're not thinking," Fog God said.

"Do not question me!"

"We need her!"

"Hardly!"

"What about the other masks—?"

"We don't need them. Now that I am back in possession," Lily said, "I am all that is required." Her roots climbed up the walls, weaving a latticework over the threshold behind them. Josie tugged at the roots, but couldn't move.

The ground began to quake.

"I'm not going to let you do this," Fog God said.

"Oh, dear," Lily said. "You haven't grown fond of her, have you?"

"You're going to ruin everything!" he said. "You can't just throw all our plans out the window, because you're feeling a little bloodlust."

The quaking increased. The sheer netting above the bed began to sway. The TV on the wall rocked in its mounting, slipping askew.

Roiling curls of fog drifted around Josie.

"What is that?" Lily roared as the quaking grew more violent, forcing Josie to grab hold of Fog God's shoulder to keep from falling into the pit of snares. He wrapped his arm around her waist and pulled her closer.

"They can't have found her already!" Lily swung her sword back around towards the Granite God. "Send out the—"

Another god pushed open the door. A god of swirling red sand.

"The volcano!" Sand God cried. "It's erupting!"

"That's not possible! The volcano is extinct!"

"There's a god up on the mountain!" Sand God pointed in the opposite direction of the ocean.

"Where are the others?"

"We haven't picked up any others. Only him."

Josie swore under her breath. Judah.

"Is that so?" Lily said, cocking her head thoughtfully at Josie. The roots began to loosen and coil back towards Lily. "The mystery Fire God comes to the rescue again I see." Her form grew and grew, threatening to bust through the high ceiling. "Let's see how he fares against a time bender and the Sword of Eternity."

"No!" Josie surged forward. Fog God held her tighter.

"Take her to the rendezvous and don't think I'll change my mind about killing her. Do not defy me," Lily said to him, "or you will be sorry."

Her form collapsed as she translocated.

"I already am sorry," Fog God muttered.

Fog wrapped around Josie. She swung and kicked, hoping to connect to something solid in the cloud of damp air shrouding her.

"Not a good time for this," he said.

"Piss off."

His arm closed around her throat and yanked her back against his chest. "Let's talk about this later."

A deafening crack, like the ground splitting open, was the last thing she heard before they translocated.

He released her the moment they arrived.

She stumbled away from him.

Squinting against the glare of the sun, her head spun from the heat pushing down on her. White sand shifted under her feet. Glittering blue waves were crashing in beside her, growing bigger and choppier with each pass. On the distant horizon rose a green mound of an island. A plume of black smoke marred the serene blue sky.

She raked her hair back. Judah was fighting Lily, and there was nothing Josie could do.

The fog retreated, concentrating around the summoner's form. The hollow pits of his eyes seemed to be staring past her towards the volcano.

She retreated from him. "Why didn't you let her kill me?"

"My mother's experiencing a little power madness after being bedridden for the last few months. Once she calms down, I'll be able to reason with her—"

Josie shook her head, turning back towards the volcano. The waves were coming in bigger. Water crashed against her knees and soaked her shoes, forcing her back.

"We need to leave," he said. "It just shows how little my mother is thinking that she sent us here."

"She's not thinking at all!" Josie shouted at him. "She's insane! You'll never be able to reason with her. You're delusional if you think you can!"

Turning, she charged up the beach and into the shade of the palms, scrambling up a slope onto higher ground.

He snagged her arm. She whipped around, ripping free.

"Why don't you just give up?" he asked. "Stop fighting all the time. You're not going to win."

"I'm not trying to win." She stared hard at the swirling face, studying its shape, trying to pick apart the summoner's voice from the god's. "I know you, don't I?"

"You don't know anything," he said. "Acquiesce and you might live."

"What do you care?" she said.

"I don't."

"I don't believe you," she said. "You ... don't want to kill me, because we know each other, don't we? Who are you?"

"Believe it or not, murdering people isn't actually high up on my list of good times."

"But you helped her murder my mother. You're planning on murdering billions of people!"

"People are already dying! They're already murdering each other," he said. "We're reaching critical mass here. Big time destruction is inevitable. You're lying to yourself if you think the earth can handle much more abuse. If we don't act now, there won't be a habitable place left for any of us to live. You'd rather sit back and do nothing and let everyone die a slow death when there's no more water to drink or food to eat, like your mother did, that's fine. We're not. We're not wiping out humanity. We're preserving it. Yeah, a few billion people have to die. But it's now or later. At least now, we still have a chance to save the planet, to save ourselves. There's no other way."

"There's always another way."

"Like what? Recycle? Come on, Josie. You're not naïve. You've been around. You know how bad it really is. You've touched the faces of the old gods. You know their power. You know that the new gods are weak because we've made them weak. We're killing the gods because we're killing the earth. What's more important? Saving a few billion self-centered murderers or saving the only home we have? Maybe the

Triune can escape to her island, but the rest of us aren't so lucky. You know what I'm saying is true."

"It might be true, but it's not right," she said. "And it's not your decision to make, who lives and who dies."

"Yes, it is, Josie. We are the voices of the gods. That's exactly what we're supposed to do."

"Now who's the self-centered murderer?"

An ear-popping boom seemed to shake the air itself. She stumbled back, bumping up against a palm tree. Fog God turned towards the horizon. Another plume of smoke punched into the sky.

The rhythm of her heart skipped and stuttered. Judah was using the power of the Fire God in a big bad way. Every time he did, it put him at greater risk.

Then she heard another voice. A deeper, hotter voice, from behind her.

"Enjoying the view?"

She flinched, spinning. She nearly cried with relief when she saw Judah standing next to her. Before the tears could appear though, she realized that something was wrong.

Fog God turned too. "Well, look who it is." The fog of his guise shifted back, curling inwards. "What the—?"

Josie knew what he was stunned by. Judah's eyes were on fire. Godly fire. Sapphire blue. Bluer than the water. Bluer than the sky. The tips of the flames licked at his temples and brow.

"I know you," Judah said to Fog God, but it wasn't Judah's voice. Only the faintest trace of Judah's voice remained—a ghost of a ghost. "Now I will kill you."

Josie grabbed for Judah's arm, but never got hold. Her fingers grazed his skin and she hissed, reflexively pulling back. He was hot—too hot

Panic convulsed in her chest, making it difficult to breathe.

The god wasn't manifest. He couldn't be.

Judah was still in there, somewhere. He had to be.

"But you're not in possession," Fog God said, backing up. He glanced over his shoulder at the spreading cloud of ash, then back at Judah and Josie. He seemed to hesitate for a second. Then he said, "Catch you next time."

The fog thinned and dissipated. Fog God was gone.

Josie's mouth was dry, her body slick with sweat. She stared at the Fire God's profile.

He turned to her.

"Where is Judah?" she demanded.

The eyes of fire regarded her. "He left."

"What do you me—?"

"He thought you were dead," the Fire God said. "He just couldn't live without you. So he left."

She shook her head. "No . . ."

Then she remembered the whisper. The glimmer she'd seen in the Beyond.

Could it have been? Was it?

A sob lodged in her throat, unable to release because she couldn't breathe.

The Fire God moved closer. The heat around him distorted the already overheated air. "You had to know I would prevail in the end. Now you may thank me for saving you."

A wave of water rushed towards the shore, threatening to crash down on them.

The Fire God pulled her to him, and they translocated away.

When they reappeared they were in Judah's backyard.

The clear blue sky was hazy and pale compared to the tropical one they'd just been under. The air might've been cooler too, but Josie didn't know because she was burning up.

She struggled away from the Fire God's embrace.

"You're burning me," she said when he wouldn't let her go.

"Is that all?"

The burn receded and disappeared.

He still held her. Her forearms were pinned between her chest and his. Something hard was pressing against her breast ... the Chain.

She worked her fingers into her sleeve.

"You're not Judah," she said.

"You may beg my forgiveness for claiming you prefer him to me," he said imperiously. He tightened his hold, crushing the air from her. "And then you may express it to me physically. Once I am satisfied ... if I am satisfied, then you will again put yourself in my thrall."

"Sounds like you've been thinking about this," she said, giving the Chain a yank to dislodge it from her bra.

Apparently he thought she was trying to push him away because he held her even tighter. She cringed as her spine popped.

"You don't have to do that," she said. "I'll do what you want."

His hold relaxed slightly. "I knew you would. Why not? Now you have the best of both realms. This body you desired and me, whom you also desire."

"You're right," she said, softening her voice and forcing herself to gaze up into his eyes of nothing but flame. "I did want you." She brought her hand up, stroking his chest.

Inside, she was trembling and wailing and tearing out her hair. At the same time, she was also numb and silent and calculating. Finally, she was getting some real use out of her Triune training. When dealing with the gods, it was better to be cold, distant, emotionless—emotions were liabilities. Down into the oubliette. Into the darkness.

"I never doubted it," the Fire God said. "The boy was full of doubts—never sure how you truly felt about him, even at the end—"

A tidal wave of agony rose up within her.

No time for that now. First the Chain.

"I told him what he wanted to hear," she said, running her fingers along his neck. Judah's neck . . .

She closed her eyes, biting her lip until she could force herself to continue.

"I knew that too," the god said, his hands sliding down her back.

Her other hand moved up his chest. She pasted a smile on her face that she'd practiced a thousand times over. A Triune needed to have a good fake smile. Josie's barely passed, but she hoped, at this moment when she really needed it, it was good enough.

Her hands came together at the hollow of his throat. She found the ends of the cord—the clasps.

"Aren't you going to kiss me?" she asked.

"I'd prefer if you kissed me," he said. "You are begging forgiveness, aren't you?"

"You're right," she said, rising up to kiss his lips. Judah's lips . . .

Pain flooded her as her lips met his, but she threw a wall up against it.

Time for pain was never.

Her hands circled around his neck, like she was embracing him. And then she connected the clasp of the necklace, chaining him. He jerked back.

She snagged the pendant clip and unhooked it just as he shoved her away.

His skin began to glow like an ember. His eyes blazed. "You ungrateful little—"

"Shut up!"

His mouth closed. Steam began to rise from his skin.

"Cool off," she said. "You're not going to hurt that body. You're not going to hurt me or anyone unless I tell you to hurt them, got it?" She held up her fist, the pendant wrapped tight inside. She had to keep it safe and away from him. "I'm in control now."

His eyes flared again. Flames ghosted up Judah's legs and around his arms. She didn't know if they were real enough to do damage or like most guises, more effect than substance, but she wasn't willing to find out.

"Stop it! You're going to treat that body as well as Judah did—better."

The Fire God remained unresponsive, as she'd instructed. She glanced down at the pendant. Though it looked like Judah's—a blue stone wrapped in copperish wire—the weight was much heavier than common quartz and copper. And it had a surreal depth, a fluid sheen, it almost seemed alive.

Trapped in its sapphire prism was a glimmer of a flame, a ghostly white ripple.

So long as she had the pendant, she controlled the Fire God.

The flames had retreated. The steam was gone. He was beginning to look like Judah again. But he wasn't Judah.

Judah's soul had been taken by that shadowy bastard Death.

Gone.

She closed her eyes and took one last breath.

In the lush green backyard of a yellow craftsman-style house, in a quiet Portland neighborhood, under a clear blue sky on a warm summer day . . . Josie Day died.

Then her eyes opened and her breathing resumed and her heart began beating.

She clutched the pendant to her chest.

Dead.

For now.

EPILOGUE

LOST WITH FOG GOD

"TELL ME WHY I SHOULDN'T KILL YOU," his mother asked.

Her TemperMentals swooped around him, hissing and whispering about betrayal.

"Good question," he said. "I don't suppose motherly love is anywhere in the answer."

"You let her get away!"

"Judah showed up. I know when I'm outmatched. He buried your entire island. Even you couldn't stop him—"

"You defied me," she said.

"Not for the first time."

"But it will be the last."

"Go ahead. Kill me. Why not? You killed my father—"

"Don't speak to me about your father!"

His lips pressed together. Under his guise, his heart was palpitating. Normally, wearing the guise of a god was invigorating, empowering, but lately, this fog was starting to feel smothering.

Why hadn't he let her kill Josie?

Plans were already underway. His mother's dreams were finally becoming reality.

The end of the world as they knew it, except ... the more he thought about it, the less he was interested in avenging Mother Earth.

He was losing interest in everything that had anything to do with his mother. All those years they'd been preparing, gathering followers, plotting the end of the human plague, she'd promised she would spare the people he cared about.

At the time, the list had been pretty short and he'd made sure to keep it that way. Not that he cared about Josie. Or ... he hadn't meant to care about her. But his mother had never said anything about killing her, at least not since they'd found out she was a mask-maker and not the Triune.

In her guise, his mother, bigger and badder since Josie had brought back her mask—Gaia 2.0—filled up the dank temple ruins in Central America where she'd retreated after Judah had blown the island off the map.

Now Mommie Dearest was extra pissed. And it seemed like he was the one to blame, but he wasn't sure he wanted to take that blame. Or to play anymore of her reindeer games.

The Sword of Eternity appeared in the woody black roots that were her fingers.

He would've stepped back, but couldn't, not with the TemperMentals swirling a phantom cage around him.

Firelight, from the torches on the wall, ran over the blade like blood.

"You are too much like him," his mother said.

Her voice was low, perilous, unhinged.

"You're not thinking," he said, searching for possible exits.

A heap of dirt and broken stone had filled in the entrance behind him as soon as he'd come in, but they weren't entirely sealed off. He could slip through.

"Don't talk back to me—"

"Someone has to," he said, sweat rolled down his temple. He was sick to his stomach as she approached, sword in hand.

He'd always thought he knew how to handle his mother, but ever since she'd killed the Triune, she'd become unpredictable.

"You're going to destroy everything we've worked for if you keep acting like this—" he started.

Her tone was high, it reminded him of a stone teetering on a needle. "Acting like what, dear heart? Acting like what?"

Gods, she had lost it. This wasn't how it was supposed to be.

"Mom, look at yourself. You're pointing a sword at me!"

"You've proven unreliable. As unfaithful as your father . . . I should've known you'd betray me, just like he did!"

He stiffened. "What?"

Her worm-laden face of dirt churned with fury. The TemperMentals picked up speed and started darting away from him, bouncing off the walls in agitation. The sword dropped to her side. He knew this was a good chance for him to escape, but he couldn't.

"He lied to me. From the beginning!" she roared, but then her voice dropped into a low dark register. "He thought I didn't know, but I found out. He laughed at me when I told him he'd regret what he'd done—"

"You told me he gave himself up willingly because he was sick. He was dying." His head throbbed. "You murdered him because he cheated on you?"

The TemperMentals stalled, hovering in the air like brown shadows.

"That's not important—"

"It's important to me," he said.

"What does it matter? He was like the rest of the humans in the world, selfish, greedy, lustful. He didn't care about anyone but himself. He deserved his fate."

He stared at his mother. She was there, somewhere beneath the guise. Or was she?

He'd never really known her. She hadn't raised him. She'd sent him to live with friends for a time after he was born and then, when the opportunity came, she had him sent to his foster family in Portland. She'd visited with him. She'd given him the fog god mask in secret. He'd always known she was his real mother. There had been a time when he'd wanted everyone else to know it too, to know that he belonged in the tribe as much as any of them. But he'd never really felt a part of it. At least, not until . . .

"It's her, isn't it?" his mother said, like she was reading his thoughts. "I knew she would do this to you. I never should've let you become involved with her."

"This isn't about her."

"Prove it. Bring her. Sacrifice her to me."

He stepped back. A TemperMental swept behind him, shoving him forward again.

"That wasn't part of the deal," he said.

"You care more for her than you do for me, your own mother."

"You've got to be kidding me."

She lifted the sword again, pointing it at him. "You have a choice. Her life or yours."

"You don't really mean that."

"Don't I?"

"Don't make me choose."

She thrust the sword forward. He lunged to the side. The blade cut through the guise of his god and sliced into his arm. He swore. Blood ran over his skin. She'd actually cut him. She could've killed him.

Crazy bitch.

"Don't return without her," she said. "If you do, you know what will happen. And if you don't return, I will reveal you and then you will have nowhere to go and then you will die, like the rest of them. Her included."

The tunnel behind him began to rumble and groan as the dirt moved away. Light shone distant and weak at the far end.

"Fly away, my son," she said, turning her back to him.

And he did.

Fast as he could.

ACKNOWLEDGMENTS

I must first thank my editorial team. Renae, she is my first and best reader, fan, and friend. Chad A. Clark, fellow indie author, whose feedback and insights are invaluable. My proofreader, Kris, who wrestled my prose into submission with good humor, generosity, and grace. And my editor and partner-in-crime, Pam House Caster—she asked all the hard questions and always inspires me to get my butt back in the chair.

Thank you to all the family, friends, and teachers who have loved, encouraged, and guided me.

Finally, my boys. I had dreams before you came into my life, but it wasn't until you were in my life that my dreams actually started to come true.

Works by
A.M. Yates

Summoners Series

Minor Gods: Book One
Lost Gods: Book Two
Fated Gods: Book Three

The Horizon Cycle

Shield and the Shadow
Stoneheart and the Axe
Sparrow and the Dagger

Stealer
Hunter (Stealer #2)
Unraveler (Stealer #3)

Find out more and sign up
for the new release
newsletter at
www.amyates.com

Hear the playlists that
inspired this book and the
entire series by following
A.M. yates on Spotify

Read exclusive stories from
AM Yates by following on
Wattpad

AM Yates can also be found
on facebook, instagram,
goodreads, and twitter